THE
RETRIBUTION
COMMITTEE

TERRY RICHARDSON

ASPIRE
PUBLISHING HUB LLC.

The Retribution Committee
Copyright © 2022 by Terry Richardson

All rights reserved. No part of this publication may be reproduced, distributed, or transmitted in any form or by any means, including photocopying, recording, or other electronic or mechanical methods, without the prior written permission of the author, except in the case of brief quotations embodied in critical reviews and certain other non-commercial uses permitted by copyright law.

ISBN
978-1-958692-17-2 (Paperback)
978-1-958692-19-6 (eBook)
978-1-958692-17-2 (Hardcover)

"For Linda, my reason for being here."

TABLE OF CONTENTS

PART ONE 1

    CHAPTER ONE 2
    CHAPTER TWO 14
    CHAPTER THREE 30
    CHAPTER FOUR..38
    CHAPTER FIVE..48
    CHAPTER SIX 56
    CHAPTER SEVEN 64
    CHAPTER EIGHT 70
    CHAPTER NINE...80
    CHAPTER TEN 90
    CHAPTER ELEVEN 104
    CHAPTER TWELVE 110
    CHAPTER THIRTEEN 122
    CHAPTER FOURTEEN 134
    CHAPTER FIFTEEN 144
    CHAPTER SIXTEEN 156
    CHAPTER SEVENTEEN 162
    CHAPTER EIGHTEEN 168
    CHAPTER NINETEEN 180

PART ONE

CHAPTER TWENTY 190
CHAPTER TWENTY ONE 196
CHAPTER TWENTY TWO 204

PART TWO 213

CHAPTER ONE 214
CHAPTER TWO 224
CHAPTER THREE 230
CHAPTER FOUR 238
CHAPTER FIVE 252
CHAPTER SIX 266
CHAPTER SEVEN 278
CHAPTER EIGHT 290
CHAPTER NINE...302
CHAPTER TEN 314
CHAPTER ELEVEN 324
CHAPTER TWELVE 336
CHAPTER THIRTEEN 348
CHAPTER FOURTEEN 360
CHAPTER FIFTEEN 370
CHAPTER SIXTEEN 380
CHAPTER SEVENTEEN 396
CHAPTER EIGHTEEN 404
CHAPTER NINETEEN 412
CHAPTER TWENTY 422

ABOUT THE AUTHOR 437

CHAPTER ONE

∞

SYDNEY, AUSTRALIA, February, 1980, Friday

Old Billy sweated profusely as he waited for his bus in George Street, directly outside the entrance to Wynyard underground railway station. The hot blast of the afternoon sun was matched by the constant flow of fetid, warm air issuing from the concrete pedestrian walkway which was packed with commuters.

The long queue of intending bus passengers was being compressed tighter and tighter as more hopefuls joined the line. When each tired office worker lined up, they pushed gently into the back of the weary traveller in front, firming up the queue just that fraction more. The afternoon heat was close to unbearable and the constant pressure from the queue was adding to the tension in Old Billy. To make the situation worse, the footpath seemed to be a solid wall of humanity, with half of Sydney's population shuffling southward up George Street, and the other half trudging down hill to the north, before disappearing into the underground rail system.

Old Billy was a crook.

A career criminal, who lived constantly outside society's rules. He knew it, happily admitted it, and was even proud of it.

Almost everyone who had met him in his sixty-three years on earth was also aware of it. He had been a crook as child, and he knew, and craved no other lifestyle.

His earliest childhood memories were of stealing fruit from the market stallholders in Pyrmont, mainly for the fun of it. As he grew into early school age, he had stood over younger kids for their pocket money, before graduating to the most lucrative of junior crimes, lifting the neighbour's milk money. This was foolishly left out each night in the forlorn hope that the coins would still be beside the empty bottles when "Charlie the Italian" made his rounds in the wee small hours.

It had been one cold, dark night in 1928 when Charlie had caught Billy and his thin, sickly little brother, Patrick, red handed. The two dirty boys attempted to scamper off with old Miss McKenzie's one shilling and threepence. Billy was eleven at the time, and Patrick only eight. Their young ages didn't help them on that occasion, as Charlie held both boys tightly by their grubby collars while he dragged them, protesting and swearing, into the light of a corner street lamp. Soon the massive hands of Constable Bernard Fry, the local beat walker, took over from the milkman. When Charlie told Fry his story, in his broken English, the huge policeman had grinned evilly at the boys before ordering the little Italian to continue his rounds. Fry had first handcuffed Billy to a railing, then picked up Patrick by his ankles and shook the terrified urchin up and down for a full minute. When several coins rattled out of Patrick's clothing and onto the stone roadway, Fry gathered them up and slid them into his own pocket. Then he manacled Patrick to the railing, and it was Billy's turn to be inverted and shaken.

He was carrying the bulk of the night's pickings, and almost ten shillings was soon tinkling and rattling onto the road. Fry placed this windfall in his pocket, and then delivered his size sixteen boot into the centre of Billy's buttocks. The child was lifted two foot clear of the pavement and a streak of white-hot agony invaded his lower back. He fell forward, landing face first in the rough gutter, and lay there sobbing in pain and fright. He heard Patrick receive the same treatment, and watched in terrified frustration as his brother's tiny, pale body flew past him, to land in the gutter, six feet further down the street. The harsh, cruel voice of Fry boomed down at the pair of terrified little boys.

'Now don't let me see you pair of buggers anywhere near anyone's front door, or I'll really do me block next time. Understand me, you pair of miserable little curs?'

Both boys were too frightened and in too much pain to answer. They simply lay were they had landed, each clutching at their own aching buttocks.

The slow, deliberate tread of Fry's footsteps eventually retreated into the darkness.

When silence returned to the street, Patrick sobbed and mumbled a promise to God that he would never steal again. Billy, despite his pain and concern for Patrick, mumbled a promise to himself to one day gain retribution.

When he was able to roll over and get painfully to his feet, Billy had already decided both the "*dago*" milkman and Constable Fry would pay dearly for this night.

As he progressed through the ranks of criminality, Billy learned all the skills he needed to ply his trade and extract his revenge. He became an expert pickpocket, learned to trick strangers into handing over money for false business schemes, and also knew how to break into almost any premises without leaving a trace of evidence.

But his reputation as a ruthless stand-over merchant was his most prized title.

At the age of nineteen, Billy was the head of a six-man gang, and the most feared thug around the waterfront suburbs of inner Sydney.

By the time he reached his thirties, he had amassed a sizeable wealth, including shares, houses and a string of almost legitimate businesses. With the wealth came the trimmings of success, such as pleasure boats, race horses and several motor cars.

But all the while, his excellent memory never strayed far from that cold, dark morning when he and his late brother, Patrick, were roughed up by Charlie the Italian, and severely injured by Constable Fry's mighty boot.

Around Sydney's waterfront, 1947 had been a memorable year for several reasons. In February there was the "Wharfies" prolonged strike, and the ensuing violent clashes with the police. When the "Wharfies" eventually resumed work, most things returned to normal until May, when a small freighter inexplicably capsized and sunk in Darling Harbour, drowning six of the crew and two dockworkers. A few other occurrences made the year one to remember, not the least of which was the unsolved, mysterious disappearance of two of the district's best known characters. One was the little old foreign milkman who had served the area for over twenty-five years, and the other was the burly, rough-diamond of a beat policeman who had patrolled those same streets over a similar time span.

Maybe one day in the future, some curious SCUBA diver might be enjoying himself forty feet below the surface near the southern pylons of the Sydney Harbour Bridge. He might encounter a tangle of cartwheels, iron hoops and rotting timber lying in the mud, and wonder what they once were. If this diver makes a closer investigation, he will probably notice the few remaining bones of a horse's skeleton, and maybe some slimy leather harness still attached. If he gets even more curious, he will probably find a small human skeleton, tied with thick copper wire to the bottom of a once serviceable milk cart. The entire pile of wreckage would be found to be weighed down by a dozen large milk churns, all filled with rocks. Maybe all this debris will be found, brought to the surface and investigated by the state's finest. The police may even, by some scientific means, identify Charlie the Italian.

But the remains of Constable Fry will never be discovered.

When fed, bound tightly hand and foot, into the roaring coal fired furnace of a cargo ship's boiler, even the largest of human bodies eventually stops screaming and disappears up the ship's funnel. The uniform and accoutrements soon cease to exist as well, and no trace is left, not even a silver button.

That was all ancient history as Old Billy Greene perspired in the bus queue.

Most of his original gang were either long dead, dribbling through their remaining days in some state-run old age institution, or securely locked away in Parramatta prison.

Billy had also spent some time in Parramatta, as well as Long Bay Jail.

His criminal career had always continued unabated, even during these interruptions and his evil empire continued to grow. There always seemed to be a ready supply of young thugs who wanted to work for Billy and run his errands. His wealth continued to grow as his business interests diversified into illegal gambling, prostitution, and the most lucrative of all, drug supply and distribution.

Billy had recently evaded a long stretch inside when the ruthless '21st' Division had raided his home unit in Alexandria.

Although a trio of tough Detectives questioned the old thug all night in a tiny room at Redfern police station, including resorting to a bit of rough treatment, he merely replied with a grin and a 'No comment'.

Eventually they had charged him with eighteen different offences, including living off immoral activities, goods in custody suspected of being stolen, and numerous drugs charges. When Billy's solicitor, the notorious Richard Oaks, had produced a wad of notes and counted out the required ten thousand dollars bail, the old criminal had grinned widely at the Detectives, enjoying their frustration as the lawyer demanded a receipt. While Billy signed the bail documents, the red-faced Detective Inspector Packard had leaned down and muttered fiercely in Billy's left ear,

'My teenage daughter is in hospital, half dead, because she was silly enough to take drugs. I've already lost a nephew to it, so I'm gunna push this all the way, you scum! That crap you bastards peddle is lethal, you bloody filthy little parasite. Try thinking about my daughter and her dead cousin, and see if you reckon your stinking money and your filthy rich lifestyle is worth it, ya mongrel dog!'

Old Billy had smirked, and replied from behind the safety of his solicitor and two of his biggest henchmen,

'You know what Packy? You shoulda told 'em to get their stuff from me. I only deal in quality gear, guaranteed. I would even organise a discount for a bulk order.'

Several other Detectives had had to restrain Packard as Old Billy and his entourage walked quickly away to a waiting car.

Billy had several Detectives on his payroll, and he made sure they earned their commissions this time. When he appeared in court to answer the charges three weeks later, the police were made to look foolish and incompetent when the prosecutor was forced to drop all charges. Apparently every shred of evidence gathered during and after that raid on Billy's home unit, had been destroyed or severely damaged in a small fire that had broken out in the division's offices late one night.

An internal investigation was underway, and several Detectives were under suspicion, but further action had yet to be taken.

After shaking his head and muttering a few quiet oaths, the fat, red faced old magistrate discharged Billy as reporters and cameramen formed up outside.

The case had been making front page headlines for three weeks, with the general expectation that one of Sydney's most notorious criminals was about to retire to Long Bay or Parramatta, permanently.

Billy had held press conference after press conference, all the while grinning and proclaiming innocence. He was interviewed by all the television stations, and made sure he wore a different coloured Italian silk suit for each program.

It was after the last television interview that some unseen hand had slipped a note to one of Billy's top men. The note stated, none too subtly, that each of Billy's four cars were now targets of an unknown bomber.

'You think getting off those charges was clever? Watch how clever we are at ridding the world of another parasite. It will be a real 'BLAST' Billy. For you as well as us. Which car, Billy? Ford Galaxy HUZ 453, Chrysler BBY 609, Jaguar XXO 559 or Holden ute ALO 163. It will be a 'BLAST' of justice at last. And if it isn't the dynamite, it will be another method that you won't see coming. Bye bye, Billy'

The henchman handed Billy the note and immediately the old crook panicked. The message was clear, and the listing of his four cars, complete with the registration plate details shook him deeply. All of the cars were registered in relative's or gang member's names, to guard against this sort of thing.

It was a well known fact that four members of the Public-Enemy-Number-One club had mysteriously perished in the previous two years. It always occurred right after they had beaten near certain convictions of major proportions, then boasted about it publicly. All of the deaths were mysterious, and the state Coroner had returned an open verdict on every single one. All the doctors and scientists who participated in the autopsies remained baffled by the sudden cessation of life in these famous crooks. The newsboys had even tried to run a scare campaign, using the words 'Vigilante' and 'Justice Seekers'. Comparisons were made to Charles Bronson's movie, 'Death Wish', but the campaign fizzled out when the last of those four criminals had been buried.

After riding home in a taxi, Billy, his solicitor and his two most trusted henchmen had devised a plan to keep Billy breathing for a few more years. They initially tried to talk him into fleeing overseas, or staying on his luxurious boat for at least twelve months.

He ruled both ideas out instantly, his old bravado coming to the fore. The old crime boss was eventually convinced to dispose of the cars, drop the flamboyant clothes and lifestyle, and conduct his business affairs in secret. This included moving from the Alexandria apartment, and using public transport exclusively. At least two of his gang were to be with him at all times, remaining discreetly in the background, ready to rush in and protect their boss should anything nasty take place.

Old Billy had set up house in a modest home unit in North Sydney, and he became very familiar with bus and train timetables between the city and Milson's Point. The flash suits were replaced with ordinary, everyday clothing, and he grew a fine moustache and a small, goatee beard to complete the new look.

Now, he cursed the unknown mob who had threatened him, as he lined up with the common herd to board a stinking bus, full of stinking people, driven by a stinking wog who probably couldn't even speak English. At least he was first in the line, so if any seats were still unoccupied, he would not have to stand up all the way home.

He casually glanced around him, grunting in satisfaction as he noticed big Jeff, his trusted number one body guard, about fifth or sixth in line. Jeff was pretending to read a newspaper, but Billy knew he would be alert for any trouble. He also knew 'Knifey' the vicious little Maltese thug who could stab, slice and dice you before you saw him coming, would be in the queue, a little further down from Jeff, but equally as watchful. The tall, solidly built man in a business suit behind Billy was attempting to complete a crossword in his folded newspaper. He seemed to have his fountain pen clenched between his teeth more often than scribbling words into the crossword puzzle. At least he wasn't pushing into Billy from behind like the smelly little old foreign woman who had been in that spot up until a few minutes ago. She had eventually become tired of the waiting, and stomped away, loudly cursing Sydney's buses, and all who travelled in them.

A bus appeared from around the corner, with the sign 'Not In Service' on its headboard.

It wouldn't be stopping, and Billy instinctively drew back slightly from the kerb as the big vehicle rushed towards the mass of humanity gathered on the footpath.

The bus was travelling at nearly forty kilometres an hour as it drew level with Billy.

The old criminal felt the slightest of tingles at the back of his neck, and thought it was nothing more than a slight muscle twinge. It was his final thought. A split second later his eyes went watery and his entire muscular system relaxed. He buckled, head first, toward the road and his face had almost made it to the bitumen surface when the front of the bus invaded the same space. A loud thump was the first sign of tragedy, then the bus leapt slightly into the air as the front wheels passed over the body. The driver applied his brakes, but momentum carried the rear wheels over the remains of Billy, now oozing blood from a dozen fresh openings in his skin.

Men shouted, women screamed and the crowd formed an instant circle around the smashed pile of flesh that had been a living, breathing human.

Big Jeff pushed his way through the circle, closely followed by Knifey. With mouths gaping they stared down at the tangle of skin and bones that had been their boss. Both thugs were initially too shocked to do anything but stare at the corpse. Jeff re-organised himself first, and began searching the crowd for anyone familiar. A rival gang member perhaps, a known hit man, a guilty looking face, anything. But all he saw was the sea of curious faces, all looking shocked and sickened, but still ogling the body.

The distressed bus driver joined the circle of onlookers. He appealed to the crowd, waving both arms as he shouted,

'He just-a fell inna front-a me! Did anybody a-witness it? Please, somebody, you must-a seen him just-a fall inna front-a my bus, please?'

Some members of the mumbling crowd nodded agreement, but most spared the distraught bus driver little more than a passing glance. The battered, bleeding body lying on the bitumen was much more interesting.

Jeff signalled covertly to Knifey. The two thugs slowly backed into the swelling crowd as two uniformed Policemen thrust their way through the throng. One was saying loudly,

'Make way, please. Police here. Make way.'

The other officer held a notebook aloft as he shouted,

'Did anybody see it? Any witnesses? Anyone?'

The distraught bus driver nodded vigorously and yelled,

'Please, anyone? You musta seen it. Tella the policeman, yes?'

Jeff and Knifey slowly and un-obtrusively made their way back to the footpath and disappeared down the entrance tunnel to the railway station. Jeff knew they could do nothing for their boss, and the best thing to do now was get out of the area as quickly as possible. More police were arriving and he knew sooner or later one of them would recognise either him or Knifey. Besides, Jake O'Rourke, Billy's second in command would be wanting a full explanation immediately.

CHAPTER TWO

Detective Constable Mike Walker re-read the crime bulletin for the third time as he sat at his desk in the Criminal Investigation Department of Wagga Wagga's ancient police station. The internal news-sheet, which had arrived via teleprinter less than half an hour ago, contained details of four major incidents which had occurred in Sydney over the previous twenty-four hours. An armed hold-up of a credit union, two rapes and the sudden death of a well-known criminal.

All these events took place over five hundred kilometres away, and were of only passing interest to the other Detectives in the upstairs offices.

They were more interested in finding out who was duffing cattle from out near North Wagga, or who was responsible for the break and enter at the railway station, and which particular local villain had lifted the three tons of copper wire from Southern Riverina County Council's depot during the weekend.

Normally the bulletin would hardly rate a second glance among any of Wagga's eight Detectives, unless it contained a warning that some offender might be heading for the Riverina. Mike Walker, however, felt compelled to study the bulletin more closely, even though he could not explain, even to himself, why it had captivated his interest so deeply. He studied the blurry text as he absently stirred his tea with a cheap pen.

The loud, gruff voice of his superior jerked him back to attention.

' 'mornin', Mikey, me lad. C'mon, we got a visit to make. Whatcha doin', staring at that thing?'

Detective Sergeant Lindsay Johnson pointed at the bulletin as he barked his greeting, orders and enquiry all in one authoritive sentence.

The tall, thickset sergeant was approaching fifty-five years of age, sported an expanding paunch, balding head and a large red nose which told any observer that this thirty year veteran of the NSW Police Force liked a drink. His grey trousers and pure white shirt did their best to hide the sure signs of ageing and bad living, but the bright red face and gravely voice confirmed heavy and regular intakes of alcohol and tobacco.

Johnson was also partial to a punt, and could often be found in the poker machine rooms at Wagga Leagues Club, or in the local Totaliser office or at the Wagga Wagga races whenever a meeting was scheduled. A good, thorough investigator, a hard man to beat in the courtroom and a tough, almost ruthless pursuer of criminals, Johnson was a respected figure around New South Wales' largest inland city. His character flaws were easily out pointed by his impressive record of catches and convictions. He was old school, right down to his lace-up shoes and the button-up fly in his suit trousers.

The veteran police officer also subscribed to the view that a belt around the ear hole was often warranted, either to prevent a young crook continuing in a life of crime, or to jog the memory of an experienced criminal who was having trouble remembering some detail or other.

Mike Walker loved working with Johnson, and had been thrilled to receive his first plain clothes assignment as junior partner to him. In the eight months since Walker had transferred from the Traffic Branch to C.I.B., he had learned more from Johnson than he ever expected to. Some of the sergeant's methods went against his grain, but Walker shared Johnson's belief that the ends usually justified the means.

'Just reading up on what's been happening in the big smoke, Sarg,' Mike replied. 'Old Billy Greene dropped dead yesterday. It says here he was waiting in a bus queue at Wynyard when he fainted or something, right in front of a dirty great bus.'

Johnson took the bulletin and read the article.

'Yeah, well, what dya think would happen if the old bastard gets run over by a bus? Those things weigh about ten tons, so if that old crook decides to play speed humps with 'em, he ain't likely to come out of it feeling too good, is he?'

Walker reclaimed the paper and said, pointing to the second page of the bulletin,

'Yeah, I know. But look. It says the Coroner is investigating, and the police doctor who attended reckons he was either dead or unconscious before the bus hit him. And three eyewitnesses have given statements saying Old Billy pitched forward just before the bus arrived, but the doctor has already ruled out a heart attack or stroke. That makes it a very suspicious death, in my book. And on top of that, this makes the fifth big time crook who has fallen off his perch in the past couple of years. And each of these buggers has just been found not guilty or the prosecutors lost the exhibits or something. In other words, all five of these birds slipped off the hook somehow. I tell you, Sarg, there's a definite pattern emerging here, if I'm any judge.'

'Which you aren't, Mikey. You're a bloody country Detective, not Sherlock Holmes or any kind of judge. Now, forget about that city stuff, and grab the car keys, will ya? We gotta go down to the railway and see the Station Master, because some bastard broke into the parcels office last night and lifted a heap of gear. C'mon, let's get going before those dopey railway blokes put their fingerprints all over everything. George is already on his way down there, so let's move.'

Johnson made it clear to his subordinate that the city matters were off limits, and he wanted to get started on their local case. The two men descended the wooden staircase and Walker fingered a set of keys as he headed for the trio of unmarked police cars parked in a rickety timber carport.

After clambering into the driver's seat of a shiny, white Holden sedan, Walker started the engine and waited for his superior. When Johnson eased his massive bulk into the passenger's seat, he turned to Mike and said sternly,

'Look, Mikey. What goes on in the big smoke is none of our business. You just let it lie, OK? We got enough to worry about here, ya got me? I don't want you wasting time and energy on shit that don't concern you, all right?'

'Sure, Sarg! It just caught my eye that every one of the mainline crooks that died over the last couple of years has just beaten some serious charges, then was seen to be skiting about it on the television or in the papers. And all of the deaths are still unsolved. Anyway, I'm not wasting any more time on those bastards. What's the story on this caper we're heading to?'

'Ok, as long as you understand. I don't want you sticking your nose into other section's business. They got their stuff to handle, we got ours. No more of it, right?'

Walker started the engine and reversed out of the carport. He nodded agreement but in his own thoughts he was puzzled at the Sergeant's emphatic instructions to lose interest in the deaths of the notorious criminals.

As the Holden cruised slowly down Baylis Street, Johnson explained to his junior,

'Apparently, just after the Tumbarumba rail motor left at around four thirty this morning, the night shift Assistant Station Master decided to take a walk around the station. He came to the parcels office and noticed the door was slightly open. He says there had been no parcels for Tumba, so he wondered why the parcels office door was even unlocked, let alone open. When he had a good look inside, he noticed some gear missing. That's all I got from the occurrence pad this morning. Greg Daley and his mate were on the night car, and they went down to do the initial report about five o'clock. Young Greg is pretty thorough, for a uniform, but him and his mate had about ten jobs to handle during the night, so we'll be starting from scratch. The boss has sent George down ahead and he gave the paperwork to us. That's all I know, so far.'

By the time Johnson had explained the few known facts to Walker, they had reached the car park outside the impressive building which served as Wagga Wagga's railway station. A pale blue Holden police car was in the adjacent parking bay, it's boot fully open and a shortish, middle-aged man dressed in a wrinkled suit was bending over the rear sill. The man's ill-fitting trousers looked like they badly needed ironing, and the un-buttoned coat was in dire need of a dry-clean. A grubby collar protruded from the top of the coat and a pair of scuffed desert boots completed the ensemble.

As Walker and Johnson approached from behind, the shabby figure stood upright and turned, smiling a greeting at the new arrivals.

'Morning, Sarg. Mike. Youse blokes got this one?'

Detective George Somersby was a brilliant Detective, a likeable, smiling man, Wagga Wagga's only trained fingerprint officer, and the most scruffily dressed individual in the local sectional command. Over the past ten years several senior officers had tried smartening up Somersby's appearance, but his constant good humour, as well as his competence and dedication to the job had soon distracted their efforts. He had been a scruff as a child, at high school, through his uniform days, and currently, after eight years as a Detective, was still in a constant state of dishevelment. His value to the police force in Wagga Wagga was more than apparent to the senior officers and they soon realised he was best left alone to perform his work.

'Yeah. They needed a couple of top notch men on this one, so here we are,' the big old Detective grinned as he informed the fingerprints man.

Somersby smiled and nodded to Walker.

'No doubt about it, then. How're you going, Mikey?'

'Great, thanks George. Found anything, yet?' Walker replied.

Somersby picked up two small suitcases before he closed his car boot. As the three Detectives walked through the waiting room, and onto the platform, he said cheerfully,

'I haven't started yet. As soon as I got here, old Jimmy, the Station Master, dragged me into his office for a cup of tea. He's really worried about this, poor old bugger. I had a quick squiz in the parcels office, but it all looks fine to me. I just told Jimmy to tell his staff to keep out of there until I do me work. He's stuck a porter on guard there for us.'

Johnson nodded agreement as they made their way to the parcels office. A uniformed, youthful railway porter stood slouching at the doorway, a cigarette drooping from his mouth as he watched a small diesel engine shunting some wagons into a siding opposite the platform. He straightened as the Detectives reached him, saying slowly,

'Youse the coppers?'

'*Police*, to you, sonny!' Johnson barked.

The railwayman immediately assumed a formal manner.

'Sorry, sir. 'Police', then. Are you the police?' he asked.

'Yes, we are. Where's ya boss? Go get him, will ya? 'n hurry up about it,' Johnson growled. Then he grinned as the youngster scuttled down the platform and disappeared into the Station Master's office.

Somersby said, as he slid the heavy parcels room door open,

'Jimmy says there was a couple of small parcels addressed to Hyde's Jewellers on the shelves. He reckons the suppliers sometimes send small boxes of precious stones and gold to the jewellers in ordinary parcels, to throw off any thieving buggers that might like to knock it off. Instead of using heavy security, which would attract attention, they try their luck through the normal passenger rail method.'

'Yeah?' Johnson said with mild surprise. 'Bloody silly risk to take, I reckon.'

'Yeah, I suppose so. But, it's been working, at least up 'til now,' said Somersby.

They were joined by a worried Station Master. He showed the Detectives where the parcels had been sitting on a shelf, and produced a record book which listed the arrival dates and consignee of every parcel. A column showed the name of the railway employee receiving the items, and another listed if or when notification was made to the intended receiver. Johnson studied the book and questioned the Station Master about the entries, while Somersby dusted the shelf, doors, windows and the few other parcels left in the room with his special fingerprint powder.

The trio of Detectives spent nearly two hours at the railway station, questioning some employees, photographing, dusting for fingerprints and searching for clues. It appeared as if some-one knew exactly what was in the two small parcels. Only the Station Master and the recipient were supposed to know, and so Johnson questioned the railwayman for a full half hour. The Detective was eventually satisfied that the man had nothing more to answer for and thanked him for his co-operation. Somersby packed up his mysterious kit of powder and brushes, before heading back to the police station. Johnson and Walker sat in their car and reviewed the facts.

'Trouble with this sort of thing is the stuff, being so small and easily hidden, could be in bloody Sydney, or Melbourne, or bloody Timbuktu by now,' Johnson growled.

Walker nodded as he fitted the key into the ignition switch and started the engine.

'Yeah, that's what I was thinking. But what about the other stuff that they got? A box of pump parts for 'Riverina Ag' and something addressed to the council. If some crook was after the jeweller's stuff, why would they bother to take the other junk?'

'To throw us off the scent, Mikey, me boy,' Johnson replied. 'I reckon we should have a little cruise around the streets near here, and I wouldn't mind bettin' we find the rest of the haul. It's worth a try, anyhow. Head up the lane there, beside the pub.'

Walker steered the Holden into a narrow lane and parked behind a small truck. The two Detectives alighted from the car and walked slowly along the lane, one on each side, searching for any signs of the discarded parcels. It wasn't long before Johnson called across to Walker, a tone of satisfaction and triumph in his voice.

'Hey, Mikey! Cop this.' He was pointing into a slender opening between two buildings.

Mike hurried across the roadway and peered into the dark recess.

A metre-long cardboard tube, with several large railway parcels stamps attached, was lying amongst the old soft drink cans, lolly papers and other rubbish. It was addressed to the local shire council, and, unlike the other dust covered items in the small space, the tube was clean and still glowing with newness. Johnson used a pen and a small stick to grasp the tube, and gently withdrew it into full daylight. He grunted in satisfaction and said to Walker,

'Jump on the radio, Mikey. Tell 'em to get old George back down here to dust this thing. I told ya we'd probably come across somethin' like this, didn't I?'

Walker smiled and shook his head slowly in amazement.

'You sure did, Sarg. Good on you. You picked it in one.'

His voice was full of admiration and respect for his superior. Still smiling, the young man hurried to the police car and radioed his message back to base.

Later, after the fingerprints man had dusted the tube and it was safely secured away in the evidence room at Wagga police station, Johnson and Walker drove back into the business district and parked in front of a glass fronted jeweller's shop. Before getting out of the car, Johnson outlined his strategy to the junior Detective.

'First up, we'd better tell old man Hyde that he's short two parcels of gold or diamonds or what-ever they were. Be a good time to ask him an' his staff a few questions while we're at it. It's got all the hallmarks of an inside job, this one. Either from here, or from the railway. I'm betting it's come from one of those two ends. You be the goodie for this mob, and I'll be the hard bastard. If we come up empty, we'll swap places when we question the railway boys again, later on. Ok, Mikey?'

The jeweller was distraught about the loss, but admitted he carried insurance on the consignment. The old man's face showed genuine distress and his breathing became rapid and shallow. Miss Cousins, his senior saleswoman, was far more concerned about her employer, than the missing shipment. She fussed over the old man, insisting he sit down and relax. She ordered a younger salesgirl to fetch a cool glass of water for the little jeweller. Walker eased the woman to one side and quietly asked her the routine questions. She snapped back her mono-syllabic answers with an air of annoyance and impatience, all the while keeping one eye on her elderly boss.

The first of the younger girls expressed shock and indignation that she should be questioned. Johnson knew her father, who was a leading criminal lawyer in the area. He had no time for the fast-talking solicitor, and now even less for his pompous, arrogant daughter. Although Walker and Johnson soon eliminated her from their list of suspects, both Detectives would have enjoyed embarrassing her some more. Her attitude was one of contempt and indifference, and Walker was glad to dismiss her and move on to the next salesgirl. The second young girl was nervous and twitchy when questioned about any knowledge of the missing parcels, and their contents. She spoke with a slight stutter, and appeared on the brink of tears several times. When Mike tried to settle her down with quiet, re-assuring words, she stammered quickly, 'It….it's just that…that…that I've never been questioned by a…a policeman before.'

Johnson allowed Mike to play the "good cop" and remained silent while his young colleague said quietly,

'That's ok, Rachel. I understand. Don't think of me as a policeman. Just as a bloke who wants to help you get through this thing. Take it easy, now. It'll be all right. Take your time. When did you find out that Mister Hyde sometimes gets his gold sent through the railways? Did he tell you, or did you find out some other way?'

'I..I..I j…j…just saw him opening a p…p.. parcel a few w..weeks ago……………..' The girl stopped talking abruptly as she realised she had been trapped.

The two Detectives exchanged looks, and Johnson asked firmly.

'How old are you, Rachel? Are you over eighteen, Girl?'

'I'm…I'm…I'm nearly.. seventeen, Sir,' the girl said, sobbing slightly.

'All right, you just calm down. Is there anything else you want to tell us? Anything at all?' Walker spoke quietly.

The girl had her head down, looking at the floor. She shrugged her shoulders before shaking her head. Walker said quietly,

'Ok, then, Rachel. If we need to speak to you again, we'll be in touch. I'll get your address from Mister Hyde, ok?'

She raised her head and tried to smile at Walker. She nodded agreement and Mike gestured her to leave. She hurried away to the back of the shop and busied herself arranging some fancy figurines on a glass shelf.

The two Detectives exchanged knowing looks, and returned to Hyde.

'We've got a few lines of inquiry to follow, Mister Hyde. Mike will need to get a few details from you, and we'll be in touch shortly. See ya.'

Johnson shook hands with the old man, smiled at the scowling head saleswoman and walked outside to the waiting police car.

Walker joined him after a few minutes and they drove to the police station, discussing their theories and ideas. They agreed the young girl named Rachel was worthy of further questioning.

As the diesel engine coughed and wound down to a vibrating stop, the driver pushed in the clutch pedal, allowing the tractor to roll a few more metres until all momentum was spent. He slumped forward and leaned his upper torso against the steering wheel. Andy Keyes stared at the dusty fuel gauge for ten seconds, noting the position of the white needle. It was hard up against the 'E', and told him he should have topped up the steel tank on which his right foot rested, when he had paused for a quick lunch, just over two hours ago. He sighed to himself and unfolded his long legs from their driving position, then swung them to the ground.

Far to the south, barely visible on the shimmering horizon, was the outline of a battered old Valiant utility. The cargo area of the old ute contained a forty-four gallon drum, half full of dieseline, and a quick action hand pump. He glanced up at the blazing sun, re-positioned his sweat stained old hat then set off in a long striding walk towards the distant vehicle.

His mind came alive as his body settled in for the long trek.

The recent visit to the big city had allowed him and his wife to enjoy some time at the beach, cleansing their souls of the hot, tedious lifestyle of mixed farming. After a half day observing the city sights the couple had found their way to Circular Quay, where they boarded a creaking old wooden ferry. The pleasant harbour crossing was over soon enough and they had made their way directly to Manly beach. Andy had changed into a pair of blue nylon swimming trunks, then chose to lie on the soft sand for half an hour, listening to the soothing sound of waves pounding the shore. He had thought over the task he still had to attend to, and planned his schedule for the next day. They had business to attend to which might take up the full day tomorrow, and he needed to be fully rested and alert, ready for the challenge.

Anita, his beautiful Malaysian wife, had turned quite a few heads in her bright green bikini as she swam and paddled in the small waves near the water's edge. He had watched her as she enjoyed the cool salt water caressing her tiny, brown body. Her smile and suggestive gestures proved too much for him to resist, and he had soon joined her in the shallow waves, holding her firmly to him as they were tossed gently up and down by the cool salt water.

By the following evening, their third day in Sydney, their business dealings were completed and the brief respite was over. They had boarded the Riverina Express at Central station, to return to Wagga Wagga and the drudgery of farm life.

Now, as he trudged across the ploughed paddock towards the old utility, he grinned as he pictured his wife this morning. Gone was the tiny bikini and the sexy demeanour, replaced by a pair of dirty denim jeans, loose fitting shirt and old sandshoes. She had risen, as usual, with the sun, and had his breakfast cooked and waiting when he dragged himself into the kitchen at around seven o'clock. As Andy slowly ate his meal, Anita was already into her second hour of housework, polishing the furniture and dusting some framed photographs which adorned three book cases in their spacious lounge room. His many football and cricket trophies were next, each one being picked up from a shelf, carefully dusted and wiped, then lovingly replaced in exactly the same position as it had been. Her cleaning routine was both repetitive and thorough. Any speck of dust had little or no chance in the home as she completed her daily, self-imposed tasks.

He finished his breakfast and mentally prepared for the next few hours, ploughing the lucerne paddock with the old tractor. The local radio newsreader had gleefully told his audience that midday temperatures would be around the forty-three degrees Celsius today. Keyes had grimaced as he thought of the hours ahead, sitting on the hard, unsprung seat of the old Fordson tractor, exposed to all that sun. He made sure he grabbed the water bottle Anita had prepared for him, before heading for the large open shed twenty metres from the homestead. As he was loading the fuel drum into the old utility, he saw Anita already outside, tossing wheat to the three dozen fowls and pair of Chinese geese in a long wire pen behind the shed.

She had looked around, a huge grin on her pretty face, beaming from under a ridiculously large straw sombrero. He blew her a kiss and she had pretended to catch it and blow it back to him. Smiling contentedly, he drove the old vehicle out into the paddocks, following a rough track along the fences until he came to the tractor parked within the large area set aside for the next lucerne crop.

Now, as his long legs carried him across the ploughed ground towards the ute, he admonished himself for not topping up the tractor's diesel tank earlier. Then he excused himself, remembering that he did have other matters on his mind this fine, hot morning.

Another yellow envelope had arrived unexpectedly in yesterday's post.

This was the second one this year, and only a few weeks after the previous one.

As he had always done, Keyes had decided not to open it last night, and instead concentrate his thoughts on the urgent farming tasks that needed attending to. After all, he had told Anita they both knew what was in the plain yellow envelope.

He pursed his lips and shook his head slightly as his long legs covered the ground quickly towards the old ute. As he walked, his gloomy thoughts continued,

'If only this bloody farming paid more for the effort we put in! And if only a decent price for the wheat wasn't constantly eroded by transport and other costs. And if the lazy bloody auctioneers would hold out for better prices when selling our sheep.'

Then, he was sure, he wouldn't have to fret and worry about when that next dreaded envelope would arrive.

He reached the old Valiant and quickly started the engine. His thoughts were still on the envelope which was sitting on the mantle piece above the marble fireplace in his lounge room. As he drove along the rough track which circumnavigated the paddock, his fertile mind began planning his response to the correspondence he knew would be contained within the envelope. The beautiful Anita would listen silently as he read aloud the contents, and only offer her suggestions when he asked her for them.

Which he would, as he always did. Seeking her opinion and thoughts were always an integral part of his response to the arrival of the dreaded yellow envelopes.

As the old vehicle drew alongside the stalled tractor, Andy glared sourly at the faded paintwork and surface rust on the machine. Despite the absolute reliability of the tractor, he hated it intensely. It was the most tangible representation of his failings as a farmer.

Most of the neighbouring farmers possessed sparkling new tractors, flash cars and large, imposing homesteads. Andy's determination, fully supported by Anita, not to go into more debt had stood them in good stead up until now. However lately he had noticed most of the larger tasks were taking twice as long as the other farmers to complete and the tractor was the prime cause. The neighbour's machines were much larger, more powerful and multi-tooled. They therefore made short work of the ploughing, sowing or harvesting work while Andy slaved away with the little old Fordson.

It all came down to money, and he believed the best way to acquire any degree of wealth was to stay away from debts.

In recent times, when the yellow envelopes arrived, he found himself doubting this philosophy more and more.

CHAPTER THREE

Mike Walker studied his notebook, frowning at his own handwriting. Some of the hastily scrawled words needed a degree of deciphering, even by their author.

He eventually made enough sense of the mess to transfer the entries onto his typewriter. His report on the progress made into the solving of the railway station break and enter listed all of the facts, summary of interviews and the follow up action proposed by Sergeant Johnson. A formal, recorded interview with Rachel Morris, the junior employee of Hyde's Jewellers, was scheduled for the following morning. Enquiries by Walker had revealed Rachel was currently being squired around town by a certain Robert Wayne Metters. Metters was known to police as a petty criminal and had in fact been convicted in the local court only last month on a charge of 'Goods in custody, suspected of being stolen'.

He was also known as a minor drug dealer, often selling small bags of marijuana to high school students or other young people around the town.

Walker had not encountered Metters before, but Johnson had had several meetings with the lightweight member of Wagga's criminal element.

'Yeah, I know that piece of *"shite",*' the grizzled old sergeant growled when Walker told him of the latest development. 'He's one of these bludgers who hasn't worked a day in his miserable life. I first caught the bastard lifting a couple of pushbikes from a school, about four years ago. That's his go. Stealing from school kids, or standin' over 'em for their bloody lunch money. I gave him a good wallop over the ear hole, and made him put the bikes back. Then I frog marched him into the school and made him apologise to the Headmaster and the kids who owned the bikes. I was gonna let it go at that, but the stupid bastard rung the Inspector and tried to lodge a complaint about me. We had old Harry Stower as the boss then. Harry tells him to come in and see him. When the idiot fronted at the counter, old Harry grabs him by the collar, waltzes him upstairs and tells me to charge him with stealing the bikes. We done him on the stealing charge but he got away with a bond. Ever since then he's slowly added to his repertoire. I been hearing various things about him over the last coupla years and I seen him in court a few times since then. Seen him in the holding cell a coupla times, too. Who told you he was hanging around with our young Rachel?'

Walker stopped typing his report. He swung his chair around to face his superior, and pointed across the room towards another Detective's desk.

'Sergeant Mashman told me. He saw Metters with Rachel at the football on Sunday, then him and the boss clocked the two of 'em walking hand in hand down the main street later that night. When we were talking about the job, and I mentioned Rachel,

'Masho' told me about her new boyfriend. I checked him out in the records and reckoned he might have something to contribute.'

Johnson glanced at Mashman's empty desk, then read the report. He nodded as he said, 'Ah, a great light begins to shine. Bob Metters, eh? That's a good job, young Mikey. We'll make a Detective outta you yet. I reckon this little case just got simplified a bit. Hopefully George has deciphered the finger prints by now, because I know we got Metters's dabs on file here. When we interview Rachel, leave out any mention of Bob Metters. Then I'll drop it on her when she leasts expects it. As soon as we break her, which shouldn't be long, we'll pick up her low-life boyfriend and hopefully wrap it all up. I don't think, assuming we're right, of course, that Mister Metters would have worked out how to get rid of the gold yet. He's cunning, but pretty stupid as well. He'll probably try to flog it in a pub, or at the pawn shop. You knock off and go home as soon as you finish the progress report. I'll call in and see Billy Flegg at the pawn shop. He owes me a bit of a favour, so I'll get him to let us know if the gold turns up at his shop. He can put the word around at the pubs for us, too. Tomorrow, assuming young Rachel opens her gob, we can pick up Metters and give him a bit of a grilling. If none of that works, we'll put a bit of pressure on the railway blokes. I'm bloody certain one of those two ends is where we'll find our gold thief, but I'm betting on Mister Metters. Orright? I'm off. See ya Mikey.'

The big Detective slapped Walker lightly on his shoulder, and left the office.

Alone, Walker thought about the Sergeant's information. He grinned to himself when he recalled Johnson's phrase, "he owes me a bit of a favour". He could only wonder how a shifty pawn broker could come to owe a senior Detective like Johnson a favour.

Still grinning slightly, Walker continued typing the report, adding the information about Robert Wayne Metters to the story.

Seated at the huge old kitchen table, Andy Keyes stared at the yellow envelope as he held it in his right hand. In his left hand was a shiny letter opening knife, poised to slice through the thick paper and reveal the contents. He looked up and saw Anita watching him. She smiled her assurance, nodding her head once at him.

'I wish I didn't have to open this, Sweetie. I really don't want to. It gives me the willies, honest it does. And you deserve a much better existence than this, Beautiful.'

The little Asian woman shrugged her shoulders, and, still smiling at him, said quietly, 'It is ok, my husband. We will get through it together, as always. Like you always say, we are a team, and as a team we will deal with it, ok, yes?'

He looked into her pretty face and drew strength from her confidence. As he inserted the paper knife into the envelope, his thoughts were more on how his love for this tiny beauty grew stronger daily, rather than on the dreaded contents of the letter.

He slowly withdrew the two sheets of paper and three photographs. After he read the entire letter several times, his shoulders slumped as the he absorbed the text, and it's meaning. After another re-read, Keyes handed the papers to his wife, and she, too, read the letter several times, her lips pursed and her brow furrowed.

He stood up eventually and sighed.

'I'd better see what I can do. How much cash have we got in the safe, Love?'

She arose from her seat, placing the letter on the table as she did.

'I think about three hundred, maybe a little more. I check now for you, my husband.'

Her faint accent was enhanced by her method of expression. Although Anita had an excellent understanding of the English language, her speech still somehow conveyed the underlying submissiveness bred into the women of her birth country.

He had fallen madly in love with the beautiful young girl when he had first laid eyes on her in Malaysia, over eight years ago. He was a visiting soldier, a temporary liaison officer, representing the Special Air Service Commando Regiment, to the Malaysian Secret Police. Anita had been appointed as his contact, guide and interpreter. He was a tall, athletic Captain, and a member of Australia's most elite group of Commandos. His group were trained to kill with bare hands, guns, knives or just about any implement which could be utilised. They also had expertise in infiltration, undercover spying and code work. Deep water S.C.U.B.A. diving was also part of their repertoire. The training included an intensive physical fitness regime. Keyes' Company of fifty-two Australians had been temporarily attached to the Malaysian Army's SAS equivalent, to carry out joint operations against an underground group of Islamic revolutionaries. The rebel group had declared their intentions of overthrowing the Malaysian government, and then closing the country's borders to all non-Islamic states, including Australia. As there were two full regiments of Australian troops stationed throughout Malaysia, numerous trade missions operating as well as hundreds of Australian citizens working in the country at the time, the threat was taken seriously, and a secret mission to destroy the militants from within was commenced. Although two Australian SAS members, and at least twenty Malaysian troops had perished, the joint operation, lasting nearly two years, had been spectacularly successful. Over two thousand rebels had been eliminated, with around five hundred captured and handed over to the Secret Police. The whereabouts of those captives was not known outside the ranks of the Malaysian Secret Police, and not many others cared. Andy Keyes, for one, was certain they had met with a slow, painful death. After witnessing the cowardly bomb attacks and raids on innocent families these individuals had perpetrated, Andy decided they deserved everything they received. He had quickly put them, and their fate, from his mind.

Anita had been a front line member of the Malaysian squad, and Andy had witnessed her talents whilst the two participated in joint operations. At first he had found her skills in the art of self defence, torture and even killing, very confronting. Her beautiful face, sparkling eyes, perfect figure and quiet demeanour, combined with her tiny stature, put one in mind of a fashion model, or high school beauty queen, rather than a highly trained and ruthless commando.

He gradually came to admire her, not just for her physical attributes, but also her dedication and integrity. As a liaison officer, he had shared many 'after operations' debriefings with her, and each time he felt helpless as he fell more and more in love with her. They were supposed to be colleagues: aloof, professional and devoid of emotions. When he finally confessed to her his true feelings, she had responded by standing up on her tip toes, hugging him tightly and kissing his lips with a passion that nearly took away his breath. Then she revealed that she had exactly the same feelings for him, but her training and breeding had prevented her from making the first move.

When, six months later, he had completed his final mission, and was given his orders to return to Australia, he had immediately asked her to marry him. Her enthusiastic acceptance had been tempered by the knowledge that each of them would require the permission of their respective superiors. After some diplomatic negotiations between the two leaders, permission was granted, and Australian citizenship for Anita had been hastily arranged. The happy couple were married under Malaysian law, and a reception that lasted two and a half days was held in the SAS canteen. They were then transported to Perth, Western Australia, where the newlyweds lived on base at SAS headquarters. Andy underwent three intense months of debriefs and retraining, before final discharge from the army.

Combining what funds they had between them, the couple had headed to the east coast and on down to Andy's childhood home, the Riverina district of New South Wales. They immediately began resurrecting his deceased parent's derelict farm. The farm, named 'Rocky Crop', had first to be cleared of Paterson's Curse and other weeds.

The happy couple had lived in a tent as they gradually restored the large homestead.

In the first year they had bred sufficient sheep to barely survive, before turning their hands to wheat and lucerne crops, as well as a few cattle. A large bank mortgage allowed them to re-stock and equip the farm, and the books showed they were only just managing to keep their business afloat. Now, after four seasons, the transport costs and low livestock prices were starting to eat into the finances. Andy was sure the farm could pay it's way, and even provide a decent living, if he could get some breathing space.

The bank had initially been sympathetic, allowing deferred payments and even granting a healthy overdraught to the young couple. But now he was beginning to understand the reality of owing large sums of money and he did not like it at all.

The cure for all of his ills was simple. Another source of income was required.

He knew that that is always easier said than done. The farm allowed very little spare time for other careers, and his talents and skills outside of farming did not exactly place him in high demand on the open job market.

His one bright spot in his life was the beautiful little woman who was always there for him, supporting, smiling, reassuring. She deserved so much more than this lifestyle.

Then, after nearly two years of struggling, two strangers had visited the farm on a bright spring day. The men had produced identification, showing them as representatives of Australia's leading bank, which held the mortgage over their farm. They said that they had come to see what assistance the young couple could be offered to allow them to retain the property. After a full day of explanations and discussion, along with some persuasion, an agreement had been reached between the men and Andy and Anita.

Despite this un-expected development, the farm continued to incur more costs than revenue, and Andy felt he was slipping behind again.

And then the first of the distinctive yellow envelopes had arrived.

Then another, and ten months later, the third. Andy and Anita dealt with the correspondence as soon as possible, but then a fourth envelope arrived two months ago. Now, just as he felt his stress levels returning to normal, this latest one had been delivered in last night's mail bag.

CHAPTER FOUR

A large crowd had gathered outside the old court house. Wollongong's main street was lined with television and radio vans, all with multiple antennae and aerials sticking up at different heights and angles. Newspaper reporters, distinguished from the electronic media representatives by their more dishevelled appearance, pushed and shoved one another, or climbed onto the old sandstone wall surrounding the court house entrance. The newspaper men waved cameras or notebooks, while the radio and television reporters brandished microphones as their weapons of choice. Uniformed and plain clothed police officers mingled with the media men, trying to keep a lid on the excitement. Around two hundred members of the general public craned their necks, or strained other parts of their bodies, attempting to see over the tops or through the legs of the massive media scrum. The pushing, shoving, jockeying and manoeuvring reached a crescendo as the heavy wooden doors of the court house swung open, and a tight group of men emerged, completely surrounding a tall, grey haired individual. Reporters shouted questions, photographers snapped shot after shot, and the majority of the general public began muttering amongst themselves.

The cordon of lawyers parted slightly, and the grey haired man held up his hand, indicating he wished for silence. Almost immediately the large crowd began to quieten. When the sea of sound had subsided, the man drew himself up to his full height and addressed the crowd, 'Ladies and gentlemen. First let me thank Judge Gordon for bringing down his verdict, which vindicated my stance, and my claim of innocence. It was the right verdict, the proper verdict, and the only verdict that could be reached in our free and democratic society. Secondly, allow me to thank my legal team. Mister Wilkinson here, his associate, Mister John Collins, and my solicitor Larry Kind This efficient team has worked tirelessly on this matter, exposing not only the stupidity of the police case, and the incompetence of the particular Detectives who staged this futile vendetta against me. But also the rampant, entrenched corruption within the New South Wales Police Force. Now, after wasting so much of taxpayers money pursuing me, knowing in their own minds I was an innocent man, those same policemen have the audacity to request a 'gag' order be placed on me and my team. They do not want you, the honest citizens of Wollongong, and their employers, to know what a miscarriage of justice they tried so hard to perpetrate. Ladies and gentlemen, the truth is now out, and hopefully, these corrupt officers will see the error of their ways, and either go about their duty with a bit more honesty and integrity or better still, resign their positions and let some honest men do the job.'

The was some applause, and a few shouts of encouragement, but most of the assembled crowd focussed their attention on the group of Detectives standing to the side of the grey haired man and his legal team. The press men turned as one to catch the reaction of the grim faced policemen. Detective Chief Inspector

Allan Muscatt, the leader of the group, glared at the man, and tried to ignore the numerous microphones which were being thrust into his face.

'Chief Inspector Muscatt, do you have anything to say about that?' a voice called.

'Inspector Muscatt, what do you say to Ian Carter's statement, that you and your team are corrupt?' another reporter shouted.

'Any comment on Mister Carter's allegations, Detective Muscatt?' a red-faced newspaperman asked desperately.

Despite the temptation, Muscatt and the other Detectives remained silent. The group of policemen walked away from the courthouse, heading for a pair of un-marked police cars. As they descended the steps, the smirking Carter, said loudly to the media crowd, 'You won't get anything from them, Gentlemen. They have made a massive error in attacking me, and laying those scandalous false charges against me, and they know it. I sincerely hope they think twice before harassing an honest, innocent citizen again.'

The gloating self-confidence of Carter was in stark contrast to his demeanour when he entered the court a little over two hours ago. Despite the assurances of his legal team, particularly the sun-tanned, blonde haired solicitor, Larry Kind, Carter had been genuinely concerned about the eleven charges which were to be heard. The police had charged him with six counts of supplying prohibited drugs, three charges of carnal knowledge of a minor, and the Australian Commonwealth Police had chipped in with two charges of sheltering an illegal immigrant.

Carter's brother was a prominent pharmacist, who owned a string of Chemist's shops. It had long been suspected by the majority of the populace of New South Wales's third largest city that the Carter brothers liked to experiment with various drugs, and were not too shy in supplying a dope-induced thrill to selected young people of either gender, in return for sexual favours. Although the rumours had circulated for nearly ten years, no charges had ever been laid, and no solid accusations had ever been broadcast. Until two weeks ago. For the last six months Ian Carter had been seen around the city in the company of a young Asian girl. The girl was always seen clinging to Carter's arm, and even the most casual observer would have noted her age to be little over twelve, or perhaps thirteen at the most. The rumour mill went into overdrive, but no-one had actually come out publicly and said what most people were thinking.

That all changed when Detective Inspector Allan Muscatt had been promoted to Chief Inspector and transferred to Wollongong. The tea-total Muscatt was a former member of the Consorting Squad, an experienced Drug Squad investigator and a staunch believer in family values. He had taken an instant dislike to the Carter brothers at their first encounter. That had been at a Chamber of Commerce meeting when Muscatt was invited to meet the city's leading citizens and council members. He had already heard the rumours from other police, but after meeting Ian and Tony Carter, Muscatt had experienced the 'gut feeling' that these men were persons possessed of extremely low morals. After the little Asian girl had appeared, Muscatt decided to place Ian Carter under regular surveillance. When a Detective observed him on Fairy Meadow beach giving the girl some pills, then undressing her in the back of his Mercedes Benz car, Muscatt ordered his men to move in and make the arrest. The police case had alleged Wollongong's best known Real Estate agent, former mayor and current councillor had been harbouring the young Vietnamese girl who had arrived by fishing boat, along with fifty or so other refugees, about ten months ago. The girl had told them through an interpreter that Carter regularly gave her the pills, then, when she was in a semi-conscious state, would have sex with her, sometimes twice a day. She admitted she did not know her exact age, but she thought she was either twelve or thirteen. The girl provided a written statement to Muscatt before being whisked away by the immigration people. The sensational news of Carter's arrest spread quickly and the local press had enthusiastically followed every stage of the case. When the hearing date arrived, the heavyweights of the Sydney, Canberra and Melbourne media descended on Wollongong to cover every sordid detail.

Larry Kind was a shady lawyer, who always seemed to turn up when a rich or famous person was accused of a serious crime. His smooth Italian suits, complete with colourful silk scarf and handmade shoes, were a semi-permanent feature of the district courts in Sydney, Wollongong or Goulburn. Always seen with a huge cigar between his lips, Kind could be relied upon to magically appear at the side of any minor celebrity who found himself up against the law.

After quickly negotiating a healthy fee from Carter, Kind had marshalled an impressive team of like-minded lawyers, and assured his client that an acquittal was as good as done. When each piece of evidence was presented to the court, either Queens Counsel Albert Wilkinson or Barrister John Collins would take the presenter through every detail, gradually extracting tiny discrepancies or doubts. This alone would not be enough to bring about the collapse of the police case, but when the immigration representative took the stand things swung around dramatically. The senior officer was forced, under intense questioning by Wilkinson, to reveal that the little Vietnamese girl had fled the safe house in Melbourne where they had installed her, and had not yet been located. Kind had then played his trump card. A well-known Victorian private investigator was called to the stand, and happily told the court he had found the girl, now living with a gang of petty criminals, in the suburb of Coburg. He produced a short, 16mm film which was shown to the stunned, silent court. The film depicted the same innocent little girl helping some males shredding marijuana and placing it in small 'deal' bags. Later she is seen smiling sleepily at the camera as she swallows a handful of pills. Then she is seen outside a co-ed high school, passing out 'deals' of the illegal weed to excited school students. Finally

Barrister Collins had produced a Medico Legal report, signed by one of Melbourne's most noted celebrity doctors. The report stated that the girl was examined, found to be at least seventeen, or even eighteen years of age, had been sexually active for several years, and was, in the good doctor's opinion, a long time user of various barbiturates.

With the police case faltering, then collapsing around them, Collins went for the final assault. He had gleefully offered to produce the doctor, and even the girl if necessary, for cross examination, should the judge deem it appropriate. The judge declined, instead ordering the girl's whereabouts be revealed to the Immigration Department.

As the charges were formally dismissed, Carter had shaken hands with his legal team, and grinned widely over at the furious Muscatt.

The experienced Detective knew that he had been robbed, denied of a simple victory by some underhanded means. His instincts were to stand up, draw his service pistol and plant one right into the smirking mouth of Carter. He forced himself to turn away and stare at his notes for a full thirty seconds, allowing his rage to cool as Carter and his entourage left the courtroom.

Outside, as the press had swarmed towards Carter, Larry Kind stood congratulating himself. The few thousand dollars spent on recruiting a corrupt immigration officer and a gang of Ex-Vietnamese 'refugees' who had formed themselves into a successful little drug supply organisation, had been a very wise investment. The five thousand dollars paid to the doctor for a carefully scripted report had also been worthwhile.

Now, as the frustrated police team drove away, and Carter gave his gloating interview, the solicitor stood beside his two legal colleagues, basking just out of the limelight and visualising the large amount of figures written on the cheque he was to receive from his thankful client.

As he chewed lightly on his cigar, he felt a tug on his coat sleeve. He turned and noted an old man, dressed in casual shirt and trousers, topped by a white straw sun hat. The old man said nothing, but smiled as he handed a plain white envelope to Kind. The solicitor looked down at the envelope as he took it, and the old man slipped back into the crowd.

The envelope had just three words written on the front, "Ian Carter. Confidential"

Kind looked around for the little old man, but there was no sign of him. If he had looked beyond the crowd of media men, and the curious crowd of citizens, he may have observed the old man, now sitting in the back seat of a pale green Holden sedan, watching him closely as the car drove slowly away from the kerb.

Seeing no sign of the envelope deliverer, Kind waited until the press finally tired of Carter's bragging and began to disperse. When his client and his two colleagues had seated themselves in Carter's Mercedes-Benz limousine, he handed the envelope to the still smirking man. After a quick glance at the envelope, Carter asked, 'What's this, Larry? Your bill, already? Isn't my credit any good?'

'Nope! None of that. Some old geezer handed it to me a few minutes ago. He didn't say anything, just gave me the envelope and disappeared like a fart in the wind. Don't know what it's about, but it's addressed to you, so I didn't want to open it,' Kind said.

Carter opened the envelope and withdrew a single sheet of paper. He read the hand-written words, and his face paled. His lips dried as he read the words again.

His three companions noticed the re-action, but said nothing, waiting for Carter to explain. Eventually the shaken man handed it to Kind, who read aloud to the others.

'*Got off this time, eh Ian? We anticipated that you would. Pity about the misery you have brought down on the innocent 'Gook' girl, though. Her life is as good as over, now. Your turn next! Time to rid* this world of one more Parasite. When you least expect us, we'll be waiting. Bye bye Low Life.'

'Hang on a minute!' Kind suddenly exclaimed. 'I just remembered. I reckon I saw that old bastard sitting in the gallery today. I seem to remember his silly bloody hat. He was twirling it around in his hands, and watching you, Ian, all the time. Then I saw him writing furiously when Johnny was reading out our Doctor's report. He was in court all day, the old bugger.'

'So, who is he?' Carter almost screamed. 'Who is this old mongrel? There's a very firm threat in that note. What do you blokes reckon I ought to do? Take it to the coppers, or what? C'mon, you lot. You're the experts, aren't you?'

There was silence inside the car for a short while, then Collins said quietly, 'I wouldn't think you'll get much help from the Police, Ian. You've just handed them a damn good hiding in court, then bragged about it on camera, and made 'em look silly. I don't think they're likely to bust a gut watching out for you. Maybe you should hire a bodyguard or two, at least for the next few months. Can you afford that?'

Carter looked at each member of his legal team, seeking an answer from each.

'I can afford the monstrous bills you three bastards are charging me, so yeah, I could cop that. But will that be enough? And, more importantly, who is this old bloke, and why is he threatening me? And besides, I ain't frightened of some old bastard who likes to write notes. I mean, did he look like a thug or anything, Larry?'

The solicitor shook his head before saying, 'Nope! He was just a little old bloke, wearing a silly bloody hat. He didn't look too frightening to me. It could be he's just some local nut case, who has bugger all to do with his time, other than hang around the court house.'

Carter looked from Kind, to Collins, and Wilkinson, then back to Kind. He said contemptuously,

'Ok, so he disagrees with the good judge's decision. Stuff him, I say! Let's go celebrate. My brother has organised a little party in the rooms behind his shop. Plenty of grog, plenty of girls, and plenty of anything else you blokes fancy.'

Carter started the Mercedes-Benz and drove away from the kerb.

As the car gathered speed, Collins said quietly, almost to himself, 'I still think you would be wise to organise some protection, Ian. You could be in some real danger.'

'Yeah, could be,' Carter replied. 'But right now I feel like celebrating. I've been waiting to get one over that arrogant bloody Muscatt ever since the bastard came to Wollongong. Almost from the outset he damn near accused me and my brother of being the crime bosses of the area. I mean, he's never shown any proof of any of his accusations. He thinks because he's the top 'D' down here he can run off at the mouth any time he pleases. So, stuff him, I say. I won, he lost, and you three had a lot to do with it. So let's forget Muscatt, the old prick with the silly hat, and that stupid fat old judge. We got some partying to do.'

Collins shook his head and glanced across at Carter before saying firmly, 'I think you had still better consider a bit of protection, Ian. I know a bit about Muscatt and believe me, he is not a copper to be trifled with. I must say, no disrespect intended, but bigger fish than you have tangled with him and came off second best.'

Carter grinned and said loudly, 'Ah, you're getting soft, Mate. Muscatt don't worry me and he shouldn't worry you either. As you would know full well, the silly bloody coppers have to play by the rules but blokes like me can make up our own rules. Stop fretting, we'll be alright.'

Wilkinson and Kind remained silent merely watching the two men in the front seat. Collins had one final try at getting his point across, 'I still say you would be better off hiring some protection muscle, at least for the foreseeable future.'

CHAPTER FIVE

∞

Walker closed the flyscreen door behind him, and dropped his briefcase noisily on the tiled floor. The sound echoed along the short hallway as he swung the main door closed.

'That you, Mike?' an Irish-accented female voice called from inside the house.

'No! It's Jack the Ripper. Any young women live here?' he replied, grinning.

Carmen Walker appeared from the hallway and kissed her husband softly as she threw her arms around his thick neck.

'Jack the Ripper, eh? I thought you only operated on the streets of London,' she teased.

Carmen Walker was a tall woman, with a slim figure and long, lean legs. She stood exactly one centimetre shorter than her husband, but weighed thirty-five kilograms less. Her freckled face and ginger coloured hair, combined with a pale skin told any observer that her origins lay in the far off British Isles. Carmen had arrived, with her school teacher parents, in Australia as a lively Irish teenager in the summer of nineteen sixty- three. The tall youngster with the plain, but pleasant features, had topped all of her classes in a Melbourne high school, before entering Monash University to study forensic science. After graduating with honours, she had moved to Wagga Wagga and continued her career at Charles Sturt University. At Charles Sturt she taught forensics and lectured in applied science to a variety groups, including New South Wales Police personnel.

It was during a police course that she had first met then traffic constable Mike Walker, and the two had hit it off immediately. After a whirlwind romance and three month engagement, they had married in Wagga Wagga's Catholic church on a wintry Sunday in nineteen seventy eight. When he had spent another two years in uniform, Mike was accepted into the Criminal Investigations Branch, finally getting his opportunity to utilise the knowledge and skills he had gained in the university course which his wife had delivered several years earlier.

He took her hands in his and said sternly, 'I could just as well have been old Jack. You have to remember to lock the flyscreen door. Any type of bloody weirdo could walk in off the street, you know.'

'Yeah, so I see,' she continued teasing. 'So, how was your day, Mister Ripper? Solve all of Wagga's crimes today?' Her Irish accent leant additional humour to her teasing. He released his grasp of her hands and slapped her lightly on her backside as she led the way into the large kitchen.

'Oh, you know. The usual stuff. Crooks, their lawyers, the press and everybody else on one side, us silly bloody coppers on the other. What's for dinner?' he asked her as he reached into the refrigerator and obtained two cans of beer.

'Have you forgotten? We're supposed to be going to the club for dinner, with Andy and Anita. You set the whole thing up, you dodo! You don't remember?' she scolded.

He rolled one of the chilled cans of beer across his forehead, and nodded.

'Oh, yeah! That's right. I had forgotten it was Friday today. Here, have a coldie and tell me what a wonderful husband I am.' He passed the other can to her and sat heavily in a large armchair. As he opened his can and took a deep drink, Carmen opened her can and poured the contents into a tall glass.

'Do you really think you can talk him out of retiring from cricket? And should you? He works jolly hard on that old farm of theirs. You having him bowling a silly cricket ball weekend after weekend must be wearing him out, don't you think?' she asked quietly.

Mike looked at his beer for a few seconds, then answered,

'I don't think so. Andy's the best quick bowler we've got, and he's one of the fittest blokes I know. I reckon he's got at least another three good years in him. Look at the football. He retired last year and we only won four games all season this year. If I had him at fullback like in previous seasons, we would have made the semis for sure. He gave footy away too early, and now he wants to give cricket away while he's still the most feared "quickie" in the district.'

Carmen drank some of her beer and smiled across at her husband.

'I still think you ought to leave the decision to him, and Anita. They work hard enough to earn their living, without you badgering them about silly games. You could do with a bit less activity, as well, you know? You aren't as young as you were. Cricket might be alright for another year or two, but you ought to think about giving the Rugby away yourself. That body can't take the hits like it used to you know, you old thug.'

He laughed and swatted at her with a cushion from the lounge.

'It's not "Rugby". It's Rugby League! There's a big difference. And who are you calling 'old'? Plenty of life left in these muscles yet. What time are we meeting them?'

'As soon as you shower and change. I've left some good clothes on the bed for you.'

By seven o'clock that evening the two couples were sitting at a square table in the dining room of Wagga Wagga Returned Services Club. Both men had large glasses of beer in front of them, while the two women were sharing a carafe of white wine. After a flighty young waitress had taken their meal order, Mike Walker spoke.

'Listen, Andy. We really want you to reconsider about giving cricket away. Not only do we need your expertise, but I reckon I'm right when I say you are still enjoying the game. Last week you got...., what was it? Four for twenty something. Come on. You know that shows how bloody good you are. What d'ya reckon, Mate?'

Andy Keyes smiled at his best friend and shrugged his powerful shoulders.

'Aw, I dunno, Skipper.'

He had called Mike 'Skipper' since they first met, in deference to Walker being his captain in Cricket and Rugby League.

'Last week it was only poor old Yerong Creek. That mob battle to field a team every week. I'm just about sick of it. The farm needs my time more than any damn cricket team. That's why I gave footy away. I just haven't got the time, plus the old body is starting to protest a bit, you know Skipper?'

Carmen Walker swallowed the last of her wine and said,

'That's what I told Mikey this afternoon. He won't admit it, but his manly frame is getting too old for Rugby League, and for Cricket, too. He needs to grow up a bit, and leave the games to the young men. I also told the stubborn mule he has no right to try to force you to keep playing. What do you think, Anita? Time they both grew up?'

The tiny Malaysian woman was sipping her wine, and watching each speaker.

'Oh, I don't think I can tell my husband this much. I like to watch them play the rough football, but I also think he could get hurt. I think the cricket is too slow. That game makes me bored, sometimes. But if Andy, my husband, wants to play this cricket, that is oakey with me.'

The other three seated at the table laughed. The little woman's pretty brown face screwed up in a smile as she reached out and grasped Keyes' strong hands.

Walker finished his beer and signalled the drink waiter for replacements.

'I can sort of understand the footy, although I still say you could go round again next year. But with the old cricket, surely you have to admit, it's great fun, and you love it? Besides, we need you. I need you. While-ever I'm captain, I want the good old East Wagga Seconds to have the Riverina's best bowling attack around. And you're a big part of it!'

Carmen clapped and said with fake sincerity,

'Wow! What an inspirational speech! You been practicing your motivational style?'

'Quiet, you lot in the cheap seats!' Mike said with false sternness. He turned to Keyes.

'Ignore her, Mate. What d'ya reckon? At least another season?'

The tall farmer grinned and shrugged, then took a long swallow of his beer.

'We'll see, Skipper. We'll see. I'm just so busy with the farm that sport may have to take a back seat. For now, let's enjoy the grog and the tucker, if it ever gets here.'

Walker and Keyes had hit it off as soon as they had met, at football registration day four years earlier. Both were relatively new in town, although Andy had spent his entire childhood in the district. At the age of nine his parents had sent him to boarding school in Canberra and therefore he knew no other boys his own age in Wagga Wagga. The school holidays were either spent with distant aunts and uncles on the coast, or helping his ageing parents with the farm, so his inter-action with locals was absolutely nil. After graduating from his exclusive Canberra grammar and high schools, Andy Keyes had entered the Military Officers' college, Duntroon. After passing out as a Captain in the Australian army, he had quickly transferred to the Special Air Service, which had eventually lead to his appointment in Malaysia.

Whilst serving in Malaysia both his parents had been killed in a tragic car crash. He eventually recovered from the shock, but spared little or no thought for the family farm.

The previously thriving property was left to wither and die as it lay abandoned and the livestock either wandered away or were slowly purloined by other farmers.

When he had finally returned to the region of his birth, he had no intention of participating in sports of any kind. He had starred in the rugby union and cricket teams at boarding school. He had even been noticed by district selectors who were searching for a new fast bowler. There was also a couple of approaches from a few Rugby clubs in the Canberra district. Despite all the early promise, it wasn't until Keyes had been posted to Malaysia that his competitiveness and sporting desire had begun to blossom.

Within his regiment there had been fierce rivalry between the platoons in any competition that could be imagined. Tennis matches, boxing tournaments, darts games, running races and golf games were held, although Andy Keyes had little or no interest in any of these sports. When the new commanding officer arrived in June, nineteen seventy-one, to assume leadership of the regiment, he had immediately established an inter platoon rugby union tournament. The senior officer, who hailed from Brisbane, believed the harsh body contact and tactical thinking of the old game would help his men to maintain peak fitness, both physically and mentally. After just one season, many of the troops requested the game be switched to the more popular rugby league, with even harsher body contact but less thinking required. The request was reluctantly approved, and Andy Keyes found himself learning a new game, which satisfied his inner desire to compete, as well as serving as an outlet for his natural aggression. He starred as a full back, centre or winger, and was his unit's best player and toughest competitor.

Cricket was already well established as the summer sport within the S.A.S. detachment, and again Captain Andrew Keyes was the standout player. His fast bowling and athletic fielding earned him numerous Man of the Match awards and trophies.

When he had returned to the Riverina four years ago to resurrect the family farm, it was not long before he sought out the representatives of local cricket and rugby league clubs. The tedium of farming life, and the worry of the overhanging debt, were easily forgotten once he was out in the sporting field.

However, this last year had been a particularly harsh one, with the downturn in farming profits, and those cursed envelopes arriving at almost regular intervals, adding to his worries He had decided it was time to leave the sporting to the younger men, and concentrate on achieving other, more tangible goals.

Now his best friend Mike Walker, who was also his cricket and football teams captain, was treating him and Anita to dinner, and trying to dissuade him from his plans of complete sporting retirement.

The arrival of their meals provided a welcome distraction from the battle for his intentions. As he chewed thankfully on his T bone steak, Andy Keyes thought about the arrival of the latest yellow envelope, and the implications contained in the professionally typed text on the sheets of paper within.

He looked across at Anita, and caught her staring into his eyes as she nibbled at her grilled fish. He winked, and she smiled slightly before winking back.

"If only you knew the whole truth, Skipper!" he thought as he glanced at Walker. His best friend had no idea of the torture and turmoil he was enduring.

Mike was a respected policeman, who had an educated wife, a nice house and no debts. Both enjoyed the benefits of secure, well-paying careers, which delivered a relatively carefree lifestyle.

Not for them the long hours, the seven day-a-week drudgery and the constant worry of obtaining suitable reward for efforts expended.

Not for them the concern of enough feed for several hundred animals who represented your livelihood.

And not for them the semi-regular arrival of those envelopes.

CHAPTER SIX

Richard Oaks sipped his coffee as he listened to his friend and colleague.

Larry Kind had been talking earnestly in a muffled tone as the two solicitors dined on sweet cakes and coffee at Kings Cross's best known coffee house, "The Roasted Bean".

The glass fronted shop was a well-known haunt of Kind, Oaks, and most other high profile lawyers and judges, who usually plied their trade at the nearby District Court.

Outside, Darlinghurst Road swarmed with bustling activity as office workers, shopkeepers and all night party goers filled the footpath. Some hopeful prostitutes strolled easily among the mass of humanity, smiling at any man who so much as glanced their way. A few sick looking individuals staggered from post to garbage bin to street sign, trying to understand what sort of a night they had just enjoyed, or perhaps why they did it, and more importantly, how to find the way to their homes.

Oaks waited until Kind had finished, and had taken another drink from his large coffee cup. It was obvious to Oaks that his friend was extremely concerned. Larry Kind had spent the last fifteen minutes explaining why to him.

'I don't know, Larry. It sounds a bit far fetched to me......, And besides, it's not exactly a new theory. The bloody newspapers were saying something similar when old Eddie Miller was found dead a couple of years ago. And they reckoned something odd occurred when 'Brother' Thompson was found dead as a door knob on a country train, out near Dubbo. But that's what the newsboys do best. Stir up trouble and sensationalise the facts. You sure you're not just letting your imagination go a bit wild?'

Kind shook his head vigorously. He removed the huge cigar from his mouth.

'Not a bit, Richie. I been giving it a lot of thought. After what happened to your bloke, and the others before, I wondered if it might just be co-incidence. But I was there in bloody Wollongong when my client copped a threatening note. It was me who actually received it. Some old geezer pulled on my coat sleeve. When I looked at him, he just grinned, and handed me an envelope. When my client read it out to us, it sounded very similar to that note you lot copped just before old Billy fell off his perch. I discussed it briefly with Collins and Wilkinson, but you know those two. It's all about the dollars, and stuff everything else. I tell ya, mate. I'm starting to wonder about that conspiracy theory that the news boys were pushing a while ago.'

Kind shoved the cigar between his teeth for emphasis and watched his friend.

Oaks smiled at him before swallowing the last of his coffee.

'Conspiracy theory! Bloody hell, Larry. You've gotta be kidding? Maybe you need a break, you know? Take a week at the Gold Coast or something. Give yourself a rest.'

Kind was not smiling as he peered closely at Oaks. He said slowly, deliberately,

'All right then, Mate, tell me this. What did Billy Greene die of? The bloody Coroner couldn't work it out, could he? And you mentioned Eddie Miller. If you recall, the same Coroner couldn't come up with a creditable cause of death for him, either. And we both know 'Brother' Thompson's death was recorded as an open finding, as was 'Scotch Tommy' McCleod. And before all of them, big Errol from Redfern was found floating in the harbour, after some witnesses saw him suddenly topple off a bloody ferry. His death was found to be 'misadventure', but he was the fittest bloke in Sydney, a super strong swimmer and a non-drinker. How does a geezer like that suddenly fall asleep, fall overboard and drown? I tell you, it's all just too bloody convenient for my liking.'

Oaks reached for one of his Turkish cigars and fumbled in a coat pocket for his lighter.

When he had the thin stick of flavoured tobacco smouldering, he said to Kind, 'Well, to answer your questions in order, Billy Greene died from 'terminal bus'. When a ten ton vehicle drives over you, you usually die, unless you're Superman. I admit they don't know why he collapsed the way he did, but he sure picked a bastard of a place to do it. The bus couldn't have stopped, even if the driver had seen old Billy. As for Eddie Miller, well he was about seventy years old, full of grog most of the time and smoked unfiltered cigarettes all his miserable life. He was a death just looking for somewhere to occur. 'Brother' Thompson I don't know much about, but I hardly think he was a candidate for 'Citizen of the Year'. I recall they found him in a sleeper bunk, dead as a dodo, on the 'Western Mail', or whatever that bloody train's called. The Dubbo Coroner found that he died in his sleep during the train journey, and that was that! And we both know 'Scotch Tommy' liked the dope a bit, sometimes sniffing more than he sold. That coulda killed him. As for Redfern Errol, well, maybe he bumped his silly looking head as he fell overboard. I don't know, and I ain't no doctor. They're all dead as door knobs, and your client in Wollongong is alive and well, so I don't know why you're so uptight about it all. Like I said earlier, maybe you just need a little holiday yourself. What do you reckon?'

Kind waited patiently until his friend had finished, then he said firmly,

'Can't you see the common theme, Rich? In fact, several common themes? Each of those blokes is as dead as mutton, for sure. But each of them died in un-explained circumstances. It's as if they just suddenly stopped living! And, if you think back, every one of those birds had just walked away from a serious charge, or several. And every one of them took the time to skite about it, and rubbish the police into the bargain. Now, I've been doing a lot of research into these matters, ever since my client was acquitted in Wollongong. Right after the hearing he stood on the courthouse steps, skiting and bragging to the TV and radio reporters like a stupid bloody school kid. He had a go at Muscatt, the top 'D' who charged him, putting all sorts of shit on him and his men. Just like Billy Greene did, and just like Eddie Miller, 'Brother' Thompson, 'Scotch' Tommy and Redfern Errol. They all got off, bragged about it, put shit on the coppers, and then wound up dead in strange circumstances. Still reckon they're all co-incidences?'

Oaks was silent for a time, digesting what his friend had said. The tension between the two men was almost tangible as they sat watching each other, the odorous smoke from Oaks' cigar providing a thin, grey divide between them. Eventually Oaks spoke.

'You know what, mate? You just could be right! I hadn't realised there might be some sort of connection. Eddie Miller was the first of them to go, wasn't he?'

'Yep! About three years ago. He was walking his dog on Cronulla beach, and they found him, stiff as a board in the sand hills, with his bloody stinking dog sitting beside his corpse. His mouth was full of sand, but the Coroner found that his heart, lungs and most other organs had simply shut down, killing the bastard within seconds. There were no witnesses, no suspects and no clues. And not a mark on his body. Plus, his bloody dog was a trained attack dog, so if anybody had attacked him, the dog would've gone for 'em. But it was just lying there beside him, with no sign of a scuffle or anything. Because he was a big-time crook, and had recently been on TV and radio skiting about being found not guilty on a raft of charges, including attempted murder, not too many people were too worried about him.'

'So, what about this client of yours in Wollongong? It's been three weeks or more since you were down there. He's still breathing, isn't he?' Oaks asked.

'Yeah, he is. For now. But after reading that note, I'm worried as hell,' Kind said.

Oaks grinned through the smoke and shrugged his narrow shoulders.

'Why are you worried? He paid his bill, hasn't he?'

'Oh, yes. He's paid the bill, in full. And a beauty it was, too. But that's not the point. I already told you I've been digging into the facts a bit, and I don't like what I'm seeing. A definite pattern is appearing, I'm fully convinced of that. Also, I got to thinking. If what I think is occurring, what's to stop them going after us, their lawyers. After all, we are the smart bastards who get 'em off, aren't we?'

Oaks' smile slowly faded as he digested this latest theme. Both men were quiet as they became lost in their own thoughts. Oaks said finally, 'All right, Mate. Suppose you're right? What can we do about it? I mean, if some do-gooder or vigilante is going around bumping off crims, what is there that blokes like us can do? And as for your theory about him, or them, starting on the lawyers, surely some of us would be pushing up daisies by now if that was their intention? Nah, I won't cop that part. If that was true, you and me would be shaking hands with the Devil by now!'

Kind smiled at Oaks joke, but immediately resumed his seriousness.

'Well, I don't know for certain, but I'm going to keep on digging. Some-one must know something. And in the meantime, I am going to try like hell to convince my Wollongong client to hire a bodyguard. Which brings me to my next point. Are any of Billy Greene's thugs looking for work? I thought, with Billy gone, most of 'em would be out of work.'

Oaks looked at Kind and smirked.

'What do you care about this Wollongong mug for? You just told me he paid, and the matter is finished. You shouldn't give a bugger what happens to him now, should you?'

Kind stubbed out his big cigar and shoved it in his coat pocket.

'He's got quite a few outstanding matters, plus an on-going feud with the police down there, and he wants to retain my services on a semi-permanent basis. He has seen enough American movies where the baddie has a lawyer on tap all the time. You know, where he can ring at any time for immediate legal advice and representation? Well, he was so impressed with the way we handled his case, he asked me to be his flunkie. I told him what it would cost, and he never batted an eyelid. The prick is loaded with dough. So, with that in mind, I thought it would be nice if I help keep him alive. Dead men can't sign cheques, you know. And, as I have just spent the last hour explaining, I believe there is a chance of a genuine threat to him. Of course, the first thing I need to get him to do is stop skiting, and baiting the coppers. Especially bloody Allan Muscatt. I had some dealings with him a few years ago. He's a hard bastard, and damned good at his job. I told him once he should have been a solicitor. You what the bastard said? He said 'No thanks! I sooner wipe a pig's arse with me bare hands. The smell is sweeter' Bloody charming, eh? A real smart arse, but one to be watched'.

Oaks threw back his head and laughed. He puffed on his cigar as he giggled then said,

'Hell, we've both been insulted worse than that. I been called everything from a thief to human excrement. That stuff shouldn't bother you. Is that what's got you so jumpy?'

'Nope! The stuff about a conspiracy to eliminate our clientele is based on my research, and what happened in Wollongong. Anyway, what about some muscle? Who's available that you know?' Kind replied.

Oaks stood up and indicated Kind to follow him outside. When the two lawyers were standing on the footpath, Oaks said,

'Well, Big Jeff and Knifey were Billy Greene's favourites. They were with Billy when he dropped in front of that bus, so Jake O'Rourke sacked them both. Even though the pair of 'em agreed it was their responsibility, they took it pretty hard. However, Jake did relent a bit. He hires the pair of 'em for odd jobs now and again. Last week he had them on the door at a party in Billy's old flat at Alexandria. I could get them to call in and see you if you like. I reckon you'd get them for a long-term deal at a bargain rate at the moment. Their esteem is a little low, so is their asking price. O'Rourke won't mind. I think he'd probably like to see the back of them. Ok?'

'Yeah, that would be fine, Rich. I appreciate it. All right, have 'em come see me at my office. And see if you can find out anything about what's happening to our clients when they have a win, then skite about it. I reckon I'm right, and I reckon you will too, when you think about it. Ok, see ya.'

The two men shook hands and walked away in opposite directions.

Back in the coffee shop, a little old man lowered the newspaper he had been holding up to his face and watched as the two lawyers parted and headed away from each other.

He smirked to himself as he stood, then he reached into his coat pocket. There was an audible 'click' as the mini tape recorder was switched off. The old man walked from the shop, passing the table where Kind and Oaks had sat. No-one saw him quickly retrieve a tiny microphone, with short radio antenna attached, from the cheap vase stuffed with plastic flowers in the centre of the table.

It had been a calculated gamble that the two flashy lawyers would be shown to the table by the window, when the old man had entered the coffee shop a few minutes before the next two customers. A twenty dollar note slipped to the waiter had guaranteed the result.

Whistling softly, the old man walked slowly along Darlinghurst road until a pale green Holden sedan cruised toward him. The car stopped beside the kerb, and he quickly opened the back door. He pushed aside a wide brimmed white straw hat which was on the back seat and settled into the car. After giving the driver a central city address, he watched the footpath carefully as the car moved off, threading through the heavy traffic of Kings Cross.

The smartly dressed figure of Larry Kind strode purposefully through the crowd, and the old man smiled to himself as he noted the arrogance and confidence exuding from the lawyer.

CHAPTER SEVEN

In the brilliant white beams projected from the twin spotlights mounted on the front of his Land Rover, Andy Keyes identified his farm's front entrance. As gently as he could, Keyes brought the rugged little vehicle to a stop two metres from the white painted steel gates. Anita was still dozing, her head resting on a rolled up woollen jumper which was protecting her face from the metal 'B' pillar of the car.

Despite his skilful attempt to stop the car with minimum of jerking, she woke as he opened his door.

'Where are we? We are at our home already?' she asked sleepily.

'Yeah, we're home, Baby. You stay there, and I'll just get the gates,' he told her softly.

She smiled and settled her head back into the jumper as he unfolded his long legs and strode to the gates. The night was pleasantly cool, with the southern sky lit by a half moon and a few million stars. He shoved both gates wide open, then stood, hands on hips, gazing up at the night sky, enjoying the wide panorama of twinkling lights. A soft gentle breeze made a few leaves and blades of grass dance slowly around his feet. In the distance an owl broadcast an early morning bulletin to whom-ever was up and about. From his freshly ploughed lucerne paddock a pair of galahs answered back. Over to his right he heard the distinct heavy rumble as a long goods train struggled up the steep grade from Uranquinty, heading south to Albury and probably on to Melbourne.

The sound of the train brought him back from his appreciation of the night. With long strides he returned to the Land Rover and clambered behind the wheel. When he had driven through the gateway, Anita surprised him by quickly jumping from the car.

'You stay there, Big Man. I'll close the gates. You too slow!' she teased with a smile.

The tiny woman wasted no time in securing the gates closed, and returning to her seat.

'A big train is going past,' she told him. 'I like the trains.'

'Yeah! Maybe it's time I took you on another train trip soon, eh?' he answered.

'Yes, I think so. Very soon,' Anita agreed quietly. She slid her tiny backside across to the centre seat, and snuggled into his left shoulder. He smiled down at her as he drove the car along the dirt track which led from the Olympic Highway to their homestead. He parked the car inside the huge, open machinery shed, and switched off the engine. Anita gripped his muscular arm and pulled his face toward hers. She smiled before engulfing his mouth with hers, kissing him hungrily. He returned her enthusiasm, reaching inside her blouse as their lips massaged each other's.

Andy broke off the embrace and withdrew his right hand from her loose fitting blouse.

Giggling, Anita scrambled out the left door and said teasingly,

'You can have me, if you can catch me, mister big slow Australian man.'

'You cheeky little bugger!' he replied as he left the driver's seat. 'I'll catch you all right. And when I do, I'll more than have you. I'll devour you!'

She shrieked with delight as she ran to the back door of their homestead, threw it open and entered the house. Andy was five metres behind her as she ran, laughing and giggling, to the main bedroom. She slammed the door shut, and dived onto the bed. As Andy flung the door open, Anita was covering herself with the cotton eiderdown, still giggling uncontrollably. He turned on the light, then quickly ripped the bedcover from his tiny wife. She lay there, fully clothed and smiling, as he slowly stripped off his clothing, all the while staring at her. When Andy was down to his underpants, Anita quickly kicked off her shoes, sat up and removed her blouse, brassier and hair band in what seemed to her husband to be one smooth movement. As he advanced on her, a smile of anticipation on his face, she stood on the bed, wriggled out of her skirt and peeled off her stockings. Clad now only in her tiny briefs, she reached for him, and they came together, slowly collapsing onto the bed as their lips met once more.

Mike Walker swallowed the last of his water, then refilled the glass from the kitchen tap. He usually finished a night of alcohol consumption with a few glasses of water.

Experience had taught him that it helped fight the gremlins and goblins who would wage an artillery battle in his head the next morning.

He stood, clad only in boxer shorts, watching the night sky through the large kitchen windows. A few pairs of headlights slashed through the darkness on the busy road that ran behind his back yard. He was glad he and Carmen had taken a taxi to the club for dinner with Andy and Anita. The traffic boys would be out and about tonight, playing with their latest toy, a breath analyser. It was said that one long breath into the strange new machine could tell the operator what percentage of alcohol was in the participants blood. The local Traffic Branch Inspector had made it clear that anyone caught by the machine would face definite prosecution. He had gone out of his way to make sure all police personnel in Wagga Wagga understood that he meant ALL persons caught, including colleagues, would be paraded before the courts. Mike, along with most other police in the big town, doubted the constables and sergeants running traffic would lumber a serving colleague. Despite this doubt, Walker was not prepared to take the chance, so a taxi had been booked and his new Ford Falcon had remained locked in the garage, along with Carmen's little red Italian motor scooter.

Walker checked the time on the electric clock mounted in the stove. Twelve forty-five.

Despite the late hour, and Carmen's soft snoring already floating down from the upstairs bedroom, Mike was not sleepy. They had enjoyed a delightful evening with Andy and Anita, even though he had failed to gain any firm commitment from his best friend for the following cricket season. After his usual two beers, big Andy had switched to orange juice, which he always did, even on football or cricket trips away. The two women had downed several carafes of the house wine, then went away to play the poker machines, leaving the men to talk. Mike had used all of his well-rehearsed arguments to try and convince his friend not to retire from cricket at the end of the season. Andy had remained non-committal, merely stating several times that he needed to devote more time to his farm if he was to make a decent living from the property.

Mike grinned as he pictured Andy, complaining about wheat and mutton prices, and crying poor mouth, whilst his beautiful little wife fed the poker machines buckets of coins. Carmen had told him as they were driven home in a taxi, that Anita had lost about thirty dollars, and did not seem perturbed.

'*Bloody farmers. I'll never understand them*', Walker thought to himself as he finished his water. He placed the glass on the sink edge and turned off the light. As he trudged quickly to the stairs leading to the three bedrooms of the two-storey house, his policeman's mind pondered the puzzle of his best friend's financial position.

He was sure Andy and Anita were in some kind of financial bind, but then reminded himself it was none of his business. He quietly climbed the carpeted staircase and entered their bedroom. As he peeled back the bedclothes and laid down beside his sleeping wife, the issue of Andy's financial situation returned to his thoughts. Something in his instincts nagged away at him, making him feel uncomfortable.

Sleep would not come quickly to him this night.

CHAPTER EIGHT

∞

Several pelicans bobbed up and down on the waves and a dozen seagulls glided lazily over head as the sun continued to heat the ocean slowly. Most early morning surfers had left the water, and were either drying themselves with enormous towels or already scurrying up the sand towards the carpark, clutching their fibreglass boards under one arm as they searched shirt and trouser pockets for car keys with the other hand.

Scarborough beach was a favourite with the many local residents who liked to start their day with a few surfboard rides or a refreshing dip in the mighty Pacific Ocean.

Now, as the hour of eight o'clock approached, most of the young men were hurrying off to work, or, in some cases, to attend lessons at nearby high schools.

As the half dozen Kombi vans and small cars raced from the carpark, the remaining dozen swimmers continued to enjoy the cool freshness of the slowly undulating salt water. A solitary

Lifesaver patrolled slowly along the sand, watching the swimmers and a trio of board riders paddling out past the breakers, intent on mastering the next sizeable wave to roll in. All of the swimmers were well within the flags, except the three men who had arrived in a white Mercedes Benz, about half an hour ago. The big young blonde man was dog-paddling in waist-deep water, but nearly twenty feet outside the line of the north flag. His older companion, whom the Lifesaver thought seemed vaguely familiar, was snorkelling a few yards from the blonde. The third member, a rat faced little foreigner, was slowly walking up and down at the water's edge, keeping in line with his two more adventurous friends. This small man had remained fully dressed when the other two had stripped to bathing costumes. To the Lifesaver it appeared as if the big blonde man and the little foreigner were bodyguards for the older man. When the trio had made their way to the water, about ten minutes ago, the Lifesaver had smiled, as he cautioned them.

'G'day, fellas. Lovely morning for it. Stay between the flags now, won't ya gents?'

The big blonde had merely grinned at him, while the older man ignored him, busy fitting rubber flippers to his large feet and a mask and snorkel to his head. The little foreigner appeared not to hear him at all, instead sweeping his gaze up and down the beach, seemingly looking for some-one or something.

Now, here they were, disobeying the flags and swimming further away with every stroke. The Lifesaver cupped his hands to his mouth and shouted, 'Hoy! You blokes! Come back between the flags.'

The big blonde man glanced at him, then returned his attention to the area where his companion was swimming. The older man submerged and carried on with his snorkelling. The little man at the water's edge turned, looked disdainfully at the Lifesaver, then resumed his walking beat of the shoreline.

The Lifesaver withdrew a shiny whistle from his shirt pocket and was about to blow it when his eyes detected movement near the snorkeler. He stared at the spot for another five seconds before he saw the object again. It was only a quick glance, but a long dark shape appeared, right on top of the submerged snorkeler. Then he spotted another dark shape just behind the first one.

The Lifesaver blew as hard as he could on the whistle, running to the water's edge as he did. The little foreign man swung around as the Lifesaver's footsteps sounded behind him. His right hand instinctively reached inside his shirt and clutched the butt of a long, thin razor-sharp dagger. The Lifesaver ignored him and took the whistle from his mouth. He shouted to the two men in the water, 'Shark! Shark! Get out of the water. I think there's a bloody pair of sharks near you!'

He waved his hands frantically as he shouted, signalling all swimmers and the board riders, as well as the troublesome snorkeler. He was beside the little foreign man now.

'Where shark? What shark? I see no shark,' the man barked to the Lifesaver.

'I thought I saw a pair of the bastards, right next to your mate, the bloke with the snorkel on.' He resumed his whistle blowing, and waving.

The swimmers began to emerge from the water now. Some were screaming, others saving all their energy for the efforts to vacate the water. The smaller and slower ones were knocked into the shallow water as the bigger and stronger surged past, seeking the safety of the dry sand. The three board riders hurriedly stood up on their surfboards, each anxiously looking into the waves, seeking the whereabouts of every surfer's nightmare.

Big Jeff stood in waist deep water, watching the commotion for a few seconds as he tried to comprehend what the whistle blowing Lifesaver was indicating. He saw the rest of the swimmers scurrying up onto the sand, and noticed the three surfers standing upright on the boards. He looked towards 'Knifey' and spread his long arms, silently asking for an explanation. The short, swarthy man mouthed the word 'Shark' at Jeff.

He pointed first to the lifesaver, then to the water where their new boss, Ian Carter, was still floating about a foot below the surface, face down, apparently observing the ocean floor through his mask. Ignoring any danger and thoughts of self-preservation, Jeff pushed his way through the water to Carter and touched him lightly in the middle of his back. The older man did not re-act, so Jeff grabbed Carter's right arm, which was now floating up, towards the surface. Again there was no re-action, and Jeff became concerned. He took a deep breath and plunged his head into the water, and shoved his face up against the mask. He recoiled in horror as he saw the vacant, lifeless eyes and gaping mouth of Carter. The mouthpiece of his snorkel was hanging loosely in the water, still attached to the mask but clearly serving no purpose to its owner.

Jeff stood up and grasped the waistband of Carter's brief swimming trunks. When the water cleared from his eyes he signalled 'Knifey' to help him as he dragged the heavy body to the shoreline. The little Maltese entered the shallows and together they heaved Carter's unmoving body onto the sand. A quick check by Jeff showed no pulse and no breathing. The Lifesaver joined them and most of the crowd of swimmers began to gather around. The Lifesaver turned Carter onto his right side and prised his jaws open. A tiny trickle of water flowed out of the mouth, as the Lifesaver screamed at the crowd.

'Somebody get up to the clubhouse and ring for an ambulance! Quick! Any-one else know first aid? Any-one?'

Without waiting for an answer, he rolled the body onto its back and commenced mouth to mouth resuscitation. No-one else volunteered to help, so he continued his attempts, alternatively breathing into the mouth of Carter, then compressing the man's chest in a regular ratio.

A young woman detached herself from the crowd and ran to the open clubhouse door.

She saw the telephone on a cluttered desk and dialled three zeros.

Back on the beach, Jeff and 'Knifey' watched anxiously as the Lifesaver continued his urgent attempt to restore life to one of Wollongong's most colourful identities.

Some women in the small crowd began crying, while the men simply watched the drama with grim expressions. Jeff and 'Knifey' exchanged worried looks as the pantomime continued. The three surfboard riders had paddled quietly to shore and, each carrying their boards under an arm, joined the crowd of onlookers watching the young Lifesaver working frantically to resuscitate the large man lying prone in the sand.

No-one saw the two dark shapes gliding two feet below the surface, moving slowly and steadily away from Scarborough beach in a southerly direction. No-one saw them round the rocky outcrop which protruded into the Pacific Ocean, and divided Scarborough beach from Wombarra rock pools. No-one saw the constant stream of bubbles drifting up from these two dark shapes as they continued southward, parallel to the almost deserted Wombarra pool, around a hundred yards from the water's edge.

When the two shapes drifted into the shoreline at the southern end of Wombarra, only a young couple and an old man saw them emerge from the waves and stand up in the shallows. The first one helped his companion undo a heavy divers weight belt, then the air tank, and then the S.C.U.B.A. mask. Then they changed places as the first one was assisted to shed the heavy diving equipment. Each diver then peeled off a pair of rubber flippers. As the two figures, still clad in black rubber wetsuits, walked briskly to a parked Ford Falcon sedan, a wailing siren shattered the peaceful rhythm of the ocean.

A white ambulance sped past northbound on the nearby Lawrence Hargraves Drive, and turned into the tiny carpark adjacent to Scarborough beach.

The two divers watched the ambulance come to a stop as they helped each other out of their wetsuits, then dried themselves with towels from the boot of the car. After closing the boot lid, the taller figure entered the drivers' seat while his companion scrambled in beside him. After a final glance around the area, the driver started the engine and drove from the carpark.

The old man, paddling quietly in the shallow water, watched carefully as the car drove away, noting the number plate and the hire-car sticker attached to the rear window.

Nodding slowly to himself, the old man smiled slightly before standing and heading for his towel, which was spread on the ground not ten feet from the water's edge. He dried himself and donned a pair of Bermuda shorts, a loud Hawaiian shirt and a clean white straw sun hat. He then walked slowly to a pale green Holden sedan and entered the back seat. The waiting driver started the engine and the car quietly left the car park.

Larry Kind flicked through his appointment diary as he stirred a large cup of coffee with a shiny, sterling silver spoon. He frowned as he noted there were three appointments before midday. Two were routine criminal matters, with both clients as guilty as sin of several felonies, and expecting him to work some sort of miracle with a court room full of do-gooders and vigilantes. He grunted as he considered the healthy fees he would invoice both criminals. He was doubtful either would pay him another cent after they were convicted, as he was sure they would be. Despite this, he smirked when he recalled the over-billing he had organised when each of these two habitual offenders had used his talents in earlier matters. He was already well ahead, so the potential loss of fees for the up-coming matters was not a worry for Kind.

The third appointment was a new client, who wanted him to represent a building consortium trying to pull a massive con on the Wollongong council. The appointment was with a well-known private investigator who was the face of the consortium, and was as famous for his frequent brushes with the law as he was for his numerous television appearances.

No matter what the cause, big Albert Tuckey seemed to always be in the picture, usually acting as bodyguard or minder to the cause's spokesperson. The word around the legal world was that any-one who crossed or displeased Tuckey, usually found themselves having a severe accident soon after.

Kind was not a coward, and in fact he enjoyed a physical confrontation now and again. Even at fifty-two years of age, the high living lawyer kept himself fit, and retained a lot of physical toughness from his Rugby Union days at university.

But Albert Tuckey frightened him.

There were simply too many rumours of injuries and maimings delivered by Tuckey for all of them to be fairy tales. Even a couple of tough Detectives from the Armed Hold-Up Squad had sought early retirement after crossing swords with Albert Tuckey.

Kind read his secretary's hand written notes beside the Tuckey appointment. The thug had been referred to Kind by none other than Ian Carter, and immediately the lawyer was on alert. He had had a few minor matters to attend to on behalf of Carter since the major trial in Wollongong several months ago. The last contact Kind had had with Carter was just over two weeks ago' when he convinced the real estate man to hire Big Jeff and 'Knifey' as personal protectors. Carter had eventually agreed to take on the bodyguards for a six month period, with an option to continue the employment afterwards, subject to a full review of their performances in the role.

Kind had negotiated a reasonable wage for the pair of minders, along with a healthy commission for himself.

Referring Albert Tuckey and his business to him was probably Carter's way of returning the favour.

'Thanks for nothing, Carter!', the lawyer thought to himself. Aloud he said,

'I need a bastard like Tuckey around here like I need a hole in the head!'

His secretary looked up from her desk in the adjacent office, wondering what her boss was talking to himself about. She had caught him mumbling to himself a lot lately, which was a habit he had only developed since the big Wollongong case two months ago. She smiled to herself and returned to the letter she was typing, after noting Kind was reaching for the 'hidden' bottle of scotch whisky he kept in his bottom drawer.

Four uniformed policemen were in the front office of the Wollongong police station when Detective Chief Inspector Allan Muscatt entered via the twin glass doors. The large clock above the counter showed ten thirty, and all four policemen observed their watches as the senior Detective rushed in, obviously running late again.

The tall young constable who was standing in front of an electric typewriter, making a lengthy entry in the daily occurrence pad, looked up. He immediately stopped typing and said good naturedly,

' 'morning, Sir.'

Muscatt smiled and replied cheerily, 'Good morning, Dave. How yer going?'

The other three constables called, almost in unison,

' 'afternoon, Sir.'

'G'day, boys. How youse going, all right?' Muscatt replied, with a friendly wave. 'No need for the sarcasm. I know what time it is!'

He opened a frosted glass door beside the counter which led to the stairs to the first floor. The station's senior uniformed officers and all of the Detectives were housed in the upstairs section of the building. Muscatt's own office was right at the top of the stairs. He placed his brief case on a spare chair, and crossed to an electric kettle sitting on a side board. He was still in the process of checking the water level in the kettle when a voice called from the doorway.

'Good morning, Allan. Or should I say "Happy birthday"?'

Muscatt swung around and saw the uniformed figure of Superintendent Sam Raynor.

'Hello, Boss. Eh? Birthday? It's not my birthday,' Muscatt replied. 'What makes you think it's my birthday?'

'I take it you have not yet checked the occurrence pad?' Raynor said, grinning.

'No. I usually leave that for Bob or Jimmy. They're my squad leaders. Why?'

'Why? Well, I thought it must be your birthday 'cause it's got a nice little present for you. A bit after eight o'clock, the day shift was called to Scarborough where a bloke had drowned. When they got there, the "Ambos" had already declared him dead. We've got a few witness statements, and a young Lifesaver, who tried to resuscitate the victim, is in the interview room giving his account of the incident as we speak.'

Muscatt was puzzled. The Superintendent was taking a long time to get to the point.

'Ok, Sam. You got me interested. Do we know the name of the bloke who drowned?'

'I thought you'd never ask. You ready for this? I told you it was a nice little present for ya. The good citizen who unfortunately passed away this morning was one Mister Ian Carter, formerly of Carter Real Estate agency, and formerly of the District Court.'

Muscatt's eyes bulged and he sat down heavily in his padded chair.

After a few seconds of silence, the Chief Inspector said softly, almost to himself,

'Well, well, well! Carter dead, eh? What a damn shame. Drowned, you say?'

'Probably! He was swimming or snorkelling or something. Had his two new body guards with him, but they musta taken their eyes orf him for a few seconds. Next thing they know, Carter has swallowed half the Pacific Ocean. Right now, he's measuring his length on a cold slab up at the hospital. Best place for him, I reckon.'

Muscatt slowly shook his head, smiling as he listened to his superior.

'I think I might like a word with these two body guards. Even if it's just to hear a full description as how the bastard died,' he said.

Raynor laughed and turned to leave.

'Yeah, I thought you would. Ok, I'll leave it with you,' he called as he stepped through the doorway. 'Funny! I was certain it must be your birthday.'

CHAPTER NINE

∞

Anita Keyes watched through the large window of the carriage as the countryside flashed past. The last station had been Junee, so she knew it would be a little over half an hour before they would be at Wagga Wagga. From there it was just on twenty minutes to The Rock, the closest station on the main southern line to their farm.

She turned to her right and observed her husband, dozing lightly as the train sped through the upper reaches of the Riverina district. The gently rolling plains between Junee and Wagga reminded Anita of the lowlands near her old home town, in the Royal Province of Manitra, in northern Malaysia. The land form was almost identical, but the colour was quite different. In Manitra, constant rainfall rendered the countryside a bright green, with bamboo and sugar cane filling the landscape, and the planted crops growing right up to the edge of the thick jungle.

Colour was the main difference in the two areas.

The low hills and shallow valleys might appear similar, but Malaysia's greens were replaced out here as the wheat fields and lucerne paddocks tendered to colour their world a dull yellow as the plants matured.

She sighed and reached for Andy's muscular arm. He was awake instantly, sitting upright and tensing his body. She smiled at him and said quietly,

'We are between Junee and Wagga, Andy. I thought you might like to get ready to leave the train, soon.'

He yawned and stretched his long legs in front of him. There were only two other passengers left in the carriage. A young lady who sat reading near the front and the elderly gentleman who seemed to be in a deep sleep, his grey hair pressed against the window, and his right hand cushioning his cheek from the vibrating glass.

Anita returned her gaze to the outside as Andy picked up the newspaper he had previously discarded, and resumed his study of the sporting section. He read a back page article about the proposed tour of Australia by the South African cricket team.

'Looks like the South African tour is gunna be cancelled. Bloody protesters and do-gooders! I wish they'd stick to politics and leave cricket alone. I was looking forward to the test matches, and I couldn't care less about Apartheid, or any other bloody policy.'

Anita whispered to him,

'It is a bad policy, though, isn't it, Andy? Black and white should both be able to do as they wish, should they not?'

'For certain!' he growled softly. 'And that includes play cricket!'

She smiled into his eyes and nodded. Their quiet exchange was interrupted by a booming voice from the overhead speakers as the train's Guard made an announcement.

'The next stop will be Wagga Wagga. Change at Wagga for the Tumbarumba line. Please ensure you do not leave any luggage on your seats, or in the racks. Next stop Wagga Wagga, in approximately six minutes. Thank you.'

After the stop at Wagga's large station, the train was soon gathering speed as it covered the short distance to the tiny village of Uranquinty. Andy watched as two young women stepped off onto the gravel platform, and the train moved off again, hardly giving the women time to leave the carriage. He stood and stretched his powerful arms and shoulders. Then he reached up to the overhead rack and retrieved a vinyl suitcase.

Anita also stood, gathering her handbag and a small overnight bag.

Their other luggage, Andy's heavy Ex-Army metal trunk, was booked through as cargo, and was riding in the guard's compartment. It's rounded shape made it awkward to handle and Andy knew the railway staff would be unable, and unwilling to carry it any great distance. He turned to his wife and asked,

'Can you get the 'Rover, Sweetheart? You got your key?'

'Yes, Andy, my husband. I will drive over the car for you,' she answered, nodding.

When the train slowed to stop at The Rock station, Andy helped Anita down from the carriage before striding quickly to the rear of the train. The old train guard was struggling with the heavy trunk, sweat dripping from his wrinkled brow as he tried to slide it to the doorway.

'She's right, mate,' Andy told him. 'I'll get it.' He stepped into the guard's compartment and grasped a handle attached to the end of the trunk. The guard straightened and happily stepped back out of the big man's way.

'You'll have to sign for it, ya know?' he croaked.

'Yeah, yeah! Let's get it off the train first, eh?' Andy replied.

The guard watched with a considerable degree of awe as Andy dragged the trunk into the doorway, picked it up by the two handles, then laid it gently on the gravel platform and straightened up. He signed the book which the guard thrust at him, and noticed the Stationmaster approaching, wheeling an ancient, steel-wheeled wooden trolley.

'Watcha got in there, Big Fella? A load of rocks or sumpin?' the old guard asked.

'Yeah, that's it. Rocks. I collect 'em,' Andy replied, as the Stationmaster joined them.

Shaking his grey head, the guard waved at the stationmaster as he held a white flag aloft, signalling to the engine driver. A loud blast from the big diesel told them the signal had been received, and the train began moving, heading further south to Albury.

Andy and the Stationmaster manoeuvred the trunk onto the trolley, and together they trundled it to a space between the station building and the parcel shed.

'Where's ya car, Andy?' the Stationmaster asked, puffing from his effort.

'Over at the pub. Anita's gone to fetch it. Here she is,' he said, pointing as the Land Rover came slowly into the rail yard. She backed the vehicle up to the space, and Andy opened the tailgate. With only token help from the Stationmaster, he manhandled the weighty trunk into the cargo area of the Land Rover, then tossed the vinyl suitcase in beside it.

'Thanks, Frank. Here, here's our tickets.'

He handed the railwayman the two paper tickets, and climbed in behind the steering wheel. Anita was already in her seat, and they drove off, across the Olympic Highway, towards 'Rocky Crop', anxious to be home.

As the vehicle bounced and bumped along the side road, heading north-east away from the rail line, Andy glanced across at his beautiful little wife. He thought she looked tired, her eyes half closed and her pretty face creased in numerous wrinkles as she rested her head on the 'B' pillar of the rugged station sedan.

'We'll be home soon, Cutie!' said softly, not expecting an answer.

She opened her eyes and smiled at him.

'I know, Handsome. And when we get there, I'm going to make a big pot of tea for you.

And, if you are a good boy, I might make some of your pikelets for you. How does that sound to you, Sexy Man?'

'Sounds pretty good to me. I love you, you know?' he reached over and clasped her tiny fingers in his huge hand as he drove along the dusty track.

Mike Walker read the bulletin for the third time and then simply stared at the blurry text. The Crime Update had disgorged itself from the teleprinter not more than five minutes ago, just as Walker was passing by. The first article grabbed his attention and he had snatched the paper from the machine almost before it had finished printing. The first article read,

"Wollongong Identity found dead at Scarborough beach."

"Ian Carter, Wollongong Real Estate agent, and recent attendee at the District Court was pulled from the surf at Scarborough beach, North of Wollongong at around eight fifteen yesterday morning. The colourful South Coast identity had been snorkelling with two other males, believed to be his personal assistants or even his bodyguards. A local Lifesaver attempted to revive Carter, and an ambulance was called. When Wollongong Section members arrived, the ambulance personnel had already declared him deceased, and the body was transferred to Wollongong Hospital mortuary. A preliminary examination has suggested cause of death could be drowning, however X-rays have since revealed no fluid in the lungs or stomach. The Coroner's office has ordered an autopsy which will be carried out today. Carter was recently charged with numerous offences, including Canal Knowledge, Supply prohibited substances, living off immoral earnings and some Federal offences, how-ever he was acquitted in the Wollongong District Court when all evidence was either discredited or disputed. Wollongong Detectives, under DCI Allan Muscatt are investigating the death."

Mike sat down heavily at his desk, fingering the sheet of paper as he absorbed the contents. The other crimes mentioned in the bulletin were routine. A couple of armed hold-ups, two serious assaults and the theft of a Porsche racing car from Liverpool.

He recalled reading an internal account of Carter's court attendance, and a newspaper report detailing the taunts and slanderous comments he made to Muscatt and his team. He had kept a copy of that bulletin, which was issued as a training notice, and stapled it to the press clipping. He sorted through the contents of the bottom drawer in his desk.

A grunt of satisfaction escaped his lips as he located a school exercise book. In this he had summarised the earlier un-explained deaths of the criminals who had beaten serious charges then spent time boasting about their victories in the various media. The training bulletin and press clipping were folded neatly inside, awaiting his summarisation. Despite the words of caution, and even veiled direct order from Sergeant Johnson to leave the subject alone, Walker had continued to pry and study the events. His interest in the Carter matter had been sharpened when he had seen Allan Muscatt's name in the training notice. He had served with then Sergeant Muscatt in General Duties several years ago, in the City Section Command area. He had enormous respect for the now Chief Inspector, and his ability. The two men had hit it off from their first meeting, despite the wide gap in their respective ranks.

As an idea began to take shape in his mind, Mike Walker looked around the office.

There were no other Detectives at their desks, just the civilian clerk tapping away at her electric typewriter. He walked to the copying machine and quickly made a copy of the Crime Update, and placed it inside his exercise book. He returned to his desk and dialled the switchboard. A tired female voice answered,

'Switch. Who's calling please?'

'Detective Mike Walker here. Could you get the Wollongong DCI for me, please?'

'Wollongong DCI. Hold on Mike.'

After a few seconds a clicking sound was followed by a familiar voice.

'Chief Inspector Muscatt. Yes, Wagga?'

' 'morning, Sir. This is Mike Walker. Long time, no see.' Walker answered cheerily.

There was a brief pause, then Muscatt replied warmly,

'Mikey! How are you, mate? You still in Wagga, eh? Still chasing the speedsters?'

Walker smiled as he re-checked the office, again making sure there were no listeners.

'Yeah, still here. Not in Traffic anymore though. I'm doing your thing. Plain clothes now. Look, Sir, I don't have much time, so I'll get to the point. I want to discuss a matter with you, but here and now isn't the time. Can you give me a secure number I can call? It's important, but I can't say much at the moment.'

Muscatt supplied a telephone number, adding a comment that he could be reached on the number anytime today before four pm.

'I'll be about ten minutes, Sir,' Walker told him, and hung up.

The Detective gathered his exercise book and tucked it inside his shirt. There was still no sign of Lindsay Johnson, or any other Detectives, so he rose and casually stretched his arms, faking a yawn as he did so.

'I'm just going across the street to grab a coffee, Sandra. If Johnno turns up, will you tell him I'll be back in about twenty minutes?' The girl nodded and returned to her typing. Walker donned his suit coat and strolled to the staircase. After descending the wooden stairs, he stepped out into the street, before hurrying around the corner and on to the Post Office. He noted with satisfaction that all three telephone booths were vacant, and he swung open the door of the nearest one.

Once inside the telephone cubicle, he dialled the number Muscatt had given him. Soon the two Detectives were deep in conversation, with Walker doing most of the talking.

When he paused, Muscatt took the opportunity to throw in some thoughts.

'Ok, Mike, I see what you mean. But, if you're correct, where do you want to go from here? I mean, I am starting to think you might be onto something, but Jeez, how do we prove anything? Some great investigative minds have their hands all over some of these cases, and they've come up empty. How can we take it further?'

'Well,' replied Walker. 'The next step, I think, would be the results of the autopsy on this Carter bloke. Can you get hold of them? And after you analyse them, we should talk further, to see if he fits the same bill as those others I told you about. OK?'

Muscatt thought for a few seconds, then replied firmly.

'Yeah, right-o. I will get the results, that's for certain. The report comes to my office in the first instance. I'll go over it with a fine tooth comb. Actually, I'll make a copy, and get it you, somehow. How's that?'

'Great! How about I come up to see you. I'm due four rest days at the end of this week. I'll bring the missus. You still married to Heather, Sir?'

'Yeah, we're still going strong. Right-o! Good idea. Bring everything you've got, and we'll stick our heads together. I live at a joint called Thirroul. 57 Wilke Road. It's right across from the beach. And listen, Mike. In this matter, drop the 'Sir' will ya? It's Allan and Mike, ok?'

Walker acknowledged, and hung up the black receiver. He remained in the booth, going over the conversation. The realisation of what he was getting into was well and truly at the forefront of his thoughts. And if Sergeant Lindsay Johnson found out, he would be in for a huge reprimand, or even worse. Johnson's earlier warning to stay away from the subject had not only shaken the young Detective, but had also been the catalyst for his increased interest and subsequent secret probing.

He strolled slowly back to the police station, mulling over his conversation with Muscatt. He knew he could trust the Detective Chief Inspector, and was anxious to meet up with him again. Muscatt's words about the other investigative minds kept coming back to his thoughts. A degree of self-doubt invaded his mind as he digested those facts. He was a newcomer as a Detective, and here he was preparing to go up against career investigators. Not one legitimate cause of death had been established in these cases, despite an apparent thorough probing by some of the states finest.

He was engrossed in his thoughts and did not see the ample form of Lindsay Johnson until they almost collided.

'Hey! Mikey! Watch where ya walking,' the sergeant's voice boomed.

'Uh? Oh, sorry Sarg! I was daydreaming,' Walker replied, stopping suddenly.

'Yeah? Well, you wanta give the daydreamin' away, me boy! You'll dream your life away. Ok, we got work to do. George just told me those finger prints from the railway job belong to Bob Metters. So, soon as you're ready, we're going to bring young Rachel in and get her statement, assuming she'll give us one. And then, if she says what we want her to say, we'll go and invite Mister Metters over for a chat. I happen to know that he's been hangin' around with the Spano brothers, either at their dirty bloody hovel in North Wagga, or wasting their dole money playin' pool at the 'Bottom Pub'.'

'Ready when you are, Sarg. Let's go get young Rachel,' Walker replied.

The two Detectives walked together to their unmarked Holden police car, and Mike entered the driver's seat before starting the engine.

They covered the short drive to Hyde's Jewellers without speaking. Neither man relished the task ahead. Their investigations had led them to the conclusion that the simple-minded young girl was being led into a criminal life by her older, street-wise boyfriend. Both Detectives were determined to go easy on the girl, but they knew her testimony was vital if they were to charge Metters with the break, enter and steal from the railway station.

The girl sobbed as she was led to the police car, and sat with her face covered by her hands as Walker drove slowly back to the police station. Once upstairs, she made a tearful confession, revealing that she had told her new boyfriend about the unmarked gold shipments. Walker typed rapidly as she spoke, noting every detail as the tough old sergeant quietly asked the questions in as gentle a voice as he could muster. She told the Detectives about accidentally finding out how the gold arrived in the plain wrapped parcels, and then casually mentioning this to Metters. She had seen nothing suspicious when the petty criminal had insisted she tell him when the next shipment was due. When it had gone missing from the railway station, and old Mister Hyde had reacted in panic at the news, she had realised the truth. When the two Detectives had called at the shop to ask their initial questions, Rachel had tried to hide her involvement. Later that night she had confronted her boyfriend as they had a few drinks in an hotel. Metters had almost succeeded in convincing her she was mistaken.

It had been one quick little sentence from his lips that removed her last doubts.

'Who'd know what was in a plain white paper wrapped parcel, anyway?'

Rachel realised then that she had not told him anything about how the gold was packaged. She had seen Hyde and Mrs. Cousins unwrapping the parcels a few times before, but was certain she had not mentioned the white paper packaging to Metters.

Walker finished typing up her statement and handed it to her. Johnson looked up at Mike and nodded. The next step, arresting Metters, would be far more pleasurable.

CHAPTER TEN

∞

Larry Kind jumped as the intercom crackled and the soft voice of Linda, his secretary reached him.

'Mr Tuckey for you. Are you ready for him?'

Kind took several deep breaths, and subconsciously straightened his tie. He pushed a button on the intercom panel and spoke with a voice full of false confidence.

'Yes. Show him in.'

After several seconds the frosted glass door swung open and the huge form of Albert Tuckey entered the spacious office.

The two men shook hands and Kind waved his left hand at a padded seat.

'Please sit down, Mister Tuckey.'

Kind closed the slat blinds at the glass wall between the inner and outer offices.

'I won't be staying long. I assume you've heard the news?', the large man said in a hoarse, throaty voice.

Kind was in the act of sitting back into his plush chair when Tuckey spoke.

He remained in a half crouch, frozen in mid action.

'News? What news, Mister Tuckey?' he asked his visitor.

'About Carter! You mean you don't know?' Tuckey growled.

'No, I haven't heard anything. What about Mister Carter?' Kind asked as he sat down.

Tuckey waited until Kind had seated himself fully then rasped in his dry, croaky voice,

'He was pulled from the surf at some beach near Wollongong this morning, dead as mutton. Apparently a lifesaver gave him mouth to mouth but couldn't revive him. Even a couple of ambulance drivers had a go, but he was pronounced dead when they took him to hospital. You mean to tell me you didn't know about any of this?'

The look of complete shock on Kind's face told Tuckey that the lawyer had been taken entirely by surprise. The colour had drained from his rugged face and Tuckey detected a slight drooping of the powerful shoulders as he slumped into his chair.

There was silence in the room for nearly ten seconds. Kind stared out of the office window, as Tuckey stared at him. Eventually Kind spoke.

'Any other details? I mean, is there anything suspicious about the death? Are the coppers talking to anybody? Any witnesses?'

Tuckey did not like lawyers, of any calibre, and he was beginning to enjoy himself watching Kind as the confusion and discomfort showed in his features.

'Well,' he croaked, 'to answer your questions one at a time, the police have impounded the body, because the cause of death is as yet unknown. My contact in Wollongong coppers says the police medical officer won't reveal his thoughts. That tells me that some bugger is suspicious about something. No, the cops are not talking, including to their uniformed colleagues, one of which is my contact. There were at least a dozen witnesses. Two blokes in particular, disregarding the lifesaver who was on duty, were very close to the action. They are, or were, Carter's two new bodyguards. A pair of jaspers who were formally Billy Greene's minders. First, they lost old Billy, now they've gone and lost Carter. I reckon they oughta consider another line of work, 'cause they won't be able to get a job minding a puppy after this debacle. Apparently the cops took them into custody at the time of the death, and as of about an hour ago, they were still cooling their heels in separate cells in the Wollongong slammer. Now, Mister Kind, my reason for this visit is twofold. Obviously, with Carter falling off the perch, the deal we had planned has fallen over with him, so we can kiss that all goodbye. Pure courtesy on my part to go ahead with this appointment. The other reason is that I have been told you organised for these pair of dopes to be employed by Carter. Is that right?'

Tuckey's voice had assumed an even hasher tone as he asked this last question.

Kind gulped and thought rapidly for a few seconds. He quickly regained his self composure and hitched his shoulders before replying.

'Yeah, that's right. I talked Carter into hiring bodyguards. You see, Mister Tuckey, I have this theory about all the mysterious deaths of some of our more colourful clientele have been suffering over the past couple of years. I thought Carter made himself a prime candidate for an un-explained death when he beat the police in his famous case a while ago. Billy Greene and a few others did the same thing as Carter. Made the police look foolish, skited about it to the media, then wound up dead in strange circumstances. Too many co-incidences for my liking, I'm afraid. That's why I wanted Carter to hire some protective muscle. As for the fact that he picked those two, well, he interviewed some others and he chose Big Jeff and 'Knifey' himself. Not me, you understand?'

Tuckey stood, looking down at the lawyer as he considered the explanation.

Kind mistook the pause as a lack of confidence. His bravado returned and he stood up.

'Anyway, Mister Tuckey. What business is it of yours, may I ask? Any dealings I had with Ian Carter was, and is, purely between my client and me. You must surely be aware of the privacy conditions under which we work.'

With blinding speed, Tuckey's right hand reached out and grabbed Kind's paisley printed tie, dragging the stocky lawyer across the desk and up to the larger man's height.

'Listen, you fancy pants punk!' the harsh voice croaked. 'You arranged for those pair of incompetent idiots to guard Carter, knowing they couldn't look after a nun at a poofter's convention! Now Carter's dead, the cops are sniffing around, and a bloody lucrative deal has fallen over, which will finish up costing me, and some of my associates, hundreds of thousands of dollars. So just watch your mouth. Understand me, Mister?'

His huge hand had been slowly twisting the tie as he spoke, and Kind was starting to choke. His courage had left him completely and his face had changed colour to a bright red. He nodded his head vigorously as he gripped Tuckey's wrist in a feeble attempt to break the larger man's grip.

The sound of the office door swinging open made both men turn their heads. Kind's secretary stood wide-eyed, a hand covering her open mouth.

She removed her hand and asked loudly, distress obvious in her voice, 'Mister Kind! What's going on? Are you all right?'

Tuckey slowly released the tie and shoved Kind in the chest. The lawyer stumbled back into his seat, gasping for breath as he recovered from the assault.

He nodded his head slowly as he regained his breath.

'Yeah, I'm OK, Linda. Please return to your desk, and shut the door. Please.'

With a final angry glare at Tuckey, the young woman withdrew, pulling the frosted glass door closed behind her. Tuckey smirked down at the dishevelled lawyer and said,

'OK! Now that we understand each other, tell me more about your theory. For a start, who do you think is organising these murders, if, indeed, any murders are being done?'

The lawyer gasped a deep breath, while glaring resentfully at Tuckey.

The physical attack had taken him by surprise and he was already planning revenge.

He recovered his composure but remained silent.

Tuckey smiled across the desk at the lawyer as he sat down.

'Well? Speak up! If you can offer any evidence, maybe I can help. I've done a bit of investigating in my time, you know?' he rasped.

After another long pause, Kind sighed and allowed his shoulders to slump. Before speaking, he clamped a large cigar between his teeth. The cigar remained unlit.

'Well, I haven't really got any proof of anything, just a theory. Billy Greene was a client of a close friend and colleague of mine. When he got killed, I happened to read the Coroner's report. It said that he couldn't determine the exact cause of death, and it looked like old Billy simply stopped living, just before the bus ran over him. If that isn't strange enough, I also happened to recall reading a report about Redfern Errol's death. It said almost word for word what Greene's report said. Then I was talking to my friend, who had a couple of other well-known clients, who also had significant victories over the police, then went to the media skiting and bragging about their wins. Not long afterwards, they each died in un-explained circumstances. Now you tell me Ian Carter is dead, and I'll bet you London to a brick that his death turns out to be unsolved.'

Tuckey listened quietly to Kind's story, taking notes in a leather bound notebook which he had withdrawn from his coat pocket.

'OK, Larry. What makes you so sure there is anything special about these deaths?'

Kind spread his arms and his eyes bulged slightly as his courage began to return.

'I just told you, Man. Weren't you listening, for Christ's sake? Every one of these villains died after bragging about beating the police, then their deaths are all recorded without definite causes. Something strange is going on, and, to tell the truth, I am a little concerned that successful lawyers like myself, and a few mates, might become the next targets. We're the smart buggers who've been getting these blokes the acquittals.'

Tuckey looked up from his notebook and growled,

'Ok, Buster! I heard ya! I reckon you might be over-stating your own importance, but let's put that aside for now. You reckon Carter might be the latest target! Target of whom, Mister Kind?'

'*THAT*, I don't know. Whether it's a group of rogue coppers who don't like being laughed at, bunch of rednecks, or maybe a vigilante mob. Who-ever it is, they know how to kill without leaving a trace. There are never any bruises, no trace of a poison, and no clue as to why these bastards just simply stopped living. What-ever, I'm starting to see a pattern here, and I don't like it. I tried talking to my colleague but he doesn't seem to grasp the significance. Maybe we can do business together after all, Mister Tuckey. How about I retain your services, and you do a little probing? Would you be interested in that sort of deal?'

Tuckey leaned back in his chair, grinning at Kind as he reached for a cigarette. After lighting up with a gold lighter, the big man blew a cloud of smoke at the ceiling.

'Well, I suppose we could get our heads together. See what's what, as they say. I assume you will be providing my fee?'

'If it's reasonable, then yes, I'll stump up the required funds. But first, tell me this, Mister Tuckey. Where are you going to look? And if you find any evidence to back up my theory, can I rely on you bringing it to me, and no-one else?'

Tuckey stood and offered his giant hand. He said, as Kind reluctantly shook hands,

'I will bring any evidence to you, and to you only, Larry. As for where I intend to start looking, well, you just leave that to me. I've already got a few ideas.'

With a final smirk, Tuckey turned and left the office, deliberately leaving the glass door wide open. Grinning wolfishly, he winked at the secretary as he left the outer office, leaving the street door open as well.

Linda rose and closed the street door, then hurried to the inner office.

'Is everything still all right, Mister Kind?' she asked her employer.

The lawyer looked at her and forced a smile.

'Yeah, everything is fine, Linda. How about ducking across the road and grabbing us both a fresh coffee? Use some petty cash, and grab us both a doughnut, too eh?'

When the woman left, Kind looked down at his hands and realised they were shaking.

'What the bloody hell have I done, throwing in with that bastard?' he thought to himself. *'I should have kept my silly bloody gob shut.'*

He reached into his desk and withdrew the half empty bottle of whisky. After taking a large swallow, he slumped into his chair. He engrossed himself in gloomy thoughts as he waited for Linda to return with the snacks and coffee.

Mike Walker watched as the girl tried to read her copy of the statement.

Tears continued to run down her cheeks, eventually dripping onto the paper.

She signed at the bottom on the three copies of the typewritten sheets, and handed them, and Walker's gold pen, back to the

Detective. She wiped her eyes with a tiny, floral patterned handkerchief.

Johnson took one copy and countersigned it. Then he handed it to the distraught girl.

'Here, Rachel. This is your copy. You keep it, won't you? I want you to understand a few things, now. First, you are not under arrest. You are free to go, how-ever I would like you to wait here in our office for a while. We have a few matters to see to. If you agree to wait here, I will personally speak to Mister Hyde for you. I'll let him know you were not involved in the theft, and that you merely slipped up a bit when talking to your boyfriend. I'll strongly suggest he let you keep your job, as you have provided some valuable information that should lead to the guilty person being arrested, and hopefully the goods returned to Mister Hyde. How's that sound? We have a deal?'

The terrified girl stared at Johnson with her eyes wide.

Eventually she spoke between sobs.

'Does that mean you're gunna arrest Rob? Is that it?'

Johnson nodded to Walker, indicating he wished the junior Detective to answer.

'Yes, Rachel, that's right. We will arrest Metters, and question him. If he tells us what we want to hear, we may charge him. If his story matches yours, then there will be no charges for you to answer. But we want you to remain here at the Police Station until we pick him up. That way he can't trick you into saying anything that isn't right.'

Walker pointed to a plain door which led to a vacant room. 'If you wait here, in the spare office over there, he will never know you were here. On top of that, Sergeant Johnson will convince Mister Hyde you knew nothing of Metters's actions, and see if he will let you keep your job. That's a pretty good deal, considering what trouble you could have been in, if we decided to put the blame your way?'

The girl's shoulders slumped, and she nodded her head. After wiping her eyes once more, she stood and followed Johnson to the small room. The big Detective smiled roughly at her and closed the door.

'Sally!' Johnson called to the stenographer who was busy thumping at a typewriter near the front of the offices. 'Can you get our girlfriend in there a cold drink or a cuppa tea?'

The young woman nodded and headed for the closed door.

Johnson returned to Walker's desk as Mike was placing the statements and data sheets into a new cardboard folder. He stood up and tucked the folder under his arm, then took his suit coat from the back of the chair.

'We going to get Metters now?' Walker asked Johnson hopefully.

'Yep!' the senior man growled. He grinned evilly as he added 'And just between you 'n' me, Mikey, I hope the bastard puts up a fight.'

Walker smiled and replied,

'Me too. I just been reading his form. He ain't much good is he?'

'No good at all,' Johnson agreed. 'He's about as useful as a one-legged man in an arse kicking contest.'

Walker grinned as the two men strode to the caryard and entered the car.

Mike drove to an address in the southern suburbs of Wagga Wagga, but there was no answer to their numerous door knocks. Both men looked around at the grubby house, before Mike went to the back door, noting several stripped car bodies and piles of rubbish scattered about the fenced yard.

Their next try was the home of Metters's associates, the Spano brothers. They had to traverse the large town and cross the Murrumbidgee River to find the Spano residence in North Wagga. Only a pair of snarling, salivating Doberman Pinscher dogs answered their calls from the side gates. Walker stood back from the steel gates as Johnson beat loudly on the front door. When he joined Mike at the gate, Johnson looked at the savage dogs and slowly opened his coat, revealing his Baretta pistol nestled snugly in a shoulder holster.

'For two bob I'd put a bullet in the head of the pair of mongrel things,' he muttered.

'Who, the dogs or the Spanos?' Walker asked, grinning as they backed away and returned to the car.

'Both!' Johnson growled. 'And bloody Metters, too. It'd save a heap of taxpayer's dough, and make me feel bloody terrific. Ok, the next port of call is The Bottom. That's where they drink at the moment, until old Charlie wakes up an' bars the bloody three of 'em. Let's go, matey.'

Walker drove back to the business district of town and parked the police car directly outside the bar doors of the large old hotel.

'They'll be here, for sure. Drinking their dole money, and planning some more mischief if I'm any judge. Right, you go in the far door, Mikey. Give me the paper work, an' I'll go in this door. If he's there, and he runs, give it to him proper. And watch out for the Spanos' if they're with 'im. They're a couple of dingos, but they're also stupid. If Metters tells 'em to, they'll try to help him get away. Got your 'cuffs?'

Walker nodded as he grinned at his superior.

'You're really looking forward to this, aren't you Sarg?'

Johnson smiled widely as he checked his own handcuffs.

'You betcha I am. Let's go, matey.'

Both Detectives exited the car and Walker strolled to the second barroom door. When he saw Johnson step in through the main door, he entered the cool bar and swept his gaze around the room. Two elderly men were sitting on stools at the bar, glasses of beer in their hands. Another man was standing at the bar, studying a horse racing form guide.

An elderly barmaid sat behind the bar, polishing beer glasses with a white tea towel.

The only other occupants were a trio of younger men gathered around a quarter-size pool table. Two of the youths were dressed in checked shirts, denim jeans and filthy running shoes. Their faces bore a slightly swarthy skin tone, and their eyes were noticeably dark. Mike guessed that the pair would be the Spano brothers.

The third pool player sported a black tee-shirt, black corduroy trousers, heavy boots and his head was adorned with dark blue baseball cap. This was undoubtedly the notorious Robert Metters. Walker noted all three wore their unkempt hair long, with the two brothers dark locks secured in pony tails. The tee-shirt wearer allowed his curly, brown hair to dangle freely over his narrow shoulders.

All of the bar room occupants, except the form guide reader, turned towards the main doors as Johnson's huge frame temporarily blocked out the bright sun light.

The reader stayed interested only in his horse racing document.

Nobody appeared to notice Walker at the second door.

Seeing he had their attention, Johnson said loudly to the trio of pool players,

'Police! You three, put those cues down and stay where you are.'

He walked purposefully to the pool table as he spoke, his keen eyes not wavering from the youths as he noted their positions and likely escape paths.

Johnson stopped at the edge of the pool table and addressed Metters.

'Robert Metters. I am Detective Sergeant Johnson, Wagga Wagga C.I.B. I would like you to accompany me to the Police Station, where I intend to ask you some questions regarding a certain matter, Ok?'

Metters's re-action took everybody in the room by surprise.

'Get stuffed, Fatso!' he yelled. As he spoke, he swung his pool cue in a wide arc, aiming for the side of Johnson's head. Johnson reeled back as the tip of the cue caught him a glancing blow across the top of his head, merely ruffling the grey hair. Metters dropped the cue and sprinted for the second door. He had almost reached the narrow doorway when he became aware of Mike. Walker was blocking the door with his body, and the fugitive quickly decided force was the best option to clear the way. He turned his left shoulder towards the Detective and cocked his arm as he ran towards the door. The attempted shoulder charge might have been effective if Walker had not recognised the manoeuvre. Years of playing Rugby League had taught Walker the optimum defensive technique for negating a shoulder charge. He braced himself and took the full force directly on his own right shoulder. While the Detective barely moved after the collision, Metters was flung backwards, ricocheting away to the side wall. With superior speed, Walker delivered a left hand punch which caught Metters flush on the point of his small nose. Blood gushed from the wound, and Mike followed up with a right cross which connected with Metters's torso. The petty criminal staggered backward before crumpling to the floor. He called feebly to his companions,

'Come on you blokes, give us a hand. Help me, quick!'

Johnson's voice boomed around the room, stopping the Spanos instantly as they attempted to join their friend.

'You scum stay where you are, or I'll flatten the pair of ya. Just try anything and see.'

Mike saw Johnson standing close to the brothers, pointing menacingly in their faces, a slight grin on his craggy face. Both youths appeared pale and frightened of the big man.

Metters was sitting up, holding his smashed nose with his right hand as the blood flow slowly abated. He looked up at Walker, then around the room. When he saw the other drinkers and the barmaid all watching with shocked expressions, he regained some of his bravado.

'You all seen it. I been assaulted by this bastard.' He turned to look up at Mike. 'Who are you, Mate? You a copper or what? I'm gunna have you for assault, no matter who ya are. You hit me for no reason. You've had it, Mate, I tell ya.'

Walker reached down and grabbed the tee shirt in his powerful grip. He hoisted the bleeding man to his feet, and spun him around, holding both arms tightly, then reached for his handcuffs from his trouser pocket. When the cuffs had snapped shut, he turned Metters back around to face him. The Detective sneered at the criminal and muttered,

'Shut your gob, Pigs Breath! I am Detective Walker. You are under arrest for assaulting a policeman, resisting arrest and a few other things I'll think of soon. In the meantime, just keep your sewer shut and listen. I'm arresting you and I'm taking you to Wagga Police Station. I'm going to ask you some questions about these and some other matters. You don't have to answer my questions. You don't have to say anything, but anything you do say will be taken down in writing and may later be given in evidence. You understand me?'

The brief show of cockiness was nowhere to be seen as Metters looked fearfully into Mike's face. He said quietly, with a plea in his wavering voice,

'What other matters? I ain't done nuffin, and I only had a go at you 'cause I didn't know who you was. What are you gunna question me about? I ain't done nuffin, honest!'

'That's about the only truthful thing you ever said, Metters!' Johnson's voice, full of authority, sounded from behind the handcuffed man. 'You ain't done nothing honest your entire miserable life. Now, you been told to shut up by Detective Walker, so shut up. If I want any shit outta you, I'll squeeze ya head. And wipe that blood on your sleeve. I don't want it all over the police car. Your stench will be bad enough.'

Walker suppressed a grin and pointed to Metters's arms. He informed his superior,

'He can't Sarge. I already cuffed him. Anyway, it's stopped bleeding for now.'

Johnson inspected Metters's bloodied nose, then the handcuffed wrists.

'Ok, Mikey. Good job. Right-o, let's go.' He indicated the main doors, then turned to face the still petrified Spano brothers. 'You pair of useless apparitions get out of here, and get home. Go feed them mongrel dogs you got caged up in your backyard. Better still, go drown 'em in the river. Drown yourselves while you're at it. Do us all a favour. Go on, git!' He watched as the terrified brothers slunk quickly to the main doors and disappeared out onto the street. Then Johnson turned to the barmaid and the drinkers.

'Ok, Beryl? You see anything you want to talk about?'

'No, Sergeant, nothing. I just saw you and your mate arrest a bloke and that's all I seen,' the street-wise barmaid replied, ignoring the glare from Metters.

'How about you blokes? Everything all right with youse?' Johnson called.

The three drinkers all nodded vigorously and the two elderly men even raised their glasses. The racing fan nodded once more and returned to his paper.

'Good. Good,' Johnson smiled. 'Be seeing you, then. C'mon Mikey. Bring that garbage with you. You drive. I'll sit with the garbage to make sure it don't get hurt.'

The three left the hotel and Mike opened the back door of the car. Johnson stepped around him and shoved Metters roughly onto the rear seat.

'Move over, ya scum!' Johnson growled. Metters wriggled to the other side of the car, clearly terrified of the big Detective. Johnson entered the car and grinned evilly at his prisoner. Mike was about to say something, but thought better of it. He shrugged to himself and entered the driver's seat. During the short drive to the police station, none of the car occupants spoke, but Johnson whistled cheerfully for the entire journey.

CHAPTER ELEVEN

Allan Muscatt re-read a copy of the same bulletin which had excited Mike Walker.

He grunted and smiled grimly as he read the description of Ian Carter's death. Muscatt had never been a religious man, but at this moment he looked up at the ceiling and winked, a wide grin spreading across his face. He whispered to the heavens,

'I dunno if you're real or not, Big Fella, but you, or somebody, sure got this one right.'

The printed sheet of paper remained clutched in his right fist as he closed his eyes and re-lived that horrible day when Carter's team of slick lawyers produced witnesses, testimonials and sworn statements which combined to discredit every piece of evidence the police had amassed in their six-month investigation into the affairs of the showy real estate agent. The memories of Carter gloating to the spellbound press on the front steps of Wollongong's court house after his acquittal, the smug looks of his law team, and the overwhelming desire to reach for his pistol, were feelings Muscatt had thought he would have to live with for the rest of his days.

Now, he felt a mixture of glee at the sudden demise of Carter, but also a sense of being robbed. A feeling of being denied the chance of a conviction touched a nerve with the dedicated Detective. He had anticipated watching Carter squirm and cry as prison staff led him away to spend the next few years enduring regular beltings and dodging the queers in the communal showers at one of the state's more rugged jails. The image of Carter dressed in prison greens, with a number printed across his back, flashed briefly into the Detective's mind. Then it was gone, replaced by the grisly sight of the dead man laid out on a stainless-steel table, still sporting his swimming trunks, as well as several ornate gold rings on his thick fingers.

His thoughts turned to Mike Walker, and the clandestine telephone call. Muscatt remembered the young constable as a keen and competent policeman, who was well liked by everyone, and respected for his integrity, intelligence and thoroughness. Even as a Probationary Constable, fresh from the academy, Walker was recognised as a shining light for the City Section Command. His physical fitness level also made him a target for the local police sports council representatives. In very short time Mike Walker was a regular member of the police rugby league team, the local police golf club and he was the city area police boxing champion.

But it was his attention to detail and dedication to the task at hand that Muscatt recalled most. As a general duties officer, Mike Walker soon gained a reputation as one whose card was marked for future greatness. Muscatt had observed the young policeman investigate the crimes he was assigned to with the thoroughness of an old hand, and recalled his feelings of disappointment when Walker had opted for the traffic branch, which included a transfer to the Wagga Wagga Section. His loss as a potential Detective to Sydney City was one Muscatt had felt personally, such was his belief in Mike's ability. Knowing that a talented person like Walker was now a Detective filled him with a sense of satisfaction. He read the crime bulletin again, this time making notes in the margin and smiling to himself as he pictured Carter's lifeless body on that cold, dull stainless steel table at Wollongong hospital.

Andy Keyes lay awake on his back, his huge hands clasped together behind his head. He stared at the ceiling, his mind going over the events of their latest trip to the city. His sharp eyes spied a black spider crawling slowly across the flat plaster, past the glass chandelier, now hanging dark and motionless from the bedroom ceiling. Despite his thoughts being focussed on occurrences in Sydney, he spared time to marvel at the spider's ability to defy gravity as it clung, upside down, to the smooth surface.

Beside him, the tiny form of Anita stirred briefly as she turned her naked body from her left side onto her right. Even in deep sleep her beautiful face seemed to smile up at him.

The couple had arrived home in the late afternoon and quickly unloaded their luggage before changing into work clothes. While Andy had spent nearly four hours fixing a gate in the lower paddock fence, Anita had swept through the homestead, cleaning, dusting and polishing furniture and fittings. Then she had cooked a roast beef meal for the two of them as Andy hand fed the domestic animals and the farm birds.

After eating, both had showered before retiring to their bedroom. In spite of his fatigue, Andy was soon aroused by Anita's teasing and touching, her child-like features smiling up at him, daring him to try to satisfy her. For the next forty minutes he had tried his best, and she had responded with enthusiasm to his almost violent thrusts.

Then, hot, tired and spent, both had lain spreadeagled over the king-sized bed and individually drifted into slumber.

Now, four hours later, Andy had woken and his mind was full of thoughts of Anita, and her unwavering support of him, particularly when the yellow envelopes arrived. Although the trips to the city which followed were always undertaken as a shared venture, he felt the prime responsibility lay across his shoulders. The clean cut, suit wearing individuals they were required to deal with all gave Andy the impression that they considered themselves a class above the farmer and his wife. If it was not for the mortgage on the farm, he would have brushed these suit-wearers aside long ago and taken his chances elsewhere. Sometimes he considered travelling alone, and dealing with the business matters without involving Anita. Each time he suggested this, she merely laughed, and then reminded him of their original agreement after settling into farm life. *'There is no 'I' in teamwork. We are a team. We act as a team, think as a team, and we survive or fail as a team'.*

It sounded like a motto from one of the S.A.S. or Secret Police Units they had belonged to in Malaysia, but it was a constant theme in everything the couple attempted.

When-ever one of the dreaded envelopes arrived in the mail, Anita would immediately show it to him and declare that it was a problem for them both. Without her, he knew he could not cope with the pressures, yet some-how, if he was without her, there might not be the pressure at all.

If it wasn't for his lovely little wife, he would not have the situation to deal with, but if he did not have Anita, he would be hard pressed to think of a single pleasure in his life.

The irony of it all caused him to grunt a false laugh. Anita stirred and draped her arm over his rigid chest. Her breathing soon resumed a slow rhythm and he watched her in the darkness, his feelings of love and admiration contrasting with his angst over those yellow envelopes. As fatigue began to wash its effects over him again, his thoughts focussed again on the envelopes, and the worries their arrival always caused him. His final thought before slumber reclaimed him was...

'the next one to arrive would be the last, no matter what. If that meant moving, leaving this farm, then so be it!'

The early morning sun sent fingers of light into the bedroom, and soon the little woman was awakened by the strengthening brightness.

Anita slowly slid her naked body out from under her sleeping husband's brawny arm. She dropped silently to the floor and quietly slid open the top drawer of a bedside table.

As she slipped quickly into her undergarments, Andy grunted and rolled onto his left side. A snort, followed by another grunt signalled to Anita that he was still in a deep sleep, so she collected a pair of jeans and an old, starched shirt from the huge wardrobe, and crept silently into the kitchen.

After donning her work clothes, Anita prepared a pot of tea and set about organising some breakfast. As she moved about the kitchen she heard a cough and other noises from the end of the hallway which indicated Andy had stirred from his slumber.

When the tea was ready she called down the hallway to Andy,

'Hey, you big lazy sleeping man! You want some tea and food or do you want me to feed it all to the dogs?'

'You do and I'll feed *you* to the dogs, Cheeky,' the gruff reply came from the doorway.

The big man had padded silently down the hallway and his voice startled her.

'Oh!' Anita exclaimed. 'You frightened me. You shouldn't sneak up on me like that.'

He laughed as she pretended to scold him.

'Just shows you, doesn't it? I've still got all the old skills. I can sneak up on you anytime I want, so just watch yourself.'

As Anita grinned and poured two cups of tea, she told him,

'You are not the only one with all your skills, big man Andy. I could sneak up on you, too, if I wish to. Now, my husband, the sneaky man, please sit down and eat.'

They ate in silence for a time until Anita realised he was staring at the floor.

She stopped chewing her toast and placed a hand on his brawny forearm.

'What is it, Andy? You are almost in a trance, when you stare like that. You are ok?'

He grasped her hand, and looked into her beautiful face.

'I been thinking a bit. I reckon you must be just about fed up with our current lifestyle. I was thinking that if we get another one of those bloody envelopes this year, it should be the last. I'm ready to pull the pin on this and try to live a normal, decent life for a change. I mean, the strain must be getting to you, because it sure is getting to me.'

She swallowed her food, took a long drink of her tea and faced her husband.

'Listen to me, my Andy. I took on this farm with you, because I wanted to, not because you forced me. I will stay here and try to survive as long as you do. If you wish to walk away, then this woman, your wife, walks with you. I love this farm, and I love you. But if you wish to live elsewhere, then elsewhere we live together. We both know we cannot do anything about those envelopes. Maybe one day they will no longer arrive to bother us, but for now, we both must deal with them. You and me, together as one. Ok? That is the truth, my husband, and I think you know it well, yes?'

He looked into her beautiful eyes and squeezed her tiny hand. Smiling, he said, 'All right, bossy-boots. We'll stick it out a while longer. But tell me! Isn't it getting to you just a little bit? Don't you ever feel like giving it all away?'

She grinned mischievously and he was reminded of their joint training sessions in Malaysia. During the un-armed combat training she had grinned just like that as she approached her opponents on the mats, regardless of gender or physical size.

'I take what is offered, and deal with it the best I know,' she said quietly.

CHAPTER TWELVE

Mike Walker pulled on the handbrake, securing the Ford Falcon against the steep slope. He leaned over towards his wife and peered out of her window.

'Does that say fifty-four? I can't see because of your boobs,' he grinned at her.

'Something's wrong with your eyesight, then, you cheeky spalpine!' Carmen shot back. 'I been telling you so, haven't I?'

Walker cuffed her lightly on her right shoulder.

'Is it fifty-four, or not?', he asked again, a faked look of exasperation on his face.

'Well, let's see now. There's a five and a four right next to it, fastened on the letter box. I'm thinking it could well be number fifty-four.'

'A simple "yes" would've done. Right-o then. Out you get and I'll take you to meet one of the nicest blokes in the New South Wales Police Force,' Mike replied.

'Ah, a nice copper eh? That'll be a welcome change, then,' she answered as she opened her door and stepped out. Walker joined her on the footpath and together they walked up the steep driveway. Mike carried a cream coloured folder and his battered exercise book. As the couple drew near the steps leading to the house, the front door opened. The powerful, stocky figure of Muscat, dressed casually in football shorts and a tee-shirt, filled the doorway. He extended his right hand and a wide grin split his pleasant face.

'G'day Mike. Long time, no see. Howya been keeping?'

The two men shook hands warmly, then Walker introduced Carmen.

Muscatt shook the tall woman's hand lightly then ushered his guests into the spacious living room. From a doorway a small woman entered the room just as Muscatt was offering drinks from an ornate wooden bar.

'And this is my better half, Heather. Darl, this is Carmen and Mike. You should remember Mike when he was with us in the city, working at a real Police Station. He takes it easier these days, relaxing down Wagga way.'

The smiling woman shook both newcomers hands briefly, and said to Mike,

'Oh, yes. I do remember you, Mike. I seem to recall you were one of the rising stars he was always telling me about. How are you?'

The pleasantries continued as Muscatt poured soft drink for himself and a beer for Mike. After checking with Carmen, he poured two white wines for the women.

Heather Muscatt had been briefed by her husband and after only a short session of small talk, she swung the conversation around to cooking.

'I'm doing a roast leg of pork for lunch. I'd better get stuck into the vegetables. Excuse me, now if you would.'

Carmen Walker took the bait. She stood up with the other woman.

'Can I give you a hand, Heather? I'd like to help if I can.'

'That'd be great. Thanks, Carmen.'

The two women left the living room and Muscatt grinned over at Mike.

'Great girl, my Heather. Right on cue. Let's go into my study and see what we've got.'

'Yeah, she's a nice lady alright. I see you're still not a drinker, Al. And I seem to remember you had a couple of "joeys". Two little boys, weren't they?' Mike asked, looking around the spacious lounge room and seeing no sign of the presence of children.

'That's right. I found out many years ago I can do without alcohol. As for the boys, Daniel is nearly fifteen, and the young bloke, Trevor, just turned thirteen. Both of 'em are at boarding school over near a joint called Campbelltown. It's an Anglican based school and it specialises in Rugby League. Both boys are on League scholarships. They're hoping to make it into the big time, and it's a distinct possibility. They are both captains of their age teams, and both are doing well in the school side of things. Dan wants to be a bloody doctor, and Trev has his sights set on either medicine or school teaching. Last term they were both at or near the top of their grades, so anything is possible for 'em.'

'Really?' Mike said, pleased for the boys he remembered as barely of walking and talking age. 'Not a pair of dills, then, are they?' he joked.

'Long as they don't think about becoming coppers. I'll skin 'em alive if they ever mention it,' Muscat said, smiling. 'C'mon. Let's go and do some sticky-beaking.'

The two policemen took up their drinks and Mike followed Muscatt into an adjoining room. The Chief Inspector had laid out several folders on a large wooden desk. Each one was labelled with a deceased criminal's name.

Walker looked at the folders and then produced his exercise book, complete with the newspaper clippings stapled inside.

'Looks like you're a bit ahead of me, Allan. All I've got is this old book,' Walker said as he laid the book on the desk.

'I've got copies of the various criminal records and also copies of the death reports and Coroner's finding from the 'Open Case Register'. I'm lucky there. I got a mate who works in O.C.R. and he owed me a favour. Luckily he also knows how to keep his gob shut,' Muscatt replied.

Both men sat down on plush easy chairs, facing each other across the large desk.

Muscatt opened the first folder with the name 'William Greene' written in large black letters across the top.

'Let's start with Billy Greene. He was a tough old bugger, and as crooked as a dog's back leg. I know a 'D' who came up against him a few times, and got a couple of convictions on him. None was enough to send him away, but. He was into just about everything you can think of, going right back to the 'thirties and 'forties. He died on the streets of Sydney, run over by a government bus right outside Wynyard railway station. There were hundreds of witnesses, but only a couple of blokes came forward. Both reckoned he passed out just before the bus ran over him. The interesting bit is that the bloody Coroner ruled the trauma caused by the bus could not be guaranteed as the cause of death. It says in the notes that they are pretty certain his heart stopped beating and his lungs collapsed before any force trauma was inflicted, but both witnesses stated he was simply standing in a queue when he went down. Strange stuff, I suppose, when you think about it.'

Walker perused the documents from the folder as Muscatt spoke. He looked up from the folder and pointed to his entry in the exercise book listing the facts of Greene's demise.

'It was Greene's death that convinced me something was up,' he told his colleague. 'When I saw the open finding, I realised it matched up with the others I had been looking into. Just like Greene, these other crims had got off serious charges, then went skiting to the media. Next thing you know, they're dead as doorknobs.'

Muscatt nodded and read Mike's notes. He closed the book eventually and said grimly,

'It sure is strange, alright.' After a few seconds of silence, he asked Walker. 'Tell me this, though. What do your bosses in Wagga have to say about it? You said you'd been looking into these matters, so are they offering any help, any clues?'

'Well, that's another strange thing. I work mostly with a crusty old bastard named Lindsay Johnson. Real old school 'DS', who is teaching me heaps. Always ready with advice, thoughts and any guidance I need. But when I mentioned this stuff to him, he not only clammed up tighter than a fish's bum, he actually warned me off.'

'He warned you off? What, warned you off investigating, or keeping those notes of yours?' Muscatt asked.

'He warned me off the whole bloody subject. And he wasn't kidding. He was most emphatic that I drop the subject, and leave it dropped. He even said something about keeping out of things that don't directly concern me. He used very strong words, too.'

Muscatt took a large swallow of his soft drink before replying.

'Really? Now I find that extremely strange. I encourage all of my blokes, especially the new ones like you, to get their teeth into anything that isn't cleared up, regardless of what it is or what 'Section' it occurred in. For an experienced 'DS' to try to warn off a junior from a particular set of cases, where he might learn a great deal, is very odd, to say the least. Tell me more about this DS Lindsay Johnson.'

Mike told him about Johnson, some of the cases they worked together and Johnson's methods of investigating, including his rough house tactics.

'Sounds to me like he's a good, *old school* Detective, who you can learn a lot from. I'd be a bit careful when it comes to the rough stuff, though, Mate. That sort of thing is starting to be frowned upon by the hierarchy who are copping more and more political pressure these days. As you probably know, the crooks and the bloody "do-gooders" seem to be able to grab the ears of politicians anytime and "Police brutality" is becoming a catch-cry for these bleeding hearts,' Muscatt said. 'Just watch that aspect, ok?'

Waker listened carefully, nodding as he accepted the advice from the veteran cop.

'Yes, I will watch that. I just thought it was a bit strange that he was so forceful when he told me to leave this matter alone. I thought he'd be right behind me.'

'Yeah, it's a bit odd,' Muscatt agreed. He made a few notes about Detective Sergeant Lindsay Johnson as Mike looked on. 'I might have a little look into him, just to see if there is anything that might explain his attitude. Don't worry, I won't let your name come into it. I can't think why he would worry about you snooping around. Ok, let's have a look at these other birds. Tommy McLeod. He beat three charges of larceny, one of attempting to bribe a Detective and one of consorting. He got an acquittal, then gave an interview to the Daily Mirror, in which he rubbished the Newtown Detectives. Two weeks later he's found dead in the front seat of his truck in Quay Street, and no-one, from police surgeons to the Coroner or even the University can name a cause of death. It was noted his heart had stopped beating about five to ten minutes before his lungs, liver and brain shut down. Coronial finding... cause of death unknown.'

For the next hour they discussed aspects of each case listed in the folders, and Muscatt recorded most of their facts and revelations in a large spreadsheet book.

He finally closed the big book and, with a grim expression, said quietly,

'The one thing that is becoming as obvious as the nose on your face, is that there is a common link in these cases. No doubt about it. As you say, all of these crims had beaten serious charges, skited about it loudly in the press, then finished up dead. And no bastard can come up with a direct cause of death. Redfern Errol did not drown, Eddie Miller did not choke on sand, Brother Thompson did not die of motion sickness and old Billy Greene was dead before that big bloody bus ran over him. Scotch Tommy might have hit the dope a bit but there were no traces of any rubbish in his body when it was pulled from that old truck of his. And now we have my good friend Ian Carter fitting the same bill. So far, the Docs have no idea what killed him, except to say he might've drowned. That's what we know for sure. So, what actually killed all these bastards, how were they killed, and more importantly, who killed them?'

Mike nodded as Muscatt made each point, knowing the senior Detective was now as intrigued by the deaths as he was. A thought ran through his mind and he said slowly,

'I reckon the common theme is some sort of poisonous substance. I mean, a substance that somehow shuts down the heart, or lungs or something. There's plenty of poisons around that can do all that, but this stuff, if we're right, is completely un-traceable. These blokes all appear to have stopped breathing or their hearts stopped beating, but for no apparent reason. The findings of the Coroner all suggest that, but don't go as far as saying it outright, probably because they haven't a bloody clue as to what it is. We also don't know how this mystery substance is applied. Do they breathe it in? Do they eat or drink it? There is no mention anywhere of any wounds or entry marks or needle point scars on any of the bodies.'

Muscatt nodded agreement as he re-filled Mike's beer and his own soft drink.

'Yeah, but what are we looking for? I don't know of any substance that can do all that, and remain completely untraceable. There's a number of potions and drugs that will give the same result, but the smart buggers at the universities and hospitals can always detect traces of the stuff. This is something different, how-ever. And, as I said, who the bloody hell has access to this mystery substance, and why are they knocking off our crims? And where do *we* go from here? I'm buggered if I know!'

Walker smiled grimly as he shrugged his powerful shoulders.

Both men stared silently at the spreadsheet book, each sipping their drinks, lost in streams of private thoughts.

Walker looked across the desk at the older man.

'How about telling me all about this Carter bloke who recently joined our gang in criminal heaven. How much did you have to do with him?'

Muscatt smiled as he leaned back in his chair. After swallowing his drink, he said,

'The worst type of scum you could come across. Filthy rich, moderately popular, and involved, behind the scenes, in just about anything shady. He and his rotten brother were generally suspected of distributing most of the illicit drugs around Wollongong. The brother is a pharmacist, with a string of Chemist shops throughout the Illawarra coast. Carter himself was a real estate agent. The police have had them both under surveillance stacks of times, and we've looked into their books, their businesses and even planted an illegal bug in Carter's Mercedes. Nothing! Not a hint of evidence. Until he turned up with a little Vietnamese girl on his arm. We reckoned she was no more than twelve or thirteen, and she clung to him like a bloody limpet. The fact he was bonking the poor little thing was an open secret, but proving it was harder than we thought. Then one day he slipped up, big time. One of my blokes was tailing the bastard when he drove the girl to a beach car park. Through binoculars my man saw Carter feed her some pills before stripping off her dress and undies. In the back seat of his car, this was, in broad daylight. The Detective radioed in and I was informed as to what was going on. I ordered the boys in, and he was arrested just as he finished doing the dirty deed. It turned out the girl was under age alright, but apparently was one of those Vietnamese boat people. How Carter latched onto her was any-one's guess. She was full of drugs, had no idea where she was or even what her name was. We hit the mongrel with a heap of charges, including Carnal Knowledge, a few drugs offences and the Commonwealth boys hit him with some charges to do with harbouring an illegal. When we get him into court, though, his mouthpiece has a stack of false statements, bullshit doctor's reports and even 'proof' that she was part of a drug dealing gang of Gooks from bloody Melbourne. Wiped the floor with us, even though the **beak** could see it was all bullshit. The bastard walked away clean as a whistle, while we looked for all purposes like a bunch of incompetent idiots. Then he stood on the front steps of the court house and spouted off the greatest load of garbage you'd ever heard. Bagged the hell out of me and all the boys, all the time saying how innocent he was. I tell you, Mikey, at one stage I actually reached inside my coat and had my hand on the butt of my pistol! I had to make a conscious effort to pull my hand away. The first round was going into the bastards temple, and the next one into his nuts. I probably would've let the next one go into the guts of his slimy lawyer. Geez, it was a terrible time, especially knowing what a miscarriage of justice it was, him getting off like that.'

Muscatt finished his words with an angry gesture and Mike could see he was furious.

'But he got his come-uppance in the end, didn't he? So, somehow, by some-one, the ledger is square, isn't it?' Walker said quietly.

Muscatt smiled faintly, and nodded.

'Yeah, sort of, I suppose. But hell, I wanted to see his face when I nailed the bastard. Even the way he went was an anti-climax. What-ever it was, it was far too good for the likes of him. He should have taken weeks to die, hopefully in severe pain.'

Walker opened the Carter file again and thumbed through the loose sheets of paper.

'That reminds me. Exactly what was his official cause of death? Was it eventually put down as drowning? Last time I read anything about it, it was still open.'

Muscatt shook his head and told Walker,

'My boss, Superintendent Raynor, told me a few days ago it was recorded as drowning. Also, I questioned his two so-called bodyguards, Sammut and Honey. Their statements are in that file somewhere. They both told how he was floating along, snorkelling, then he sank to the bottom. Then the bloody shark alarm or something went off, so, Jeff Honey dove down to grab him. He says he found the snorkel mouth piece already out of the bastard's mouth. I reckoned he must have copped a gobful of sea water when the mask slipped out, and was too slow getting it back in. I sure wish I had of been there. I would have shoved him further under and stood on his bloody neck.........'

Muscatt broke off his tirade when he looked at Walker. The younger man was shaking his head and his eyes showed puzzlement and surprise.

'What is it, Mike? You found something?'

Walker pointed to a small paragraph at the bottom of the police surgeon's statement.

'Yeah, I think so. Look at this. It says *'although drowning was initially suspected, no foreign fluid or water was found in the lungs. Heart, lung, liver and kidney functions appear to have ceased **pre** mortem'*. And you say your boss told you it was definitely drowning? That's a bit strange, isn't it?'

Muscatt took the sheet and read it thoroughly for himself. His eyes showed the same surprise and he read the document again before speaking.

'Something's wrong here Mike! Something is very wrong. Old Sam Raynor made a point of telling me the Surgeon had declared death by drowning. This is a copy of the doc's report, signed and marked 'Final', and, as you say, it says quite the opposite to what I've been told. Old Sam went to great lengths to get me to believe there was no point in me studying these reports too closely. Now I think it might be worth our while to stick our noses into this particular case a bit more thoroughly, and note any other discrepancies. Then we should go over the other five cases and look for similar odd bits. What do you reckon?'

'I reckon we've found the first chink of light. I also reckon we've dumped a hell of a lot of work on ourselves. A couple of days worth, at least,' Walker replied.

'Yeah, I agree. When are you and your missus due back at Wagga?' Muscatt asked.

'Not for two more days,' Mike said.

'Care to stay the night? I've got a few rest days due, and right now I feel like taking 'em. We've got two spare double rooms. How about it?'

'Sounds good. Carmen will enjoy not having the long drive back to Wagga tonight.'

After another five minutes of reading the various case notes, Walker suddenly felt his pulse quicken. He re-read the Billy Greene file then the Carter folder.

'Hey! Look at this. I knew there was something else sticking out at me. Those two bodyguards of your mate Carter. Honey and Sammutt. They were also two of Billy Greene's top men. And a statement from Jake O'Rourke, Greene's side kick, said they were with him at the time he croaked. And now the same two were with Carter when he bought it. That's a hell of a coincidence, I reckon, Mate. Don't you?'

Muscatt nodded and reached for the file. Neither man said anything as they read the papers one more time. Muscatt smiled grimly as he said quietly,

'I reckon I'll be having another long, cosy chat with Mister Honey and Mister Sammut. They just became my prime suspects in Carter's murder. Not that that should be a crime. They should get bloody medals if they turn out to be the bunnies.'

Mike grinned at Muscat and pointed to the other files spread out over the table.

'I wonder if we've found our murderers? Let's see if Misters Sammutt and Honey were hanging around these other bastards when they fell off their respective perches.'

The conversation was interrupted by Carmen who opened the door and said pleasantly,

'Ok, you two. Heather has laid out a lovely spread, and you had better be fronting up.'

With a final glance at the open files, Muscatt stood and drained his drink.

Walker followed suit and both men left the study and headed for the dining room.

CHAPTER THIRTEEN

Andy Keyes stared at the two heaps of rotting, stinking kangaroo and sheep carcasses piled into a large ditch. The ditch had been gouged into the earth at the very back of his northern-most paddock. Even using the widest blade he could fit to his old tractor, it had taken Keyes a full day to deepen the hole to six feet. It was also six feet wide and ten feet long. Several jute wool bales, which were stuffed full of household garbage, were in the hole, adding to the stench. In the bucket attached to the old Fordson tractor were two more wool bales of rubbish. Andy pulled a lever and the bucket was raised higher and higher, until it reached it's upper limit. He pushed another lever forward and the bucket tipped, depositing the wool bales deep in the hole, and on top of the exposed animal carcasses. Some of the swollen kangaroo and sheep bodies burst under the additional weight, and the added stench soon reached the tall man sitting on the tractor.

He pulled a hand kerchief from his shirt pocket and wrapped it around his head, making doubly sure it covered his large nose. With his makeshift mask now in place, he lowered the bucket and began pushing the piles of loose dirt into the hole. After half an hour he had replaced sufficient soil from one side of the hole, and drove the tractor around to the opposite side. He immediately began repeating his actions, and soon had the entire reeking contents of the hole covered with freshly turned soil. He ran the tractor over the loose dirt, levelling the soil with the bucket, leaving a smooth finish. Andy turned in his seat and opened a valve in the square tank attached to the rear of the tractor. Green, foul smelling liquid sprayed from two nozzles at the base of the tank. He drove slowly up and down the patch until it was soaked with the green liquid. For good measure he sprayed several yards of untouched ground around all four sides of the hole. The quick acting fertiliser liquid would ensure a healthy covering of grass would soon blanket the entire sprayed area. Within a few short weeks there would be no trace of the hole, or its foul-smelling contents.

Satisfied, Andy removed his mask and drove away, heading in the direction of his homestead, some twelve miles to the east. The sun was rapidly sinking at his back as he arrived in the house yard and steered towards the huge machinery shed.

Anita appeared at the kitchen door and waved, smiling cheerfully and brandishing a brown bottle of cold beer. He returned her wave and quickly parked the tractor next to his Land Rover inside the shed. The sight of his beautiful wife and her welcoming smile, together with the offer of a cold beer, made Andy dismiss thoughts of further tasks and he strode quickly to the house, smiling in anticipation.

'You get it all done, my big husband?' Anita asked as he reached the door.

'Yeah, it's all dead and buried. God, the stink was awful. Some of the 'roos exploded when the house garbage hit them. I tell you, that upped the smell level quite a bit'

He trudged through the doorway and sat down at the large kitchen table. She followed him and quietly slipped the cap off the beer bottle. After pouring a generous glass for her husband, the tiny woman put the bottle back on the table.

'You look troubled, Andy. Is there something which is a big problem for you? If there is, then it bothers us both, my dear husband,' Anita asked, concern on her pretty face.

'Oh, it's just the business, you know, Love. I told you a few days ago, I've decided to put a stop to those darned envelopes, even if it means abandoning this farm again. I mean, we can't go on like this. I'm not sleeping and I feel you twitching and turning most nights. It's definitely time for a massive change in our lifestyle!'
'What is 'twitching', Andy?' she asked, with a quizzical smile.
'It's what you do to keep me awake every night,' he teased. Anita smiled seductively and stroked his muscular fore-arm. 'Maybe I can find something else to keep you awake, my lover? Or maybe it put you to sleep, instead? What do you think, big Andy-man?' He reached for her tiny hand and clasped it in both of his. He whispered, 'I think you are about the cheekiest little sexpot I've ever heard of, that's what I think.'

'So, I'll interview Honey and Sammutt again, and try to find a connection, other than the death of their two bosses. You're certainly right, it's too much of a co-incidence to ignore. The best bet will be to discover who actually hired the bastards. Billy Greene, as far as I recall, always left the hiring and firing to Jake O'Rourke. I don't think Carter had a 'second-in-command' so he probably hired them himself. Either way, I should find out by talking to 'em separately. Honey seems ready to talk but that little Maltese prick hasn't said a word. That's what's keeping the pair of them on remand.'

Muscatt smiled grimly as he finished.

'Ok, that's a good start,' Walker said. 'Somehow, though, we have to get to the bottom of what is killing these bloody crooks. It's the un-explained deaths that I would like to know about. It's by far the most intriguing aspect to me, but what is it?'

The two Detectives had enjoyed a hearty meal of roast pork and vegetables, followed by a dessert of home-made apple pie and cream. As soon as the women had cleared the table, both men obtained another drink and returned to Muscatt's study.

'Let's look at the facts again,' Mike Walker opened. 'These crims have all died suddenly, and not one of our experts in the Coroner's department can give a certain cause of death. The only thing we seem to know for sure is they're being bumped off at regular intervals.'

Muscatt nodded as he glanced at the files spread around the table.

'But **who** is organising the killing of these monkeys? It seems like some sort of vigilante or something, if we're right. Sammutt and Honey are probably only the trigger men. I mean, most of the population would want these bastards dead, but some-one, somehow, is knocking them off, and using a method that is, so far, undetectable.'

The room became silent as both Detectives ran the known facts through their minds.

Muscatt was the first to speak.

'I just remembered something. A mate of mine has just scored a job as the Commissioner's Staff Officer. A bloke named Jeff Parkinson. He gets promoted to Inspector as part of the job, otherwise he wouldn't have applied for it. He's a real good bloke and a real knockabout. I might get him to see if the 'Commish', or any bugger in the hierarchy has noticed our little pattern of events, and if any of 'em are thinking the same as us.'

'But what would that prove, Allan? It would only mean there are other blokes as smart as us in the job. Seriously, though, I don't see how us knowing some-one else has noticed the pattern can possibly help us find out what's going on,' Walker replied.

'All the same, I'll talk to Parkinson. It can't hurt,' Muscatt said firmly.

The two Detectives each raised their glasses and sipped, while a thoughtful silence again invaded the room.

Mike Walker steered the big Ford Falcon around the tight, twisting bends as they climbed higher and higher towards the small town of Robertson. The southern coast of New South Wales was still visible in the rear-view mirrors but the dense forest of trees and bushes was gradually obscuring the pleasant vista.

They had left the Muscatt home at nine that morning and Mike calculated they should be home in Wagga Wagga by late that afternoon.

Carmen was silent, watching the spectacular scenery slide past as the Falcon's powerful vee-eight engine hurried them up the steep road. She had rolled her window down, enjoying the rush of fresh, clean mountain air and even picking up the sounds of the bush animals and birds above the healthy growl of the engine.

On the drive down the coast Mike had filled her in on the topics of his discussions with Muscatt. She seemed genuinely interested and asked several questions when Mike had finished his story. Now she was quiet as they made swift progress towards their home.

After another twenty minutes they reached the summit of the mountain range and the road flattened out. As the engine note subsided with the less effort required on the plateau, Mike turned to Carmen and said,

'You're a bit quiet, Love. Anything the matter or have you just run out of cheek?'

She smiled softly at him and rolled her window up.

'No, everything's fine, thank you. But I was having a bit of a think. That business you were talking about, with those well-known criminals dropping dead with no reason.'

Mike grinned at her and winked as he said,

'Oh, they had reasons all right. Their rotten hearts and brains stopped working, along with all their other organs. We just don't know why, or how, or by who, that's all'

'Yeah, well, as I said, I've been thinking. Somewhere, deep in the back of my mind, I seem to recall reading somewhere in an old text book or something about that very subject. I just can't remember exactly where and what the details are. But I'm sure it was something about a rare poison that leaves no trace what-so-ever of itself. And it has an instant effect on all mammals. Instant death via shut down of all muscles, and absolutely undetectable via bloodstream, lymph system or anything else. I'm trying to think where I read it, but at the moment it's avoiding me,' she said thoughtfully.

Walker sat more upright and glanced at his wife.

'Really?' he exclaimed. 'That sounds promising! Is it a gas, a liquid or what? And what's it's origin?' he demanded.

'As I just said, if you'd been listening, I can't quite put my finger on it at the moment,' Carmen replied. 'I need to put my mind to it, but I'm sure it's in one of my books at home. I'll give it some more thought when we get home.'

'Yeah, please do. It's the first clue, or even a hint of a clue, that we've got about what this stuff could be. I'll give you a hand as soon as we get home,' Mike said keenly.

She shook her head, making her gold earrings dance and glint in the morning sunshine.

'You just leave it me, Mister Detective. You wouldn't know where to start and you wouldn't recognise it if you saw it. For now, just tell me more about what you and Allan know from reading the forensic reports and death certificates and all that.'

Walker sighed and shrugged his powerful shoulders.

'Ok, I'll start with the most recent death, of Carter in Wollongong,' he said.

For the next two hours they discussed the cases, with Mike reminding his wife several times that he should not be revealing most of the facts, and that confidentiality was paramount. Carmen remained quiet and thoughtful, only asking a few short questions as Mike detailed the circumstances of the sudden deaths of New South Wales's most notorious criminals.

They reached the Hume Highway after another hour and joined the endless stream of traffic, mostly large trucks and semi-trailers, heading south.

Carmen dozed as Mike drove and soon he felt the first traces of fatigue starting to set in.

As they entered the large city of Goulburn, Mike slowed to the speed limit and changed down a gear. This woke Carmen and she sat upright in her seat.

'Where are we?' she asked sleepily.

'Goulburn. I'm starting to get the wearies so I reckoned we ought to stop and grab a coffee and a bite. What dya reckon, Sleepy-Head?' he replied.

'Finally a good idea from you,' she teased.

He looked across at her and said in mock indignation,

'Well, here's another good idea. You can pay. Keep your eyes open for a decent looking café or something. How about that joint up there?' he pointed ahead to a large café with its doors wide open. There were many people inside but they spotted a few vacant tables when he pulled the car into the kerb right outside the entrance.

A flighty young waitress scribbled down their order of coffee and toast, flashed an insincere smile and hurried away toward the kitchen. Mike looked around the crowded café, noting several couples and some families, as well as a few large men in working clothes who were sitting on stools at the long counter. He reasoned these men would be long distance truck drivers, slaking their thirsts and filling their stomachs before tackling the next leg of the arduous journey to Melbourne or Adelaide. The place was noisy, with several dozen conversations going on at once. Mike jumped slightly as Carmen pinched his forearm, unaware that his wife had been speaking to him.

'Hey there, Deafy!' she exclaimed. 'Has your hearing gone completely? I was talking to you, you deaf bat. Stop trying to eavesdrop on other people's chatter and listen to me.'

'Huh? What? Oh, sorry love. I was miles away. What were you saying?' he replied.

'I was saying I just remembered where that information is about your mysterious poison. It is on some microfiche and I'm sure I've got it at home. So, how about that?'

Mike was instantly alert. He grinned as he gripped her wrist and said excitedly,

'That's terrific, Babe. Can you remember anything about it at all? Like, where's it come from or what form it's in?'

Carmen held up her hands and said forcefully,

'Now hold your horses, Mister Detective. I've got something like fifty slides of microfiche in my files, and no viewer to read them on. It will have to wait until I go back to work and see if I can borrow a reader from the office. In the meantime, you'll just have to be patient. I do seem to recall it's from somewhere in Asia that it comes from, and that's all the recollection I can come up with for now. Let's now leave it until we're home, OK?'

Walker nodded reluctantly just as the waitress brought their coffee to the table.

'Ok, I'll wait. But please understand how import this is, won't you Honey?'

Allan Muscatt listened impatiently to the ring tones of the internal police telephone. Eventually the tones stopped and a loud click sounded. A stern female voice barked in his ear and he grinned to himself in spite of the unfriendly greeting.

'Commissioners suite. Good morning. My name is Elizabeth. How can I help you?'

'Yeah, g'day Elizabeth. I'd like to talk to Jeff Parkinson, please.'

'Is that 'Acting Inspector Parkinson' you mean?' came the clipped reply.

'Yeah, that's him.' Muscatt answered, already growing tired of the woman's manner.

'And you are?' was the next demand.

'I am Chief Inspector Muscatt, from Wollongong Section' he supplied with as much insolence as he muster. *these bloody self-important civilian sheilas, they give me the shits,'* he thought to himself.

'Hold while I see if he can talk to you,' she ordered.

While Muscatt sat at his desk waiting, he fumed at the total lack of respect the civilian clerks and office helpers were famous for. It seemed they felt because they were working at Police Headquarters, and regularly inter-faced with the Commissioner, the deputy Commissioners and various high ranking politicians, they were above the real Police Officers on the ground, doing the real job. He was composing a sarcastic comment when a deep male voice came on the line.

'Jeff Parkinson! Is that you, Allan?'

'Yeah, it's me Parko. How ya goin', Mate?' Muscatt answered.

'Going great, thanks, Al. What can I do you for?'

Muscatt grinned to himself as he pictured his friend working amongst the Police hierarchy and spending most of his day in an air-conditioned office. He knew Parkinson was a much more outdoors type who preferred 'hands-on' policing to office work.

'I was wondering if I can arrange a meet with you. There's a matter I need to discuss and I also need your help with. Any chance you can get away from your desk for a while? I mean, we need to talk face-to-face and the matter is a bit delicate.'

There was several seconds of silence before Parkinson replied.

'Can you give me a hint what this matter is, Allan? I'm fairly pushed for time these days but if it's important I might be able to nick off for an hour or so. No more, though and you would have to come up here. There's no way I could sneak down to Wollongong without a very good reason.'

'Ok, no worries. How about tomorrow? I can drive up to Sydney and meet you. I can't tell you any more over the 'phone. How about that little café near Regent Street? The one we always went to after night shift, remember? That alright?' Muscatt asked.

There was the prolonged silence before Parkinson said quietly, 'Well, alright. It'll have to be late though. I'm flat out until about three o'clock. Want to make it three-thirty, tomorrow arvo?'

'Beauty! Three-thirty it is. See you then, Jeff. I really appreciate it.'

As he hung the receiver back in it's cradle, Muscatt became aware of another presence in his office. He looked into the tinted glass of the large picture window and recognised the reflection as the burly form of his superior, Superintendent Sam Raynor. He swung his chair around and said as he smiled a greeting,

'Hello Boss. What're you doing, sneaking up on me like that?'

Raynor did not return the smile and walked slowly to Muscatt's desk. He seated himself in a padded chair which was drawn up to the desk, and faced the Chief Inspector. 'Where are you off to, Allan? And who was that you were arranging to meet in Sydney? Your position is here in Wollongong, not gallivanting around the big smoke having cosy chats with your mates. What are you up to?'

The unfriendly nature and the questioning of his movements took Muscatt completely by surprise. The two senior officers had always enjoyed a cordial relationship, and Muscatt was one of the few police officers to have been invited to the Raynor house for a social drink. Now, all that seemed to have dissolved as the two men faced each other.

'I was just organising a meeting with a colleague, Sam. I didn't think you wanted me to clear each and every trip with you. I don't ask that of my blokes, so I don't see the problem now. Why, what's up?'

Raynor stared at Muscatt for a few seconds before he said sternly,

'You know the protocols as well as I do, Allan. If you want to talk to The Commissioner or any member of the executive, you should go through me. I don't like anyone, least of all my senior officers, disregarding procedure when-ever it suits them. I'm disappointed, Allan.'

Muscatt was shocked and momentarily dumbstruck. He and Raynor had never had a harsh word between them. Ever since he had taken up his position as Officer-in-Charge of Detectives, he believed he enjoyed complete trust from his superior. Then another thought occupied his confused mind.

'Can I ask you, Boss, how you knew I was calling the big office? I mean, I dialled the number myself, so the switchboard couldn't have known. Is my telephone bugged or something? I would like to know that before I explain to you what I was doing.'

Raynor slowly shook his head and placed his massive hands on the edge of the desk.

'Your 'phone isn't tapped. I knew you were talking to the Commissioners suite because some woman from there just called me to tell me so. For your information, that has just become standard procedure. If any officer telephones or drops into the suite, the Section Commander has to authorise it first. I assume you did not tell them I authorised the call, so they got straight onto me. Ok? Now that you know, please remember it. What is most important to me is that you are looking after your duties here, and not getting involved in other section's matters.'

Although still shocked at the mild reprimand, Muscatt relaxed and nodded.

'Alright, Sam. Now that I know, it won't happen again. Do you have any objections to my trip to Sydney tomorrow, even if I don't discuss the details with you?'

The big old Superintendent peered at Muscatt for a few seconds the smiled thinly.

'Right-o! You do what you got to, but remember what I said about other section's cases. Have a safe journey and I'll see ya later.'

The Superintendent left the office and Muscatt stared after him as he closed the adjoining door. Something about Raynor's sudden appearance and the following terse warning was unsettling the Chief Inspector and he did not like the feeling of not being trusted.

CHAPTER FOURTEEN

Ten men sat silently around the huge table. With the exception of one small, old gentleman, all were smoking. Some had cigarettes, one or two had cigars and a large, gruff individual seated at the head of the table sucked noisily on an ornate clay pipe.

The non-smoker sat watching the rest through a cloud of wispy tobacco smoke. He was dressed in a pale blue safari suit, clean sandshoes and a silk cravat decorated his throat

In his hands was a white straw hat which he slowly twirled through his bony fingers.

Just as the pipe smoker began another fit of coughing, an oak panelled door opened and the final member of the group strode into the room and took his place at the table.

The late arrival nodded greetings to each of his companions and sat heavily into his allotted chair. He removed an off-white, powdered wig from his head and placed it on the table in front of him.

The pipe smoker cleared his throat and addressed the gathering in a deep, croaky voice.

'Right-oh, then. We're all here at last. First item for discussion is the latest field report from our operative. I have it here and as usual you will all get a copy at the end of general business. It basically says, and I quote, *'the subject was enjoying a swim at Scarborough beach with his two bodyguards watching over him. He was snorkelling and concentrating on the sea bed. Approaching him presented no difficulty. He was dealt with quickly and we were not detected, either during operations or during our withdrawal. Press reports confirm a satisfactory conclusion to this operation.'*

That seems to be the case alright. I read all the articles in the Sydney and Wollongong papers and they confirm the operative's report. Seems satisfactory, as per usual, Commander?'

He addressed the question to the little old non-smoker in the safari suit.

The small man stood slowly and withdrew a notebook from his coat pocket.

Before speaking he placed the white hat gently on his seat.

'Yes,' he replied in a high, almost feminine voice. 'As the 'ops' report says, this one went off smoothly. I watched them from an adjoining beach. I was able to walk slowly and un-obtrusively onto the southern end of Scarborough to observe the hit. It seems they were spotted, but mistaken for a couple of sharks. In the following confusion, the operatives made a very clean get-away while the lifesavers were busy trying, in vain, I might add, to revive our friend. I then returned to my previous position and saw the 'ops' re-emerge from the water, change clothes and decamp without raising any suspicions. A good, clean job all round, I'd say.'

Cries of 'Hear! Hear!' and grunts of approval came from various members of the group.

The little old man sat down, smiling as he acknowledged the agreements.

The pipe smoker then growled to the man sitting next to him,

'And the payment, Mister Treasurer? It has been paid in the normal manner?'

The man stood and consulted a sheet of paper in front of him.

'Yes, it's all been paid. As agreed at our last meeting, the new rate of twenty-five thousand was placed into the operatives account, and I note that it has already been transferred to the operative's personal account in a different bank. No problem there.'

Again the 'Hear! Hear!s and approval grunts followed. The man returned to his seat.

'Right, then! Those matters in hand, it seems,' the pipe smoker croaked. 'Anyone got anything to report, particularly regarding the security aspect? Or anything at all before we move on to the future?'

The little old man with the white hat rose to his feet again. He pulled a tiny tape recorder from his shirt pocket and checked the condition of the battery via a small meter on the machine. All eyes in the room turned to him and there was complete silence.

'I acted on the suggestion from the last meeting, and decided to ear-wig on a conversation between our two lawyer friends as they shared a coffee in their usual café at 'The Cross'. Please listen closely, as the recorder has limited volume.'

In one movement the entire group leaned forward and all attention was on the tiny tape recorder. A slight hum was followed by a scratchy noise as the tape began and the muffled voice of Larry Kind became audible.

'…..and it's far too much of a coincidence. They all have been acquitted, mouthed off to the bloody media and then suddenly died. I reckon some-one, either a vigilante or a group of do-gooders, are organising to bump 'em off, somehow.'

'I don't know, Larry. It sounds a bit far fetched to me……,' Richard Oaks' voice was well known by the group seated around the table.

After another twelve minutes of the two voices, the sound of chairs scraping, followed by fading footsteps was all to be heard from the little machine. The old man stood up and switched it off. He looked slowly from man to man before saying quietly,

'Although I am certain he is unaware of us at this time, it is obvious our friend Mister Kind has detected our pattern of operations. If he continues to garner support from his colleagues, our entire existence may be in jeopardy. It was very easy for me to eavesdrop on this conversation, and neither of them gave me a second glance. However, I suggest a method of dealing with this situation be discussed now, as a matter of urgency! These two discussed, in detail, our last five operations. They are clever men and Kind is well known for his persistence, I am sure you will agree.'

There was a chorus of 'Agreed's and 'Hear Hear's, then the large man with the ornate pipe rose from his position at the head of the table. He coughed loudly once, gaining the immediate attention of the remainder of the group.

'As your chairman I thoroughly endorse what the Commander has just said. His tape recording proves beyond doubt that our operations are becoming noticed. Whilst I remind the club that it was never our intention to include the lawyers in our activities, it seems that the situation may have altered some-what. So, question one is, should we now spread our field of operation to include these gutter dwellers, or should we stick to our original charter? What say you, gentlemen?'

There was a chorus of grunts and murmuring as the nine others thought the problem through. The small man in the safari suit merely watched and listened as he twirled his white hat through his bony hands.

After five more minutes the chairman banged his pipe loudly on the table, in the manner of a judge calling for order in a courtroom.

'Right, gentlemen. Any thoughts?'

A tall, dignified man wearing a dark suit stood up and addressed the gathering.

'I have talked it over with Gerald and Peter.'

His cultured, deep voice resonated throughout the room as he indicated the men seated either side of him. 'We believe we would be foolish to extend our activities to include other persons. We, that is, us three, would be opposed to any such expansion.'

There was general agreement around the huge table, with some comments as to the necessity of 'keeping our options open' or 'we can always look at it again in the future'.

When the mutterings had died down the pipe smoker banged his makeshift gavel on the table again, calling for silence.

'Right-o, then. That's settled for now. Next is the matter of subscriptions. Mister Northey. Your party promised fifteen thousand dollars. Has it been agreed?'

The tall, thin man seated at the opposite end of the table smiled as he passed an envelope into the centre.

'There she is Your Honour, in cash, exactly as promised. I trust the socialists from the opposition can match it?' He smirked across the table at a large man who grinned back at him while he stubbed out his cigarette.

'Match it?' the big man snorted. 'We've more than bloody matched, Bert. You tell your leader he might be the big boss, but he belongs to a stingey party. Our union brothers have contributed to my party's donation, and I hereby present the sum of twenty-five thousand.' He, too, slid a thick envelope into the centre.

If any of the other members were impressed, they kept their feelings hidden. After a few seconds of silence, the chairman shoved his unlit pipe into his mouth, and growled around it to his colleagues,

'Who else? Vernon?'

The late arrival lifted the powdered wig from the table and reached underneath it.

He withdrew a crumpled envelope and tossed it onto the first two.

'Ten grand, as arranged. I tell you, though, some of the junior blokes were a bit reluctant to cough up. We had to convince them of the destination of the dough. They mostly think it's for a good intending charity. I suppose it is, really, eh?'

His ample stomach shook slightly as he giggled at his own joke. Most others either grinned or chuckled quietly to themselves.

'Here's mine!' declared a tall, powerfully built man who sat next to the chairman.

He was dressed in a uniform and the shoulders of his jacket were decorated with numerous silver oak leaves and crowns. His tunic's breast sported half a dozen ribbands depicting various service and bravery awards.

'Your lot might be a bit reluctant, Vern. But squeezing five grand out of informant funds is always bloody tricky. Me and Roger had to all but commit fraud to get it, didn't we, Mate?' He asked the question of the man sitting next to him as he passed over yet another envelope to the centre of the table. The second man was dressed in a uniform almost as ornate as his companion.

This man nodded thoughtfully as he screwed a cigarette into a small holder. After lighting up, he gestured at the members around him and said, pointing briefly at his friend and colleague.

'If, when Paul retires next month, and I DO get the big job, I might have to bow out of these meetings and appoint one of the Assistants as my proxy. I haven't the nerve of Paul to run the job and take part in this as well. Still, I'll cross that bridge when I come to it. I might not even get the job, yet.'

'You'll get it, Rog. I have the Premier's, and Minister's words on it. If we can take the word of any politicians.'

There was more quiet laughter until the man who had handed in the first envelope said, with faked indignation,

'Hey, hey, hey. Hang on a minute. I hope you are excluding present company? My word is my bond, otherwise I wouldn't be here. I don't know if that goes for Mick, though. The 'lefties' are renowned for breaking promises, as we all know.'

'You're just jealous because I topped your contribution,' said the portly man. 'When you can produce twenty-five thou, come talk to me.'

Although the entire group grinned at the good natured exchange, an undercurrent of ill feeling between the two politicians from opposite sides was easily detected.

'Ok, I reckon that's enough school boy sledging. Anyone else?' the pipe smoker said.

A thickset man dressed in a fine silk suit threw an envelope to the centre of the table where it skidded into the others. He stated bombastically as he sat down,

'Here's thirty grand, as promised. We'll stump up the same amount next month and there will be no whingeing from any of my colleagues. We recognise the good cause and the improvement to society we're all achieving.'

'Ah, the Banking Sector tops us all again!' the pipe smoker beamed as he gathered the envelopes to him. He stacked them one on top of each other and admired his handiwork.

Then he slowly withdrew an envelope from his own coat pocket and added it to the top of the stack. As he pushed the lot over to the treasurer at his side he commented,

'This seven from the bar completes the set, I fancy.'

They all watched as the treasurer opened each envelope, quickly and expertly tallying the amounts. He wrote each figure into a small account book and then looked up.

'Well, chaps. With this ninety-two thousand our credit balance now stands at one hundred and fifty thousand, six hundred and fifty-three dollars, and seventeen cents.'

'Let's not forget that all important seventeen cents,' Bert Northey said loudly.

The rest either grinned or laughed out loud at the politician's sarcastic joke.

Northey was a sitting member in the state parliament, and although his tenet was deeply etched in conservatism, his hilarious sense of humour enabled him to find a joke in most situations. He represented not only the Premier in this little club, but most of the hierarchy of his ruling political party. His humour and gregarious nature masked a constitution of steel and a deep sense of right and wrong. It was Northey who had first imagined the concept of the 'Retribution Committee', as the club called itself.

Justice meant fair punishment, and this gathering was determined to see things put right.

That was the dogma by which the club operated. When an 'operation' was conducted, they all referred to it as a '***Proper Sentence***' for the criminal involved.

After convincing his Premier and party, he had then set about recruiting the other members, including a representative from the opposite side of the political spectrum. The judicial members came next. A supreme court judge, the state's chief magistrate, the president of the bar association and finally the Police Commissioner, who elected to have his senior Assistant Commissioner join him, to spread the guilt.

The Police contingent had been the most difficult to convince. Breaking a few laws whilst running the country's largest police force was one thing, but selecting, organising and funding murders was a whole new set of circumstances. It had taken many weeks of meetings and many case studies of major criminals who had walked away scot-free, before the state's Commissioner agreed to come on board. Obtaining the funds from the Police budget, and somehow masking the payments had proven relatively easy, especially when it became known that both sides of state parliament were represented in the club.

At the last moment, Sydney's leading business entrepreneur and property developer was added to the target list. Despite being New South Wales's wealthiest man by a huge margin, extracting the necessary subscriptions had proven difficult. It was only when this man had convinced several other of Sydney's elite bankers to contribute had the task of collecting the funds been made easier.

Now, after two full years of existence and numerous successful operations, the club was running smoothly, reaching its goals and satisfactorily fulfilling its potential.

The matter of a couple of lawyers getting suspicious was the only dark spot on their otherwise bright horizon. Then the Commander dropped his bombshell.

He coughed loudly to attract the attention of the chairman.

The pipe was once more used as a gavel and the room became silent as the chairman spoke.

'You have something to add, Commander?'

'Yes, I have,' the small man said quietly. 'I have it on good authority that another of our friends has been asking awkward questions around the underworld. I am sure you are all aware of one Mister Albert Tuckey. Well, apparently he has been making somewhat of a nuisance of himself by enquiring at the Coroners' court, and other places, regarding the circumstances of the demise of our last five targets. Would anyone care to comment on that?'

There was a general upsurge in mutterings and chatter as each member discussed this latest revelation. Finally the chairman banged his makeshift gavel several times on the table and called for silence. When the talk subsided he drew a deep breath and said,

'Well, Gentlemen. I rather feel this puts a very different light on our earlier discussion regarding Kind and Oakes. My first thought is where is the leak, if any? And the next thought is, will Mister Tuckey be a candidate for our next operation, as we don't, at present, have a target planned?. Give me your thoughts, Gentlemen.'

There was an immediate animated conversation as each member tried to put his own opinions forward. The Commander was questioned at length as to the authenticity of his information, but each man knew he would never have breathed a word if the facts were not checked upon first. After several theories and suggestions were tabled, it was eventually agreed the 'Commander' would double check the information, and if it was authentic, Albert Tuckey would be the subject of the next Proper Sentence.

The decision was left to the old man, but every member present knew the outcome.

Within a few short weeks, Albert Tuckey would join the list of shady characters who had presented the state's Coroner with an unsolved, mystery death.

CHAPTER FIFTEEN

Mike Walker watched as his wife set up the microfiche reader on the bar top in the corner of their large lounge room. When she had connected the last cable and turned on the power, the screen flashed and crackled as it warmed up and gradually came to life. The machine gave a soft buzzing sound, then a series of pops.

Carmen smiled at her husband and said confidently,

'Now we can start. These first few slides are the oldest, and I rather fancy the info you want is in one of them. Ok, let's see.'

Mike watched as she moved the slide up, then down, then across to the right. Carmen hovered the slide at a list of known chemicals, then ever so slowly moved the viewer as she read the brief details of each substance. It took almost a full hour to wade through all the data before Carmen removed the slide and returned it to its cardboard sleeve.

'Well, that's one down, about thirty to go,' she said with a sigh. 'How about a nice cup of tea for the researcher, waiter?'

'Right-o, I'll get you a cuppa, but you keep looking. If this stuff is in there, the sooner we find it, the sooner you can relax. Go on, get searching,' he said with mock sternness.

'Slave driver!' she retorted as she fitted the next slide to the viewer.

Mike went to the kitchen and made tea for the two of them. He grabbed a packet of biscuits from the pantry and headed back to the lounge.

'Any thing?' he asked hopefully. Carmen turned to face him and said sarcastically,

'Well now, d'you think I would be sitting here still staring at this thing if I'd found something, you foolish Dodo? Don't worry, Mister Anxious. If I find what we're after, you'll be the first to know. Now, pass me my tea and shut your cake hole, will you?'

He grinned at her and placed the teacup beside her hand.

'Hope it burns all the way down, you cheeky bugger,' he replied. He sat on a bar stool and resumed watching her move the slide, read, move the slide further and read some more. The only sound was the ticking of the large clock which was hung on the opposite wall, and the occasional metallic click as Carmen moved the slide.

The waiting became too much for Walker and after another forty minutes he announced,

'Bugger this. I'm going for my run. If the station calls, tell them I'm not taking tomorrow as another rest day because Johnno and me are due in court on the Metters case, with the break and enter at the railway.'

'Uh-huh,' Carmen grunted, her eyes not leaving the screen as she perused more data.

He quickly changed into football shorts and socks, running shoes and an old Tee-shirt.

After stretching his calf and thigh muscles at the front door for five minutes, he set off at a slow jog, gradually increasing his speed as he headed for the nearby sports fields.

He ran on the wrong side of the road, facing on-coming traffic. To ensure safety, he turned his head at the sound of any approaching motor vehicle, fully aware of the numerous joggers who fell victim to errant motorists every year.

As he jogged his thoughts returned to the mysterious deaths of the criminals. Allan Muscatt was due to call him tonight, after his meeting with Inspector Parkinson, the Commissioner's Staff Officer. Muscatt said he would telephone around nine so he hoped Carmen would have found the elusive poison by then. He reminded himself to buy her something nice to show his appreciation for her efforts. He reached the sports val and began a series of sprints, up and down the faded side lines. At the end of each sprint he dropped to the ground and performed ten push-ups. After nearly an hour he paused and walked to the dressing sheds where several water taps dripped slowly onto the parched earth. He turned one on full and doused his sweat covered head under the cool flow. Then he removed the Tee-shirt, soaked it under the tap and replaced the garment on his body. As he wriggled into the shirt, and the residue water cleared from his eyes, Mike became aware of a car parked in the shade of some trees, on the opposite side of the field. It was a sporty red Mazda RX7 and there was something familiar about the car.

He pretended to carry out more stretching as he carefully studied the car and its occupant. His keen eyes soon detected a man sitting at the wheel, a pair of binoculars held to his face and pointing at Mike. Suddenly he recalled the Mazda. It had followed him as he jogged along the streets, turning into a side street when he swivelled his head to check for traffic. He had thought no more about it, even though the car had rejoined the main road ahead of him, stopped, then resumed cruising slowly behind him until he turned his head again. The driver had turned off again into the nearest side street, which Mike happened to know was a small cul-de-sac. Slowly following and turning off when likely to be spotted was classic surveillance technique.

He decided to attempt to confront this mystery spy, and quickly leapt to his feet, running smoothly as if circumnavigating the oval. As he expected, when he began nearing the Mazda, it quickly reversed out from under the trees and sped toward the open gates. Mike pretended to ignore the car but he noted the number plate and committed it to his memory. The car stopped across the road from the gates and Mike continued jogging, completing the circuit of the oval. He jumped the low fence at the far end of the oval and sprinted for the cover of the adjoining street. A large electricity kiosk was set on a concrete slab just beyond the corner, and he crouched behind it, listening for the car.

After nearly ten minutes there was no sound of an approaching vehicle so Mike slowly raised his head above the kiosk. The street was deserted. He resumed his run, taking a round-about route back to his house. The front door opened as he approached and Carmen stood in the doorway, a huge smile beaming across her face.

'Guess what, Dearest? I think I've found your mystery poison,' she announced proudly.

Looking around the nearby intersection and noting the details of any parked cars, Mike nodded to his wife as he ushered her inside.

'That's great, Love. Has there been any strange cars cruising the street while I was out?'

'The only strange thing in this street is you, you plonker!' Carmen retorted, shrugging free of Mike's grip on her elbow. 'What's got into you? I was believing this toxic substance you and Allan were seeking was indeed the most crucial matter on earth, or at least to be finding it. And, you ungrateful spalpine, I've been slaving over that cursed screen for the last three hours and making comprehensive notes, but you.........'

Carmen's tirade trailed off as she watched Mike stride to the large windows, draw the heavy drapes, then peer out at the street through a small opening between the curtains.

'What's occurring, Mikey? Is the Bogey Man chasing you, or what?'

He turned and faced her, a grim look on his sweat stained face.

'Some bugger is. I was working out up at the oval when I clocked some bloke sitting in a car, watching me through binoculars. I think he had a camera, too. By the way, thanks heaps for the research, and I am excited and grateful. This other business just took priority for the moment. Just let me do a couple of tasks then I want you to give us all the information you have. Right now I need to write down the rego number before I forget it.'

He busied himself obtaining a notepad and pencil, then scrawling down the number and description of the car. Carmen walked over and stood beside him, taking his free arm in her hand. She grinned mischievously and whispered,

'He was probably a pervert, simply ogling your manly body. Can't say I blame him for that, you handsome rogue. You're always telling me how gorgeous you are.'

Mike looked unsmilingly at her and immediately she realised how serious he was.

'No, this wasn't any sort of weirdo. He followed me along Glenfield Road, and each time I turned to look at him, he drove into a side street. Then I spotted him parked under those big trees on the far side of the oval, and he took off when I approached him. Something really weird is going on, and I'm going to find out what.'

He crossed to the telephone and dialled the number for the Police Station. A friendly voice answered after half a dozen rings.

'Wagga Police. Sergeant Brady.'

'G'day Lenny. Mike Walker. Can you switch me through to Traffic thanks mate?'

'Hello Mikey. Hey, it's not 'Traffic' anymore. It's 'Highway Patrol'. You should know that. Anyhow, there's no-one home up there. They're all out chasing 'hoons'. What's up, mate? Can I help you with anything?'

Mike thought for a moment then decided to take a chance.

'Do you have access to the Transport Department Computer, Len? I need to check a rego number and I don't want too many bodies knowing about it.'

The old Sergeant hesitated for some seconds then said cautiously,

'Yeah, I can get in. Give us the number and I'll see what I can do. But why the secrecy? I mean, I'll have to write something in the log, as you well know.'

Mike had been hoping Brady would not insist on making an entry into the computer log book but decided the result would be worth the risk. He supplied the registration plate details and agreed to hold on the line while Sergeant Brady made the computer entry.

Experience told Mike that the entire transaction would only take a matter of seconds.

'You there, Mikey?' the familiar voice came shortly. Walker held his pencil ready.

'It should be a nineteen seventy-nine Mazda RX 7. Bloody hell! Hang on a minute!' After the exclamation Mike heard the Sergeant draw a deep breath as the clicking of the computer's printer sounded in the background.

'Believe it or not, it's one of ours! Owned by the Government Stores, Pyrmont. It's a bloody unmarked cop car. Says it's allotted to Police Headquarters.'

Walker sat down heavily on a bar stool as the information sunk in. An un-marked car belonging to Headquarters was almost certainly Internal Affairs.

He was being followed and spied upon by his own department.

'You still there, Mike? Hello?' the Sergeant's voice sounded from the telephone.

Mike recovered from his surprise and spoke into the handpiece. 'Ah, yeah, I'm here, Lenny. Thanks, Mate. Look, is there any way you can keep quiet about this, at least until I get the chance to sort something out and talk to a few blokes? It's important, but nothing illegal or untoward is happening. I just need some breathing space. Can you help me out?'

Again the old Sergeant was silent for a few seconds before replying.

'All right, young Mikey. I won't say a word but I have to put your name in the log. Either yours or mine, and I haven't put forty-two years into this job to get crapped on at the last moment. I'll just write 'Walker' with no other details, and if any shit hits the fan, I'll say I accessed it on your behalf, because you lost your access when you changed from 'Traffic' to plain clothes. Ok? That's the best I can do for ya!'

Walker knew he would get no further concessions from the experienced old cop.

'That'll have to do, then, thanks Sarg. I'll explain it better to you as soon as I can.'

'No, don't bother. I don't want to know any more. You take care, now. See ya!'

The line went dead and Mike realised the Sergeant had hung up the receiver.

He thought for a short while before realising Carmen was standing behind him. He turned to face her and decided to reveal the entire episode to her.

He told her of the car following him, the man behind the wheel spying on him, how he hid behind the electricity kiosk in the hope of bailing up his pursuer, and finally that the car was a Police vehicle and was probably staffed by Internal Affairs.

Carmen initially looked shocked, then adopted a philosophical attitude.

'Maybe it's routine stuff. You are only new to the Detective ranks. Maybe they want to know more about their new 'Golden Boy'.'

'No! I think it might have something to do with what me and Al Muscatt are sticking our noses into. He's supposed to ring us tonight about nine. I'll fill him in with this latest happening when he does. Meantime, give us all you've got on what-ever this poison stuff is. I'll write down as much as I can so you won't have to repeat it to Al.'

'Right you are, then,' Carmen agreed. She placed her notes in front of herself and began to read. 'A group of French scientists were studying flora and fauna in Malaysia in the late nineteen thirties. The locals told them about a particular beetle that can kill a horse if it wanted to. Naturally, the scientists were extremely sceptical, as this beetle was no bigger than half a centimetre across. The natives, who could speak a bit of French, by the way, eventually showed one scientist and an aide to a small tree where a tiny colony of these beetles lived. It says there were only seven of the creatures and the silly twit of a scientist let one climb on his hand. They were studying its form when the beetle apparently stood on its two hind legs, the scientist looked closer and dropped dead in less than a second. The natives decamped with all speed, leaving the poor damn aide to report the death. The other scientists, including two qualified medical doctors, no less, returned to the scene, dragging a couple of natives kicking and screaming along with them. They retrieved the body and conducted an on-the-spot autopsy. None of the suspected causes of death were manifested in the examination and subsequent toxicology tests which they performed. The natives described to the group how this tiny little beetle carries a rare poison in glands attached to its back pair of legs. When the aide said the killer beetle stood on its back legs, the natives told them that was the beetle declaring war.'

Mike was listening intently and taking notes. He held up a hand to interrupt.

'Hold on, how did these uneducated Malaysian natives know so much about this little bastard? I mean, they must have found out the hard way or something, eh?'

Carmen nodded and pointed to her notes.

'I was just getting to that. This whole report was compiled by Doctor Peire Montblino, who was a biological scientist, and co-written by a Doctor Phillipe Catilan, who was a medical doctor. The report says the local natives were aware of the beetle and his lethal venom for generations. They used to sneak into the villages of other tribes they were warring with, and release hundreds of the little swine all over town. Apparently they wrapped them in banana leaves to guard against being bitten. There was plenty of tales about losing several warriors, obviously the careless ones, during the trek into the jungle to attack the neighbours. When they snuck in, they simply opened up the leaves, scattered the rotten little blighters around and retreated to the trees. From there they watched the enemy drop like flies until there were few enough fighting men left standing. Then they calmly speared the remainder, took over the village, including the women and kids, and that little war was over. This carried on until the Christian missionaries arrived and talked them all into living peacefully. Despite this, the local tribe concerned here kept the secret and only used the poison to bump off the occasional baddie who stumbled into their village and started throwing their weight around on the missionaries. The secret of the killer beetles was passed down to each head man and his sons for ages. Why some-one decided to let these visiting scientists in on the secret, well, the report doesn't say. 'tis a pity the first fool didn't heed the warning and refrain from touching the beetle.'

Mike was scribbling furiously and only paused when Carmen stopped to have a drink of water. She waited until he was ready again and then continued.

'Now, the report goes on to say the party captured around a dozen of the beetles and secured them in their cash box. They took their departed friend, the beetles and one of the more adventurous natives and headed back to Paris. Once back at the university, the scientists soon worked out how to 'milk' the little horrors for their venom. Unfortunately three more of the bright sparks managed to somehow come into contact with the stuff and died on their feet, again within one or two seconds. Each of these chaps, along with the imbecile who played with a beetle in Malaysia, were thoroughly examined under autopsy, and not one recognised cause of death was found.'

'Exactly like our friends from Sydney and now Allan's mate from Wollongong,' Mike said quietly. 'Does the article say why the toxic stuff wasn't revealed to the world?'

'It certainly does, Mister Brilliant Detective!' Carmen answered, smiling at him. 'For one thing, it was thought the whole of the western world would go charging in, trying to get hold of some venom to use as they saw fit. Also there was the promise they had made to the villagers, that they would keep the secret. I wondered about that, you know? The Froggies doing the right thing? Anyway, they did, apparently. And the main reason they kept quiet was World War Two had kicked off and France knew it was about to be occupied by the Krauts. The big fear was, if the 'Jerries' found out about it, they would use it on the French population, the Pommy army and the poor bloody Jews. So, the good scientists of Paris University kept their collective cake holes, or should I say *garlic* holes, closed. The detailed report was recorded on primitive microfilm, placed in the pages of a nondescript old text book and planted in an underground book depository. According to the side notes on that microfiche, it was only unearthed in nineteen fifty-five. The archaeologist who found it had, and still has, no idea of the significance of his find. He simply microfiched it, along with hundreds of other similar documents he found during his dig. It also says the archaeologist, a Doctor Wilson Boyd, went into a mental institution at Palm Springs, USA, in nineteen sixty and is probably still there, star-gazing his days away.'

Mike finished his note taking and looked at her, grinning.

'That is fantastic stuff, Love. Great work. I reckon you've pinned down the method. We now have to find out who, what and why. Now, do we know if any-one has access to these nasty little beetles, or their poison, these days. I mean, it looks like some-one has, but do we have any chance of finding out who?'

Carmen had reached the end of her notes. She returned to the microfiche reader and moved the slide slowly across the screen.

'Ah!' she exclaimed. 'I nearly missed this last bit. The nineteen fifty-five notes say the original tribe, now civilised and thoroughly 'westernised', still have the secret and are the only people on Earth who can locate, capture and milk the beetles. Only the good folk who hail from the Royal Province of Manitra, in northern Malaysia, can access the insects and their poison. A few expeditions have journeyed to Malaysia to extract information from the people, and all have come away empty handed. The last attempt was in nineteen sixty, and that was a joint French English mob. They, too, got nothing for their troubles except total denial from the Malays that such a beetle even exists. And that, my love, is the lot. So, what's next, Sherlock?'

Mike looked at her and slowly shook his head. He grabbed her hand and kissed it.

'You sweet, sweet darling. God I'm lucky to have such a smart, resourceful and beautiful missus.'

'I've been telling you so, have I not?' she chuckled.

'I can't wait to tell Allan. When he rings tonight he'll get the shock of his life. We've not only nailed down the lethal substance, but I reckon we've trodden on some toes, too because I've got the rotten Internal Affairs bastards following me.'

'Aren't you worried about that, Mike? I thought you said they play rough, those 'I A' muppets. You maybe should tread a little carefully,' Carmen cautioned.

'Nah!' Mike replied. 'I know I have done nothing wrong, and, so far neither has Al. It will take a lot more than some spook who has too much time on his hands to worry me.'

Although outwardly he displayed all the bravado he could muster, mentally he was concerned about the Internal Affairs. His own honesty had never been questioned and it would take a very smart expert to fit him up for something he had not done.

Amongst these mixed thoughts, something else was nagging at him. Something from the revelations by Carmen in the matter of the killer beetles from Malaysia was not sitting right. He sighed as the prospect of another sleepless night loomed.

CHAPTER SIXTEEN

∞

Allan Muscatt turned his unmarked police car into Wilke Road and pushed the accelerator pedal harder. The steep slope fought the power of his engine all the way to the apex, where the road flattened out temporarily. He parked across his own driveway and secured the car. As he gathered his brief case and a large folder from the passenger seat, he glanced across the street and froze. Parked opposite him was a familiar dark blue Holden sedan, with several radio aerials protruding in line along the roof. He knew this car well as it was usually parked beside his own in the police station car park.

As he watched, the driver's door opened and the burly figure of Superintendent Raynor stepped out. As Raynor crossed the road, Muscatt alighted from his car and smiled.

'Hello, Boss. What're you doing down this way? Slumming among the peasants?'

Raynor drew up in front of him, and he noticed the big man was not returning his smile.

'Allan, what I have to say is very serious, but at this stage is also off the record. You've been talking to certain people about matters that don't directly concern you. Well, you've shot yourself in the foot, I'm afraid to say. Me, and several influential Seniors are fully aware of what you've been doing with your spare time. I'm here to tell you right now, you have one chance, and one chance only to drop it, and stick to your proper duties. Do I make myself perfectly clear?'

Muscatt was stunned into silence as he listened to the Superintendent. Eventually he recovered from the shock and said hesitantly.

'What do you mean, Sam? You knew I was going to the city to talk to a mate and.........'

Raynor cut him off with a frustrated wave of his huge hand.

'You spoke to Acting Inspector Parkinson. You questioned him about certain unsolved murders and enquired as to whether or not the Commissioner of any of the Deps were aware of a pattern of events. You should be aware that Mister Parkinson reports directly to the Commissioner and nothing gets by the big boss. I'm not going to debate the matter with you anymore, except to repeat you are to drop it, and drop it now.'

Muscatt was too stunned to speak at first, realising everything he and Parkinson had discussed had probably been recorded and played to the Commissioner.

He found his voice and said as he shook his head slowly.

'So, it goes that far up, does it Sam? And we were right. These bloody crims are being bumped off intentionally, probably with some kind of official or semi-official sanction.'

Raynor grimaced and coughed behind his hand before replying.

'You mentioned we just then. That's another thing, Al. You get in the ear of young Detective Walker, your little mate from Wagga.

He's gunna be watched for a while now and his cards are marked the same as yours. Tell him to keep out of other matters, you do the same and you both just might get to collect your pensions. Mark my words, Allan. What-ever is going on is to be left to those who are the experts. Leave it alone, get your mate to do likewise, and go back to being the good, honest copper you can be.'

Muscatt slumped back into the seat of his police car, confusion and defeat showing on his face. He thought for a few seconds and was about to speak when Raynor said.

'That's all I'm gunna say, Al. You tie up your loose ends, talk to Walker, and be very careful how you word it. That's it. Good night, and see you at work tomorrow.'

Raynor turned on his heels and strode back to his car. Without looking sideways or waving, the big Superintendent drove away and the car disappeared down the hill.

Muscatt sat in his car for ten minutes, going over the one-sided conversation and weighing up the enormity of what Raynor had said. Reluctantly he came to a decision.

He would first tell his wife Heather all about the cases, starting with the unsolved death of Ian Carter. Then he would telephone Walker as arranged, relate his conversation with Raynor to Mike and discuss their next move. He understood Raynor's veiled threat, but Allan Muscatt was not a man who took threats kindly. And the core fact of the matter, the multiple murders, was still something he was reluctant to let go.

Andy Keyes sat in his armchair reading a newspaper while the television muttered quietly to itself in the corner of the lounge room. Anita entered the room and stood with hands on hips, pretending to glare at him.

'Hey, you, Mister Newspaper Reading Man! You wanted to watch something on the television that was so important I could not watch the show I had picked out.'

'Oh, sorry, Darling. I forgot about the TV and got caught up reading about the Sydney football. You go ahead and watch whatever you like. You know me. I'm easy.'

'Thanks a lot to you,' she replied. 'My show is long finished now, all gone!' she said.

'Orr, come on. Don't be like that, Beautiful. Give us a kiss,' he grinned at her.

Anita poked her tongue out at him and turned away, returning to her sewing in the kitchen. He knew she was not really angry and smiled to himself as he resumed reading.

Ten minutes later Anita returned to the lounge room carrying the latest yellow envelope.

'Are you ready to deal with this, Andy?' she asked quietly as she turned off the television set. Anita crossed the room and sat on the floor in front of him. He placed his newspaper on the arm of his chair and took the envelope from her tiny hand.

He looked at the envelope then said to her.

'Well, we both read it last night, and we know what we have to do. I really am fed up with it all, you know Sweetie.'

Anita nodded sympathetically at Andy and said,

'Yes, I guess I could do without it too, Andy my husband. But first we need to deal with this one. I have noted the requirements, and I have just checked the safe. There is just over three hundred dollars in there. Do you think that is enough money?'

'There's never enough money in our safe. But, we'll manage, as always, won't we?'

They read the contents of the envelope together, discussing some of the details as they went through each of the paragraphs.

'We ought to send them the bill for the train tickets and the hotel accommodation. That would stir the camp up a bit, wouldn't it?' Andy commented.

'I don't think they would be paying it. Anyway, we can manage, as you said,' Anita replied, smiling lovingly at her husband. He reached out and drew her into him and they kissed long and deeply. She pulled back from him eventually and stood up. Even standing next to Andy while he was seated, her face was only slightly higher than his. She reached down to his hands and urged him to his feet. With an impish smile she led him away from his lounge chair and onto the long sofa. As he undid his shirt and peeled off the garment, she wriggled from her clothing. Then she furiously undid his belt, zipper and trouser buttons.

The room shook slightly as they moved together, their sexual moaning the only sounds above the gathering wind from outside.

Albert Tucker's thick fingers fumbled with the rotary dial on the Public Telephone. The traffic outside on Parramatta Road was easing, making hearing slightly easier. The warm day had surrendered to nightfall and the only light came from a dull bulb inside the telephone booth. The ringing tones continued until a loud 'click' sounded, and a familiar voice answered.

'Hello! Larry Kind speaking.'

Tuckey grinned to himself as he pushed button 'A' and listened as his coins dropped.

'G'day Mister Kind. You know who this is, so there's no need to identify meself. Just giving youse a bit of an update. I spoke to a contact I have at the Coroner's Court, and he told me some interesting facts. It seems you could be right. The blokes who we discussed all have their files marked 'OPEN' in big red letters. That includes the latest scumbag, your mate Carter from Wollongong. Now, that tells me there is definitely something mighty fishy going on. I've got a contact at the copper's Forensic Lab. I'm gunna get him to copy the Police Surgeon's reports for me, and I'll come over to yours and we'll have a little chat. How's that sound? By the way,

I want two hundred green men in payment for expenses so far. Have that with ya, won't ya?'

'You seem to have contacts everywhere. Ok, I'll be in my office Thursday. Is that alright? I'm in court from Monday to Wednesday, all day every day,' Kind replied.

'Yep! That's fine. Just don't forget the money. You know how agro I can get if I'm pissed off, don't ya? See ya Thursday, around four o'clock.'

Tuckey hung the receiver back into the cradle and smirked to himself. He wrote a brief entry in his pocket notebook and left the phone booth, whistling to himself. His stylish apartment was only two hundred metres from the booth, and he enjoyed the casual stroll back to his home. Despite his experience and natural caution, he did not notice the pale green Holden sedan parked discretely a hundred metres down the road with it's two occupants watching him closely. The old man in the back seat held a pair of night vision binoculars to his eyes as he leaned slightly out of the side window.

Beside him on the seat, beside a white straw sun hat, was a powerful military style amplifier. This device allowed the operator to listen into conversations being held up to three hundred metres away, and hear every word as clearly as if they were right alongside the speaker.

When Tuckey entered a building via an electronically locked foyer, and disappeared into a lift, the old man made some notes in his diary with the aid of a small, battery powered torch, then said quietly to his driver,

'Ok, Harold. We found out what we had to. Drop me home now, thanks.'

The car's headlights came on and it cruised away, heading west along Parramatta Road. They had been following and observing the huge figure of Albert Tuckey for the past five days. The entries in the old man's diary described in detail his habits, his preferred travelling methods and his usual day-time eateries. More than enough information for the operative to complete the mission.

CHAPTER SEVENTEEN

∞

Mike Walker jumped as the telephone rang, dropping his magazine onto a side table.

Even though he had been expecting the call, it still managed to startle him. As he rose and crossed the lounge room floor, Carmen called after him,

'Good Lord, Mikey! Your nerves have gone and left you. Settle down, my love'

He nodded and smiled re-assuredly at her. Two hours earlier they had heard the front iron gate squeak and Mike had rushed outside to investigate. It seemed the wind had blown the gate open slightly, and Carmen told him then to relax.

'Hello, Mike speaking,' he spoke into the receiver. His powerful shoulders slumped and he relaxed when he recognised Allan Muscatt's voice.

'Mikey. I won't beat around the bush mate. Either one of our 'phones could be tapped. I don't know, but there's been some strange things going on. How are you, by the way?'

'I'm fine, Al. There's been strange goings on down here, too. You want to go first or shall I? You sound like you're a little stressed out,' Mike replied.

'I'll go first. Listen closely, will you Mate? It all started when I got home yesterday from my visit with what I thought was a trusted mate, bloody Jeff Parkinson. That's the bloke who just got the job as the Commissioner's Staff Officer. Seems he can no longer be trusted. When I got home there was a visitor waiting to talk to me......'

He went on to tell Walker all about Superintendent Raynor's visit, and the strong warning to keep out of the case of the dying criminals. He explained that it was clear Parkinson had reported straight to either the Commissioner or another very high ranking officer, and the message had filtered, with great speed, to Raynor. They discussed the implications, and the obvious fact now that the hierarchy of the force was well aware of the pattern. Muscatt put forward his theory that the hits were probably being arranged from up high. Mike had reached the same conclusion and was about to voice his thoughts when Muscatt dropped another bombshell.

'......and the last thing Big Sam said to me was, and I quote, '***get in the ear of young Detective Walker, your mate from Wagga, and tell him he's going to be watched.***' Like me, apparently, to use his words, our cards are marked from here on in.'

He heard Walker take a sudden deep breath as he imparted this last piece of information to the younger man.

'Shit!' Walker exclaimed. 'I had no idea we were treading on such big pairs of toes. I'm starting to get a bit concerned about the whole thing, now. Especially in light of what occurred here this arvo. First up, though, the good news. Carmen found out about the mystery poison the hit man must be using. It fits all the criteria and is virtually unknown. It comes from Malaysia and has never been detected. She's got all the dope on it, and when I hand the 'phone over to her, get ready to take heaps of notes. That's great news, eh?' he paused as Muscatt cut in and acknowledged it was a giant breakthrough and would probably answer the baffling question of 'how'.

Mike then continued, relating the incident where he was followed, and the later information that the car was an unmarked Internal Affairs Police car.

Muscatt was quiet at first when Walker finished speaking. Then he asked Mike the question that had formed in both their minds.

'Well, Mikey. What do you think? You want to drop it and return to normal, or do we shove it up the bastards? My thoughts are twofold. First, who-ever is bumping the crooks off is doing society a big favour. I have no doubt about that. But the other side of the coin is, I don't like being told what to do, especially by bastards who are breaking the law themselves. And I never have taken too kindly to being threatened, again by mongrels who are happily smashing through the law themselves. So, what do you think? It's obvious now that we are in fairly deep. I reckon it's now a case of sink, or swim.'

Walker thought for a few seconds then looked at Carmen. Via an extension speaker she had listened to the entire conversation. Now she smiled at Mike and whispered,

'Your call. I'm with you either way, but think it through carefully. You have **right** on your side, my love, but you may be going up against a superior enemy.'

Mike nodded to her and then spoke into the telephone.

'Al, I reckon we should take the tip and butt out. When I first noticed the pattern of the crooks dying and no medical explanation was forthcoming, it really took my interest. But first my partner, Lindsay Johnson warned me off, then there was another death, your mate in Wollongong, and now your boss warns you off in no uncertain manner. And, to top it all, I get followed and spied on by bloody Internal Affairs. I'm really worried, Allan. I mean, it sure appears as if the big knobs in the job are not only onto it, they are, as you say, probably organising the whole thing. I think it's time to drop it, and I'm bloody sorry I ever got you involved. From now on I'm going to keep my mouth shut and just concentrate on learning how to be a good Detective. I've had enough. What about you, mate?'

The answer from Muscatt was a surprise to Walker.

'I'm not so sure, Mike. It is still a major crime to be bumping blokes off, even if they are career crims. And now you tell me Carmen has the info on the poison, I reckon we should box on for a while. At least we can rattle a few cages and see who opens the door. I really want to know all about the secret poison. Can you get that to me?'

Carmen spoke so Muscatt knew she was listening.

'I'll print it all out for you, Allan, and Mikey can mail it to you. But listen Allan, although this isn't any of my business, don't you think Mike might be right? Maybe it's time to forget all about it and stick to your jobs. And have you discussed any of this with Heather? She surely has every right to know, if either your reputation or career, or maybe even your well-being is in jeopardy?'

'Hello, Carmen,' Muscatt answered. 'Yes, I have talked it over with Heather. She has pretty well left it to me. I must say, though, I'm surprised and a bit disappointed at you, Mike. Don't tell me they've got you rattled? A young, fearless buck like you?'

'They've got me rattled, for sure. I've hopefully got a long career ahead of me and I think I just might have overstepped the mark a bit. And who wants the "Internals" hanging around, especially at my time of life. No, I'm out, mate. I hope you are, too.'

Muscatt tried in vain to keep Walker interested in pursuing the cases. Eventually he conceded and the two Detectives agreed to disagree. Walker promised to finalise the research on the Malaysian poison and send everything to Muscatt's private address.

Secretly Mike hoped Muscatt would rethink his plans and return to normal work.

When the call ended, Carmen added more data to her notes, including pinpointing the exact region in Malaysia where the poison was found, then handed the notebook to him.

'It's all there, Mike. If we were true friends of Allan and Heather, we would toss it all in the fire, including the microfiche slide, and never think of it again.'

'I am hoping that he'll give it a bit more thought, particularly when he gets this, and realises it's best left alone. God, I hope so. He's too fine a fellow to get mixed up in this sort of a mess. But, you heard me promise to send him the stuff you've uncovered. As soon as we send it, I suggest we dispose of the microfiche and at least **we** can move on.'

Carmen moved to his side and placed her long arms around his neck. She kissed him lightly then said, as she rubbed her breasts across his bare chest,

'Yes, I totally agree. It is for the best, and I'm sure Allan will see it that way when he thinks it through thoroughly. Now, you go shower and we'll have an early night, OK?'

'Right-o, Love. It's been a hell of a day. It started out fine with you finding the poison, but it sure deteriorated rapidly, didn't it?'

'I'll have to see if I can improve on your day then, won't I, you handsome hunk?'

He grinned and slapped her lightly on her backside. He walked to the staircase and called over his shoulder as he began climbing the steps,

'I won't be long. See you in the love chamber'

Her girl-like giggles reached him as he turned into the bathroom.

Across the road and nearly two hundred metres from the Walker house, two men alighted from a brown Ford Falcon panel van. As they walked quietly through the dark to the house, the taller one whispered to his companion,

'Looks like Detective Walker is in for a good night. Kinda makes you want to leave the equipment in place. It could make for good listening later, eh?'

The shorter man chuckled and shook his head.

'Maybe, but you know our orders. Ok, let's get our stuff and piss off as quick as we can. Don't forget, watch out for that squeaky gate that nearly gave us away earlier.'

Without any more talking, the two figures stepped over the low fence and approached the house. The tall one squatted down beside a small flower garden and located the telephone connection to the premises. He expertly disconnected a fine, plastic coated wire and backed toward the fence, rolling the wire around his hand as he went. When he reached the street, he picked up a small wooden box from beside the fence, into which the wire disappeared. Out of the other side of the box, a long black lead, much thicker than the first, ran all the way across the road, to the panel van.

On the opposite side of the house, the shorter man slowly eased a thin radio microphone from inside the lounge room window. The aluminium window was opened just four millimetres. After retrieving the microphone, he gently closed the sliding window, restoring everything as it was before darkness had fallen. He padded silently to the front of the house, stepped cautiously over the fence and joined his companion in the panel van. Both men busied themselves rewinding a pair of magnetic tapes which were housed in two large recorders. Satisfied, the shorter man made several notes in an official Occurrence Book while the tall man started the engine and they drove out of the street.

They refuelled the car at an all-night service station, indulged in some take-away food and headed for the highway leading to Sydney.

CHAPTER EIGHTEEN

∞

The ringing telephone woke Mike Walker, startling him into full wakefulness. He groped for the instrument on his bedside table. Carmen also woke and they sat up together. He shook the sleep from his brain and grasped the handset.

'Hello, Mike speaking,'

' 'morning', Mikey,' the grizzled voice of Sergeant Lindsay Johnson intoned. ' I had to ring ya early 'cause I'm giving ya a lift to work. I got our car, ya see. We got Metters in court today and we got another little job to look into before we go. I'll pick ya up about eight, OK?'

'Yeah, right-o, Serg. I'll be ready. What's the other job?' Walker replied.

'Tell ya all about it when I see ya. 'bye now,' was the answer before the line went dead.

Carmen had risen and was washing her face in the ensuite. He told her about the call as he began laying out a suit and tie.

Half an hour later they were finishing their coffee when a car horn sounded from outside. He rose, collected his brief case and kissed Carmen on the cheek.

'See you later, Sexy. I should be ready to come home about four thirty or five.'

'Right then, Lover-boy,' she smiled her reply. 'Now, don't go thinking any more about that other business with Allan, will you? By now I suspect he might have realised you were right and he needs to drop it all. You do like you promised, and stick to what you should be doing. Concentrate your considerable talents on what-ever this latest case is that Lindsay mentioned. Off you go, and enjoy yourself in court.'

He grinned at her, turned and opened the front door. The Holden Police car was parked in his driveway, with Sergeant Johnson just settling into the passenger seat.

'G'day, Sarg. Don't you wanna drive?' he asked as he placed his case on the back seat.

'No, you can drive. Besides, as soon as we finish in court, you can drop me at the trotting track. They're having a twilight meeting and I've been given some good oil.'

'Yeah?' Mike answered. 'I might come with you. I could use some extra dough.'

The big Sergeant smirked and shook his head as he fastened his seat belt.

'No, you won't, young fella. As soon as we're out, and you drop me off, you're going back to the station to do a computer course. But first, head over to the Turvey Park shops. The bloke who runs the hardware joint has caught a staff member knocking off gear. He made an official complaint yesterday, and the boss let me leave it until you returned to duty. Apparently he's got a C.C. T.V. set up and has this joker dead to rights. Should be an easy matter. We'll do the preliminary now, arrest the bugger if there's anything to go on, and lock him up before we go to court. How's that for a day's programme? Happy with that?'

'Ok, sounds fine to me. What's this course I have to do? It's the first I've heard of it.'

'It's a new thing we just got. There's a big new computer in that little room behind Sally's desk. I'll give you the drum now. The room has to be kept locked. They'll give you a key. The programme is a bloody beauty. It's all about bank accounts. Once you've got the guts of it, you'll be able to access any bank account, or credit union and building society. We can track any money trail and see what our crooked friends are doing with their money. It's fantastic, and even an old dinosaur like me can handle it.'

'Beauty!' Walker exclaimed. 'Maybe we can do a bit of funds transferring, eh?' he joked. Johnson shook his head again and informed his junior.

'We all made comments along those lines. For a start, it's a "View Only" programme, and another thing, the bloke delivering the course has absolutely no sense of humour. Bloody Masho finished up asking him did he leave his personality in the motel, or did a computer virus kill it? Gees, we laughed. He didn't, but. Miserable bugger. Bloody good course, anyhow. The thing to remember, it's very hush-hush because of the obvious ramifications. There was a memo given to every Detective last week, but you were away. Kenny Jenkins was sick last week so it'll only be you, Kenny and the instructor. Ok, you can worry about that later. For now, let's see what this bloke at the hardware has to say. This paperwork says his name is Joe Miller. You know him?'

'No. I don't get over this way much. Certainly not to shop, anyway,' Walker replied.

They had arrived at the small village style shopping centre and Mike parked the car outside the shop front. Both Detectives alighted and Johnson led the way into the shop.

They were met by a small man of middle age and Johnson quietly told him who they were and asked if he was the manager. The man immediately called to a young girl and had her take over at the cash register. He led the Detectives into a cluttered office and introduced himself.

'Hello, Gents. I'm Joe Miller and this is my shop. Thanks for coming', he said softly.

Johnson showed the man his badge, introduced Mike and asked,

'Right, Mister Miller. Tell us what's been happening.'

Mike took out his notebook and wrote in shorthand as the man spoke.

'Well, I'm sorry to say, one of my blokes has been robbing me. I first noticed the stuff missing last week, so I switched on the security tapes. They hadn't been used for a few months after the shop lifting stopped. But now, I reckoned they would help me work out where they were going. I mean, it's adding up to quite a few dollars worth now.'

Johnson held up his hand and interrupted the man.

'What d'ya mean they? What're 'they', Mister Miller?'

'Oh, sorry,' Miller said. 'I mean knives, Mister Johnson. Good quality knives, all of them. Most are made in Switzerland, some in Japan. I carry a large selection of knives for hunters, fishermen and, of course, farmers. They're worth anything from ten dollars up to about two hundred. I had one of each of them displayed in the glass case next to the till. When I noticed a couple missing, I replaced them from stock, thinking some-one else must have sold them.'

'Who else works here?' Johnson asked.

'Well, outside of me, there's my wife, Patricia. There's young Carol, who's out there on the till now. Andrew McIntosh is off today, but he usually runs the loading dock, drives the fork lift and handles the builder's orders. I've got a young bloke called Tommy Bice who mainly drives our delivery truck. That's where he is at the moment, out delivering. There's a nice woman, our next-door neighbour, called Lexie. She works Thursday and Friday only. The only other one is Kevin Post. He's the one on the security tape. It is pretty clear, showing him lifting a really nice Swiss number. It was worth about seventy dollars wholesale, so I had a price ticket of a hundred and twenty on it.'

Johnson whistled softly and commented to no-one in particular,

'Bloody nice mark-up on knives. Ok, Mister Miller, we'd better see the tapes now, eh?'

'Yes, of course. I would like to tell you, Gentlemen, this gives me no pleasure at all. Kevin has been with me for three years and I always thought he was salt of the earth.'

The man opened a locked cupboard and slid out a video tape player. A portable television set was on the sliding shelf beside the player. He switched the machines on and the television screen lit up. They watched the pictures which showed shoppers coming and going, making purchases and paying at the cash register. The girl Carol was clearly depicted, then Miller appeared and relieved the girl. Another man appeared and stood behind the counter, seeming to be sorting through a bundle of dockets. Miller is seen to talk briefly to the man, point to the till, and then disappear out of camera shot.

Walker noted the time and date which was displayed across the bottom of the screen.

'Here!' Miller said suddenly. 'Here it is, watch this.'

The three men watched as the man on screen looked to his left, then to his right. He then leaned to his left, reached into the glass case and withdrew a large knife, enclosed in a leather sheath. He opened two of his shirt buttons, slipped the knife inside before re-buttoning the shirt. Three minutes later Miller appeared and resumed his position at the cash register as the other man left the area. Several other scenes appeared on the screen showing the loading dock, the front door and a shot from the rear of the store.

Johnson nodded to himself and looked at Walker.

'You get it all, Mike?'

When Walker stopped writing, he looked up and spoke to Miller for the first time.

'Can we have the tape, Mister Miller? It will be required as evidence, right Sergeant?'

'Yeah, that's right,' Johnson answered. 'Tell me, why wouldn't he simply lift one from your stock, rather than the ones on display?'

Miller pointed to a large bunch of keys attached to his trouser belt.

'I'm the only one with access to the locked area where the valuable items are kept. Good quality hand tools, power tools, stainless-steel bolts, and of course, the knives.'

'Fair enough. Where is our friend now, Mister Miller?' Johnson asked.

Miller had withdrawn the tape and placed it in its cardboard container. He handed it to Johnson and replied with obvious sadness.

'He's in the yard, sorting out some stock that arrived this morning. Shall I get him?'

'No, you stay away, for now. We'll have to take him to the station straight away, and you will probably have to appear in court unless he confesses and pleads guilty.' Johnson was being as gentle as he could with the distressed shop-keeper.

Miller simply nodded and waved towards the office door.

Johnson indicated to Walker to follow him and they left the office, walking through the shop to the rear door. Both Detectives recognised Post as he lifted rolls of wire onto steel racks. They walked up to the man who had his back to them. Johnson spoke.

'Kevin Post?'

The man whirled around and looked at Johnson and Walker.

'Yeah, that's right. What can I do for you?' His manner was pleasant but some uncertainty showed on his face. His eyes widened as they showed their badges to him.

'Mister Post, I am Detective Sergeant Johnson, from Wagga Police. This is Detective Walker. We would like you to come down to the Police Station with us. We have a few questions for you.'

The man dropped the wire he was holding, swallowed hard and asked,

'What about?'

'Knives, Mister Post. A few knives that have gone missing from this shop. We'd like to ask you a few things about them, OK?'

Post's shoulders slumped and he simply nodded. Walker took hold of his elbow,

'Come on, Kevin,' Mike said, aware of several people, including Miller and the girl Carol, watching from the rear of the building. They led Post through an open side gate, and around to the car park. Without speaking, Mike opened the rear door of the Holden and indicated to Post to enter. After the man was seated, Johnson squeezed his bulk in beside him and Walker entered the driver's seat. When the car was moving, Post spoke.

'I've been an idiot, haven't I? God, why was I so stupid?'

'We all get tempted, now and again,' Johnson said. 'It's best you don't say anything more, just yet, Kevin. Wait 'til we get to the station and we'll talk properly.'

The man kept his head down, alternatively shaking it from side to side or clamping his hands to his face. When they arrived at the Police Station, the Detectives escorted Post into an interview room. Johnson indicated a chair and sat in another opposite. Mike checked a double tape recorder mounted on the table, then switched the machine on. Johnson waited until the tapes were turning, then spoke directly into a microphone.

'This is a record of interview between Detective Sergeant Lindsay Johnson, and Mister Kevin Post. Also present is Detective Michael Walker, Wagga Wagga C.I.D. I must tell you, Mister Post. I am investigating the matter of several expensive hand knives, reported missing from Millers Hardware, of Fearnley

Road, Turvey Park. I am going to ask you certain questions about this matter, Mister Post. You do not have to answer my questions. You do not have to say anything. If you do say anything, it will be taken down in writing and may later be given in evidence. Also our conversation will be recorded on magnetic tape. You will be given a copy of that tape. Do you understand?'

The man nodded without looking up. Mike had been fitting three sheets of blank paper with carbon between each, into a typewriter and he nudged Post softly, pointing to the recorder.

'Uh? Oh yes, I understand.' Post said glumly. Johnson said loudly,

'Good. Do you wish to make any statement about this matter, Mister Post?'

'Will it do me any good?' Post asked.

'It is entirely a matter for yourself. If you make a statement voluntarily, it will speed up the process and your co-operation will be mentioned favourably in court, should the matter go that far,' was Johnson's answer.

'Ok, I'll do a statement. I've done something stupid. I may as well face it,' he replied.

Walker typed as Post spoke, admitting all guilt, telling them he was always short of money and he easily found a ready market for the knives. He was unable or unwilling to name his customers, but otherwise made a full confession.

When it was over, Johnson signed each copy, Mike signed under Johnson and the three sheets were given to Post to read and sign. Post had said that there may be some of the knives at his house, so Johnson informed him,

'We will arrange for some uniformed Police to take you home, and they will need to have a look through the house, OK?'

Post nodded, and Johnson continued.

'Good boy. You show the uniformed officers where any of the knives are, and anything else that you shouldn't have, and then they will bring you back here. You will then be formally charged and given a court date. You will be released on Police bail, provided you can satisfy the Custody Sergeant that you'll be staying in town and will present yourself to court when told.'

The man was led into the front reception area and the arrangements made. They left Post sitting in a small cell, with the door locked.

After checking his watch, Johnson told Walker, 'C'mon, Mikey. We're due in court now. Harry said he'd put us on either first or second. I saw Metters as we pulled in earlier. Naturally he was with the Spanos and the three of them were talking to bloody Malcolm Dutton. Fair dinkum, Dutton is exactly the type of solicitor that gives 'em all a bad name. I love beating him, as I usually do.'

They entered the court house just as the case was being called. Johnson and Walker stood aside, allowing Metters and his solicitor to walk in first. When the Spano brothers attempted to follow, Johnson subtly shoved them aside and brushed past them. Mike sat on a seat outside the door as he knew he would be called as a witness. Johnson strode straight to the prosecutors table, said something to the man in a brown suit seated at the table, then rejoined Mike on the bench seat outside the court. The Spano brothers were directed by Dutton to remain outside until called and sat opposite, both looking slightly frightened. Johnson grinned evilly across at them, thoroughly enjoying himself.

Andy Keyes opened his eyes and blinked as the early morning sun sent its filtered rays through the slatted blinds into the bedroom. He stretched his powerful arms and then his legs and feet. There was no sign of Anita in the bed but that did not surprise him. It was rare that he awoke and rose before his wife, even though he was normally up and about by seven or seven-thirty each morning. He heard the rattle of crockery coming from the kitchen and guessed Anita would be organising a cooked breakfast for him and a small bowl of fresh fruit for herself. He stood up from the bed, located his working clothes and dressed. After a visit to the bathroom he joined Anita in the large, open kitchen.

She turned from the stove and flashed a wide grin at him.

'Hello, Big Mister Sleepy-Head. The tea is made and for you I have ready some lamb chops and some eggs. How is that for you, My Husband?'

'Sounds good enough to eat, like you, Sexy Bum,' he replied. He encircled her in his arms and reached down, grasping her buttocks in one huge hand.

She pushed into him, giggling with delight. They had made love on a sofa the previous night, then again when they went to the bedroom. Finally satisfied and spent, both had drifted into a deep sleep until Anita's internal body clock woke her at six am.

Andy released her and sat heavily at the table. As Anita placed a steaming dinner plate in front of him, Andy poured two cups of tea into delicate china cups. They ate breakfast in companionable silence, each lost in their own thoughts.

Finally Anita asked,

'What are your jobs today? I have to plant some more radish, carrots and those herbs. Then I am going into town for some groceries. What about you, Big Man?'

'I've got the north paddock to plough, then, if there's time or daylight left, I'm going to move the cattle into the holding paddock. The truck will be here two days from now, so I want to get them ready for loading. There isn't too much feed in the holder, so I'm leaving them in the stubble paddock as long as I can,' he told her.

They discussed farming matters for the next half hour as they sipped their tea. Eventually Andy's eyes drifted to the sideboard. He stared at the yellow envelope, wishing it would disappear. Anita soon picked up on his feelings and her eyes also drifted to the envelope.

'And, of course, we have that rotten thing to deal with. When you go into The Rock, are you going to the Railway Station?' he asked.

'Yes, I will book our seats. Three days from now, isn't it, and back two days after that?'

'Yeah, that's it, Sweetie. God, I hate this shit!' Andy cursed. He rarely swore in front of his wife, but she was always totalling forgiving.

She collected the breakfast plates, kissed him on the top of his head and set about the washing up. He stood, grabbed his hat from a peg behind the door and said to her,

'I'm off now. See ya about lunch time. Take care crossing that highway, won't you?'

'See you, Handsome. I will be careful. You take care, too,' she replied, blowing him a kiss and showing him her widest smile.

CHAPTER NINETEEN

Mike Walker listened as the Instructor read from a training manual. At the end of each paragraph, the three men in the room turned to the new computer and either Walker or Detective Ken Jenkins carried out the function which the text had just described. After three and a half hours, both Detectives felt they had a reasonable mental grip on the capabilities and intended purposes of the computer. The Instructor finished the last paragraph and snapped his book closed.

'Is there any questions before you sit for the assessment?' he said purposefully.

Both Detectives shook their heads and looked at each other.

'Right!' the Instructor continued. 'Who wants to go first?'

'I will, if you don't mind, Mike, I'll have a go, 'cause I got training in about an hour.'

Walker knew Jenkins was a local Karate Master and waved agreement to him.

'Fine,' the humourless Instructor said. 'Mister Walker, would you leave the room, please? It will only take about fifteen minutes.'

Walker left the room and sat at his desk. While he was waiting he completed the paperwork from today's cases. The Metters matter had gone well for the police, with the defendant being found guilty, despite an hour-long rant by solicitor Malcolm Dutton. The Magistrate was totally un-impressed by the pleas to consider Metters' harsh and deprived upbringing, his supposed low intellect and the implied guilt of his ex-girlfriend, Rachel Morris. After dismissing the solicitor's arguments, and studying Metter's previous crimes, Magistrate Joseph Greenberg convicted Metters and sentenced him to thirty days jail in Goulburn, fined him two hundred dollars and ordered him to pay seven hundred and twelve dollars restitution to Hydes Jewellers.

After the completion of the hearing, Walker had driven Lindsay Johnson to the trotting track in Wagga Wagga's showground. He had then hurried back to the court house in time to present the facts in the case of Kevin Post's charge of stealing. Post was remanded to appear again in three weeks. Even though Post indicated he would plead guilty, Johnson instructed Mike to ask for an adjournment to allow them to arrange the evidence, and obtain full statements from Miller, and other staff members of the hardware store. The adjournment was granted and Post given court bail.

Mike completed the paperwork just as the computer room door opened and Jenkins walked out. He winked at Walker and brandished a newly completed certificate.

'Look what I won, Mike,' he joked. 'I'm so happy now that I've achieved something.'

Walker laughed at his sarcastic comments as he made his way to the room.

He seated himself at the computer desk and awaited instructions. He was given a sheet of questions to answer in writing and made short work of the exercise. Then the unsmiling instructor sat beside him and dictated several practical operations for Mike to carry out on the computer. When he had completed them all successfully, the Instructor offered his hand and said solemnly,

'Congratulations, Detective. You have passed with one hundred per cent. The only one to do so. Feel free to practice if you like, while I fill in your certificate of competency.'

Mike worked on the computer, enjoying himself as he pried into various bank accounts of people he knew. He concentrated on the names of criminals and was perusing the six accounts held by one of Wagga's most notorious villains, a certain Gregory Wayne East. He was reading through the deposits and withdrawals in a local credit union when the Instructor handed him his new certificate and key to the room. Without another word, the Instructor stood, packed his instructional manuals and left.

Mike continued to access ordinary people's bank accounts, and then decided to check his own. The first account was their joint savings, reserved for holidays or special purchases. It showed a credit balance of almost eleven thousand dollars. Then he looked at Carmen's personal account in the same bank. He felt a pang of guilt as he noted she had three thousand and thirty dollars of her own. Clicking his tongue against his teeth in self admonishment, he quickly closed that entry and opened his own cheque account. This was the account where his Police salary was paid into. He smiled ironically to himself when he noted the credit balance of only six hundred dollars. He was about to close down the computer when, on a sudden whim, he decided to sneak a look at his best friend's account.

He typed in Andrew Keyes, Rocky Crop Farm, The Rock, NSW and waited for a hit.

The script appeared on the screen with the various links listed along the bottom.

The feeling of guilt ran through him again as he spied on his friend. He tried to tell himself it was only for the sake of practice and no harm was being done.

Then he saw the total balance of Keyes' everyday account.

It clearly showed a credit balance of over six thousand dollars. He stared at the figure for a long time, trying to make sense of it.

Andy and Anita had always given the impression that they were flat broke and were never sure where their next meal was coming from.

'Six grand!' he exclaimed out loud to himself.

'Where the hell did that loot come from?' he thought. *'Maybe he sold some cattle, or perhaps a cheque from his wheat sales came in?'*

Then he remembered how to follow the links to see where and when the deposits or withdrawals occurred. He carefully typed in the instructions to the computer and watched as the various screens popped up and then changed to the final picture.

As he watched, a fascinating money trail revealed itself to him. The majority of the six thousand was the residue of a twenty-five thousand dollar deposit. Another account, referred to as 'No 3 Account' showed regular payments to a well-known farm mortgage company. He then followed the links and accessed 'No 4 Account'.

He read the details and reeled back in shock when he read the bottom line.

It showed a credit balance of one hundred and forty-three thousand dollars.

The most stunning aspect of this account was a semi-regular string of deposits, all in cash and all for twenty-five thousand dollars. The only detail not shown was the source of the deposits. Each time he attempted to ascertain the source of Andy's deposits, the computer automatically blocked the access. He tried every method he had learned from the course but each time the computer placed its bar on the transaction.

He noticed another link to the main account and tried it. This link easily led him to an account in Anita's name only. It showed a credit balance of thirty thousand dollars.

Mike sat in the chair, staring at the screen, changing from the everyday account, to the numbered accounts and back to Anita's. When finally his subconscious accepted the facts, his mind raced as he attempted to reconcile what the computer was telling him with Andy's situation as he thought he knew it. It simply did not make any sense.

As the computer would not allow printing of the data or transfer to any other computer or programme, Walker decided to make some notes, although the reasons why weren't clear to him. He took out the exercise book from his bottom drawer and copied down the dates, amounts and progressive totals of all accounts belonging to his best friends.

The book also contained his notes on the mystery deaths of the criminals, along with the newspaper clippings and photocopies of the Police Crime bulletins.

The dates of the deposits showed no strict pattern but were mostly between three and four months apart. Something in his developing Policeman's instincts forced him to pay particular attention to the dates. After reading through the dates several times, he glanced at the list of dates of the deaths of the criminals. He quickly noted a similar pattern of three to four months apart. The implications started to hit home and he drew a sharp breath as a sudden thought struck him.

He groped in his brief case and found his personal, five-year diary. Hurriedly flipping through the pages, he soon found the first entry he was seeking. It showed the date of an important cricket match, against the crack team from Junee. At the bottom was the entry, in his hand writing, 'Andy not available, Going for a train trip to the city'.

He checked the date against the dates of the deaths.

The day after Andy went to Sydney, the first of the criminals was found dead.

The next death coincided with Andy and Anita's next train journey, As did the next and the next. Their last trip, just over three weeks ago, started two days before Ian Carter was found dead in the waters off Scarborough beach. His friends had returned to The Rock the following day.

'No way!' Mike said aloud and to himself. 'No bloody way. There's another explanation. There has to be. Nothing more than a strange co-incidence, I'll bet.'

He looked around, making doubly sure he was alone in the Detective's Office.

After completing his notes, he gathered up his brief case and coat and left quickly. Johnson had given him permission to take their Police car home so he had called Carmen during the day, telling her not to bother driving into t own to collect him.

He drove home in a slight daze as the possibilities ran constantly through his mind.

After parking the Holden in his driveway, Mike was glad to see Carmen waiting for him at the door, smiling a welcome.

He walked quickly to her, brushed his lips across hers and said grimly,

'Come in and sit down, Honey. We've got something serious to talk about.'

Carmen followed him inside, closing the front door behind her.

'What the devil is in your undies, Dearest? We won the lottery or something?'

'Grab us both a coldie, will ya Sweetheart? Then sit down and be prepared to have your socks knocked off. I've got what I reckon is the bombshell of all bombshells.'

Andy Keyes had finished ploughing and was almost back at the homestead, the old Fordson tractor chugging reliably along the track which led to the huge machinery shed.

He rounded the corner of the shed and his eyes widened. His Land Rover was parked inside the shed, in the normal position beside the battered old Valiant Utility.

Just outside the shed a dust covered Ford sedan was parked. Two men dressed in suits were standing beside the front door of the homestead. He saw Anita's tiny figure behind the men, who had turned to face him when they heard the sound of the tractor. Andy secured the machine and swung his long legs to the ground. One of the men walked towards Andy, his right hand extended.

'Mister Keyes, how are you?' the man said pleasantly.

Andy shook the man's hand, noting the stranger did not offer his own name.

'I'm OK. And just who might you and your friend be?'

'Call me Stan. This is Matthew. We're here to see and your good wife. We want to discuss some business. In particular, we need to talk to you about your situation, including your on-going existence on this farm. May we go inside? It's a little hot for us city-slickers out here.'

Andy eased the man aside and looked at Anita.

'You ok, Babe?'

The little woman nodded vigorously as she replied. She became aware that Andy had assumed an aggressive stance, ready to act swiftly if required.

'Yes, Andy. I am fine. I met these two gentlemen just as I was coming home through the main gate. I told them to wait in their motor car until you arrived home, my Andy.'

'Good!' he said. 'You mind telling me who the hell you pair are, and what you want? We don't like mysteries here. What's going on?' Andy addressed the men sternly.

The first man did not appear bothered. He glanced at his companion who spoke then.

'Please, Mister and Missus Keyes. Could we go inside and sit down. We'll tell you everything you need to know then, OK?'

Andy looked at his wife. She shrugged, then gave a slight nod, which Andy observed.

He indicated for her to step inside, then motioned to the two men to follow her.

Once inside, he pointed to the lounge room and the men complied. Anita busied herself collecting a large jug of lemon juice and water from the refrigerator. She placed the jug and four glasses on a tray and carried it into the lounge room. Andy said to the men,

'Take a seat, gentlemen. Anywhere you like. All the same price.'

Both men smiled at his joke as they sat on the long sofa. Andy sat himself on the short sofa while Anita poured the drinks and handed one to Andy and the two visitors.

'Well, Mister Keyes, I think we should get straight down to 'brass tacks'. You have probably guessed who Matthew and I represent, so let's not have any unnecessary questioning. We are here to inform you that a serious situation has arisen. It is one we cannot ignore, and it has changed dramatically our mutual circumstances. When you first entered into the current arrangement you were both warned this may happen. Well, the worst has happened and our employers can no longer take the risks on you. We all know what this means, and you will have to accept what we are about to recommend. Two separate persons have compromised your position. I will tell you who they are and what actions they have taken, but for now, please begin preparing for the final solution. All the assistance you will need will arrive here early tomorrow.'

Andy and Anita exchanged looks as they held hands. He noticed her eyes reddening and squeezed her tiny hand before addressing 'Stan'.

'I know you said no questions, Sport, but I'm going to ask some anyway. First, how can you be so certain of what you told us? Secondly, what if we demand more time?'

Stan looked across at his companion and then back to Andy and Anita.

'You know we cannot reveal the source, Mister Keyes. You are well aware of that. As for time, I'm sorry, but tomorrow it is. That is final. Any other comments?'

Both Andy and Anita had plenty of comments and questions, but after another hour of heated discussion, and some explanations from the two visitors, the Keyes' conceded.

After another half hour the two men left. They both offered their hands to Andy as they left, but he chose to ignore them. He stood, hands on hips, glaring after them while Anita simply watched the ground clutching Andy's muscular right arm as men drove away.

CHAPTER TWENTY

Mike Walker had finished telling Carmen of his discoveries and his suspicions. She had listened, stunned into silence as he revealed details and backed them up with the notes in his old book. He closed his talk with a shrug and asked,

'What do you reckon, Love? It is all there in black and white. I mean, it all fits far too nicely. I keep telling myself it can't be, but the facts are there.'

Carmen had tears in her eyes as she mentally digested the information. She shook her head and wiped tears from her eyes with a paper tissue.

'I can't believe it, Mikey. I know you think you have it all sewn up, but how could it be? There just has to be another explanation. Those deposits, could they be some kind of super pension from the army or similar? Andy is such a quiet type, and a thorough gentleman. And Anita is a sweet, gentle little thing. They couldn't be mass murderers. They're our friends. Our best friends, for God's sake!'

Mike nodded agreement and re-read his notes, particularly the bank account details.

'So, how do they explain the massive amounts of dough they own? I always thought they were as poor as church mice,' he said almost to himself. Carmen asked him,

'Well, **why** do they have to explain it? To us, or anybody else? It's their business.'

'I reckon we both know the co-incidence is too much. There just doesn't seem to be any other way they could acquire that wealth. And I was.........'

Mike's voice trailed off as another thought came to him.

'What were you going to say, Mikey?' Carmen asked.

He looked at her, then perused his note book again. He crossed to the bar.

'Have we still got that microfiche? The one that told us all about the secret poison?'

'For sure I have. It's there on top of the pile, right at your left hand, there. Why?' she asked, still upset and confused.

'Can you remember the name of the little area where it comes from?' he said.

Carmen gasped and clasped her hand to her mouth.

'Yes, and I know what you're thinking. It is called 'Manitra'' she replied. 'And we both know that is the exact region where Anita hails from. She's told us so, many times.'

Mike snapped his fingers and said,

'I knew something hit home when you first read out the details. It has been nagging away at me, even after I told Allan Muscatt I was dropping out. The strange place name rang a bell, but I put it to one side, too excited about your information. Now it's clear as anything. Anita mentions 'Manitra' when-ever we talk about her homeland. And another thing you might or might not know, Pet. Both she and Andy are trained killers. I don't know if either of 'em have actually killed any-one, but Andy has told me a couple of times how effective little sweet Anita would be if push came to shove. And, of course, he's an ex S.A.S. Commando! Those blokes are trained to kill in many different ways, and he spent a few years in Malaysia while that scrap was on with some muslim rebels or something. Anita was a Malaysian equivalent of our S.A.S. Crikey, this is looking more and more ominous. What the hell do I do now?'

Mike was becoming as distressed as Carmen. The room was silent for some minutes.

Eventually Carmen moved to his side and clasped his hands in hers.

'My love, there is only one thing you can do. You have already nailed your colours to the mast when you told Allan you were dropping the matter. Now, you have to pass on all this new information, and let him deal with it. You can hardly be expected to confront your best pal with an unproven allegation and suspicion that him and Anita have been killing off the state's most notorious villains, now, could you? Give it all to Allan. Let him deal with it as he sees fit.'

He looked at her for a long time, but he came to the conclusion she was right.

'You're right, Darling. I'll phone him right now, and see what he has to say.'

He gathered his notebook, the loose notes he had made during his conversation with Carmen, and even the microfiche in its cardboard container.

As he crossed to the telephone and reached for the instrument, he realised for the first time his hands were shaking. After dialling the Muscatt home number, he turned and looked at Carmen. She smiled her encouragement as the ringing tone sounded in his ear.

The ringing continued and Mike became concerned. The ring tone ceased and was replaced with the engaged tone. He scowled at the telephone and redialled the number.

'They must be out somewhere,' he commented to Carmen.

The call rang out again so he replaced the receiver and noted the time of six o'clock.

'I'll try again in an hour,' he told her. 'I'm surprised they would go out during the week, but who knows? I hope they're home within an hour or two.'

For the next hour Mike and Carmen went over the facts and tried to convince themselves that their suspicions were wrong.

Carmen cooked a small meal of chicken and vegetables, but Mike was unable to eat more than a few morsels. At Carmen's insistence he showered and changed into shorts and T-shirt, returning to the lounge room just prior to trying to contact Muscatt again.

He swallowed the entire contents of a can of beer before dialling the number.

Once again, the number rang fully out twice before he gave up.

'That's a bit odd, you know, Love,' he said to Carmen. 'Allan told me when we stayed up there that they rarely go out, and if they do, it's only on weekends. Then it's usually to the local footy or over to Campbelltown to see the boys. I'll try again later.'

'I've been wondering if we shouldn't call Andy and Anita,' Carmen offered. 'I feel we owe it to them to at least let them in on our suspicions. They might laugh at us, or even get cross with us, but at least it would give us a better idea of what's going on.'

'Yeah, I thought about that,' Mike said. 'Two things stopped me. One, my duty as a copper. I mean, if it's true, well, friend or no friend, we're not supposed to pre-warn people before they get arrested. Secondly, and this is a bit far-fetched, but if it's true, what's to stop them from coming in here and bumping us off? Let's face it, if they are the killers, two more bods wouldn't make much difference to them. This thing is so heavy and seems to reach so far up the police food chain, they might be ordered to eliminate us, and Allan and Heather, too.'

Carmen shook her head and pointed a long finger at him.

'Aw, come on Mike. That's stretching things too far, don't you think? You just forget that particular line of thinking, or I'll be starting to think you've lost your marbles.'

He shrugged and reached for another beer from the small bar refrigerator.

'I'm going to try one more time, then I'm taking a sleeping pill and going to bed.'

'Yes, try the 'phone again, but forget the sleeping pill. That's at least three of those beers you've scoffed and I tell you, a sleeper will do you no good at all.'

For the first time since arriving home, Walker smiled.

'Ok, Bossy-Boots. No sleeping pill. Let's see if Al is home yet, shall we?'

He dialled the number three more times, each time allowing the tones to fully ring out.

It was now nearly nine o'clock and he reluctantly locked the front door and switched off the downstairs lights. Carmen had preceded him to their bedroom by ten minutes but was sitting up in the bed, fully awake. He stripped off his shorts and shirt and climbed into bed beside her. She clutched his left hand in her right and whispered,

'You try to sleep, now Mikey. There's nothing we can do tonight. Tomorrow is another day and we'll maybe plan our next move over some breakfast, Ok?'

He noted Carmen had used 'we' and 'our next move', signifying he had her full support.

'Right-oh, Sweet. If I can't get through to their home in the morning, I'll try through the departmental system when I get to work. Good night, Love.'

'Good night, Mikey. Sleep tight, Ok?' she answered.

Despite his wife's wishes, both knew it was highly unlikely he would get much sleep this night. His mind was still racing and he detected hers was at full speed as well.

Lindsay Johnson picked up the telephone and growled into the mouthpiece,

'Yeah? Johnson speaking.'

He listened to the familiar voice from the phone and reached for another cigarette.

As he lit the smoke with a gold table lighter, the voice continued in his ear.

Eventually the voice stopped and asked for his reply.

'Sick, eh? But Boss, I'm fit as a bloody fiddle. Are you sure you want me to report in sick? And young Mikey's got the car. He'll be expecting to pick me up in the morning.'

'Listen, Johnno! You just call the station now, report sick, and I'll take care of Mister Walker. I'll get the duty Sergeant to ring him first thing. I'll tell you what's going on soon, but for now, you just enjoy your sick day, Ok?'

'Ok, you're the boss. I could do with a rest, actually. I spent today out in the hot bloody sun, frying what's left of my brain,' Johnson said good naturedly.

'Yeah, I know you did. I hope you had a win, as well. Right, that's it. See you later.'

The line went dead and Johnson replaced the receiver. He chuckled to himself. This was the first time he had been ordered to report sick. And by the Police Commissioner, no less. He was slightly drunk from the numerous whiskies he had consumed at the track and back at his home. The combined effect of the afternoon spent out in the sun, and the alcohol also rendered him too tired to give the matter much more thought.

Tomorrow, he would sleep in, until he awoke naturally. With a considerable glee he switched off the electric alarm clock, grinning to himself.

CHAPTER TWENTY ONE

∞

Walker was chewing thoughtfully on his second slice of toast when the jangling of the telephone brought him to full alertness.

He dropped the toast and raced for the 'phone, hoping, as he picked up the receiver, it was Allan Muscatt calling. Instead the kindly voice of old Sergeant Brady filled his ear.

'Good morning, Young Michael. I have a message for you, Ok?'

'Oh, hello, Sarg. How ya going? A message for me? Who from?' he answered, making sure he hid his disappointment.

'Questions, questions!' Brady said. 'The message is for you to come into work as soon as you can, but don't rush. And don't worry about collecting Sergeant Johnson, because the old bugger has reported in sick. The boss just wants you in here as soon as you can, but, I repeat, leave the siren switched off. It ain't that urgent, apparently.'

'Ok!' Mike replied. 'What's wrong with Johnno? Nothing too serious, I hope.'

'I have no idea, Mikey. I'm just the telegram boy. Ok? See ya when ya get here.'

As Walker hung the receiver up, Carmen sat down at the table and sipped her coffee.

He told her about the phone call as he resumed eating.

'….and I'm going to try Allan's house once more before I go to work. I'm still troubled about them not being home last night. It doesn't seem to fit, somehow.'

Carmen nodded agreement and said, 'Good idea. You look awful, by the way. Red eyes, big bags under your eyes and blotchy skin. Anyone can tell you hardly slept last night.'

'Thanks! You look gorgeous, too, Miss Universe,' he shot back in mock seriousness.

He rose and walked back to the telephone. When there was no answer, he returned to the dining area. His instincts were telling him something was not right. He decided nothing would be gained by hanging around the house, so he went up to the bedroom, donned his suit and brushed his teeth. When he descended the stairs, Carmen was waiting for him, holding his brief case and sun glasses for him. He took the items, kissed her lips and collected the keys to the Police car. He said as he fingered the keys

'See you, Love. What time you going in?'

'Not 'til about midday. I've got a quiet day so no sense wasting it in the silly office.'

He smiled, waved to her and left via the front door.

The uneasy feeling stayed with him all the way to the Police Station. He put it down to last night's revelations and his suspicions about his best friends.

When he had parked the Holden in the rickety carport, he entered the building through the side door and climbed the wooden staircase to the Detective's office. The office was empty, except for the old lady cleaner who was mopping the vinyl floor. He was about to sit down at his desk when the immaculately dressed form of Detective Chief Inspector Norman Fisher strode quietly through the door way. Mike immediately stood up, as was the protocol, when the senior officer entered the room.

Fisher was in charge of the eight-man Detective Squad in the Wagga Wagga Section, as well as three other Detectives and the two-man Stock Squad based at nearby Junee. He was a thirty-year veteran of the Police and extremely well respected by civilians, court officials and Police Officers. He was a member of numerous committees and charitable organisations in and around New South Wales's largest inland city.

Fisher walked right up to Mike and smiled. He said kindly,

'Come into my office, Mike. We need to talk.'

Walker was immediately on his guard. Several thoughts ran through his mind at once.

'Could this business with Andy and Anita be about to explode? Have those Internal Affairs bastards been telling tales? What the hell is happening?'

He followed the Chief Inspector into his spacious office. The older man smiled at him again and indicated he should sit down. Fisher closed the door, making doubly sure it was fully shut. Then he went behind his large, ornate desk and sat.

'How are you, Mike? Enjoying the job?'

'Yes, Sir. I'm loving it. I'm learning a hell of a lot from Sergeant Johnson, and others. It beats traffic by a mile. Is everything all right, Sir?' Mike was feeling very nervous.

'Well, yes and no. I've called you in here to tell you two things. First, Sergeant Johnson has submitted a glowing report on you. You should know that. He, and me, too, have found your work to be of the highest standard. Congratulations.'

'Thank you, Sir,' Mike replied. He knew there was more to come and waited anxiously.

'That's the good news. Unfortunately, I am the bearer of some tragic news, as well. I am informed you are particularly friendly with Detective Chief Inspector Allan Muscatt, of the Wollongong Section. You even know his wife, Heather, I believe?'

Mike swallowed hard before answering.

'Yes, Sir. That's right. I've known Mister Muscatt since I graduated. My wife and I recently visited the Muscatts at their Thirroul home.'

The Chief Inspector nodded slowly, then leaned forward on his desk.

'Well, I am very sorry to tell you, Mike, but Chief Inspector Muscatt and his good wife were tragically killed in a motor vehicle accident yesterday evening. I'm very sorry.'

Mike sat back, too stunned by the news to say anything. His mind raced as he thought about their recent meeting, staying overnight with Allan and Heather, their last telephone conversation and Allan's decision to continue the investigation into the mysterious deaths of the members of Sydney's underworld.

After a long silence, he found his voice.

'What happened, Sir? Are there any details as to what occurred?'

'I have a report here from the Wollongong Traffic Inspector, a preliminary Coroner's report and a detailed report from Rescue. None of it is good reading, but I'll make it available to you, if you like. I should warn you, though, Mike, it's not very pleasant.'

Still stunned, Mike shrugged and looked at the floor. He had read through hundreds of similar documents during his days in traffic, and had compiled numerous reports himself. He eventually lifted his head and looked his superior in the eyes.

'Do you know something about the circumstances, Sir? It seems you have been trying awfully hard not to tell me something, with respect, Sir.'

The D.C.I. reached into a drawer and withdrew a slim folder. He pushed it across the desk and advised the younger man,

'Everything I know is in there. Right now, I want you to sign off, take that copy home with you and decide then if you wish to read it or not. Either way, you must return the entire folder to me, personally, this time tomorrow. By the way, the Commissioner's Office has issued a special bulletin. D.C.I. Muscatt is to be given a full Police Funeral, and the department has agreed to include Missus Muscatt as well.'

Mike said suddenly,

'What about their kids, Sir? They have two young boys at boarding school. What's happened about them?'

'All taken care of, Mike. They are in the care of relatives of Missus Muscatt, with full Police support. They are undergoing counselling by Police chaplains and a Police psychologist. At this stage everything that can be done is being done. Now you run along home. Take your departmental car. It's yours for as long as you need it, within reason. Ok? Off you go, Mike. And once again, I'm truly very sorry.'

Mike took the folder and stood. He was about to salute when Fisher waved him away with another kindly smile.

In a semi daze he walked to the car and drove to his home. As he entered the driveway he gave a thankful sigh as he noted Carmen's scooter still in the garage.

She met him at the door and immediately sensed his angst.

When he told her the tragic news, Carmen burst into tears. He soon joined her and they held each other tightly as they sobbed for ten minutes.

When they had both composed themselves, Carmen declared she was not going into work that day. She went upstairs to have another shower and freshen herself up while Mike made a pot of tea and opened the slim folder Fisher had given him.

When Carmen returned, he said flatly,

'At least we know now why the poor buggers didn't answer their phone last night.'

He sipped his tea as he read through the scant details in the folder. It was all regulation facts until he read a 'supporting report' from a Wollongong traffic officer, who was a motorcycle patrolman. This officer's report stated that he observed Muscat's car, which, unknown at the time, was his unmarked police Chrysler Valiant, 'speeding and swerving erratically'.

The report said the motorcycle officer performed a U turn and gave chase but the car was travelling too fast, so he decelerated and followed from a safer distance until back-up could assist. Mike showed this report to Carmen and stated firmly, 'That sounds like a load of bulldust to me. Al Muscatt was a slow and careful driver. He always was. When I transferred to Traffic he said to me something like 'don't become a silly rev-head, like most traffic boofheads. You'll always catch 'em eventually. If a dick head wants to speed, there's no need to join him. He'll come to grief on his own.'

'I recall him telling me that. These reports don't make sense.'

Carmen read some of the reports but she was too upset to read through them thoroughly.

After last night, both were rapidly reaching their emotional and stress limits.

'Tell me this Mikey. Is it normal procedure for your boss, or anyone else, to supply reports like this so soon after such a tragedy?'

'No, it isn't,' Mike replied. 'I hadn't thought about that aspect. It certainly isn't standard operational procedure. I wonder why.'

They both picked up sheets of the various reports.

Mike read how an eye witness told of the car trying to round a bend on Lawrence Hargrave Drive at high speed when it speared through the wooden safety rails and plunged over an eighty-foot cliff, bursting into flames as it landed on the rocks below.

Then Mike spied the notation on the preliminary Coroner's report.

'Hey, Love. I told you this was crap! The Police Doctor's report says, "Although severely burned and traumatised, the male driver's body was able to render several blood samples. An extremely high concentration of alcohol was present in this body." It goes on to state, "the other deceased person was initially too burned to determine gender. It was found by dental records to be a Missus Heather Marjorie Muscatt. The body also contained a high concentration of consumed alcohol". Now I know there's something fishy in this garbage. Heather was, at best, a light drinker. But Allan didn't drink at all! I tell you, Love, this is starting to stink to high heaven. And it's got to be connected to that other rotten business. Allan Muscatt did not drink alcohol. Some-one has blundered, big time.'

'Yes, I think you are right,' Carmen said, a worried look on her face. 'But what do we do now? I'm thinking that Allan and Heather were somehow murdered. And why? Because he was investigating those mysterious deaths, that's why. And I think that means you could be in danger, too. Oh, Mike! What are we going to do?'

'I think the reason I was given copies of this stuff is a form of warning. A warning to show me what can happen if I stick my nose in again. This is rotten to the core.'

He cuddled her to him, brushing the hair from her eyes and kissing her ear. He felt her trembling and realised for the first time in their marriage, his wife was truly frightened. He felt the anger building up inside him and soon came to a decision.

'I was going to take the blame for this, you know, Sweetie. I thought, if I hadn't of stuck my big nose in in the first place, none of this crap would have happened. But now, I'm thinking, to hell with it. If these bastards hadn't started killing people, crims or not, then Allan and Heather would be alive, Andy and Anita would be good citizens, and we would be Ok. So, I reckon it's time I confronted Andy, and his little missus, to see what sort of explanation they come up with. That's what I reckon. What about you, Darling?'

He held her at arms-length and looked into her eyes. She matched his stare then smiled slightly. She nodded her head and told him firmly, with tears still rolling slowly down her cheeks.

'You are so right, Mister Detective Constable. I think we are owed an answer, at least.'

'Right!' he said. 'Let's go now. I'll leave the work car and we'll go in the Falcon.'

He collected his note book, the microfiche and the folder and they entered the garage through the connecting door. While Carmen activated the roller door switch, Mike started the car and waited for her to get in. He reversed the car out and they watched as the garage door automatically closed and locked.

He drove along the street and turned into the main road. Mike constantly glanced into the three rear view mirrors, alert for any tailing vehicles.

No cars seemed to be following them and he drove out of town and headed south, along the Olympic Highway towards Albury.

CHAPTER TWENTY TWO

They reached the small village of Uranquinty and Mike stopped at the general store.

'I need a drink or something. What about you, Love?'

'Yes, please. An orange juice or similar would go down a treat,' she answered.

He entered the shop and soon returned with two small bottles of juice. They each drank slowly, both lost in their own private thoughts. When she had finished, Carmen said,

'You're not sure about this, are you? I mean, about confronting Andy and Anita, particularly so soon after last night's tragedy.'

'I'm just trying to work out the best way to word it. I mean, what if we're wrong? I could not only be losing my best friend, I might be accusing innocent people of horrendous crimes, or worse still, placing us, particularly you, in danger.'

'Hogwash!' she snorted. 'We both read the evidence. The train trips away, co-inciding with the timing of the deaths. Then there's the money. Thousands of dollars paid in exactly two weeks after each mystery death. And the fact that the deadly poison comes only from a tiny part of a small country, that Anita just happens to hail from. Top all that off with the likely murder of Allan and Heather. You were right, this morning. Some bastard owes the world, and us, a bloody good explanation.'

Carmen rarely swore and Mike realised she had toughened up and was now as angry as he was. Her determination and support of his viewpoint buoyed his spirits and he started the engine. They continued the drive until they reached the town of The Rock. He turned left off the highway and drove along the smooth dirt road. When they reached a sign posted intersection, Mike stopped the car again.

'Last chance, Sweetie! Last opportunity to back out,' he said looking across at her.

'Like hell!' she replied firmly. 'Let's go see them and get some answers.'

He drove on, reaching the unmarked turn off which led to the Keyes' farm.

They arrived at the large twin gates which bore a metal sign stating 'Rocky Crop'.

Carmen alighted from the car and went to open the gates. She turned and shrugged at Mike, a confused look on her face.

He stepped from the car and walked to the gate.

'Look at this,' Carmen said, pointing to the gates.

A heavy steel chain was looped between the gates, secured with a shiny new heavy duty padlock. A second chain, also very thick, was looped around the bottom of both gates.

It, too, was joined by a heavy padlock. Mike muttered almost to himself,

'I've been out here about fifty times since we've known them. I guarantee these gates have never been locked before, even when they go away. This is strange.'

Carmen examined the locks and chains, then she noticed the tracks in the dust.

'Look at this, Mike,' she said, pointing to the ground. Several sets of large truck tyres were evident in the dirt. Mike squatted down and peered at the tracks.

'Hmm! Could be a cattle truck, taking their beasts to the sales. He said last week he had a couple of dozen ready for sale, and he added they needed the cash. I wonder......'

They both looked around for another ten minutes before Mike said.

'Bugger this. I'm not going to let some chains and a few padlocks stop me. Not now.'

He went to the car, opened the boot and began searching through his tool box.

He approached the fence beside the gates, carrying a large pair of fencing pliers and a small hacksaw. While Carmen looked on he cut all six strands of wire in the fence, then set to work with the hacksaw at the base of a steel fence post.

'You're going to do a fair degree of damage to the fence. And what about any livestock who might get out and wander away?' she said to him.

'Do you see any sheep or cows?' he asked, barely pausing from his task. 'Every time we come out here, this paddock is well stocked with stupid sheep or healthy cattle. Have a look now. It's empty. That is strange enough on its own. But look across at the other paddocks. Not a sheep, cow or any other animal to be seen. Weird, eh?'

He finished the sawing and tossed the cut post to the side of the track.

'As for the damaged fence, if I'm wrong about any of this I'll happily pay for the replacement or repairs. Come on, Love. Let's go.'

They returned to the Ford and he drove around the gates through the newly created opening. The track leading to the homestead was reasonably smooth. Mike knew Andy frequently graded the road with his big old tractor. In ten minutes the homestead appeared and he swung the steering wheel, guiding the car along a fork in the track which led directly to the front door of the building. He stopped and secured the car and they both alighted.

Mike walked to the machinery shed while Carmen knocked on the front door of the house. He noted the Land Rover was missing, but the Fordson tractor was inside, with the old Valiant utility parked alongside. Various implements and trailers filled the rest of the shed. He left the shed and joined Carmen at the front door.

'Take a look, Mikey,' she said, 'Look through the windows. The place is empty!'

He pressed his face against the wide expanse of glass. The house was devoid of furniture. There were no curtains in any of the windows, and he saw the various shelves and mantles were vacant. Andy's numerous football and cricket trophies had adorned these spaces. He tried the door and found it firmly locked. He tried the windows but they were all secured. Carmen also tried the door.

'That is so unusual,' she observed. 'What about the back? Shall we try there?'

'Might as well,' Mike said. Together they walked around the house, checking each window as they went. They reached the back door and found it locked as well.

Mike stood back and considered the situation. Then another fact revealed itself.

'Listen!' he said to Carmen. 'Can you hear anything?'

She stood still and cocked her ear to her left. She shook her head.

'I don't hear a thing. What am I listening to, or for?'

'That's it. There's nothing. No sheep, no cows, but what about the chooks and the geese. They always make a racket when we arrive. No clucking, no goose screams, nothing. Come on, let's check the fowl yard.'

They walked to the machinery shed and rounded the corner. The long yard which was surrounded by four feet high chicken wire, was attached to the rear wall of the shed.

'Oh my God! Look, Mike!' Carmen exclaimed. She pointed to a large pile of feathers in the far corner of the yard. They walked slowly along the chicken wire fence until they reached the corner. They saw that the piles of feathers were actually the corpses of the two geese and the dozen fowls. Each bird appeared to have several small calibre bullet holes in its carcass. They stood staring at the mass of dead birds for a few minutes.

'Anita loved every one of those birds. She even had names for them all,' Carmen said.

'Yeah, she did, didn't she?' he replied. 'This is getting weirder by the minute. Come on. Let's try the house again. There might be a clue or two in there.'

'Won't we be breaking the law if we break in, Mike?' she asked as they walked.

'We've already broken a few laws, just by cutting the fence and entering the property. Right at this moment I couldn't give a stuff. The law is getting a bigger hiding from other parties than we can ever do to it. I'm just a little fed up with the law right now.'

They reached the back door again and Mike gave the locked door knob a violent twist.

The knob remained fast but he saw the wooden door bend slightly. He looked at Carmen, and signalled her to stand back. Using all his football skills, he charged at the door, hitting it with his powerful shoulder. The door buckled and they heard a loud crack. He stepped back and charged again. This time the door snapped open, the three hinges ripped from the frame. He straightened his shirt and stepped through the doorway, followed by Carmen. The kitchen was empty, with not so much as a tea cup or a piece of cutlery in the room. They systematically searched the cupboards and drawers, finding nothing. Then they went through the rest of the house, searching, probing, looking for any sign of furniture, clothing, or any other possession of the former occupants. The house had been completely and thoroughly emptied and cleaned. Even the carpet had been removed from the floor. They looked at each other and Mike said,

'Well, we can safely assume they have moved house. To where, and how, and more importantly, why, I wonder if we'll ever know. But they have certainly gone!'

Carmen nodded agreement, a shocked and bewildered look on her face. By unspoken mutual consent they both headed for the smashed back door and stepped outside. They walked slowly around the outside of the house, looking for any clues. When they reached Mike's car, Carmen again pointed to the ground.

'There's more lorry tracks here, Mike. They go right up to the front door. And, you can see, they are totally different from those others. What do you make of that?'

Mike examined these tracks, squatting in the dust as he peered closely at the tyre marks.

'I reckon these are from a furniture removalists truck, or similar. And those we saw at the gate were dotted with cow and sheep shit, so I reckon they were from a livestock truck, or trucks, shifting their cows and sheep. Don't ask me where to, though.'

He straightened and turned to look at the large machinery shed. Guided by some instinct, he walked over to the shed, followed by Carmen. Without a word, he began searching through the shed and its contents. He had no specific item in mind, but something in his brain was urging him to conduct a thorough search. They checked over the tractor first. The engine was cold but fresh tyre tracks indicated the machine had been driven into the shed within the last twenty-four hours. He moved to the old Valiant utility and opened the driver's door. While he searched through the cabin,

Carmen moved to the cargo area. A two hundred litre fuel drum, a hand operated pump and a small, battered toolbox occupied the tray. Then she spotted a long canvas bag, with two leather handles attached. She recognised the type of bag and called Mike.

'Hey, Mikey! Look, isn't this Andy's cricket bag?'

He quickly joined her and reached for the bag. It was heavy, indicating it was full of Keyes' bats, pads and other cricket paraphernalia. He lifted the bag out of the vehicle and placed it on the ground.

'Now that is strange. He wouldn't leave that behind, I'm sure. He always has his two favourite bats and a set of pads. Let's have a look.'

Mike unzipped the bag and began taking out the items. The set of pads were first out, then several pairs of cricket gloves. A new bat was next, which he leaned against the vehicle. Then a small canvas bag containing some cricket balls was next, and he placed this in the tray. Last out was another bat. This one was well used and Mike recognised it as the bat Andy usually favoured when playing. He checked inside the empty bag and was still searching when Carmen grabbed his wrist.

'Look, Mike!' she exclaimed, pointing to the new bat which he had leaned against the car. He followed her gaze and saw the white paper attached to the bat with a strip of clear sticky tape. He snatched up the bat and turned it over. A small, white paper envelope was adhering to the flat of the blade. There was no writing on the outside of the envelope but it was apparent a folded sheet of paper was inside. Without hesitation Mike removed the envelope and carefully forced it open. A single sheet of note paper was inside, neatly folded in half. He unfolded the sheet and his eyes widened as he read.

'*Skipper, If you are reading this then you will have worked certain things out. We are taking the actions we are under some protest. Nevertheless we have no choice, just as we had almost no choice to become involved in the first place, over three years ago. Don't try to find us, because you will be wasting your time and effort, as well as placing yourself in danger. At this time you are safe. I have a guarantee on that. Stick to being the best copper in Wagga and a great cricketer, Skip. We are truly sorry for what has occurred but you and your friend should have stayed out of it. I wish I had known earlier. Give our love to Carmen, and have a great life.'*

The note was unsigned, but written in Andy's unmistakable wide spaced scrawl.

He reread the note then passed it to Carmen. She read it twice and looked up at him.

After a third read of the note she said philosophically,

'Well, I suppose that is all the explanation we are going to get. What now, My Love?'

He took the note and replaced it in the envelope and reattached it to the bat. Then he returned all the other items to the bag, except for the new bat, and refastened the zipper. After hoisting the bag back into the utility, he shouldered the new bat, with the envelope still attached.

'What now, you ask? I'm going home, with a terrific souvenir from one of the nicest blokes I've ever met. And as of tomorrow, I'm going to concentrate on my work and try, as instructed, to be the best bloody copper in Wagga. What about you, Dearest?'

Carmen linked her arm through his and they walked towards Mike's car.

'Me? I'm going to try to be the best copper's wife in Wagga.'

He smiled at her and said,

'You already are, ya mad Irish beauty. You already are.'

THE END OF PART ONE.

PART TWO

CHAPTER ONE

The large inland city of Wagga Wagga, NSW, Australia 17th October, 1980.

Detective Mike Walker waited patiently deep in the shadows of the North Wagga wheat silos. The soft ticking of his wrist watch seemed unusually loud as he checked the time. Twenty minutes after eleven. The informant had guaranteed the meeting between the town's most notorious criminal, one Darren John Monk, and some visitors from Sydney would take place at eleven o'clock this night. The deal was to involve the sale from the proceeds of Wagga Wagga's largest break, enter and steal. The buyers from Sydney were to pay Monk in cash.

Seventy-two large boxes of cigarettes had disappeared from a wholesale warehouse last weekend, after the thieves had painstakingly removed an air-conditioning duct from the roof of the building. A small pantechnicon truck had also been taken the same weekend, from a hire firm, conveniently located next to the warehouse.

Neither the truck nor the cigarettes had been found, despite the efforts of Walker and his superior, Detective Sergeant Lindsay Johnson. Even with the hands-on assistance of their boss, Inspector Norman Fisher, they had failed to come up with a solid lead. Monk was by far the chief suspect, but when Johnson and Walker questioned him, he had smirked and denied any knowledge of the crime. Even when the considerable weight of Johnson was brought to bear on Monks forehead, via a thick telephone directory book, the career criminal had ceased smirking but still offered no information. Eventually Monk's solicitor, Malcolm Dutton, had appeared and demanded his client's immediate release. With no proof or even any hints, the Detectives had reluctantly agreed and watched in simmering anger as Monk took his time leaving. The thin, wiry criminal slowly stood, straightened his tie, and then stooped down to pick up the telephone book. With a smug grin, he handed it toward Johnson.

'Here, Mister Johnson. I think you dropped this.'

Johnson had merely glared at the criminal so Mike took the book from his hand.

Both Monk and Dutton had chuckled quietly as they left the Detective's office.

After finally calming his temper, Johnson told Mike to finish for the day and go home.

When Mike had left the office, he had seen the bulky figure of Johnson entering the bar of the Hotel across from the Police Station.

He knew that the next morning would be a difficult one with Johnson's hang-over rendering him in a foul mood until the middle of the day when the effects of the alcohol would finally have worn off.

Several other noted local villains had been questioned over the next three days but no progress resulted, leaving Johnson and Walker frustrated and puzzled. No finger prints or other clues were detected, other than a large hole in the flat roof of the warehouse where the air-conditioning duct had been attached, and six empty pallets on the racks where the boxes of cigarettes had been.

The unexpected break-through came when two General Duties policemen arrested a minor criminal for stealing a pair of portable radios from a main street electrical store.

Joseph Spano had a string of petty crime convictions and was well known in the local court. The last time he had appeared before Magistrate Benjamin Gold, after being caught in possession of a screw driver, a large hammer and a short crow bar, he had been shaken by the stern warning he was given.

'I see by your record, Mister Spano, that you are still having trouble accepting second chances. Well, let me tell you this, young man. You are now out of free kicks. You are convicted this time of possessing equipment for breaking, and fined two hundred dollars. Further, I sentence you to eight months imprisonment. How-ever, for now I will fully suspend the imprisonment provided you are of good behaviour for a period of two years. If, in that time, you again offend in any way, you shall serve that eight months in Parramatta Prison, as well as any other sentence imposed for the matter which brings you before me at that time. Do you fully understand what I am saying?'

Even his solicitor, Malcolm Dutton had warned him to go straight, at least for the next two years. As they left the court house, Dutton had advised Spano,

'I hope you got that, Joe. The old prick is fair dinkum this time. I've heard him give that warning before and believe me, he isn't joking. You'll finish up doing time if he sees you again, Ok? You keep out of mischief and try to get a job, alright?'

Despite the warnings from the Magistrate and the lawyer, Spano knew no other lifestyle and had continued with his stealing, vandalism and burglary. When he had walked past a display of transistor radios outside the electrical store in Baylis Street, the chance to grab a quick prize was too much for him to resist. Just as he tucked the radios under his flannelette shirt, two Constables on foot patrol had rounded the corner in time to witness the theft. Spano had only managed three steps when Senior Constable Glen Hall had grasped his filthy collar and halted his escape. Constable Wayne Burley joined in and quickly handcuffed the would-be fugitive.

Spano had been conveyed to Wagga Wagga Police Station and when the two uniformed officers began to question him, he suddenly remembered the Magistrate's warning. He shook with fright and then wet his trousers as the thought of jail penetrated his mind. He was being cautioned by Hall when he suddenly spoke up.

'I might have some information for youse blokes. Any chance of letting' me orf if I tells youse sumpin'?' Spano asked. 'It's got ta do wiff the smokes what was pinched.'

After a few attempts to get the man to reveal his information, Hall decided to speak to Johnson and Walker. He was aware they were investigating the huge break-in and sent Burley upstairs to inform the Detectives.

It had taken less than ten minutes for a deal to be struck between the Detectives and the criminal. As soon as Spano saw Johnson his face filled with abject fear and he wet his pants again. Johnson noted the younger man's terror and quickly turned it to his advantage. When Spano revealed his older brother, Max, had been working for Monk, the Detectives knew his information would be genuine. The terrified criminal told them that Max had revealed the cigarettes were to be sold to a crooked Sydney wholesaler that very night. The stolen truck had been secreted in an old shed at North Wagga, and the brothers had painted the white vehicle dark blue, using four inch brushes and ordinary house paint. Monk had inspected the truck the previous day and declared his satisfaction. He ordered Spano to drive him in the loaded vehicle to the disused North Wagga wheat silos, and they were to be there at exactly ten minutes to eleven that night. In return for his tip, Joe Spano was provided with accommodation in the form of a Police cell, with meals and a television set. He would be released in the morning, if the information proved correct, and no charges would be laid. The only other condition was that he accompany the arresting officers back to the electrical store and return the radios, with an apology, at nine am tomorrow.

Johnson finished the dealings with a dire warning to the young man.

'If your info is good, then that's the end of it. If not, you go before the court in the morning for pinchin' them radios. Plus, I will personally let every crim and low life in town know that you have been up here spilling you lousy guts to us, ok? Ya got me? We clear? This deal is for once only, so make up your stupid mind, Shithead.'

Spano readily agreed, realising what a good deal he was getting.

He was secured in a small holding cell and given two cans of soft drink.

Now, as Mike Walker waited silently in the shadows of the old silos, he thought about Spano, and the other criminals he had come into contact with since switching from Highway Patrol to the C.I.B. Over the past few months he had often reflected on those less stressful days of cruising the streets and highways in high performance Police cars, nabbing speedsters and unregistered or unlicensed drivers. Although less challenging, life had been considerably simpler. He was thinking of the various incidents and intriguing occurrences which had shaped his career, and his personality, since becoming a Detective, when the portable radio attached to his belt crackled.

The distinctive voice of Sergeant Johnson spoke quietly.

'All personnel! Check in by numbers.'

Mike immediately pressed the talk button and said softly 'Two.'

His transmission was quickly followed by Sergeant Mashman's 'Three,' Detective Woodrow chimed in with 'Four,' then the cage truck crew with 'Five.'

The acknowledgments were immediately followed by Johnsons urgent call.

'Smokey!' It was the pre-arranged signal that the target had been spotted.

Walker straightened up and peered along the rough access road leading to the silos. In the dark he made out the shape of a small truck moving slowly over the gravel road, its lights out and the engine barely above idle. As Walker watched from his concealed position, the truck turned a semi-circle and stopped, the front facing back the way it had come. The engine died and both cabin doors opened. The thin figure of Monk alighted from the passenger side and lit a cigarette. In the tiny glow from the smoke, Monks hooked nose and pale face were clearly identifiable. The driver also alighted and began to urinate beside the truck. Mike recognised the driver as Max Spano.

Both men were casting their gazes around the area warily and eventually Mike heard Spano say to Monk,

'Looks good, eh mate? Those other bastards should be about here, shouldn't they?'

'They'll be here, don't you fret. Just keep your bloody eyes peeled for any sort of movement or anything that looks strange. And keep quiet unless you see sumpin', ya goose.' the voice of Monk growled in the darkness.

Walker smiled to himself, knowing that the pair would be even jumpier if they knew four detectives were observing them, concealed in the shadows and surrounding the truck. An old shed next to the silos contained two unmarked police cars and the cage truck. Two uniformed officers were sitting in the cabin, listening for their coded order to swing open the shed door and drive the vehicle forward to block the stolen truck and the purchaser's vehicle.

After another five minutes, a pair of car headlights appeared at the entrance to the access road. The car paused for a full two minutes before slowly advancing toward the silo. The car stopped again a hundred metres from the pantech, and the lights went out. Mike watched Spano reach into the truck and quickly switch his headlights on and off three times. This was apparently some predetermined signal amongst the criminals, and the car proceeded to the silos. Mike noted it was a modern Ford Mustang, very expensive and very fast. The arrests would have to take place exactly as planned and with precise timing, because he knew if any of the hoods got away in the Mustang, no police car in this area would catch it.

Two men stepped from the big sports car and Mike watched them exchange handshakes and introductions. He heard Monk invite the newcomers to inspect the cargo area of the truck, and all four trudged to the rear of the vehicle.

Spano opened the two rear doors and switched on an interior light. From his vantage point Mike could see the large cigarette cartons stacked three high inside the truck body. The shorter of the two newcomers, who seemed to be in charge, tore open a box and withdrew a five packet carton. He then opened this carton and checked the five packets of cigarettes. Mike heard him order his accomplice to check another large box, and the Mustang driver clambered up into the truck. Before he could select a box to inspect, Sergeant Lindsay Johnson's voice boomed from the radio.

'Smokey Two! Smokey Two!'

It was the "GO" signal and Mike leapt from his hiding place and ran towards the truck driver. He had his new Smith and

Wesson revolver in his right hand and he quickly placed the barrel against the man's temple. Even as he locked his grip onto the left wrist he saw the small black truncheon in the man's belt.

Before Spano could reach for his weapon, Mike barked into his ear,

'Don't even think about it, Dickhead! This isn't a toy I've got at your head! Just relax and be a good boy and maybe it won't go off.'

Mike was aware of much shouting and cursing as the other three detectives grappled with their startled targets. The cage truck roared out of the shed and slid to a halt behind the Mustang, crashing lightly into the sports car's rear bumper bar. The two uniformed men rushed forward, one taking custody of Mike's catch, the other running to help Johnson who was wrestling Monk to the ground. As soon as the uniformed constable had secured his handcuffs on Max Spano, Mike went to the assistance of Sergeant Mashman who was holding on to one arm of the violently struggling Mustang driver.

Mike tackled the pair together just as the other man reached into his coat and produced a long knife. Mashman quickly drew his revolver and placed the barrel against the man's forehead.

'Go on, Stupid! Pull that thing any further out and you'll see your God much earlier than you reckoned. Now drop it!'

Utter defeat showed on the man's face and he nodded, dropping the knife onto the ground. Mike snapped his handcuffs on the man's wrists and then pushed him toward the truck. The other three criminals were now all sitting on the ground, their backs against the stolen truck and their hands all secured behind them.

Johnson went to all five of his colleagues one at a time, checking for injuries.

He then turned to face the four captives and grinned widely at them.

'In case you idiots don't know, I am Detective Sergeant Johnson, from Wagga Police. These other good chaps are Detective Sergeant Mashman, Detectives Walker and Woodrow, and these two of Wagga's finest are Senior Constable Grey and his mate Constable MacIntosh. You, on the other hand, are low life thieves and scum. I am investigating the theft of seventy-two large boxes of cigarettes from Daley's Wholesale Warehouse, in Copland Street Wagga. But you would already know that. I am also investigating the theft of a Ford Transit light truck from Riverina Hire, also of Copland Street, Wagga. But at least two of you would also know that, as well. It looks remarkably like this one, before some fool painted it.' He tapped the side of the pantechnicon as he spoke.

'Now, you four geniuses are under arrest for the purpose of questioning. We are going to take you all to Wagga Police Station, to have a cosy chat. That means we are going to ask you some questions. You remember questions, Monky? We asked you some about this matter the other day, but, you naughty boy, ya told me you knew nothing. Tut tut, Monky. Very naughty. Any of you scum got anything to say?'

The other policemen were grinning at Johnson's display, although Mike felt uncomfortable when his superior acted outside guidelines and this was one of those occasions. Monk glared up at Johnson and spat.

'I won't be saying nothing until my lawyer is present. And even then, don't expect any favours from me, Pig!'

Johnson threw back his head and roared laughing.

'Is that the best you can do, Monky? Pig? Listen, Arse-wipe. I been called worse than that by your missus when I refused to pay her. Ok, enough pleasantries. Boys, you take Mister Spano there and that other creep who thinks he's Alan Moffat, for a nice little trip in the back of your shit cart. Once ya get the door locked, one of ya drive the Transit to the station. Lock the Mustang up and leave it here. We'll radio in and get one of the Highway boys to drive her to the station. Should be plenty of volunteers for that little task, if I know our Highway Patrol lads. Masho, will you kindly convey this other gentleman to our place for tea and bikkies? Get his name and details on the way would you, Mate? As for you Mister Monk, you get to ride with me, the Pig! How's that sound, Monky, old mate? Happy to be seen riding with a real Pig? Come on, Shit-breath. Let's go.'

The prisoners were loaded into the various police vehicles and the convoy set off, the Transit leading with Constable MacIntosh driving.

CHAPTER TWO

Main Western Railway Line, 2 kilometres east of Lithgow Albert Tuckey sat behind the wheel of his Jaguar, watching the twin boom gates descend. Several red lights attached to each gate were flashing intermittently in unison with the two pairs of large red warning signals either side of the road. For good measure bells were ringing to warn one and all of an approaching train.

Tuckey was a Licenced Private Investigator, according to the government issued identification wallet nestled inside his coat pocket. He was a big man, standing exactly two metres tall, and weighing in at one hundred and fifty three kilograms. His size had been his greatest asset most of his working life and he had been determined to use this advantage from very early in his career. At the age of seventeen he had been one of Sydney's best known

Doormen, employed by licenced bars and clubs which he was not yet old enough to legally enter. His size and brute strength was usually enough to settle down any malcontents or trouble makers, although Tuckey much preferred to deliver a thick ear or split lip when-ever he could get away with it. By the time he was in his twenties, he had established his own firm and attained his coveted P.I. Licence.

Now in his early fifties, the investigators licence was merely a front as the big man dabbled in many varied activities, most of which were either outside the law, or perilously close to it. Over the past decade Tuckey had branched out into a new and extremely lucrative field. Personal protection for businessmen, sports stars, actors, singers or any individual with enough money to afford the exorbitant fees. Tuckey wasn't the first to move into this murky occupation, but he was by far the most famous. He had given many media interviews over the years regarding the allegations and innuendo surrounding private detectives, and was regarded as the self-appointed spokesman for the industry. When he moved into the personal protection field, his celebrity and fame saw many high profile men, and a few women, clamouring for his services. He also hired out this protection to heads of various causes or protest groups, provided they had the necessary funds.

Lately he had been retained by a notorious, high profile criminal lawyer, Larry Kind, to probe some mysterious and unsolved deaths of a few of New South Wales' most notable villains. Tuckey could not care less about these departed crooks, but Kind had convinced himself there existed a vigilante group who was organising the killings. He had also convinced himself that he, and his equally high profile lawyer colleagues, could become targets as a result of representing the criminals. Kind had hired Tuckey to exploit his connections at the Glebe Coroners Court and see if any substance existed to his vigilante theory. As far as Albert Tuckey was concerned, it was a pointless exercise all round, but he was determined to milk the flashy lawyer for as much money as possible. To that end, he had taken a drive to a small farmlet outside Lithgow to interview a Mister Lawrence Shortall, who worked Monday to Friday as a laboratory assistant for the Coroners Court. Other than terrifying Shortall with veiled threats of arson and personal harm, there had been no results from this trip, and now he was driving home to his stylish apartment in the inner-city suburb of Rozelle, slightly miffed at a wasted day.

A blast from the locomotive's horn added to the din as the train entered the level crossing. Moving slowly, but gradually accelerating, the heavy goods train, hauled by three massive diesels, passed in front of Tuckey's car with a mesmerising effect.

To free himself of the hypnosis, Tuckey began mentally counting the wagons as they swept past. He had reached thirty-five when he became aware of a motorcycle stopped at his driver's door. A large, leather clad figure was driving the machine, and a much smaller person rode pillion. Both individuals were completely clad in black leather riding gear, and also wore full face helmets. Tuckey gave the couple and their motorcycle a cursory glance, and assumed they were about to speed off in front of him as soon as the boom gates returned to their upright positions. He grinned to himself as his right foot eased onto the accelerator pedal whilst his left pressed firmly on the brake. The big twelve cylinder, twin turbo-charged engine was straining to launch the car forward as soon as the driver released his brakes. It was a starting maneuver he had learned many years ago from an acquaintance who drove racing cars for a hobby. It took your opponents by surprise and usually won you any traffic light drag races you had been challenged for.

Tuckey forgot about counting the rail wagons and concentrated on the upcoming contest. He noted the train's Guards Van nearing the crossing and readied himself for take-off. Just as the trailing rail van left the crossing, he heard the motorcycle horn sound. He turned to look at the bikers and noted the pillion passenger had raised the visor of the helmet. The person had what looked to Tuckey like a ball point pen in the mouth, aimed directly at the big man's face. He saw the cheeks puff out once, then felt a slight sting on the end of his large nose. As the bells ceased ringing and the boom gates began their upward journey, Tuckey felt his eyes start to water and suddenly he could not breathe. His eyes slid shut and then there was only darkness.

He did not hear the bike drive off, and he did not see the red warning lights stop flashing. The big engine returned to idle as his feet slipped off both pedals. The automatic gearbox drove the car slowly through the first set of gates, passing over both sets of rails before gently bumping into the posts on the far side of the crossing.

There was no other road traffic but the railway was a busy one.

The Jaguar was still parked up against the crossings signal post, fouling the second set of rails, when the bells began ringing again, the red lights recommenced flashing and the twin boom gates started their downward journey once more. Nine seconds later an express freight train rounded the bend at nearly eighty kilometres per hour. The driver applied an immediate full emergency brake to his train and pushed hard on his horn button. He and his observer braced themselves as the huge locomotive ploughed into the Jaguar, sending debris, car parts and a few body parts in every direction. The train lost speed rapidly but was clear of the level crossing by close to three hundred metres before it came to a complete stop. There were some small pieces of the Jaguar, and Tuckey, clinging to the front coupling and ditch lights of the leading locomotive. Dust from shattered ballast rocks was still swirling in the air as the two enginemen clambered down from the locomotive and began running towards the rear of their train. The guard stepped down and stared open-jawed at the remains of the Jaguar and the boom gates.

Traffic was getting heavier as they reached the outskirts of Penrith. The two-lane highway was gradually filling with cars and trucks and the tall man driving the motorcycle decided to remain behind a car and caravan as they descended the Blue Mountains. Earlier he had enjoyed swerving in and out of the traffic and his pillion passenger was laughing and urging him to go faster. Now the increased traffic demanded more care and caution. As the last steep hill flattened out, the expressway opened up in front of the bikers and the posted speed limit rose from eighty to one hundred and ten kilometres per hour. He twisted the throttle grip and the big Honda 1000 quickly accelerated until the speedometer needle settled on one-ten. In forty minutes they reached their turn off and were soon motoring easily along Concord Road. After crossing the Parramatta River via an old iron bridge, the bike turned right onto busy Victoria Road and joined the moving traffic jam all the way into Sydney's centre. After negotiating several turns and side streets, the bike stopped at the mouth of a tiny alley, fifty metres from Town Hall underground rail station. The pillion rider alighted as the driver cut the engine. Between them the two individuals reversed the machine into the shadows at the end of the alley. Both figures quickly stripped off the leather riding outfits, including helmets, gloves and knee-length leather boots. A large cardboard carton was sitting on top of several milk crates and bread trays in the alley. The taller figure lifted out a small suitcase, and placed the leathers and helmets, along with the keys to the bike, in the carton. From the suitcase they took standard shoes, an 'Akubra' hat, and a ladies handbag. After a quick check of their appearances in the bikes mirror, the couple strolled, hand in hand, from the alley and joined the throng of hurrying office workers heading for the trains. They purchased tickets to Wyong and settled in for the first ride to Hornsby. A change of trains there soon had them sitting quietly, each enjoying the view from the large windows as the inter-city train took them closer to their destination.

At Wyong they handed their tickets to a uniformed porter and walked briskly to the station car park. A Land Rover was parked beside a small brick wall and the tall man unlocked the back tailgate, placing his suitcase inside. Then he entered the driver's seat, and reached across to unlock the passenger's door. The small woman scrambled into the left-hand seat and they both fastened their seat belts. The vehicle reversed from the car space, then turned out of the car park and headed for the nearby coast.

A minute later a pale green Holden sedan also left the same car park, but it turned left, heading for the highway to Sydney.

A small figure wearing a white straw hat peered out of the rear window, watching the Land Rover as it disappeared down the winding road to the sea-side.

CHAPTER THREE

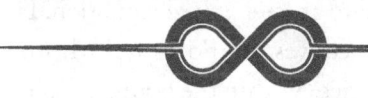

∞

The Post Office clock was showing almost four o'clock as Mike Walker drove along Fitzmaurice street, bound for his home. The street was dark and quiet, with a slight breeze disturbing a few leaves and papers in the gutter. Although the Holden Police car was fitted with air-conditioning, Mike had both front windows down and was enjoying the cool, sweet, early morning fresh air.

The four arrested criminals were safely locked in separate cells at the rear of Wagga Wagga Police Station. So far Max Spano was the only one talking, and he was saying plenty. He had provided a full statement to Walker and Sergeant Johnson, detailing his theft of the Ford Transit truck, then the step by step description of how he and Monk, accompanied by another petty criminal, William Dale Dixon, had first broken down the wire fence of the warehouse, then entered the building via the roof. He even explained how he and his brother, Joe, attended a local hardware store, purchased large brushes and blue house paint, then 're-coloured' the white Transit in an abandoned service station. Monk had organised the entire enterprise, paid for the paint and brushes, and promised Spano twenty-five per cent of the proceeds when the exchange was completed at the silos.

Spano's statement would be enough to convict Monk, but he had no information on the two buyers from Sydney who had turned up in the new Mustang.

Monk had refused to answer a single question. He had merely sneered at the two Detectives, smirking and whistling tunelessly as he ignored their queries. Within the hour Malcolm Dutton had strode into the Police Station, demanding the desk sergeant escort him to his client. Each time Johnson or Walker asked Monk a question, Dutton interjected and said loudly, 'Don't answer that!'

After three hours of getting nowhere, Johnson decided to end the night. Dutton demanded Police bail for his client, but Inspector Gary Jeffries agreed with Johnson and refused. Dutton had expected this and informed the senior officer he would be back in the morning with suitable papers and would apply to the court for a reasonable bail amount to be set. Inspector Jeffries smiled affably and suggested Dutton do that very thing. With a final contemptuous grunt, Dutton stomped out of the station, calling a warning to Monk to remain silent.

The two Sydney men had made do with the duty solicitor who was called from his bed and gave the appearance of resenting even being in the presence of his clients.

He, too, applied for Police bail on behalf of the pair. The only information Sergeant Mashman and Detective Woodrow had gleaned from them was their names, and the fact that Charles Clarence Childs had on his person the sum of four thousand six hundred dollars in fifty and twenty dollar denominations. His accomplice, Allan Frederick De-Hern, had only seventy dollars, a gold 'Cartier' wristwatch, a valid New South Wales drivers licence and a gold wedding ring.

Both of these men were advised by the duty solicitor to co-operate with the Detectives, but both chose to ignore the advice and said nothing.

The Mustang was driven into the back yard of the Police Station and thoroughly searched. Walker and Woodrow found three loaded 'Ruger' pistols, two lengths of elastic rope and a street directory of large county towns and cities. Wagga Wagga was book marked, and a neat red line was inscribed from the Sturt Highway, over the Murrumbidgee River, through Oura and terminating at the North Wagga wheat silos.

The Transit was secured in a lockable shed in the yard, awaiting the attention of Detective George Somersby, Wagga Wagga's fingerprint expert. Somersby would be asked to search the truck, it's load of cigarette cartons, and the Mustang for fingerprints and other data. He would also get to dust the pistols from the car, as well as the street directory. If any prints existed, Somersby was sure to find them.

Max Spano had been offered the counsel of the duty solicitor, but declined when Johnson suggested he make a full confession, and that that confession would be mentioned favourably in court.

Spano took this to mean he would be a star witness for the prosecution and likely walk away free. It was only when both solicitors had left that it was eventually made clear to him his statement would help, but the Police felt they had sufficient evidence to convict the four men in custody, plus Dixon. William Dixon was well known to the police and was not considered a flight risk. A day shift uniform car crew would be given the task of bringing him in.

Spano spent a restless night in his cell, wondering if he had acted a little too rashly.

Mike arrived home and parked the car in his driveway. As quietly as he could he withdrew his briefcase and locked the car. As he fitted his key into the front door lock, a light inside came on and he knew his wife Carmen had been awakened by the car's engine noise. She was a light sleeper at the best of times, but when Mike was on night duty or working late, such as now, she barely slept at all. He let himself into the house just as Carmen appeared at the top of the stairs.

'My, my, Detective Handsome. You have put a big day in, haven't you?'

Despite his fatigue, Carmen's good natured comments, delivered in her soft Irish lilting accent, made him smile and start to relax. He dropped his briefcase and said fondly,

'G'day Sexy! What are you doing up at this hour? You should be in dreamland.'

She descended the stair and placed her arms around his thick neck.

'Oh, you never know. I was waiting up, hoping to have a lover come visit me. Didn't see any good-looking hunks hanging around on your way in, did you?'

Mike kissed her tenderly on her neck, smiling to himself at her teasing.

'You brazen hussy. Seeing you're up, how about putting the kettle on? I could murder a decent cup of tea. We've been swallowing that rotten Cop-Shop coffee all night.'

'Did you want something to eat, as well? I could throw together a sandwich, or there's some of that chocolate cake left. What say you, my love?'

He sat on a stool beside the breakfast bar and said tiredly,

'A bit of that cake sounds good. It will go well with a cuppa. Thanks, Love.'

As she busied herself in the kitchen, Carmen hummed softly to herself. She always relaxed when he came home. Over the past year they had had several traumatic experiences, starting with a fellow Police Officer and his wife tragically killed in a fiery car crash, followed by the sudden disappearance their best friends from the area after coming under Mike's suspicion of committing serious crimes. Mike had also become aware that he had somehow come to the attention of the dreaded Internal Affairs Branch, which was a situation no officer relished. Even though his conscience was clear, it troubled Mike to know senior officers were watching his every move.

Only total support from Carmen and his local superiors prevented Mike from resigning his position and moving away completely.

When their lives had eventually settled down again, Mike had applied himself to his work with almost fanatical dedication. This had sometimes placed undue strain on their marriage so they had developed a system of coded messages to both encourage each other and to signal when some time out was required. Carmen had picked up a small, stuffed teddy-bear from a charity shop in Fitzmaurice Street while they were still suffering grief after the death of Mike's colleague and his wife. The little bear was dressed in tiny trousers and a checked shirt, and was topped off with a miniature straw hat. But it was the face of the toy which drew most attention. The sad expression formed by the sewn lips and downcast plastic eyes gave off a most melancholy appearance. As soon as she saw it, Carmen just had to have it and when she had shown Mike, he grinned and told her 'He looks like we feel. If we look that miserable, maybe it's time we pulled ourselves together.'

Now if he began to appear down and moody, or just became too quiet and thoughtful, Carmen would secretly take the bear from its resting place in the lounge, and place it in Mike's briefcase. He would always understand the message, and immediately apply for some rest days from work. They would then usually pack a few things and go camping on a secluded spot next to the Murrumbidgee River that they had discovered one weekend a few years ago.

When Mike detected Carmen was feeling the strain, he would place the bear on the seat of Carmen's little red Italian motor scooter. Carmen rode the scooter to her work, out at the university where she lectured in forensics and science. When she discovered her scooter occupied by the toy bear, she knew Mike thought she was in need of a break. Both realised the silly messages would seem childish to strangers, but it was a fun way of keeping watch on each other since the tumultuous events of the recent past.

'So, did you catch your villains, Mikey? I mean, was the long night worth it?' she asked as she poured tea into two cups.

Mike rarely told her the intricate details of the cases he was working, but this one had been different. The local media had covered the break-in extensively, and Mike had been interviewed on radio and by two local newspapers. Sergeant Johnson had been asked to do an interview on two local television stations for their news bulletins. He initially refused but was directed by the Detective Inspector to accede to the requests.

Like most Wagga Wagga residents, Carmen was well aware of the crime, the goods which were stolen and the investigating detectives.

'Well, we've got four bods in the cells, and by nine o'clock this morning a fifth should be joining them. We got the ciggies back, and the truck, and we've seized three firearms and a near new Mustang, as well as four and a half grand in used notes, so I suppose you could say we've had a successful nights work. Of course, the main game is to be played out in court, starting at ten o'clock today. Hopefully the 'beak' will refuse bail for the main three crooks, and restrict the movements of the two minor players. And that reminds me, have I got a fresh suit for court? I got this one a bit dirty convincing a couple of our friends to calm down and wear some bracelets.'

Carmen immediately showed concern.

'Did you manage to get hurt? You usually finish up with some bark off you when dealing with those type of spalpeens.'

'No, I'm fine. No injuries to anyone this time. About the suit?'

'Yes, you have a choice of two. Both outfits are hanging in the wardrobe. Are you going to try for a few hours sleep before you present yourself to Old Sloppy Jaws? You know how particular he is.'

'Old Sloppy Jaws' was the disrespectful nick-name the police used when referring to Magistrate Gold. He was extremely overweight and his jowls appeared to rest on his chest, so the nickname was used secretly by those who dealt with him regularly.

'Yeah, I'm going up now for a shower and try for a bit of a snooze. If I drop off, will you wake me no later than nine?' Mike replied.

It was now nearly five o'clock and Carmen knew four hours sleep would not be enough, but she reasoned it was better than none.

When he had made his way up the stairs and into the shower, she sat alone, sipping on her tea and thinking about their life. Neither had been the same since the deaths of Mike's friend and colleague, Detective Chief Inspector Allan Muscatt and his quiet, loving wife, Heather. The two had been killed in a car crash on the coast, not two kilometres from their home. Certain details of the crash still bothered Mike, not the least of which was the findings of the Police Surgeon that the Muscatts bodies had contained large quantities of alcohol. It was well known that Allan did not drink at all, and Heather was known to only imbibe in the occasional glass of wine.

Mike and Allan had been secretly working an investigation into mysterious deaths of some well-known criminals after Walker noticed a distinct pattern emerging. They had obviously trodden on some very big toes, and each was warned off from the cases. Mike had decided to accept the warnings, but Muscatt chose to plough on. Mike was sure that fact had led directly to the suspicious deaths of Allan and Heather.

While that tragedy was still fresh in their minds, Mike had stumbled upon some evidence that his best friends, Andy and Anita Keyes, might be involved in the murder plots and were living a secret double life. When he and Carmen had gone to visit the Keyes on their farm at The Rock with the intention of confronting them with Mike's evidence, and the Muscatt's deaths, they had found the farm deserted. All livestock was missing and Anita's prized egg-laying fowls were lying slaughtered in their pen. The homestead was completely empty and the only clue they found was Andy's cricket bat, which had a farewell note attached, and also contained a veiled warning not to attempt to locate them.

Carmen sighed to herself as she remembered the good times they had had with the Keyes, particularly in sport. Both Andy and Mike had played Rugby League and Cricket together. Mike was captain of both teams and Andy was a star full back and deadly fast bowler. Even when Andy retired from football, the two couples remained firm friends and socialised together often. Their sudden disappearance left a massive hole in the Walkers ring of friendship, but more seriously, it seemed to confirm Mike's suspicions regarding the Keyes' double life. All the indicators pointed to Mike being correct, but the warning left by Andy was strong enough for Mike to take heed and leave the matter of the mysterious deaths of the notorious criminals alone.

The entire experience had changed him, and Carmen often found herself wondering if their life would ever return to normal. Although Mike worked hard at his investigations, and dedicated himself to doing a thorough, clean job, he occasionally became angry at the world and sunk into depression, blaming himself for the Muscatts deaths and the Keyes' disappearance. It was at these times that the Teddy Bear was used and they took immediate steps to relieve the tension and get away for a few days.

CHAPTER FOUR

There were seven customers waiting near the front door of the Dive Shop as the manager unlocked the three padlocks and slid back the bolts. He checked his wrist watch and noted it was ten minutes to six. The shop was not due to open until six am but as it looked like another busy day ahead, he decided to make an early start.

His wife was in the back room, preparing coffee and toast for the two of them, but he wondered to himself if either of them would get a chance to enjoy the light breakfast.

As soon as the customers stepped in, "Old Henry" fronted the manager.

'Where was you yesterday, Alex? I lugged this here bottle all the way down here on me bike and youse wuz shut!' He indicated the S.C.U.B.A. air tank he was holding.

'Sorry, Mate. I had to take the missus to Sydney to see a specialist. A bit of women's trouble, you know,' the tall manager stroked his thick beard as he spoke.

'Oh, I see,' the older man said. 'Just thought it was a bit strange, a diving place being closed on a Sunday, that's all. Thought it would be ya busiest day.'

The tall man took the empty air tank from him and said,

'Nah. It sometimes is, but yesterday we had no bookings at all. Besides, we can't muck around with women's plumbing, can we?'

'No, we sure can't. How is our gorgeous little Angela? She OK now?' Henry asked.

As Alex attached the air lines and submerged the tank in the filling tub, he nodded.

'Yeah, she's fine, thanks. Here she is now.'

The manager's tiny Asian wife appeared, carrying two steaming cups of freshly brewed coffee. She smiled at each man in the shop and placed the cups on the counter.

'Who is next, please?' she asked quietly. A thick set young man stepped forward and was soon being attended to by the little woman. As they dealt with each customer's needs, they grabbed sips of coffee and one at a time stepped into the back room and ate their buttered toast. By seven-thirty the shop was again empty and Alex checked his watch. His first students were due at eight for their final diving lessons, so he went to the storeroom and laid out four wetsuits. Then he took his own wetsuit from a special drying locker and checked the garment over thoroughly.

Filling air tanks and selling diving, fishing, swimming and surfing equipment was the mainstay of the business, but the Diving Instruction School brought in the most income. It was also Alex's favourite part of running the shop. Occasionally Angela ran the school, particularly if the students were young women or children.

In the six months they had operated the business, the diving school had earned them over twice as much as the retail side.

By eight o'clock the four dive students were in the storeroom, checking their equipment and testing their air supply. Alex opened the boatshed doors and pushed the fifty foot launch out into the strengthening sunshine. He secured the boat to the jetty and went about checking fuel, oil, safety equipment and the fresh water tanks.

The students were now ready and shuffled down the timber walkway to the jetty. The two men and two women all carried flippers, weight belts and air tanks.

'Right, hop aboard, people. Take it easy, there's a bit of movement from the incoming tide. I'll just get my gear and the refreshments. Won't be tick.'

He watched as the four eased themselves over the side and settled onto the two passenger couches along either side of the boat. He went to the back door of the shop and gathered his diving outfit. Angela had placed a cardboard carton next to the doorway. He checked the contents, noting two vacuum flasks which would contain tea and coffee. There were two packets of biscuits, a plastic box full of sandwiches, some chewing gum, lollies and three large bottles of spring water. Also, the most important item in Alex's opinion, a small aluminium tube containing seasick pills.

He lifted the box onto his left shoulder, and picked up his S.C.U.B.A.

Angela came to the door and he leant down to kiss her. She responded lovingly and hungrily kissed his hairy mouth as she placed her hands around his neck. They broke apart when the four students in the boat began applauding and whistling.

He grinned at her and turned away, heading for the boat. Angela called softly to him,

'You take care, my big man. Watch out for the wild ocean. She is a jealous woman.'

He turned and smiled, then shaped his lips to a kiss. She could barely discern the gesture through his beard, but instinct told her what he was doing.

When the big man boarded his boat, the group was ready and eager to embark on the adventure. The two men smirked at Alex and one of the girls spoke.

'Nice to see old married couples openly showing their love.'

Alex just grinned at the foursome, then turned to start the boat. He set both throttles to 'Start', checked the transmission levers were in neutral, and pressed the start buttons.

The boat was fitted with twin turbo charged four cylinder diesels and when they started the entire vessel shook gently with the vibrations. Alex asked the men to undo the bow and stern lines from the jetty and then the boat drifted slowly out.

When they were safely clear, Alex engaged 'Ahead' gear and pushed the throttles up three notches. The bow rose slightly and they were soon cruising at twenty knots, away from the shore and towards a distant island. The students chatted amongst themselves, excited to be about to complete their final sessions before testing and assessments to obtain their official Divers Certificate.

Alex sat at the control panel, one hand on the carver timber and brass wheel. He constantly monitored the array of gauges, particularly the two large rev counters and the oil pressure indicators. As the boat rapidly ate up the waves, Alex allowed his thoughts to drift to other matters. The business was turning over well, despite a bank mortgage and a commercial credit card. It took up nearly all of his time, and his wife Angela was also obliged to help out most days. They could not afford to employ any staff at this point, but both considered they were making a reasonable living from the shop and dive school. Therefore they were slightly shocked when a large yellow envelope had arrived in the mail last week. These envelopes meant bother and unease, causing Alex and Angela a large degree of unwanted stress. After some discussion, they had decided they had to deal with the situation immediately. This meant closing the business for a day, with the corresponding loss of income. It seemed to Alex that they were similar to a dog chasing his own tail. The yellow envelope had financial implications, but the closing of the shop for the day meant significant dollar loss.

Alex brooded to himself as the launch skimmed the wave tops. The four young people in the rear simply took in the spectacular views and watched the island draw ever closer. When the boat was abreast of the island, Alex turned the wheel until the small landmass stood around three hundred metres off the starboard side. He returned the throttles to idle and allowed the boat to lose speed of its own accord. When he was satisfied with the vessels position, he pushed a large chrome plated pedal on the deck near his feet. The anchor chain gave a gentle rattle as it paid out, increasing pace as the heavy pick descended the depths. When the chain stopped rattling, Alex moved the selector to 'Reverse' and notched the throttles up to '1'. He felt the boat begin to go astern, then the anchor dug in and the chain tightened. He set the throttles back to idle and cut the ignitions.

'Ok, Folks,' he addressed his students. 'Don your gear and get ready to go over. As I told you, this is a deep dive, and we must stay in contact with each other at all times. You will go two at a time, with me. Who-ever remains on board, one keep a sharp lookout for other boats, any currents you see, and of course, any of our large finned friends. The other one keep these headphones on which will give you radio comms with me. Any questions?'

Dennis Stein, the tall blonde young man spoke.

'Who do you want to pair up, Alex? Do you want boy and boy or boy and girl?'

'Doesn't matter to me,' Alex answered as he assembled the 'Diver Down' buoy and tied its rope to a small stainless steel capstan mounted on the very stern of the boat.

The four played 'scissors/paper/rock' to decide the two teams.

He tossed the buoy into the sea and watched it drift away from the boat until the rope tightened. 'Right, see how the buoy drifted? What's that tell us?'

The beautiful red haired girl raised her arm and smiled.

'That's all right, Bec. If you know, just tell us. We're not in school now. You don't have to raise your hand unless you want to go to the ladies.'

The others laughed, then the girl explained how the drift of the buoy indicated the strength and direction of the prevailing wind and current.

'Yep, beauty! Well done,' Alex answered. 'Now, anyone else tell me how I can quickly judge how deep the water is?'

Dennis started to lift his arm, then dropped it as he remembered Alex's words to Bec.

'Ah, I'd check the anchor chain. That should give us an idea.'

'Correct. Well done, Den. Of course, with drift and possible hills and depressions on the sea bed, that method is not fool proof, but it gives us an indication. Ok, who's going first?' Alex was anxious to get the dive underway. The class had covered all the theory over the last five weeks and he saw no point going over it all again. Next week-end they were to be put through their assessments by an instructor from another school, and they would complete a short theory paper then. He reasoned if they did not know the theory by now, it would be pointless trying to learn it at this time.

'Adam and Julie are going first, if that's all right. Bec's gunna be on the radio and I'm gunna be lookout,' Dennis said as he helped the auburn haired Julie through her equipment check. Adam was assisted by Bec, then Alex checked both sets thoroughly.

'Right-o, lets get wet. We'll follow the anchor chain at first, Ok?' Alex said and, holding his mask to his chest, sat on the side of the boat. He leaned backwards until gravity would be denied no longer, and fell the metre and a half to the sea. The two students followed suit and all three donned their masks. Alex held his right hand high, with thumb raised, and waited until he received the same gesture from Dennis. The trio swam slowly to the bow of the launch, grasped the anchor chain and one by one sank out of sight.

The streams of bubbles eventually vanished as the divers sank deeper and deeper. The rippling waves disguised the bubbles so Dennis and Bec settled in to their allotted tasks. Bec donned the headphones, received and returned a radio check from Alex, and then settled comfortably in the Captain's Chair. Dennis yawned, stretched his arms wide and sat in a padded seat beside her. Both watched the waves and the occasional gull or tern circling above. The sun was getting brighter and hotter, having a lulling effect on both people. After twenty minutes Dennis checked his large diver's watch, noting the length of time the other three had been down.

'You want a drink, Bekky? I'm gunna have a glass of his mineral water,' he said.

'Oh, ok.' she answered. 'I'll keep my eyes peeled while you play drink waiter.'

Dennis descended the short, steep staircase into the main galley of the launch. The deck was covered by slip-proof rubber matting but the rest of the furnishings were pure luxury. Most metal fittings were polished brass, and the others were shiny stainless steel. Polished timber lined the walls and all cupboards sported smoky glass facades. The three windows down each side had been tinted a dark blue, and printed curtains, depicting underwater scenes hung from brass rods. Dennis whistled two notes softly to himself in appreciation. Although he had ridden in the launch many times over the length of the dive course, he had not ventured below before today. When-ever the class took a meal or drinks break, their host Alex had gone below to fetch the supplies and they dined or drank on the outside decks. Alex had told them there was a toilet on board and he noted a small door in the rear wall marked 'Unisex Head' to the left of the stairway. Both girls had used the on-board facility before but he and Adam preferred to relieve themselves when they were in the water.

On the right side of the stairs was an identical door, but it bore a brass plaque with the words 'Engine Room' attached with six brass screws.

Dennis was in his final year as an apprentice motor mechanic and as such was interested in all things mechanical. He reasoned no-one would be offended if he made a quick study of the engines, so he turned the brass 'T' handle and opened the door. There was a steel ladder of four steps leading into the room, and a slight smell of dieseline was apparent. He descended the little ladder and found a switch beside the door. When he flicked it on the engine room was flooded with bright white light from four overhead florescent tubes. He looked around and noted two banks of heavy duty batteries, one down each side. Two square stainless steel fuel tanks were mounted high on the rear bulkhead, and another square tank underneath labelled 'Fresh Water'. A large tool chest was bolted to the deck against the forward bulkhead. A metal shelf above the tool box held several technical manuals and other papers, all bundled together with elastic ribbon. He looked over the twin diesel engines, mounted side by side on the deck in front of him. Each was connected to a gearbox, with shiny propeller shafts protruding from the rear and disappearing through watertight seals at the very bottom of the rear bulkhead. Some rods and levers indicated the location of the boats rudders and two thick wiring harnesses carried cables up through the top deck, leading to the captain's control panel on the outside deck above.

He studied the engines again, noting they were spotlessly clean and appeared to be in first class order. There had obviously been a slight leak from the starboard engines fuel filter, judging by the stains on the deck and the diesel smell. Other than that, Dennis thought to himself you could just about eat your meals down here, such was the cleanliness and tidiness.

He was still examining the engines when a thought occurred to him. There was no name plate on either of them. Nothing to show who made them or where they were manufactured, or when. His mechanical knowledge told him this was most unusual so he conducted a closer inspection. Despite knowing where the name plates should be, he found no trace of any identification. He straightened up and turned to leave, still a little puzzled, when he spied the shelf containing the books. Surely log books, service and maintenance books or even warranty cards would be somewhere here, he thought. That should satisfy his curiosity as to the make of the diesels.

Just as he reached for the bundle of books and papers, a strong wave smacked into the side of the boat, rocking the hull and throwing him sideways. The bundle was jerked from his grip and he lost his footing. He cursed as his head collided with the shelf and his left foot struck the tool chest. Then he saw the books and papers. They had splayed out from the elastic and were strewn over the deck. He quickly began to gather them up when he heard Bec calling from above.

'Gawd, that one snuck up on us. You all right down there Dennis?'

'Yeah, I'm fine. You Ok?' he answered.

'Yes. Everything is all right. Where's my water? Did you spill it or something?'

'Be right up. Won't be a tick,' he replied.

All the while he was conversing with Bec, he was sorting the scattered books back into a logical order. Some papers were stacked between two manuals and then he saw a thin cardboard folder. He opened it up expecting to find some technical data on the boat or her mysterious engines, but instead a photograph of a man stared back at him. The colour photo was clearly several years old, but it was obvious the man was quite large and wore an almost sinister look on his face. He had the strange thought that the man was somehow familiar. Another photograph depicted the rear of a large car, clearly showing a New South Wales number plate. Without knowing why he committed the plate number to memory and looked further at the contents of the folder. An A4 sheet of yellow paper carried just two short lines of typed text. The top line read 'Total Liquidation' and the next line read 'Completion Date, 19th Dec.'

Dennis wondered briefly what this could mean, but then Bec was calling him again.

'Hey, Den. Where's my drink? There're coming back up, so get your bum up here.'

He hurriedly replaced all the books and papers, switched off the lights and ascended the ladder. After closing the engine room door fully, he grabbed two glasses from a cupboard and a bottle of water from the carton. He poured two drinks and made his way up the steep stairs to the outside. Bec was peering over the side, watching the streams of bubbles rising as the three divers carefully ascended from the depths. He handed her a glass of water and she smiled her thanks before returning her attention to the sea. The divers broke the surface one at a time and Dennis helped each one over the railings and back on deck. The divers formed a small circle as Alex had taught them, and each helped the one in front to remove air tanks and loosen face masks, as the person in their rear carried out the same function on them. When all divers had stripped off their weight belts, air tanks and flippers, Alex addressed them.

'Well, that went well, troops. No errors, no foolishness and no problems. That sea snake was only curious, and was never really a threat. You both noticed what I did to make him lose interest? If that happens again, just do as I did, hold your foot up, so all he sees is your flipper. He will soon lose interest and swim away, just as our friend did down there. What-ever you do, don't try and play with them. Now, any questions?'

There were none but Julie and Adam were clearly excited at having completed their mandatory deep dive. Adam opened his small bag attached to his wetsuit and produced a selection of shells. He passed them around and the group discussed the various types and shapes. They had not seen some of these before and Alex told them this was because the creatures which had inhabited them lived in the deeper waters.

'Ok, let's have a little snack, then we'll see how Bekky and Dennis go. I'll just grab the tucker box.'

He disappeared below and soon passed the food carton up onto the deck. They each enjoyed a light meal of a sandwich or biscuit and either tea, a cup of coffee or some water. The dangers of doing a deep dive with either a full bladder or a stuffed stomach was well known to them all, so everybody ate and drank sparingly.

When they were finished, Alex directed Dennis and Bec to don their equipment and prepare for their dive. As before, he double checked their outfits, and his own, then splashed into the sea. The two students followed him and they made their way to the anchor chain. Alex tapped Bec on the shoulder and held up two fingers. This meant she was to descend second, after him. He then held three fingers up at Dennis. After receiving their thumbs up, Alex called Julie on the radio. She replied loud and clear and the dive began. Julie watched Alex get three metres below, then she descended slowly after him. When she was a further three metres down, she looked up and was relieved to see Dennis following her. After nearly five minutes, the sea bed appeared and they gathered around the buried anchor to acclimatise. Alex indicated to them to check their depth gauges, watches and finally their large diving knives. When those checks were completed, he used gestures to tell them to swim around, explore the sandy bottom and observe the undersea world. He swam backwards a few metres, and hovered where he could watch both students and also keep look out for any visitors, welcome or unwelcome. The students swam around, each collecting some small items from the floor. A few large fish swam past, and a school of squid appeared from behind a pile of rocks. After twenty minutes, Alex signaled the two students to approach him. They swam to him and he showed them his watch before pointing up.

Both students nodded acknowledgement and the trio breast-stroked over to the anchor chain. This time Alex ascended first, followed by Bec, and then Dennis began his rise. He watched the graceful manner in which Alex and Bec slowly floated to the surface, with only the occasional kicks with their flippered feet. Although he concentrated on rising at the correct speed, his mind kept wandering back to his visit to the engine room of Alex's launch. The mystery of the unbranded motors paled when he recalled the two photographs and the strange typing on the sheet of paper. He knew that the face of the big man in the first photograph was somehow familiar, and he was confident he would ascertain the make and model of the car, particularly if he could get another look at the second photo. But the more he thought about it, the more certain he became that that he had seen that face before.

Dennis broke the surface to find Bec already on board and Alex holding onto the top of the anchor chain, waiting for him. Both men clambered on board the boat and formed the little circle again, with Bec. As soon as all three were free of air tanks, weight belts and flippers, Alex addressed them all.

'Right, that was great. You all went well, and I am very pleased with the lot of you. I reckon it is time for a bit of lunch, then you can all have a free swim around the boat if you want. After that, you all suit up again and go down as a foursome. How's that sound? This time I'll stay up here, and one of you will wear my radio mask, Ok?'

All four nodded enthusiastically and they chattered excitedly as they helped themselves to the sandwiches, biscuits and drinks.

When the break was over the two girls stripped off their wet suits then went below. Dennis and Adam also stripped off their wet suits and went over the side, swimming and frolicking in the slight swell while Alex stood on the roof of the main cabin keeping watch. The two girls emerged clad in tiny bikini swim suits. They were greeted by wolf whistles from the boys and both smiled shyly as they pretended not to hear. Julie climbed up to the roof with Alex and checked with him about diving from there. He nodded approval and she leapt high in the air, performing a perfect somersault before gliding into the water. The other three all applauded and Alex grinned widely. Bec simply dove from the side of the boat and joined her colleagues.

Alex allowed the four students to enjoy themselves for another twenty minutes before calling them back into the boat. When they were all back on board, Alex told them to don their wetsuits and check their equipment and tanks.

'We need to complete this exercise before that swell gets any rougher,' he said.

After the students had checked their gear then the gear of each other, Alex went from one to the other, to assure himself they were safe and ready. Then he addressed them.

'Ok, you all look fine. Now, when I went down the last time with Den and Bec, I took four items with me. They are plastic discs, with a lead washer glued to the back of them. That stops them floating back up, you see. They are different colours and I want you to retrieve one each. Bec, you find the green one. Julie, you want the red one. Dennis, you're on blue and Adam, you're yellow. You also take the radio mask, Adam. If you find one that isn't your colour, leave where it is and keep looking for your own, ok? And don't rush back to the surface with your find. You wait down there until you are all ready, then resurface properly at the correct rate. Any questions?'

There were none, so he indicated them to take up diving positions on the side of the boat. He nodded and one by one the four dropped backwards into the sea.

As soon as Adam had conducted his radio test, they disappeared underwater.

After noting the four streams of bubbles rising satisfactorily, Alex sat at the Captain's Chair and thought. He had noticed the traces of a pair of wet footprints at the engine room door, and wondered who had been prying around his boat. The engine room held more than the twin diesels and fuel tanks. A hidden floor safe was bolted in under the large tool box. The safe contained around twenty thousand dollars in cash, an automatic pistol and a waterproof folder which held his military service record, qualifications portfolio, citations and awards as well as his discharge papers. It also held a small rack of files which Alex wished to remain secret. Deciding he needed to check things, he rose from the chair and quickly went below. Once inside the engine room, he checked the contents of the shelf and knew instantly they had been disturbed. There were three identical folders on the shelf and he realised they had been hastily re-arranged. He placed the folders in the file rack, and lowered it into the hidden safe. When the toolbox was back in its place he returned to the deck, just in time to see the streams of bubbles breaking the surface, indicating the students were ascending. When all four were back on board and stripped of their diving equipment, and handed him their coloured discs, Alex spoke.

'Well that's it, people. You have achieved all of your tasks and completed the assignments beautifully. I'm very happy with you all. Next week is your final tests, which will be done by Colin Watkins, from Gosford Dive. So, brush up on your theory and practice your donning and shedding techniques and you'll be right. Before we head back in, are there any questions?'

Everyone had some comments but no questions, so Alex raised the anchor and started the diesels. The four students chattered to each other as the launch swung around and accelerated towards the distant shore.

CHAPTER FIVE

∞

Mike Walker mumbled and rolled back onto his right side. His wife giggled to herself and shook his shoulder more vigorously. She said loudly directly into his left ear,

'Come on, you lazy slug. Get up, you log. Magistrate Sloppy Jaws wants to see you. Come on Mike, wake up.'

He stirred again and opened his eyes. When he saw Carmen he smiled and sat up.

'What time is it, Sexy? It had better not be before nine, or you'll get a spanking.'

She picked up a pillow and swatted his head with it. Pretending sternness she said,

'Oh, yeah? You and what army, Sleepy-head? It's five past nine and time for you to get up. You don't want to be late for court, now, do you?' she said.

He reluctantly rose from the bed and made for the en-suite bathroom. Carmen straightened the bed and returned to the kitchen to prepare a snack and a pot of tea.

Mike showered, shaved then dressed in a clean suit. Tea and a sandwich was waiting for him when he descended the stairs and joined Carmen in the kitchen.

'You thinking the case will go all right, Mikey?' she asked.

'Yeah, should do. We caught the buggers red handed with the stolen truck full of the stolen cigarettes. And the blokes from Sydney that we'd been tipped off about showed up right on cue with a roll of notes that would choke a bloody draught horse. They aren't saying anything at this stage and 'Slimy' Dutton is their mouthpiece but Johnno reckons we should be able to stop the main three from getting bail. It should go our way but you never really know with old 'Sloppy Jaws'. We'll do our best. Right, I better go.'

Mikes first task was to collect Sergeant Johnson from his house in East Wagga. The senior detective was waiting for him, sitting on his front verandah reading the local newspaper. He stood and folded the paper as the unmarked police car turned into his driveway. After picking up his brief case he entered the car, greeting Mike cheerfully.

' 'morning young Mikey. Get some sleep, did ya?'

'Yeah, I grabbed a few hours. How about you? Manage any?' Mike replied as he reversed the car out carefully onto busy Lake Albert Road.

'No, didn't bother about snoozing'. I'll catch up tonight. Have you gone over your statement this morning. Old 'Sloppy' was in a shitty mood yesterday, they reckon. I hope the old bastard's in a better frame of mind today. Still, we caught Monk and his mates dead to rights last night, so the prosecutor should make easy going of it. We're not going to oppose bail for Spano and Dixon. They're both guilty as sin, but they're also small fry. Monk and his two buyers are the real fish. We're gunna ask for those three to be held on remand and see if we can get three weeks for 'em in the metro remand centre. That'll give us enough time to cross all the 'T s' and dot all the 'I s', I reckon. It was a good result. We got the truck and all the booty, as well as the crooks. The only thing I'm shitty about is Monk didn't resist. I was looking forward to that.'

Walker grinned as he steered the Holden along the road, heading for the Police Station. Johnson was totally 'Old School' when it came to dealing with career criminals, and believed a bit of roughing up was a good way to show them who was in charge. More than once in his thirty year career Johnson had had to answer complaints regarding his tactics, but so far he had emerged unscathed. Mike was sometimes uncomfortable with his superior's methods, but he also admired the crusty old Detective and marvelled at the long list of clear-ups to his credit. The younger man was determined to keep his hands to himself as much as possible, but acknowledged the fact that he was learning a great deal from Johnson.

The twelve high backed chairs arranged around the huge mahogany table were ornately carved and upholstered with highly polished red English leather. Each chair was overstuffed with wadding and horse hair but, despite their hardness, was surprisingly comfortable. They matched the table perfectly, and blended with the polished timber shelves and cabinets which completed the room's décor.

Eleven of the chairs were occupied, with the lone vacant one holding several cardboard files. At the head of the table a large, plump man read a three-page report as he puffed on a Dutch clay pipe. Most of the other men seated around the table were also smoking, some with cigars, two more pipes and the three at the bottom of the table made do with cigarettes. A small, older man wearing a light blue safari suit was seated next to the vacant seat, and was the only person not smoking. He looked scornfully at the gradually descending smoke cloud and covered his nose with a silk handkerchief. A white straw hat sat on the files next to him. He let his vision drift around the circle of men at the table, noting they were all studying copies of the same report as the pipe smoker at the head of the table. As his eyes fell upon each man, he thought of their occupations and high positions in society. The state Police Commissioner sat directly opposite the old man, his much adorned uniform barely discernable through the smoke. Next to the Commissioner was the state's justice minister, then a senior magistrate. The pipe smoker at the head of the table was a district court judge, and on his right sat the current state Deputy Leader of the Opposition. Down the bottom end of the table the three cigarette smokers were the chief executives of the state's two leading banks, and the country's richest property developer. Then came the newly appointed Deputy Commissioner of Police and, completing the circle, the chief of the state's prison system on the old man's right.

"A veritable bevy of Upstanding and Outstanding Citizens," the old man thought.

"Doing their best to right the wrongs of our useless bloody courts. And bigger crims than the bastards they sit in judgement of. Bloody hypocrites all, God bless 'em'."

He left himself out of this character analysis, reminding himself he was merely an employee of this bunch. Doing their bidding, arranging their 'Operations', carrying out any necessary research and observing the actual tasks where possible, that was his role. And at ten thousand dollars per month, his troubled conscience soon cleared.

This esteemed gathering of high powered executives referred to themselves as 'The Retribution Committee' and the little old man had chosen the title of 'Commander'.

The group had formed after several of the state's most notorious criminals had miraculously been acquitted, either by missing evidence, tiny points of law, or sometimes blatant lies and perjury. The self-imposed charter of the Retribution Committee was simply to eliminate these criminals without fanfare or ceremony, making society a better place, in their collective opinion. To date they had accounted for half a dozen of these rogues, as well as a few smaller operations where mere warnings were needed or less tougher action was warranted. The Commander had recruited just the right operative with just the right method of dealing with the villains, and he was meticulous in the planning and execution of the operations. So far not one cause of death had been determined by the greatest scientific minds and best medical science at the state's disposal. Every case remained open and unsolved, but, due to the character of the victims, no-one seemed to bother a great deal either. And not one case had drawn much more than lip service from the media.

It was only when a couple of Police Detectives had noticed the pattern and started to pry that drastic action had had to be taken. When the Police Commissioner had reported to the group that a pair of his men were digging into the unsolved cases, despite heavy warnings to desist, that the regrettable decision was taken by The Retribution Committee to eliminate the senior one, relocate the Operatives, and hope the junior Detective accepted the warning. A 'Secondary' Operative had been used to facilitate the elimination of Detective Chief Inspector Muscatt, and some subtle modifications had been made to his unmarked Police vehicle. It was unfortunate that Muscatt's wife had also perished in the firey car crash, but the 'Force' considered this no more than collateral damage. And it seemed that dramatic occurrence had had the desired effect on the junior Detective, as he had kept a low profile ever since the 'accident' and, according to all reports, was progressing nicely as a good country police officer.

The report which the gathering were now reading was of the latest operation.

A rather troublesome Private Investigator had made a nuisance of himself, probing the unsolved cases. He seemed particularly fond of hanging around Glebe Coroner's Court, were it was apparent he had several contacts. Albert Tuckey was well known to each and every member of the 'Force' and it caused some concern when his activities first came to their attention. Who had hired him, or encouraged him, was not known, and considered unimportant. The Commander told them he was fairly certain a particular flashy lawyer had engaged Tuckey, but he was confident he would back down if and when Tuckey met his fate. It was quickly decided that Mister Tuckey would be the subject of the Forces' next operation, and who-ever had caused him to take an interest in the departed criminals demises, would soon think better of it.

The report detailed Tuckey's departure from this earth, with some points supplied by The Commander, and some from his operative. A photocopy of a newspaper item carrying all the grim details of the unfortunate occurrence formed the third page of the report they were now all studying. The reporter told how 'well known Sydney underworld figure Albert Tuckey' had obviously fallen asleep behind the wheel of his expensive Jaguar saloon and had driven through an active railway crossing just as a high speed super freighter train was speeding through. An accompanying photograph showed the car wreckage, the largest piece being around the size of an ordinary wheelbarrow. The head of the gathering said as he laid the report down.

'Well, how sad ! Looks like it was a nice Jag, that one.'

The rest had also finished reading and placed their copies on the table. Most chuckled at the head man's comment. Albert Tuckey had few friends in life, and none at all in this room. The head man turned his attention to the Commander.

'How are things with your people, Commander? Settled into their new life and location? I assume the fee for Tuckey's job has been forwarded.'

The little old man stood and said softly,

'They are settled in just fine, thank you, Sir. The last operation was carried out by them without a hitch, so I think we can assume it is business as usual from now on. They used a motorcycle I obtained for them, and one of my associates watched them return to the city and replace the bike exactly as I requested. They then changed and left by train for their new home, while my man removed the motorcycle and other equipment they had utilised. A good, clean job all around, I would dare to say. The payment was transferred yesterday. I now have a related matter I wish to table.'

He immediately had the undivided attention of all of the members and they leaned forward so as to not miss a word.

'I bring to your attention the matter of that woman who discovered my operative's modus operandi. On the telephone tapes recorded by Roger's men,' he paused and indicated the Police Commissioner seated opposite him. 'The young detective is clearly heard telling our late friend, Mister Muscatt, all about the methods used and other vital details. Even though Muscatt was regrettably silenced, the information is still out there, waiting for either this woman to reveal all, or to, intentionally or not, let some-one else in on the fact. Perhaps a colleague or some such. I was wondering if any of you think, as I do, we need to deal with this situation in some way?'

He smiled at the circle of grim faced men and resumed his seat.

The discussion started straight away, with widely differing views being shouted across the table and much fist banging and pointing.

Roger Simpson, the Police Commissioner shouted above all the rest.

'That bloody woman you're referring to is the wife of one of my blokes. I can tell the lot of you right now, I am not being party to the whacking of another copper, and that's final. Or his missus, for that matter. I'll risk jail myself to blow the whistle on all of us if you come up with that for a solution. Two innocent people already taken care of is two too many! So think of something else.'

His outburst silenced the rest as they thought over his damming words. Most heads were hung as they recalled the appalling decision they had felt obliged to make six months ago. The slaughtering of a serving Police Officer had not been what any of them had wanted, but eventually it was seen as the only permanent solution.

The little old man stood again, and addressed the meeting.

'Might I be so bold as to suggest we do not have to terminate this detective or his wife. My concern is, are they sufficiently warned off at present? To me, it represents a loose end that needs tying up. I don't like loose ends, and I'm sure none of you do either. My thoughts are, we need to deliver a physical warning, just to re-enforce our earlier actions. Perhaps a minor accident, accompanied by some advice, would suffice. Roger, your connection in Wagga Wagga. Is he still telling you our keen young detective is behaving himself, and not showing too much grief over the Muscatts?'

The Commissioner glared at him for ten seconds before answering.

'Yes, Commander. I am reliably informed he is not only performing his duty above and beyond, but he has shown no interest what-so-ever in events taking place outside of the Wagga Wagga section. That good enough for you?'

The Judge at the head of the table banged his pipe on the arm of his chair, signifying he required the attention of the group.

'Sorry, Roger, but it is not quite good enough. As the Commander says, the information is still out there, and very much represents a loose end. We must address it, no matter how unpalatable it is.'

Again the room was filled with angry arguments and comments as various opinions and insults were hurled across the table. When the pipe was heard tapping again, the room gradually fell silent and they all turned their attention to the Judge.

'Commander,' he began. 'Have your operative organise an injurious, but not fatal accident for Missus Detective, will you?

Nothing too damaging, mind. Just enough to garner a few weeks off work to re-couperate and give them time to accept what we could do anytime we please. And see that Mister Detective is made aware of the reasons for the accident. I think that should do the trick. All right, Roger?'

The Police Commissioner was clearly not pleased, but eventually his shoulders slumped and he reluctantly nodded.

The charged atmosphere of the room abated noticeably and some members relaxed.'Ok, that is settled,' the Judge stated. 'As usual, we leave it to you, Commander. Has anyone got anything else? Merv, you mentioned earlier you had something.'

All eyes swung to the Chief Prison Officer, who coughed self-consciously and stood.

Mervyn Walter Harris had risen through all the ranks of a prison officer, starting in nineteen fifty-one. He had served in prisons all over the state, gaining experience with all types of criminals and misfits, from junior offenders right through to multiple murderers. He had enrolled in every available course the service offered, and put himself through University part time and now held three different University degrees, including a Masters' Degree in Public Service Administration. He had applied for the vacant Chief Officers position as soon as he reached Superintendent level. His appointment followed soon after, leaving thirty-two more senior officers to seethe in frustrated anger. This did not bother the ambitious Merv Harris at all. When the Retribution Committee decided to invite him to join their ranks, he was quick to accept.

So far, his input had been limited to offering opinions on some habits of selected targets, and contributing his monthly fees, which were diverted from Corrections Department Administration funds.

Now, though, he had a real operation to put forward.

'Most of you would know one of my current guests, a Mister Luigi Alphonse Magetti. Well, for those who don't know, Magetti is to be released tomorrow morning, from Parramatta, at eight o'clock. This delightful immigrant has served only eleven months of a double life sentence, after being convicted of the murders of two innocent teenagers. To refresh your memories, Magetti and three of his dago cronies were cruising around La Peruse one dark winter's night about two years ago. They were waiting for a cargo ship to enter Port Botany and a crew member was supposed to toss a water-proof bag overboard, presumably stuffed with bloody heroin. One of Magetti's mates, a Juliano Culissio, was all suited up in S.C.U.B.A. gear, apparently ready to retrieve the goods. Anyway, the ship was delayed for sixteen hours at sea when the rudder or something broke, so this car load of grease was at a loose end. They came up on a Volkswagen Kombi van, parked under a big tree at the end of Anzac Parade. They decided to investigate, so Magetti and another crook, Angelo Mossi, snuck up and peeked in. A young school student from Kogarah, John Taber, was busy bonking the backside off his girlfriend, a Miss Susan McKenzie, from Maroubra. To cut a long story short, Magetti and Mossi reefed open the side door and pointed knives at the previously busy young couple. Mossi tied young Taber's hands while Magetti held a knife to Susan McKenzie's throat. He then dropped his trousers and told the girl she was going to satisfy him, then Mossi, and he'd let them go. As soon as he made a move towards the girl, young Taber, who was a Karate student, kicked Mossi in the balls, and then threw another kick at Magetti. While Mossi was rolling around in agony, Magetti plunged his knife into Tabers right eye, then pulled it out and stuck it into his chest. The Police doctor reckoned Taber was dead at that time. The girl started screaming then, so Magetti knifed her in the belly, then slashed her throat and ran. He left his wounded mate, Mossi, on the ground, and made it back to his car. The three of them pissed off out of the area, and when the first Police car arrived, after neighbours reported the screaming, the cops found both teenagers dead and Mossi lying beside the Kombi, unable to even sit up after young Taber had re-arranged his knackers for him. He was taken to hospital, then to Maroubra Cop Shop. He refused to co-operate with Police, and spent four months on remand after being hit with a total of six charges, including double murder. The slimy rat eventually opened up, and done a deal with Homicide. In return for dropping the two murders, he told them the whole story, from the aborted drug pick-up, to them finding the Kombi, and finally to Magetti's sexual intentions and subsequent knifings. Even though he was rolling around in agony, he still witnessed the two stabbings and the girl screaming. But when detectives went to Magetti's known haunts, he was nowhere to be seen. He and Culissio had shot through back to Italy. It took Interpol around another year to grab the pair of them, but Culissio had contracted some form of cancer, and died in police cells in Milano. Eventually Magetti was dragged back here, faced court and copped two life sentences. Then Mossi, currently serving three years and six months for his part in the rotten scheme, suddenly confesses that it was he, not Magetti, who killed those two kids. He has been diagnosed with terminal cancer of the lungs and throat, and the docs reckon two months will see him out. In the meantime, his lawyers contacted the Attorney General, the Police Prosecutions Branch and, of course, most of the mainstream media, with his bullshit confession. We think Magetti has promised Mossi that he'll take care of his wife and five kids. It's well known the Magetti family are loaded, and Mossi has got bugger all. His family are living off welfare and stay in a converted shed on the Magetti farm at Moss Vale. Ok, that's the saga of the soon-to-be-released Luigi Magetti. He has, as I'm sure you know, been sending letters and tapes to the papers, radio stations, television stations and even to his local state member. He proclaims his innocence, scoffs at suggestions he has organised the Mossi confession and now is giving it to the Police, big time. But, most of all, the prison grapevine says he is going to organise the sudden deaths of the three detectives who put him away, plus four of my senior Prison Officers, me, and the old couple who called Police on the night of the killings. With all that in mind, I would like to suggest Mister Magetti be considered as our next client. I can't think of a better reward for him.'

Harris sat down and allowed each member his private thoughts.

As usual, it was the Judge at the head of the table who spoke first.

'I am fully aware of the Magetti story. Thanks for the update, Merv. My feeling is we should do this, and do it quick. Within a week of the mongrel's release, I'd say.'

There were cries of 'hear hear' around the room, and the Police Commissioner summed up the mood of the group when he said loudly,

'Absolutely must do. We can't have scum like this roaming the streets. I say we do it, and soon. I'll find out who three 'D's are, and have them attend a course in Tasmania or somewhere. And there will be a twenty-four hour a day Police presence at the house of that old couple. Merv, what about you and your boys? You and them need Police protection? Just say the word.'

Harris smiled and shook his head.

'We'll be right, thanks Rog. We've already organised our own protection roster. So, Gentlemen. Are we agreed? Commander? Do-able, yes?'

The little old man nodded and held out his hand for the folder Harris had read from.

The folder contained all the facts needed, including photographs, the addresses of Magetti's farm and his two apartments, plus the registration and descriptions of the four cars and three trucks currently owned by the Magetti family company.

'After my usual feasibility study, I will set up a plan and notify the Operatives of the two jobs we have allocated them.'

'Good, good. That's settled,' said the head man. 'Other than subs, any other business, Gents? I'd like to get home tonight, so let's have it. Here's mine.'

He threw a stuffed envelope onto the table. The others all did likewise and the Senior Magistrate placed them in his lockable brief case. He smiled at the group as he clicked the locks shut.

'I won't bother counting it. I know you are all honest and honourable men.'

The room was filled with laughter and giggling. The head man rose and wheeled an ornate drinks trolley to the table. It had bottles of whisky, rum, vodka, brandy and wine crowded onto the top shelf. On the second shelf, there was dry ginger ale, water, a soda syphon, lemonade and two ice buckets. Each man helped himself to a stiff alcoholic drink, except the Commander.

He settled for a small lemonade, with just one ice cube.

When his drink was finished, he gathered up the two deadly folders and his white straw hat. He smiled at a few of the men, then said, in his soft voice,

'Gentlemen. I shall see thee all anon.'

It was his usual departure saying, and the group raised their glasses toward him as he left the room, quietly closing the huge teak door behind him.

Outside, a pale green Holden sedan was parked under the shade of a cedar tree, across the road from the District Court buildings. The Commander eased himself into the back seat as the driver started the engine.

'Home, Sir?' he asked his passenger. The Commander sighed and said softly,

'Yes, Harold, straight home. I have a job of work to do. Two, in fact.'

CHAPTER SIX

Sergeant Lindsay Johnson grinned across at Mike as the three criminals were escorted from the court room, each one handcuffed to a burly Prison Officer. A senior Prison Officer led the way through a side door which opened to reveal a narrow passage. This was the direct route to a pair of holding cells, which in turn opened to a small loading dock. A plain white prison truck was backed up to the dock, and a Prison Officer was hosing out the prisoner accommodation cages inside. The line of prisoners and their escorts shuffled past and into the holding cells. Monk was shoved into one cell and his two Sydney based counterparts were pushed into the other. The handcuffs were removed and as his guard was leaving, Monk called to the senior officer,

'Hey! General! How about something to eat and a drink? We been locked up like animals since eight this morning. It must be at least morning tea time, if not lunch.'

The senior Prison Officer turned and looked disdainfully at Monk.

'General? What's this "General" business, Shit-head? You call me "Sir" and nothing else. And you'll get a feed when I say so. If you shut your gob, I just might consider it. Otherwise, sit there and keep quiet.'

He leaned sideways and addressed the other two prisoners. 'You keep quiet as well and we might give you something to eat and drink. You're not going anywhere until at least four o'clock when court finishes, because we may have some travelling companions for you.'

There was no answer from any of the three criminals who had just been remanded in custody by the court. The prison truck and the crew of five would transport them, and possibly others, to various jails around Sydney this afternoon. It meant a long night ahead for all but the officers did not mind. They were on double wages for overtime.

Johnson, Sergeant Mashman and Mike all walked from the court and stood outside in a tight circle. Johnson and Mashman lit cigarettes before Mashman said,

'Well, that bit was easy, Lindsay. A three week remand should give you all the time you need to prepare. I reckon Monk and Childs will be looking at six or seven years, with that other creep, De-Hern good for at least a couple. What are ya gunna do about Spano and Dixon, Mate?'

Johnson drew deeply on his smoke and shrugged.

'They're both small fry, really. Spano is gunna give evidence against the big three, and Dixon is so bloody scared he'll say anything I tell him to. I'm gunna suggest they get orf with bonds, and plus I'll have a cosy little private talk with the pair of 'em.'

Mike Walker and Sergeant Mashman knew that meant both petty criminals would probably end up with good behaviour bonds and a thick, swollen ear each. Mike was philosophical about Johnson's methods. He knew nothing he could say would alter the tough old sergeant, and he also knew Spano and Dixon would probably stay out of crime for a good while after their cosy little private talk with Johnson. Despite this, he would do all he could not to be present when Johnson administered his own brand of justice. He happily left the violence to the Sergeant unless absolutely necessary.

Mashman left for his residence soon after and Walker accompanied Johnson to their office, located on the top floor of Wagga Wagga Police Station. As they reached the bottom of the stairs, Johnson said,

'You go on up, Mikey. See if Sandra has typed up those crime reports an' statements for us, will ya? Then get on the big computer and start gathering the financial information on Childs and De-Hern. I already done Monk, so I know where his bank accounts are. I wanta know where Childs got that four and a half grand from. I bet the idiot drew it outta one of his own accounts. While you're doing that I'm going in to see George and get his fingerprint summary. Masho said he got all the prints we'll need orf the truck, the smokes and even the 'air con' ducts that the fools removed to get in. It looks like Spano and Dixon were too stupid to wear gloves at all, and Monk forgot to put his on when they met up with Childs and De-Hern. That should add a little spice to our evidence, eh, Mate?'

Walker smiled and nodded his acceptance. He ascended the outside fire escape stairs and entered the air-conditioned Detective's Office. The only person present was the civilian typist, busy tapping at her electric typewriter. She looked up as he asked,

'Hey, Sandy, you wouldn't have done those reports and statements, by any chance?'

'This is them now, Mike. I'm nearly finished. How did court go?' she replied.

'Oh, pretty good. We got a remand on those three, and Johnno put a good word in for Spano, Old "Sloppy Jaws" seemed to like what he heard from our prosecutor.'

He walked toward his desk as he spoke, then noticed a fresh Crime Bulletin in the tray of the teleprinter. He took the four-page bulletin to his desk and sat down to read.

The first item jumped out at him and caused a shudder to run through his body.

'Underworld Figure and suspected 'Stand-Over' man Albert Leslie Tuckey dead in mysterious circumstances.'

The article went on for three paragraphs, referring to Tuckey as "One-time Private Investigator" and "Door Keeper". The text stated he had apparently suffered an unknown medical condition and drove his car into the path of a speeding goods train at a level crossing just west of Lithgow. Mike read every detail of the first two paragraphs before his eyes fell upon the last sentences of the final stanza.

"Although the body suffered severe trauma and injury in the collision, the Forensic Examiner claimed the vital organs, including the heart, appeared healthy with no sign of infarction. Tissue samples suggest all organs were functioning normally premortem. Investigations are continuing under the leadership of Detective Inspector Newton, Western Regional Homicide".

Mike felt his stomach muscles tighten and he gripped the paper fiercely. The description of the demise of Tuckey was all too familiar. It was almost identical to several killings of underworld figures he had been studying months earlier. His friend, Detective Inspector Allan Muscatt had joined with him as they had probed these deaths, and they all had the same hallmarks as this one. Then he and Muscatt had been warned off, with no doubts they were dealing with a superior power. Walker had thought hard before deciding to drop the matter, but Muscatt insisted on continuing. Then Muscatt and his wife, Heather were killed in a firey vehicle crash. Mike suspected it was organised by the same persons who periodically removed the criminals. There had been enough clues for Mike to know something just did not sit right about the deaths of the Muscatts, and he had had no doubts who-ever was behind it would not hesitate to add Mike and probably Carmen to their list of victims.

Since these occurrences, Walker had kept his head down and worked hard to become a competent Detective, under the rough guidance of Sergeant Lindsay Johnson.

Even at home he and Carmen had only discussed the Muscatts and the Keyes briefly before agreeing to avoid the subject as much as possible.

Despite convincing himself he had made the correct decision, and thereby ensuring his own and Carmen's safety, the entire matter filled Mike with a sense of self-loathing. He had never backed down from any type of conflict, but these unseen brokers of death obviously had far reaching powers, and it scared him. He tried hard to reconcile his feelings of cowardice with the knowledge that he and Carmen would probably grow old together.

This fresh Crime Bulletin brought the memories roaring back, shaking his inner being, as well as pricking his conscience. He had felt from the outset a huge degree of guilt over the deaths of Muscatt and his wife. The mysterious disappearance of the Keyes from their farm had added to his misery, but the cryptic warnings had been sufficiently graphic for Walker to realise he was exposing himself and Carmen to a power he could not master. He forced himself to be comfortable with his decision to drop his clandestine investigation and concentrate of perfecting his craft as an investigator and Detective.

Now, as if to torment him and draw him in again, the detailed description of Tuckey's demise and the un-explained aspects of the death attached themselves to his mind.

He quietly walked to the photocopier and made a copy of the bulletin. He had just replaced the original in the teleprinter tray when Johnson entered the office. He appeared not to notice Mike's actions and instead spoke to Sandra.

'G'day, Beautiful. Got our reports 'n' statements done yet, Love?'

Sandra's lips tightened and she glared up at the towering figure of Johnson.

'They are just finished, Sergeant. And I have told you before, please call me Sandra or Miss Greene. I am not your beautiful anything and I am certainly not your love.'

Johnson was totally unmoved, as usual, and grinned widely down at the woman as he took the completed documents from her hand.

'Aw, don't be like that, Beautiful. Be nice and I'll take you out someday. Thanks for this, Sweety.'

The woman ignored him and inserted more paper into her machine, before commencing another typing task.

The exchange between Sandra and Johnson allowed Mike to slip the copied bulletin into his shirt pocket unnoticed. He heard Johnson chuckle and then his bulky figure appeared beside him.

'Righto, Young Mikey. Let's go through these and make sure we're singing from the same page. I didn't have me watch on during the arrests, so I put the same times down as you and Masho did. When you 'cuffed Spano, you cautioned him, didn't ya?'

'Ah, what? Caution? Oh, shit yeah. I sure did, and then I heard you caution the four of them together. Plus we cautioned them again back here. That's what it says in the arrest reports. Even Masho and Woody have mentioned cautions in their reports.'

Johnson eased himself into his chair and began reading through the statements. Mike went to the computer room and used his special key to enter. The large computer sat on two tables, two tiny red lights blinking in unison at him. He pushed the Activate switch and immediately the red lights were extinguished, to be replaced by two pale yellow ones. The machine gave out a whirring sound as it powered up and when the yellow lights turned to green, he switched on the television style monitor.

Mike entered his personal code words via a keyboard, which was attached to the main computer by three thick cables. The monitor's screen lit up and soon the word 'MENU' appeared in the middle of the picture. Before moving the electronic pointer to the menu, he returned to the door and looked into the main office.

Johnson had his back to Mike and was still perusing the typed documents. Sandra was focused on her typewriter and continued tapping her keys. As neither showed any sign of interest toward him, Mike quietly closed the door and sat down at the computer.

He withdrew the photocopy of the crime bulletin and re-read the details of Albert Tuckey's death. He shook noticeably as he read the details of the medical examination of the body, which told him all bodily organs were healthy, blood samples taken showed no illnesses or diseases, and the numerous skin tissue samples indicated a very healthy specimen. He circled some of the facts, before returning the papers to his shirt pocket and sat thinking for a short time, staring at the monitor's screen.

The computer had only been installed for around eight months. It was top secret and only the station's eight Detectives, the section's Superintendent and three Inspectors had access to it.

The machine had been developed and supplied by the American F.B.I. and was one of only ten in the country. New South Wales Police owned five of them, and Wagga Wagga Section was considered fortunate to receive this one. It's main attribute was that it was linked to every bank, building society, loan company and credit union in the country. By entering the targets full name, gender, date of birth, and any other known identifying facts, the operator could read details of all accounts held by any of the financial institutions in that particular name.

It was during his instructional course on this computer that Mike had stumbled upon some disturbing facts regarding his best friend, Andy Keyes. Keyes and his Malaysian wife Anita, had always given the impression of struggling farmers. They toiled day in and day out on their little farm at The Rock, around thirty kilometres from Wagga. Whilst practicing the correct procedures on the computer, Mike had entered Andy's name and details, only to be shocked when several different accounts were revealed containing hundreds of thousands of dollars collectively. When he probed deeper, he found semi-regular deposits into one particular account, and the dates corresponded to the occurrences of the mysterious deaths of the state's most notorious criminals. The discovery of his friends' hidden wealth and the regular deposits led Mike to investigate other aspects of Andy and Anita's circumstances. As captain of their cricket team, Mike had had to find a replacement for Andy on occasions when Keyes had told him he would be unavailable for certain matches. The supposed business trips had aligned with the un-explained deaths of the criminals. When Mike put all the facts together he knew his suspicions could easily be confirmed by confronting Keyes.

The only unknown component was the mysterious way the criminals had died. Doctors, scientists, toxicologists and other experts had been unable to detect the causes of the deaths, but they all agreed the victims' organs were all functioning normally until suddenly shutting down.

Mikes wife Carmen lectured at the university, and her speciality was forensics and applied science. When he eventually discussed his suspicions and findings with her, Carmen had recalled reading an account of a super-toxic beetle which was found in only one region of the world. After much painstaking research, Carmen had identified the deadly beetle, and the potent venom which was held in tiny sacs attached to their front legs. The study by a group of French scientists during the nineteen-thirties had revealed one microscopic drop of the venom could kill a fully grown human in less than two seconds, and leave no known symptoms of its existence. The body's entire lymph system and all internal organs were immediately paralysed, causing instant death. The existence of the beetles and their lethal secret was known only to a select few members of the scientific world, and to a small tribe of Malaysians. This tribe inhabited the tiny area called The Royal Province of Manitra, in the country's far north. It was this fact, when revealed by Carmen's research, which convinced Mike that his best friend Andy, and Andy's Malaysian wife Anita, might be guilty of carrying out the multiple murders of the famous criminals.

Anita came from the small Royal Province and Mike recalled both she and Andy were ex commandos and trained killers.

After the tragic deaths of Detective Inspector Allan Muscatt and his wife Heather in a suspicious car crash, Mike had decided it was time to confront the Keye's at their farm out near The Rock.

Accompanied by Carmen, Mike had driven to the farm, only to find the entire property deserted and the homestead completely empty. All livestock had been removed and the farm's egg laying fowls and a pair of turkeys were slaughtered and left in a decomposing pile at the end of the bird enclosure. After a thorough search of the house and outbuildings, Mike had found Andy's beloved cricket bag in the cargo area of his old utility truck parked in the machinery shed. He had looked through the gear bag and stumbled upon Andy's new, and as yet, unused cricket bat. Taped to the blade was a small envelope which contained a cryptic note. It partially explained to Mike that he was correct in his assumptions about the Keyes' and that he and Carmen would be safe enough if he, Mike, dropped the matter completely. The note suggested he concentrate his efforts on being a good Detective, forget about trying to solve the mysterious deaths, and to forgo any attempts to locate the Keyes.

Mike had thought the matter through and realised he was way out of his depth, but also, he and Muscatt had obviously come close to revealing some truths, and his worst suspicions were likely to be correct. If two Detectives such as Muscatt and Mike Walker could get as close as they did, then who-ever was organising the hits must surely realise their time was nearly at an end. The only firm conclusions which the two had arrived at was the mysterious organisation reached high up into the upper echelons of the Judicial system and the state Police Force.

With the disappearance of Andy and Anita, Mike had thought the secret executions would cease. Now he had in his shirt pocket evidence that the secret group of self-appointed vigilantes was not only still in existence, but continuing their activities.

That also meant Andy and Anita Keyes were alive and well, probably living in another part of the state and collecting the huge payments just as before.

Mike checked the main office again and saw Sandra still working away at her typing and Sergeant Johnson engrossed in proof reading the reports and statements.

He moved the computers pointer to the enquiry box and entered Andrew Keyes.

After nearly ten seconds the result popped into view. No Match Found he read.

Mike entered Anita Keyes and waited for the machine to conduct the search.

No Match Found appeared again. He withdrew his private notebook from his coat and looked up Andy and Anita's birth dates. He had noted these when the two couples first became close, as he and Carmen, neither having any living relatives, liked to recall special friends birthdays. He added this data to the two names and was quickly advised No Match found. Mike hurriedly wrote the results next to both names.

"Ok," he thought to himself as he returned the notebook to his shirt pocket. "So, their masters have even twigged to this aspect."

Realising this method was now useless to him, Mike entered the full name and date of birth for Childs, then the same for De-Hern. He noted down several accounts in Childs name, with a combined total of ninety-three thousand dollars. One account, held in a Marrickville branch of a nationwide bank, showed a cash withdrawal of four thousand eight hundred dollars, dated the day of the planned purchase of the stolen cigarettes and the Ford Transit truck.

De-Hern held only one account, at the same bank, with a credit balance of two thousand and six dollars.

He copied these facts neatly onto a blank statement form and switched off the computer. Just as Mike was closing the computer room door, Johnsons desk telephone jangled. The big Sergeant put down the reports and picked up the telephone.

'Yeah? Sergeant Johnson,' he growled into the mouthpiece. As he listened he waved a furious hand to Mike, indicating for him to approach.

'Right-o. Nope ! Just me an' Mike. Where is this? Right, got ya. We're on our way!'

He slammed the telephone down and reached for his suit coat.

'C'mon Mikey. An "All cars" to the "Great Eastern". Attempted Malicious Damages which has turned into a brawl. She's a signal-one job. Got ya gear, haven't ya?'

As they quickly descended the outside stairs, Mike felt for his gun and handcuffs in their respective holsters. He withdrew the car keys from his shirt pocket and ran to their car.

Johnson was already at the passenger's door, a look of anticipation on his craggy face. As Mike opened his door and sat behind the wheel, he heard the big Sergeant say,

'C'mon Mikey. It'll be all over by the time we get there. C'mon, let's go.'

Mike reached across the car and unlocked Johnsons door. As he started the engine he saw Johnson hurriedly clip his seat belt on and then open the glove box. As the car turned out of the car park and into Tarcutta Street, Mike noticed Johnson holding two short rubber batons which he had obtained from the glove box. He glanced across and noted the excited smile on Johnson's face, knowing from past experience that Detective Sergeant Lindsay Johnson liked nothing more than getting to grips physically with law breakers and hell raisers. The old cop had been a state champion wrestler in his twenties, a more than handy front row forward in a local Rugby League team, and an accomplished boxer within the Police Sports Organisation. Despite his age and the heavy drinking and smoking, Lindsay Johnson still possessed great physical strength and a well-deserved reputation for fearlessness. The possibility of an all-in brawl against a group of would-be villains was Heaven sent to him.

With siren wailing and the grille mounted blue strobe lights flashing, Mike's car sped to the end of Tarcutta Street and lurched violently as he turned right onto Edward Street. Ahead they could see several Police vehicles already scattered around the entrance to the Great Eastern Hotel, and a swarm of humanity gathered on the footpath and the roadway. Mike had barely brought the Holden to a stop when Sergeant Johnson flung open his door and leaped out, baton in hand, and hurried towards the melee.

CHAPTER SEVEN

The Stein family tradition of Sunday lunch together could be traced back to the late nineteen sixties. Old Rupert Stein had watched his six children grow into adulthood, and lamented as most of them married and moved out of the family home. He and Madeline, his loyal wife of fifty-three years had requested the four boys and two daughters to reside as near as possible to them, close to the growing town of Toukley.

Two of the boys had easily complied, and the daughters had set up house within five kilometres of the Stein waterfront home in Peel Street. The youngest member of the clan, twenty-year-old Dennis, still lived in his parent's home as he worked his way through a four year apprenticeship as a motor mechanic. Only Mark, the second eldest, had been unable to live locally. His career as an investigative journalist with a leading Sydney newspaper, necessitated he reside in the city, close to the action and drama which fueled his everyday existence.

Despite his city living, Mark managed to make the journey to Toukley most Sundays, and it was a rare Sabbath when the Stein roll call was not complete. Rupert always sat at the head of the long table, with Madeline at his right. The sons and daughters rotated their positions each Sunday, and the seven grandchildren sat with their respective parents. Dennis usually found himself next to Mark, as the two young men had always enjoyed a close sibling relationship.

This Sunday was rainy and bleak, so the long table was moved from the back patio into the extended rumpus room. As Madeline and her daughters, along with the two daughters-in-law, prepared the food, the five male members of the family sipped cold beer whilst watching over the third generation of Steins.

Mark and Dennis sat apart from the other three, initially discussing football, then women, general sport and finally back to women.

'Still haven't found "Miss Right" yet, Brother?' Dennis asked cheekily.

It was a constant topic between the only two un-married members of the clan. Both had sworn never to marry, much to the amusement of their parents and siblings.

'No way! Anyway, what would I want to tie myself down with one sheila for, when there's a smorgasbord of talent out there? I tell you, mate, there are more gorgeous dames in one city block than there is on the entire central coast. Gorgeous, available and willing, most of 'em. And those that aren't, usually have a sister or friend who is. I mean, why buy a book when you can join the library with hundreds of books? Bugger that getting married stuff. Life's too short.'

Marks new lifestyle in the city had altered his puritanical outlook. His job and his circle of friends brought him into contact with hundreds of different people almost weekly, and he embraced the faster pace of city life with open arms. He rarely brought a female friend to these family luncheons, but on the occasions which he did, the girl was usually stunningly beautiful and either a model, an actress or a glamorous reporter from his newspaper or a television station. And he had never been accompanied by the same girl twice.

'What about you, Den? Anything going on here you want to brag about?'

'I'm still seeing the lovely Linda every now and then. She's that little short-arsed chick I was telling you about before, the one who works across the road from the garage. I'm keen on her but so is just about every other randy bugger on the coast. We go out about every second weekend, but so far I haven't made too much progress, if you get my drift. Oh, and there's a cute red-head I'm doing the dive course with. Her name is Rebecca, but of course we call her 'Bec'. She's a stunner, and friendly as hell. I was starting to chat her up a bit but she didn't seem all that interested. Then a couple of weeks ago she had some car trouble. She's got a little shit box Datsun, and it wouldn't go into gear. 'Super-Den' to the rescue. I drove her home, and got Barry, my mate, to tow her car here. I put a new clutch in it for her, and because I put the parts on the garages account, told her there was no charge. I'll have to pay the fifty odd dollars when the bill comes in, but I reckon it's a worthwhile investment, if she shows the proper amount of appreciation, don't you?'

Dennis was grinning wolfishly as he finished. Mark grinned and slapped him lightly across the back of his head.

'You low life beast! The poor girl will never pay a higher price for car repairs.'

Dennis became serious and made sure no-one else was within earshot.

'That reminds me. I've been wanting to talk to you about something that's been bothering me. When we were out on the dive boat last week, I decided to have a gander at the engines while the owner was under water. While I was sticky-beaking, I accidentally knocked some folders open. They all had stuff about the boat, the engines or S.C.U.B.A. diving in 'em, except one. This other folder had a picture of some big, evil looking bastard, and another photo of the arse end of a new Jag. I don't know why, but I wrote the number plate down. The big bloke in the first photo looked familiar, but I'm buggered if I know where from. The other strange thing is, there was a sheet of paper with some weird words typed on it. I think it said something like, 'Full liquidation and must be complete by 19th December' or something very like that. I have no idea why it's worrying me so much, except this geezer looks so bloody familiar. If I give you the Jags rego number, can you use your copper connections and find out who or what owns it?'

Mark looked at him for a few seconds then shrugged.

'Yeah, I can do that. Give us the number and I'll find out for you tomorrow, probably. Seems strange, but. You worrying about something like this instead of chasing girls.'

'Yeah, I know,' Dennis replied. 'I got no idea why it's hooked me, but it has. Will you call me at work tomorrow, or here?'

'I'll call you here, because I won't be able to talk until about seven tomorrow night. That's if I can get the info you want by then. Depends on which copper I speak to. One or two will do anything for the press, hoping to get their names and pictures in print. Others clam up like a fishes arse and wouldn't tell you the time of your own funeral. Also, I've got a contact in the Main Roads Department. If I strike out with the cops, I'll call her.'

'Her?' Dennis asked. He noted the evil grin on Marks face and nodded knowingly.

'Oh, I get it. "Miss Main Roads Department" is one of the latest conquests, is she?'

Mark simply shrugged and grinned. Dennis took a slip of paper from his shirt pocket and handed it to his brother. Mark read the number written on the paper and slipped the note into his wallet.

Their sister Susan came to the doorway and said loudly,

'Right-o, you hard-working baby sitters. Bring your charges with you, all of you wash your hands and come and eat. Quick and lively or the dogs will get it.'

The five men all rose and ushered the children to the bathroom where they all washed their hands before reporting to the long table and its heavy burden of steaming roast vegetables and baked legs of lamb.

Mike Walker hurriedly yelled an 'On location' call into the radio microphone, then stepped from the car. He saw Sergeant Johnson stride briskly to a corner of the fracas where a uniformed constable was battling three heavily built youths. One youth was holding the policeman in a bear-hug while the other two swung numerous wild punches into his body and head. Johnson raised his rubber truncheon high as he roughly tapped the larger of the two assailants on the shoulder. The man turned in time to receive a heavy blow from the truncheon precisely in the centre of his forehead. As his eyes glazed over Johnson hit him again, but this time the club crashed into his right ear, drawing blood and rendering the thug unconscious. Ignoring the collapsing man, Johnson stepped closer and jabbed his weapon into the ribcage of the second assailant. This man yelped in fright and pain, whirling around to confront the big Detective. Johnson grinned at him as he swung the club in a wide arc, connecting the thug across his left temple. As his victim staggered sideways, Johnson tripped him up and punched him hard in his chest.

The removal of his two attackers allowed the uniformed constable to wriggle free of the third man. Turning to face his enemy, Constable Wayne Burley ripped three quick punches to the man's face, then tackled him to the ground. Johnson watched as Burley hand-cuffed his man, then withdrew his own manacles. He reached down and roughly grasped a wrist of his first victim.

After snapping one cuff on the unconscious man, he attached the other one to the left wrist of the second thug. With his two conquests now locked together, Johnson directed Burley to link his catch to the other pair.

'You'll have no trouble keeping these three mugs under control, Mate. If they try to scarper, just kick the legs out from under one of 'em, and all three'll collapse like a bag o' shit. You ok, by the way? You got a bit of 'claret' leaking from ya snout.'

Mike saw Johnson go to Burley's assistance and knew straightaway his uniformed colleague would be safe. Looking around at the on-going melee, he spied a pair of uniformed officers surrounded by thugs. As he ran to the assistance of the two, the smaller one reeled away, blood pouring from the head. He saw the long blonde hair flaying around and realised it was Constable Wendy Good, a well-liked and trusted female member of Wagga Wagga Foot Patrol, who had been hit on her head by a metal garbage can. With additional anger and outrage rising in him, Mike waded into the circle of assailants. He hit the nearest two with his truncheon, landing telling blows on the back of their heads. Without waiting to see the results of his initial actions, Mike grasped the next attacker by his arm and turned him around. The man faced him, stumbling slightly as he turned. Mike punched him hard, his fist crashing into the nose. Blood sprayed outwards and the man sank to his knees, crying out in pain. Mike kicked him out of his way and tackled another thug to the ground. Two other attackers fell with them and they all wrestled in a tangled mass until three more uniformed policemen joined in.

All the worry and tension of the past, his concern of the mysterious disappearance of his best friends from the farm at The Rock and the tragedy of the loss of Allan Muscatt suddenly found an outlet as Mike waded into the thugs. He found himself face to face with Gerald Braid, a known petty criminal who he and Johnson had questioned the previous week over the cigarette break in. Braid had smirked and refused to answer any questions, constantly baiting Johnson and Walker with snide comments and rude gestures. Now Mike saw his chance to gain some revenge as well as release the stress and tension of the past six months. Braid grabbed Mikes wrist and twisted it cruelly, an evil grin on the big man's face as the truncheon fell to the ground. Ignoring the pain, Mike swung his other fist at Braid, scoring a glancing blow to his sweaty forehead. Realising the danger of a severe injury to his lower arm, Mike rolled with the twist, taking the bigger and stronger man by surprise. This gave Walker a brief advantage and he kicked out with all his strength at Braids legs. The criminal gasped as his legs were knocked out from under him, and Mike wasted no time. He scrambled to his feet, reaching for his handcuffs. Braid was still clutching his knee when his arms were roughly pulled behind him and secured by the hand cuffs.

Panting slightly, Mike looked around to see if any other colleagues were in jeopardy. Wendy Good was under attack by two hoods. One had her arms pinned by her sides and his accomplice was grinning as he tore her uniform blouse from her torso. When her brassier was revealed, the thug hooked his fingers underneath the cups and tugged the undergarment free. He waved the torn brassier high in the air as he and his friend laughed loud. Wendy was kicking at her tormentors, her naked breasts now covered in her own blood from her head wound. Any embarrassment she was feeling was quickly superseded by her anger and self-preservation instincts. The thug who had been holding her arms had released her but had managed to unbutton her pistol holster. The weapon fell free of the pouch and landed on the footpath beside the gutter. The thug gleefully stooped down and retrieved the gun.

Mike observed all of this activity while running to the scene. As he passed the second thug he punched him hard on his right ear. The thug went down in a semi-conscious state and remained prone on the ground.

284

Seeing the second thug picking up Wendy's gun, Mike withdrew his own pistol and shoved the barrel hard up against his forehead.

'Drop it, you maggot, or I'll let some daylight into your worthless brain!'

The man froze, after opening his fingers to allow the gun to drop back to the footpath. His face showed fear and his eyes crossed as he stared down the barrel of Mike's gun.

'I dropped it, Sir,' he screamed. 'Don't shoot, please Sir. I dropped it. I was just picking it up for the lady, honest.'

'On your arse, Dickhead. Now!' Mike yelled at him.

Immediately the thug sat down, still looking fearfully at Mike and his pistol.

Mike straightened, but kept his eyes on the thug.

'Wendy! You ok?' he called to the distraught and dishevelled female constable.

She crossed her arms to cover her naked breasts and moved to his side.

'Yeah, I'm good, Mike. I've lost some blood, but I'll be right. Thanks for your help.'

'Here,' Mike said as he lowered his gun and unbuttoned his shirt. He shook out of the garment and handed it to her. 'Put this on for now.'

She quickly donned the shirt then stooped to collect her pistol. When it was safely restored to the belt holster, she withdrew her own handcuffs and said,

'This creep is mine, ok, Mike?'

Without waiting for his answer, she reached behind the frightened thug and snapped the cuffs on tight.

'Hey, they're too tight, Miss. Can ya loosen 'em orf, please?' he pleaded.

'Get stuffed, Cretin. If I could, I'd put them around your filthy neck. Just sit there and shut up.' Wendy had no sympathy for her attacker.

Around them the riot had all but ceased, with just one or two scuffles continuing.

Mike looked around and saw the publican and one of his barmen wrestling with a young man and Sergeant Johnson was holding a struggling youth while a uniformed Sergeant was attaching handcuffs to the youngster's wrists.

Two Constables took over from the hotel staff and soon this thug was also secured with his arms behind his back in handcuffs.

Inspector Wallace approached Mike and Wendy. His truncheon was hanging from his wrist, secured by a short leather strap. Mike noted the Inspector had some blood splattered on his otherwise immaculate uniform shirt.

'You two all right?' he asked with concern.

'Yes, we're ok, thanks Sir,' Wendy replied. Mike smiled thinly and nodded.

'Good, good. There's an ambulance across the road, Constable. Go and have that head looked at. You're covered in blood. Is it all your own?'

'Yes, Sir. I copped a garbage bin over the head. I'll be all right, Sir.'

He clicked his tongue against his teeth as he examined her head wound.

'I'm sure you will be. But get yourself over to the meat wagon, anyway. Detective Walker, you take her over to the Ambulance. We don't want her collapsing in the middle of the road. And you can re-holster your gun, now. I think the worst is over, don't you?'

Mike looked slightly embarrassed as he replaced the gun into his shoulder holster.

'Oh, yes, sorry Sir. That one has my handcuffs on him, Sir.'

He pointed to the semi-conscious thug still lying prone on the footpath.

'And this one is wearing mine, Sir,' Wendy said as she indicated the cowering man at her feet.

'Right-o. I'll see they are returned to you both in due course. Now, off you go.'

Mike shrugged and took Wendy lightly by the arm.

As they walked through the crowd, the several bystanders parted and allowed them clear access across the road to the waiting ambulance. Mike turned and counted a total of twelve prisoners, all with hands secured behind their backs. Most had bloody wounds of varying degrees and two more ambulance vehicles arrived on the scene.

Mike stayed with Wendy as the paramedics checked her over. They bandaged her head and measured her pulse and temperature. Then the older one said kindly to her,

'We're going to have to take you to the hospital, I'm afraid, Constable. That gash will need at least a dozen stitches, and your right thumb is probably fractured.'

Mike heard Wendy reply, arguing her case not to be transported.

'Hey, you!' he said with fake sternness. 'Stop being a naughty girl and do what the man says. Sit down and behave. I'll tell Wallace what's going on. And I'll organise some clothing for you.'

Two other constables attended the ambulance, eventually joining Good as passengers for the nearby Wagga Wagga Base Hospital. A total of five Police Officers and six prisoners made the journey to the casualty department.

Sergeant Johnson strolled over just as the ambulance was leaving the scene.

'How'd ya pull up, Mikey? Get a few good ones in, did ya?' he grinned.

'Oh, I assisted in quelling the disturbance, Sarge,' Walker replied with an ironic smirk. 'I was just looking after Wendy Good. She copped a decent whack on her scone. The ambo reckoned she is going to need a dozen stitches. How'd you go?'

'I also "assisted to quell the disturbance". Got a couple of the gutless bastards. Knocked two of 'em out while I was helping Burley. Good fight, eh?'

'What was it all about? There must have been at least fifteen of those pricks. The only one I recognised was stinking Jerry Braid.'

'Apparently, they're a bunch of pig hunters, come down here from Dubbo. They was grogging on in the pub, making a nuisance of 'emselves when one of 'em decided to piss down the pocket of the snooker table. Albert's head barman, Billy Hill, saw him and tried to chuck him out. This idiot bunged on a blue, and his loud-mouthed mates all joined in. There was seventeen of 'em all up, but a few pissed orf when the first car arrived. It seems Albert, Billy and young Matthew Goldberg were holding their own for a while, but then the rest of these arseholes joined in and outnumbered the pub staff about five to one. As soon as the first couple of cars arrived, the mob turned on our blokes, and some-one only just got the "Signal One" in before the shit hit the fan. I saw you give your shirt to young Wendy. She all right?'

'Other than the nasty gash in her head, she might have a broken thumb. But, she's a tough little bugger. She'll be right,' Mike answered.

Johnson nodded and checked himself over for wounds or damage to his attire.

'Well, Wallace said we can return to what we were doing. We just gotta go back to the station and do quick statements about this kerfuffle first. I suppose you wanna grab a new shirt from home? Hey, where's your handcuffs?'

'Braids wearing them, for now. I told Inspector Wallace they were mine and he said he'll get them back to me. I got some spare shirts in my locker. I might grab a quick shower back at the station, before I dress up again.'

'Good idea. Ok, let's get outta here. There's enough uniforms and cage trucks to look after this lot. The bloody television and radio mob are here and I don't wanna talk to any of 'em. Old

Reggie from the newspaper has already grabbed a photo of me, and had the audacity to ask me what happened. I pointed to one of the crooks who I knocked out an' told Reg to ask him'

Johnson chuckled as he led the way back to the car.

CHAPTER EIGHT

∞

The loud ringing of the telephone shook Dennis Stein from his doze. He heard his mother answer the phone and her subdued murmuring followed as she chatted to the caller. Dennis stretched his arms wide and then swallowed a mouthful of cool water from the beaker sitting on his bedside table. His bed was strewn with books and pamphlets, all on the subject of S.C.U.B.A. diving. With his final assessments less than a week away, Dennis was determined to achieve a high pass mark in order to obtain his 'Master Diver' certificate. His trade studies were all behind him now, and he only had to complete the final six months of his practical training to become a qualified Motor Mechanic. He intended to complete a full year as a tradesman before applying to join the New South Wales Police Force. He had obtained enough information to know that with qualifications as a mechanic and a diver, once his basic training and probation were completed, he could transfer to either Highway Patrol or the Police

Diving section of the Water Police. To find himself in a career which combined his two main interests, as well as the excitement of the varied tasks as a Police Officer, was Dennis' lifetime dream.

He picked up a text book titled 'Recovery Techniques for Deep Sea Divers' and had barely began to read when his mother appeared at his bedroom door.

'Hey, Love. It's Mark, for you. Said he's got some information you wanted.'

Dennis sprang to his feet and walked quickly to the telephone in the dark hallway.

'Hello? How ya going, Brother?' he spoke into the handpiece. Marks voice crackled back to him.

'G'day, Mate. Tell me, did you say you knew something about that Jag you wanted me to look into? I just forget exactly what you told me.'

'No. I said the photo of the big bloke which was with the photo of the Jag, reminded me of some-one. I said he was a big, evil looking bastard, who looked familiar. Why? What have you found out?' Dennis replied.

'Well, the Jag used to belong to a nasty underworld mongrel called Albert Tuckey. But the Jag, and Mister Tuckey were smashed to pieces by a train out near Lithgow about four weeks ago. Tuckey was a known stand-over man, a thug-for-hire, a former Private Detective and a bloke best avoided, if you enjoy having your knee caps where nature put them. He was described in various news reports as a colourful Sydney identity or a well-known underworld figure. Of course, this meant he was one of those vicious crims who either paid off crooked cops or was too bloody smart to ever get hooked for the major offences. Apparently, he's got a record as long as your arm, but only one Felony conviction, and that was for Grievous Bodily Harm, to a young woman, in Kings Cross sometime in nineteen sixty-eight. So, Little Brother, when did you become acquainted with this delightful piece of work?'

Dennis absorbed all the information his brother passed on, then said thoughtfully,

'I already told ya, I don't know him personally. This photo just looked so familiar. Now I reckon I know what it is. His picture was on the television news every night for about a week. It was after he was killed. They kept showing his mug and giving details about him. And I seem to remember they kept saying the cops couldn't establish his cause of death. That seems funny, doesn't it? I mean, if a train ploughed into his car while he was in it, I would have thought that would do for a cause of death. What dya reckon?'

'Yep,' Mark replied. 'I reckon 'Terminal Train' would do for a cause of death, especially when it's a scum bag like Tuckey. Anyway, that's who owned the Jag, and I presume the bloke who's photo you saw with it was Tuckey himself. So, the question now is, what is your diving instructor doing, carrying around a picture of Tuckey and his car? Are the two blokes connected in some way?'

Dennis thought for a few seconds before answering.

'I haven't the foggiest idea. It is bloody strange, though. A Central Coast S.C.U.B.A. diving instructor and a big-time Sydney stand-over man. I can't see any link, but then, I don't know either of them that well. And I guess I won't be getting to know Mister Tuckey too well any time soon. Strange, though, ain't it?'

'So, what's your interest, Mate? I can dig deeper if you want me to,' Mark said.

'It's just that I saw the photo and it triggered some thought, some interest. Then I wondered why Alex would have these photos and that sheet of paper in his boat. Combine that with what you've just told me, and we have a puzzle, don't we?'

'We would have, if it was any of our business,' Mark retorted.

'Ok, if you're too chicken,' Dennis teased.

'I'm not chicken,' Mark said. 'If you want, I'll go digging when I get the time. Do you have the full name and address of your diving buddy? That will be my starting point. Any info you can give me will help. But tell me this, what do you intend to do with anything I find out? You could be sticking your scrawny neck into a whole world of trouble. What I've read about Tuckey is, he didn't have too many friends, but those he had are all scumbag nasty buggers. You sure you want to mix with those types?'

'I don't want to mix with any of them. I'm simply curious as to why my diving instructor carries around photos and stuff concerning dead bad guys,' Dennis said.

'Ok,' Mark told him. 'Leave it with me. See ya on Sunday.'

A loud click told Dennis the call was over. He returned to his diving books but the images of Albert Tuckey and the shiny Jaguar XJ kept disturbing his concentration.

He decided to find a way of broaching the subject with Alex when he presented himself for qualification assessment at the dive shop next Saturday.

Mike Walker checked his reflection in the large mirror attached to the shower room wall. Since returning to the Police Station he had obtained a fresh shirt from his locker, showered, shaved and redonned his dark blue suit. His leather shoes had suffered a lot of scuffing so he had given them a polish and buff as well. Now, as he tied a clean tie around his thick neck he chuckled to himself when he thought of his wife Carmen. She had been listening to the local radio at home when news of the near riot had been broadcast. She had telephoned the Detectives' Office after an hour, only to be told by Sandra that Mike had returned shirtless and covered in blood. Johnson had then taken the call and assured Carmen that Mike was all right and not injured.

The big Sergeant had yelled to Walker through the shower cubicle door, suggesting he telephone his wife as soon as he could.

Johnson's desk telephone rang, and the crackly voice of Noel Brady, the kindly old desk sergeant sounded in his ear.

'G'day, Johnno. A heap of stuff just landed on my counter from the hospital. There's a set of handcuffs with a tag on them, says they're yours. Another set of 'cuffs and there's a ripped and bloody shirt, some notebooks and a gold pen, amongst other stuff. A uniform tunic and a blood-soaked tit holder. Any idea who belongs to this lot?'

'Yeah,' Johnson answered. 'The shirt and 'cuffs are young Mikey's. He's in the shower washing away the evidence of how good he can fight. I'll come and grab it.'

Johnson replaced his telephone and left the office, making for the outside staircase.

When he entered the public reception area of the station, Sergeant Brady handed him a plastic garbage bag.

'All in there, Mate. What happened to Mike? His shirt is a mess, and bloody near torn to shreds. Did the bastards get a few in on him, or what?' Brady asked.

'Nah, he's too good for that,' Johnson grinned. 'Don't worry about our boy Mikey. I saw him clock three at once during the shit-fight. But poor little Wendy Good copped a whack over her pretty little noggin. It's mostly her blood on his shirt. A pair of heroes ripped her blouse and tit-cover off her, so after he dealt with those two scum, Mikey took off his shirt and covered Wendy up. He probably won't want it back but I'll take the lot up to the office and he can please himself. Thanks, Mate.'

Johnson picked up the bag and returned to his office. He emptied the contents onto his desk and retrieved his handcuffs. He placed Walker's cuffs on Mike's desk and picked up the two notebooks. The first one was bound in a blue vinyl cover, with the New South Wales Police logo printed on the front. Walker's name was on the inside cover so Johnson tossed it onto Mike's desk. He picked up the other note book, noting it was an ordinary, non-issue little pad. There was no identifying name on it, so he began to flick through the pages. He read some meaningless notes about cricket, some scores, several telephone numbers and then a list of names which he recognised as the team members of a local Rugby League team, headed by the entry which read Mike Walker, Lock & Captain.

Realising the little pad belonged to Walker, Johnson was about to place it on Mike's desk when he spied the names, Andy & Anita Keyes on another page. These names were followed by several large amounts of money, each amount was followed by a question mark. He flipped through a dozen more pages and found Andy d.o.b. 2.4.49 then Anita d.o.b. 11.6. 51 written in Mike's neat style. After perusing the remaining dozen pages, Sergeant Johnson snapped the pad shut and sat down at his own desk. He remained seated, thinking through the facts contained in the book, until he heard the stairs creaking as Mike returned from the showers. On an impulse Johnson slipped the notebook into his coat pocket and turned his attention to restoring his handcuffs into their pouch. The outside door opened and Walker strode in.

'Ah, you look better, Mikey. All clean and tidy again. Sergeant Brady sent this stuff up. It come back from the "horse pistol" apparently. There's your handcuffs, and the shirt you so gallantly placed over young Wendy's neat little boobs. They're keeping her in, by the way. Her and two blokes are staying in casualty for a few more hours while the "docs" monitor their condition. Same with four of the scum. The rest are filling the cells downstairs. You ring Carmen yet?'

Mike replaced his handcuffs in their pouch, then examined the torn and blood soaked shirt. He picked up his official notebook and wiped the outer cover with his handkerchief, then discreetly checked the shirt pockets for his personal notebook and was disturbed to find it missing.

'I'll call her now. Just one thing, though Sarg. I don't think you should be mentioning Wendy's body like you did. She's a colleague, and a bloody good copper. I reckon you ought to show her a bit more respect than that. Sorry to nit-pick but, with all due respect, I think you're out of line. Please cut it out.'

Johnson grunted in surprise and looked at Mike, checking if he was joking. He soon realised his junior was serious and replied quietly,

'Ok, Sir Galahad. No offence to little Wendy intended. But make that the first and only time you chip me about how or what I say. I am what I am, and we'll leave it at that. Now, are you ready to resume work?'

'Yeah, thanks Sarg. Was there anything else with our stuff?' he asked quietly.

'Nope!' Johnson replied. 'Why, something missing?'

'Oh, no, it's all right. I was wondering what happened to Wendy's uniform blouse, and her brassier. Nothing else, eh?' Mike looked around the two desks as he spoke.

'Nah, that's the lot for us. Wendy's blouse and brassier were with our stuff but I left them with Brady,' Johnson answered, all the while watching Mike and noting his re-action to not finding his personal note pad.

'Oh, right-o,' Mike said. 'I'll call Carmen, let her know she isn't a widow yet.'

Johnson noted the troubled look on Mike's face. He felt a touch of sadness for his young colleague, but he knew he must not let him know about the notepad.

Other, more important personnel had to be informed, and he hoped it would not lead to too much bother for Mike, even though his duty was clear in his own mind.

As Walker dialed his home number and began speaking to Carmen, Johnson busied himself with the large pile of paperwork stacked untidily on his desk.

He heard Mike talking to his wife, assuring her he was not hurt and in good health. When Walker finished his call, Johnson said to him,

'You get to grab the bank account details for those pair of shit-heads, Mate?'

'Oh, yeah,' Mike answered. He found the statement form where he had dropped it on his desk and read aloud the figures he had obtained from the computer.

'So, Mister Childs withdrew four and a half grand, did he? Let's see him explain what that dough was for, especially when we now know he was supposed to pay old Monk four thousand for the ciggies. I'll keep this information up my sleeve until just the right moment, then I'll drop it on him. You watch him shit himself. He won't know we can get that sort of info, and how quick we do it.' Johnson grinned as he spoke.

Mike grinned at Johnson's words, then, together the two Detectives constructed a full brief of evidence for the next hearing of the Monk / Childs case. They were almost finished when Detective Senior Constable George Somersby entered the office. The fingerprint man was his usual smiling self, and his attire was also at it's normal ruffled self. His suede desert boots were scuffed and dirty, his trousers wrinkled and the light blue shirt was unbuttoned at the throat. His entire ensemble looked as if it hadn't seen an iron for many weeks.

Throughout his career, George Somersby had been verbally chastised by every one of his various supervising officers for his unkempt appearance. Despite trying his best, the likeable character had found it impossible to stay tidy. His happy disposition and easy going nature, combined with his extreme competence as a fingerprint and forensic officer, had seen every senior officer who tried eventually give up in their attempts to straighten him up and he was inevitably left to his own devices.

Somersby grinned as he tossed a folder on Johnson's desk, and greeted his colleagues.

'G'day Johnno. Hello Mikey. I got a heap of prints from that truck and it's cargo. As well as Monk's, there's plenty of dabs from Mister Spano and another set which I'm still waiting to hear back from Sydney for. They're probably either Dixon's or De Hern's. I've just been comparing the fresh sets which you took with the ones I found on the open carton in the truck. I reckon they'll be DeHern's. How's that for ya?'

'That's beaut, George. Bloody quick work. Good on ya, Mate,' Johnson answered.

'No problem. While you lot were busy getting down and dirty with the common herd at that All Cars, they forgot about me and left me alone. So, I got stuck into it and there you have it. My full report and court statement are there, so I'll leave it with you two. Any idea when their next appearance will be?'

'About three weeks. The main three are gunna be guests of the government at Parramatta until then. Thanks again, George. You're a credit to your uniform' Johnson replied.

Somersby grinned, spread his arms and looked down at his rumpled clothing.

'Always proud to serve. See ya. See ya, Mikey,' he quipped as he left the office.

Johnson grinned as he watched Somersby leave.

'He's got me buggered. The smartest forensic bloke I know, yet he looks like he wouldn't have enough brains to get a headache. And what a mess! You know, Mikey, I've seen him front up for court in a clean shirt and tie, suit nicely pressed and his face clean shaven, but still wearing them dirty old stinking desert boots. And half an hour after his court appearance, he looks like he's done ten rounds with Cassius Clay. Christ he gets untidy in a hurry. Great bloke, though, eh?'

'Yeah, a champion for sure,' Walker replied. 'What else do we need for this brief?'

Johnson scanned through the thick file before answering.

'Bugger-all, for now. I already got permission to re-interview the three of 'em when they come back down here in three weeks. We'll do that as soon as the truck arrives, then submit the supplementary records to the court. When old "Sloppy" reads the part about the bank accounts, I reckon that'll be enough to nail 'em. I don't think they'll bother to appeal, and even if they do,

"Sloppy" won't bail 'em. My guess is they will be on the same truck heading back to Parra or Long Bay for a few years rest.'

Mike nodded agreement and thumbed through his official notebook, checking his facts and committing to memory times and dates concerning the case.

'Well, I think we've had a terrific result, especially when you consider our tasks were interrupted by the riot and shit fight we attended as well. Are we going to be needed in that matter, Sarg?'

'Nope!' Johnson replied emphatically. 'Just submit our statements and arrest reports, and uniform are gunna handle it from there. Great stuff, eh? We get to bump a few dickheads on the scone, and somebody else does all the paperwork. It don't come much better than that, Mikey.'

Walker grinned in spite of himself. He knew Johnson enjoyed the physical side of arrests, but was also aware that his superior had a tendency to step over the line on occasions. The days of Johnson's type of policing were coming to an end, with more and more groups calling for restraint by the officers. Although he acknowledged the hampering nature of this trend, Walker believed the less violence involved in arresting suspects, the better, and cleaner, the task could be performed.

Checking his watch, Mike said to Johnson,

'It's just gone four thirty, Sarg. We done enough for Queen and Country today?'

'Yeah, I reckon,' Johnson answered, glancing at his own watch. 'I'm ducking across the road for a couple. You coming?'

'Ok, but just a couple,' Walker replied. 'I don't want to get lumbered by the traffic boys with their new toy, that 'Breathalyser'. You want a lift home or you going to soldier on?'

Johnson shook his head and smiled at Mike.

'Nah, I'll get the uniforms to drop me home. You just remember to pick me up about eight in the morning, all right?'

The two Detectives donned their suit coats and left the office, trudging down the rickety outdoor staircase. They crossed the street and entered the saloon bar of the Hotel. Once both men had glasses of beer in front of them they discussed the various cases they were working on as they drank.

No further mention was made of the female Constable but Walker sensed the big old Sergeant was harboring some resentment after being criticised by his underling. After finishing two glasses, Walker wished Johnson good night and returned to the Police Station. He entered their unmarked Police car and drove home through the back streets of Wagga Wagga, eager to see his wife, Carmen, and reassure her he was not hurt in the near riot.

During the short drive, he went over the events of the day in his mind, including his brief debate with Johnson over Wendy.

He wondered to himself why it meant so much to him, but concluded he was simply protecting a colleague whom he liked and admired.

CHAPTER NINE

∞

Alex stared at the typewritten sheet of paper in his huge right hand. He shook his head as if to clear away some restriction to his eyesight, then read the text again.

Two large yellow envelopes were laying empty on the kitchen table beside him. Both had arrived in the morning post, but had remained unopened until he returned from work at his dive and fishing tackle shop. Although his tiny Asian wife, Angela had stayed home this day and thoroughly cleaned their two storey house, she had refrained from opening the distinctive yellow envelopes.

Both Alex and Angela knew what the contents would be. Only the specific details would be unknown. Both also knew the envelopes would mean trouble.

The strangest aspect of today's mail was the arrival of two envelopes together. Usually they arrived singularly, and up to twelve months apart. This was the first occasion when two had turned up in the one delivery.

Alex had opened the first envelope, studied the typed text, three photographs and a press clipping from a leading Sydney newspaper. He had passed the contents to Angela and she in turn studied each item before handing them back to him.

'Ok, my husband. We will have to make the arrangements straight away. We do not have much time to attend to this. I will check the safe, but already I am thinking we have ample money in there to see to this, yes?'

'Yeah, righto, Gorgeous,' he replied, smiling lovingly at the demure woman.

While Angela moved a lounge chair and unlocked the floor safe nestled discretely underneath it, Alex opened the second envelope. He became agitated immediately as he read the single typed sheet in this one. After re-reading the letter, he passed it to his wife who had noticed his change of mood and left the safe. She stood beside him as she took the paper, a look of deep concern on her pretty face.

'What is it? What has caused you so much concern, my big man,' she asked.

'Wait 'til you read it, Love. I think we've got big trouble here,' he said softly.

The woman read the paper, and clutched at her own throat as the content became clear. He noticed tears welling in her large brown eyes and reached for her. She dropped the sheet of paper onto the table and buried her face in his chest.

He pulled her into him, becoming aware of the heaving of her body as she sobbed.

Eventually she composed herself and drew away from him a few inches. She looked up into his face, noting the look of distress which had come over him. Alex shook his head slowly, and gently squeezed her tiny shoulders.

'No way!' he said quietly. 'No way in the world are we going to do this. I'm going to contact The Commander first thing in the morning, and tell him so. And, I'll add that if they decide to go ahead using some-one else, or even try, I'll blow the whistle.'

Angela managed a weak smile before replying.

'Thank you, my husband. I was scared you might not act this way, but I should have known you much better. But why, dear husband, do you think they wish harm to her? What has she done that warrants this?'

'I think I know what they're thinking is, but it won't work. That'll be the day when I have anything to do with injuring an innocent woman, let alone some-one who we know well, and who would not hurt a fly. And I'm going to tell them so, in plain terms. They try this and they'll have me to deal with,' he stated firmly.

'Us, dear man! They will have us to deal with. As always, we are a team. They take on you, they take on me also, all right?' she said defiantly.

For the first time since opening the envelopes he smiled.

'Ok, Tough Guy! Us, then. Right, let's organise the first job, and I will make the call in the morning about the Carmen thing. It ain't happening, whether they like it or not.'

They studied the details from the first envelope, making notes occasionally and consulting a Sydney street directory. When the plan of action was decided, they went over the entire procedure again, starting with the time of the necessary train was due to depart Wyong railway station.

Angela left him then, to prepare their evening meal.

Alex sat quietly in his lounge chair, thinking over the recent past. He cursed the situation he found himself in. Since retiring from the Australian Army just short of four years ago, his life had been one giant series of highs and lows. The highs began when he was given official permission to marry his Malaysian wife, and her citizenship had been secretly fast tracked. It was helped by the fact she had been an officer in the Malaysian Special Forces, and served as liaison between her unit and the Australian Special Air Service detachment deployed in her country.

Her husband had been a captain in the S.A.S. and they had worked together in many dangerous operations. Like the rest of her unit, she could kill a large, strong man with her bare hands, and could fire any type of small arms, as well as withstand any amount of pain or discomfort. Despite her small stature, perfect figure and masculine-melting beauty, she was as lethal a weapon as her husband, and quite a few terrorists and other Malaysian traitors had regretted not taking her more seriously.

When the two officers fell hopelessly in love with each other, they kept the romance to themselves until his time was up and he was offered a discharge and repatriation back to Australia. After some raised eyebrows and a few 'tut tuts' from the S.A.S. hierarchy, the two were flown to Perth and he underwent a three month debrief and retrain. The now married couple travelled to the Wagga Wagga region of New South Wales where they occupied his parents long deserted farm. His mother and father had passed away within a week of each other while he was serving in Malaysia, and his wife had no living relatives, so they were free to follow which-ever path they chose.

After setting up as farmers, restocking with sheep and cattle, they had ploughed paddocks, mended fences and gates, sown crops and settled down to the hard work and drudgery of mixed farming.

He even found the time to resume his other two loves, Rugby League and Cricket.

He was a talented and tough fullback or winger, and in Cricket was a fearsome fast bowler. They enjoyed many weekends away from the farm, playing and watching the sport, as well as socialising with new found friends. Just when their lives seemed settled, a colleague from both of their pasts had made contact and offered them a financially attractive way of clearing farm debt and setting themselves up for the future. The deal entailed them utilising the skills learned in their previous occupations, with full protection from the law and absolute anonymity. The lucrative deal had continued until his best friend, New South Wales Police Detective Michael Walker, had begun a clandestine investigation into the results of their actions. When it came to the attention of his handlers that his friend was unknowingly on his trail, Alex and his wife were hurriedly moved, the Detective warned off and another Detective eliminated in a most brutal fashion.

Now, by the arrival of the envelopes, as well as one received three months previously, it appeared it was to be 'business as usual', and he hated himself for allowing it to continue.

His wife joined him and tossed a bundle of money onto the table.

'There is exactly five hundred dollars there. That will be enough, will it not?'

'Yeah, Beautiful. More than enough. I see our man travels regularly by train to the city from his farm at Moss Vale. That should suit our needs perfectly, don't you reckon?'

He traced the route of the railway line on a map he had spread out on the table.

She followed his thick finger, nodding slowly as the various locations were indicated.

'It says here he also has up to four of his 'gorillas' with him on these trips. That shouldn't be too much of a problem. He makes two trips a week, usually. One from Moss Vale to Sydney, after kissing his wife goodbye, and the other to Campbelltown, where he keeps a girlfriend in an apartment. Hopefully we can deal with matters quickly, probably on his next trip, and not have to involve either his mistress or any of his 'apes'. He's Italian, apparently, and we know what vicious blighters they can be. The target, Luigi Magetti, is rather rotund, smokes cigars almost constantly and when he plonks himself in his reserved seat on the train, only gets out of it if he has to go to the toilet. His 'apes' run and fetch anything else he wants, including coffee from the buffet on board the train. He has only just been released from prison, so his complexion is supposedly quite pale. Shouldn't be too hard to spot. And he is due to receive his warning of impending gloom from the Commander this very morning.

That gives us Thursday as the best day to deal with the matter. That's the day he jumps off at Campbelltown to spend a few hours with his squeeze. I hope she's not too disappointed when her "Mister Suave" fails to show up.'

While Alex and Angela were discussing their intended operation, the target was just boarding the first-class section of the Goulburn to Sydney Express at Moss Vale station. Bruno Allasotti, a huge Italian former professional wrestler, led the party as they made their way down the centre aisle of the carriage. Magetti followed, clutching the morning newspaper and a plain leather brief case. Behind him, Carlos Andre and Joey Moscano, two more Magetti henchmen, brought up the rear. All three of Magetti's men carried a pistol and a long-bladed sheath knife each, concealed beneath their crisp silk suits. Magetti was unarmed, but alert for trouble never-the-less. A tall, thin youth walked down the aisle towards them, but only made it as far as Allasotti. Without a word, the big man shoved the youth into a vacant seat, out of the way of Magetti.

'Hey, watch it, mate. Who do'ya think you're pushing, ya great galoot?' the youth protested loudly, drawing the attention of the two dozen other passengers and the railway Corridor Attendant. Moscano had reached the youth now, and leaned down, whispering into the right ear of the man.

'You justa shut up, punk, and showa some respect, eh? Or maybe you no wanta keep your furgin knees where they already are, eh?'

A look of total fear came over the youth's face, and he simply nodded.

He waited until the four Italians had reached their seats at the end of the carriage before standing up and continuing his way to the opposite end. The Corridor Attendant was waiting for the four men, busily brushing some non-existent dust from the seats with his handkerchief. He smiled nervously at Magetti, indicating the forward facing window seat.

'Good morning Mister Magetti. Your seats are ready,' he said reverently.

'Good, Trevor. Good. How is your little one, ah…..what's her name? Michelle? That's her name, is it not, Trevor?' Magetti said, smiling at the railway man.

'Yes, yes, that's it, Michelle. She is fine, thank you so much for asking. Have a good trip, Mister Magetti. And just let me know if I can get you anything.'

All four men eased into the comfortable seats and Magetti nodded to Andre. The henchman reached into his coat and withdrew a bundle of money. He peeled off a twenty dollar note and thrust it at the attendant with an ill-concealed scowl.

The railway man quickly pocketed the money and backed away, smiling and bowing as he left the passenger saloon and entered his tiny compartment.

After a whistle from outside, the locomotive horn sounded and the train began to move. Magetti watched the platform and the crowd of people disappear in a rapidly blurring image as the train accelerated out of Moss Vale. When the town had vanished from his view, he opened his newspaper and began reading the stock market reports. His three bodyguards relaxed and settled in for the journey. Every fifteen minutes Trevor the Corridor Attendant made his rounds, always stopping at Magetti's side and enquiring as to any wants or needs of the four men.

After slightly more than an hour, the train was slowing as it pulled into Campbelltown station. Andre stood and entered the toilet located near the far end of the carriage. After the train jerked to a stop at the platform, Magetti stood and stretched is arms. When the whistle sounded from outside, he resumed his seat just as the train began moving again. It was rapidly leaving the station behind when Trevor came hurrying along the aisle, clutching a white envelope. He stopped breathlessly at Magetti's side.

'Here, Mister Magetti. Something for you. I brought it straight up to you,' he panted.

He held out a standard white envelope, with one word 'Magetti' scrawled on it.

'Where did this come from, Trevor? Who gave this to you?' Magetti growled.

'Some little old geezer. He was travelling in the next car, from Goulburn. I noticed him earlier, before you got on, Mister Magetti. He got off at Campbelltown, handed this to me and said something like, "give this to Mister Magetti". The he put this silly white hat on his head and walked off into the crowd. I saw him heading up the stairs when we left the station and I brought it straight to you.'

'And you don't know who he is?' Magetti asked, puzzled.

'No Sir. Never seen him before in my life. I just know he got on at Goulburn, is all.'

With a grunt, Magetti handed the envelope to the returning Carlos Andre.

'Here Carlos. Read this to me. Ok, thank you Trevor. That's all. Go!'

The Attendant scurried back to his compartment as Andre tore open the envelope.

As he read the short letter to himself, a deep frown appeared on his face. He looked at his boss, shaking his head slightly and pointing to the note.

'I said read it, Carlos! What is wrong with you? Read it, now!' Magetti said firmly.

'Well, ok Boss. I tell you word for word, but it's what the note says, not me, all right? It says, "Hello, you greasy, murdering scum. It is time we put the record straight. You killed those two innocent kids, not Mossi. So now it is your turn to pay. We specialise in righting wrongs, and you are one of the biggest wrongs we know.

If you have any character about you, which we doubt, your last thought will be of the two kids you robbed of a long and happy life. And nowhere are you safe, even in the company of your stupid, useless thugs. Hope you've done your last will, Grease Ball. Goodbye." Sorry, Boss, but that is what it say.'

Andre was shaking with fear as he read out the contents, but Magetti was shaking with fury. He snatched the note and read it for himself, then screwed it into a tight ball.

'Get that stupid furgin porter back here. Who is this arsehole who thinks he can threaten me, eh? Get furgin Trevor the idiot-a back here, now!'

Moscano rose and quickly fetched the frightened Attendant.

'Yes, Mister Magetti? Can I get you something?' he squeaked.

Magetti glared at the quivering man before muttering quietly.

'Who is this bastard-o who gives this gutless note to you, Trevor? Tell me all you know about this imbecile. What you know, huh? Tell me now, Trevor.'

'Honestly, Mister Magetti, I know nothing of him. As I told you, he stepped off the train at Campbelltown, handed the envelope to me and told me to get it to you. I've never seen him before, and I don't know who he is or where he comes from. Honest, Sir. I am telling you the absolute truth. I swear on little Michelle's life, Sir.'

Magetti looked at the man for a full twenty seconds, and decided he must be telling the truth. He was obviously too frightened to do otherwise. He smiled at Trevor.

'All right, my friend. I believe you. But I'm-a gonna get you a telephone number. You see him again, anywhere, anytime, you call this number, let us know, Ok?'

He nodded to Andre who reached into his pocket and produced a small notebook. Magetti scribbled a six digit telephone number and handed it to Trevor.

'Anywhere, anytime, capiche?' he said forcefully.

'Yes, Mister Magetti. I understand.' Trevor nodded vigorously as he took the paper.

'Good. Now, Vamoose' Magetti dismissed him with a wave of his brawny hand.

When the railway man had left, Magetti and his three thugs discussed the threatening letter in Italian. Eventually his bravdo overcame his initial fear and outrage.

'To hell with this idiot. I have never backed down from trouble, and I won't now. Who-ever they or them are, let them come, if they got the guts. Stuff them all ways. Ok, boys, we not take them seriously. Anybody want to fight, we ready, No?'

The three henchmen all outwardly agreed, making jokes and telling their boss any attacker would have to kill them first.

Inwardly, all three had different thoughts. Anyone brazen enough to threaten Luigi Magetti so openly, so specifically, must be reasonably sure of themselves, who-ever they are. All three decided to be extra vigilant from now on. None of them wanted to lose their well-paying, lucrative meal ticket.

The Commander gently replaced the hand piece of his antique telephone. For five minutes he sat quietly, thinking over the conversation he had just had with his Operatives. In the four years he had been involved in the activities of 'The Retribution Committee', this was only the second time the Operatives had called him. The first call had come only a few months ago when they had had to relocate the husband and wife team of Operatives. On that occasion, he had been able to placate the team with a thorough explanation and get them to agree with the decision. The team had eventually seen reason and the call finished on an amicable note.

This time, the atmosphere had been much less cordial. The Operatives had even gone to the lengths of threatening the

Commander, and the entire organisation. The main fact troubling the old man was the absolute refusal of the Operatives to carry out the assignment. This had never happened before, although some assignments had been given to a casual Operative in the recent past. This was different, in that the task had been allotted to the main Operatives by the Retribution Committee directly, along with a second mission. The Operatives readily accepted the second task, but were steadfast in their refusal to even contemplate the other.

The Commander was in no doubt as to the reason for the refusal. He knew the target was well known and well-liked by the Operative team. Even though the instructions stressed this was not to be a 'Full Termination', meaning injury only, not death, the team had made it plain that the mission was not to go ahead, by them or anyone else.

"So…….the dog wants to wag the tail, eh?" he thought to himself. He had to think carefully about this one. There was no doubt in his mind the Committee will still want the job completed, and that was not a real problem for him. His casual Operative could and would easily fill in. It was how best to explain the situation to the Retribution Committee. They might take the view that he was losing his grip, or worse, decide to have the Operative team terminated. Neither option appealed to him, but he knew he must request an immediate meeting of the Retribution Committee.

With some trepidation, he dialed an unlisted number, and waited for an answer.

After a short, heated conversation, the Commander nodded as he was given the details of the emergency meeting he had asked for. It was to be tomorrow evening, usual time and place. Then there was a loud click as the call was terminated by the other party.

He wrote the date and time in his pocket diary, gathered his notes from the conversation with the Operatives, then reached for his glass of cognac sitting on the arm of his lounge chair. As he sipped the drink, he thought deeply about his lifestyle.

Lately he had been considering retirement. The constant risks and cloak and dagger aspects of his job were taking a toll on his nerves for the first time.

Only yesterday he had checked his bank balances, noting he now had slightly under one million dollars to his name, as well as complete ownership of his comfortable cottage. The suburb of Cronulla was popular with home buyers, and as he contemplated retirement and relocation, he smiled as he realised he could easily add another two hundred thousand to his wealth after selling the cottage.

He gave his reflection in the huge mirror attached to the wall a self-satisfied smile. Then, with a philosophical sigh, he picked up the telephone and dialled the number of his chauffeur. When Harold answered, he was given a time to call for the Commander the next day. That done, the old man finished his drink then rose, walking slowly to the bathroom, looking forward to a hot shower and hopefully, a good night of sleep.

CHAPTER TEN

Sergeant Lindsay Johnson replaced the telephone receiver then slipped the tattered little notebook back into his shirt pocket. He tapped his thick fingers on the desk as he thought to himself. His feelings of guilt were soon overtaken by his thoughts of right versus wrong. He knew his most recent telephone call would likely cause others some grief, but he eventually convinced himself his actions were justified.

He had ensured he was alone in the office before dialing a secret number in Sydney. When he made his verbal report, including reading from the notebook, he sensed the anger building in his companion on the other end of the line. When he had finished his report, he had braced himself for a reprimand, and he was not disappointed.

'Bloody hell, Lindsay! I thought you had that little bastard under control. I thought moving his mate on, getting him right out of your area would be enough to make him wake up to himself. Especially when you remember the fate that bloody Muscatt copped. What is the story on this young bugger? Is he a masochist or just a bloody hard head? I tell you what, he's already down for some minor treatment, or at least his university professor wife is. Now you tell me he still wants to dig around. Well, you've got one more shot at roping him in, Lindsay, or the shit will hit his fan, big time. We have an emergency meeting tonight, and I'll have to report this. You just find a way of sitting on him, or I won't be able to protect him anymore. Ok?'

Johnson winced as the information and rebuke hit home. He replied respectfully,

'Yeah, I will, somehow, Boss. Does this mean what-ever you lot had planned for his missus will be cancelled, or at least delayed?'

There was a brief pause before the authoritive voice answered.

'I don't know. I'll try, but I need to know you've done your bit and made him lose interest, Ok? Get on it and report back to me before six tonight.'

There was a loud click and the line went dead.

Johnson let out a long sigh and a slight shudder went through him. He felt a large weight on his shoulders as he recalled the conversation. Still alone in the office, he checked his watch. One-thirty. Mike should be back from lunch any minute, and he would insist the two of them go driving when they were together. He had four and a half hours to talk sense into his younger colleague, and he was determined to succeed.

After all, even an experienced old Detective Senior Sergeant did not dare disobey a direct order from the Commissioner.

Mark Stein looked at the woman standing in front of him. She was well into her forties but still sported a figure which any sixteen-year-old girl would be proud of. Her stylish navy blue mini skirt and tight fitting blouse enhanced her curves, and her pretty, unwrinkled face was topped off by thick auburn hair which always looked like it had just been attended to by a team of first class hairdressers. She wore just enough make-up and lipstick to complete the stunning look, finished off with modern diamond earrings and necklace.

'That's incredible, Jenny. How did you manage to gather all that info without giving the game away? You're bloody amazing!'

She smiled a seductive smile which almost made Mark gasp.

'Oh, you know. Smile a bit here, so a show a bit of thigh there, and pretend you find the bloke and his work interesting. then most of you blokes will tell your life story. It wasn't all that hard, really. Mister Shortall was most co-operative. I nearly had to clobber him to shut him up.'

'How did you do it? I mean, it was a bit of the old "needle in a haystack" stuff.'

'Well, I got lucky first up. I went to Glebe and I've got a pretty good contact in there, who is madly in love with me. He told me straightaway that one of his colleagues, a Mister Shortall, had told him about copping a visit from your friend Albert Tuckey. Apparently this Tuckey creature turned up at Shortall's hobby farm out near Lithgow, and tried to squeeze information out of him about a string of mysterious deaths. The deaths all involved Sydney crims, and all had a few things in common. Like, for instance, every one of the crooks had just got off serious charges. Every one of them then went public, skiting and bragging about how they beat the cops. Then each of them turned up dead, and all the scientific brains in the state can't work out what killed them. It seems some fancy pants lawyer by the name of Larry Kind hired your mate Tuckey to make some enquiries. Tuckey gets Shortall's name from his own contact at Glebe Coroners Court, because good old Mister Shortall was the only Lab Assistant who worked on all of the mysterious cases. So, Tuckey visits Shortall, who knows bugger all about the facts, other than what's in the public reports. He does manage to frighten the shit out of Shortall, but before Shorty can report the incident or what-ever, Tuckey drives his Jaguar into a freight train on his way back from Shorty's farm, and joins the list of dead baddies. And to top it all off, despite being smashed to smithereens by the train, the scientists and the cops, as well as the coroner, cannot state for certain the cause of death. Apparently, his organs show death by some unknown poison or something, exactly like the other low-lifes that Tuckey was sticky-beaking into. Just desserts, it seems, but there you have it. Happy, Marky-Boy?'

Mark shook his head in wonderment as he grinned at her.

'It's bloody amazing, Jen. You got all that in one quick visit to an old flame. Amazing! I'm buggered if I know how you do it.'

She smiled seductively, battered her long eyelashes and pulled up the hem of her skirt.

'Oh, it wasn't that hard, really. As I said, just a wink here, a flash of leg there and the rest was easy. Are you going to tell me what it's all about, or do I have to use the same torture techniques on you?'

He laughed and leered at her appreciatively.

'Please, go ahead. Look, seriously, I might be onto a big story, but I need some more facts. How about dinner tonight, and I'll fill you in?' he asked.

'I just bet you'd like to, given the chance. Ok, seven o'clock, your place. You cook, supply the wine, the after dinner mints, and the story. I'll supply me.'

Her confidence and exuberance was infectious. Mark knew she was a lively date and a willing and experienced sexual partner from office gossip, but because of their age difference, he had not ventured down her path. The prospect of a hot date with Jenny was as exciting as the size of story he was starting to sniff.

The ten members of the Retribution Committee sat around the huge mahogany table, most smoking something and all anxiously awaiting the arrival of the Commander.

District Court Judge Morwell opened the cover of his ornate pocket watch, grunted noticeably and snapped the cover closed. He was about to voice his disapproval of the late hour for the fifth time when the massive wooden door to his right opened and the diminutive figure of the Commander shuffled in.

There was silence as the little old man made his way around the table to his seat. He dropped his white straw hat on the vacant seat beside him, placed two thin folders on the table and sat down in his allotted chair. Morwell coughed loudly then spoke.

'Well, Commander. Glad you finally made it ! It is most unlike you to be tardy, so I suppose you had best start us off with an explanation or two. How come the lateness?'

The old man stood, leaned his bony hands on the table and spoke with surprising volume, immediately gaining the full and undivided attention of the other ten men.

'Well, Sir, I regret my lack of punctuality this time, but I have a valid reason. It ties in with why I requested this meeting. Firstly, as you all know, two separate missions were ordered at our last gathering. The task of dealing with Mister Magetti is in hand, and I anticipate observing the Operative Team completing the task tomorrow. Obviously a full report will be furnished to you at the next scheduled meeting. The other mission, I am afraid, has become very problematic. In fact, I fear it may be beyond us. To cut to the chase, the Operative Team have refused point blank to carry it out. And, on top of that, they have stated they will reveal everything about us, themselves, and our past missions to both the media and the federal authorities if we try to implement it. The reason I was unable to appear here on time is I have spent the last hour and a half on the telephone to him, trying, in vain I stress, to convince them to change their minds. As a compromise I even suggested I will use an alternative operative, and arrange for them to be out of the country on holidays while the mission is under way. Again they refused, and repeated the threat that if that mission went ahead, they would reveal all.'

There was a stunned silence in the room for almost ten seconds as each member digested the information. Eventually it was the Police Commissioner who spoke.

'Problematic, you say, Commander? I rather think it may be a Godsend. I mean, we're talking about a relatively innocent woman, who happens to be the wife of one of my Detectives, who happens to be one of the job's rising stars. I was against it from the start, so I'm thinking this might be a blessing in disguise, eh fellows?'

There was arguments for and against, with most against the Commissioner's view.

'What about the information she found?'

'Who the hell are these killers, telling us who they will or will not terminate? Looks like a case of the violin trying to play the fiddler.'

'We pay these bastards handsomely, don't we? We tell them, they don't tell us.'

'Maybe you're right. It might be a blessing in disguise.. I don't think….'

'Yeah, that's your problem. You don't think……'

'Perhaps it's best we back off for a while with this one?'

'She's still bloody dangerous to us, you idiot! Her knowledge could easily be let loose to other bastards. Only needs one slip……'

'What? Are we scared of one stupid bloody woman, now are we?'

While the arguments raged, the Commander sat quietly, swinging his gaze from one speaker to the next. Eventually Judge Morwell banged his ornate pipe on the table and yelled for silence. It took another twenty seconds for the insults and arguments to cease. When the uneasy silence enveloped the room, Morwell addressed the group.

'All right, gentlemen. Obviously we have a problem. We will not solve it by insulting each other like a pack of spoilt school boys.

Commander, is there any way you can convince the Operative Team of the depth of their folly?'

The little old man rose and addressed the judge.

'They do not see it as a folly, Sir. They were most adamant that the subject not be harmed in any way. They even insisted she not be contacted, and I regret I was unable to move them. I pointed out such things as the danger she poses to them and our operations. I mentioned the massive amounts of money they had made from the activities, the fact that their friend in Wagga Wagga, is still a serving Police Detective, the efficient manner in which we re-located them, and the way the late Mister Muscatt and his spouse, had been regrettably dealt with.'

'So, what do you recommend, Commander?' Judge Morwell demanded.

'It is not for me to say, Sir, but I would point out the group has already identified this woman as a significant threat. Or at least the information she possesses is,' he replied.

The Police Commissioner broke in, thumping the table hard as he spoke.

'So, what's your bloody recommendation, Commander? It's a clear enough question.'

The little old man looked at the larger man, a blank look on his face as he thought.

He waited until complete silence pervaded the room and all eyes were on him.

'Very well. I am in a position to engage a casual operative. He will carry out the mission to the letter, once I provide a feasibility report and suggested method. That will be relatively simple, but still leaves us with the problem of the main Operative Team and their threat to end our activities and expose the Retribution Committee. So, we can solve one problem but then generate another. I await your guidance, gentlemen.'

He glared at the Police Commissioner for a few seconds before resuming his seat.

After every member had aired their own thoughts on the situation, Melvin Quartermain, Chief General Manager of the Colonist Bank, stood hesitantly and coughed. All eyes swung his way and Judge Morwell tapped his pipe on the table.

'Yes, Mel? You have an idea or perhaps a suggestion for us?'

'Well, I was thinking, how about we call the Operative Team's bluff? I mean, first we authorise the Commander to facilitate the Wagga mission, then we either call their bluff, or, as an extreme, have the Commanders "Casual Operative" eliminate the team if they look like making good on their threat. We all have a lot to lose if the team is permitted to carry out their threat, and I don't believe we should allow them to start dictating terms to us. WE employ them, after all. Not the other way around !'

Again there was much debate, shouting and many insults traded before the pipe was tapped loudly. When they were all quiet, Morwell called for a formal vote on Quartermain's proposal. Following usual procedure, the Commander was excluded from the vote and sat back in his chair, watching each member as they wrote either a 'Y' or a 'N' on the slips of paper which had been passed to them by Morwell. The members then folded the slips to conceal their vote, and passed them along the table to the Judge. Morwell quickly unfolded all of the papers and began sorting them.

'Eight to two, in favour,' he declared. 'Right, Gents. That is decided, so we now hand the matter over to you, Commander. How much funding will you require for this?'

'Fifteen thousand will cover the Wagga mission, thank you. I'll need it, in cash, by tomorrow night. The team are planning to carry out the Magetti mission tomorrow, which I intend to observe. Usual twenty-five is required for that one. What shall I say if they contact me regarding the Wagga Wagga matter?'

'Tell them we're still considering it. Yeah, that's it. Tell them you brought their concerns to us and we are giving it our deepest consideration. That should at least hold them off for a while,' Morwell replied.

Cries of 'Yes', 'Hear hear' and 'Good-o' echoed around the table.

The Commander noted the Police Commissioner and his Deputy did not join the chorus of agreement, and guessed they would have been to two 'N' votes.

Duane Sharkey, rumoured to be the wealthiest property developer in Australia, raised his right hand, indicating he wished to speak.

'Mister Sharkey!' Morwell acknowledged.

All eyes were turned to the end of the table as the rich man stood.

'Ah, I have a bit of a question. Um, our so-called "Operative Team". How much do they know about us? I mean, do they know any of you blokes? Have they met any of you? Correct me if I'm wrong, but is it not so that the only method of contact is via the post? Obviously, they have the Commander's 'phone number. But, apart from that, I don't think they have a clue who we all are. Maybe we're jumping at shadows, worrying ourselves about their threat?'

He shrugged and spread his arms, waiting for any responses.

Morwell tapped his pipe and then pointed it at the Commander.

'Commander, will you answer Duane's questions, please?'

The old man nodded but remained seated.

'Mister Sharkey, on that score you have nothing to concern yourself with. The Operatives have never laid eyes on any of us, including me, although I have observed them closely on nearly every mission. They also have no idea who comprises our group, your positions, occupations or any other details. When they were recruited, it was done through an acquaintance of mine, a former internal investigator of the bank which held the mortgage of their farm. Unfortunately that chap has since passed on, and obviously poses no threat. The only other contacts they have had was the two fellows who informed them of the need to relocate. These two are trusted associates of some of us here and they possess no knowledge of our group and what we do. The twenty other men we hired to shift them from the farm to their present location were simply casual labourers, hired from Melbourne, who were paid far in excess of the going rate to carry out the move and then forget it. And as for your main question, I do contact them via mail only, and the telephone number I provided to them for emergencies has only been used twice. It is one of four numbers I control, and can be switched off and discarded with a moments notice. When I facilitate their payments after a mission, I use different methods of money transfer, and always from different locations. I believe we are as untraceable as we can be. Does that satisfy you, Mister Sharkey?'

Sharkey grinned and sat down. He said loudly as he lit another cigarette,

'Yep! I reckon that is good enough for me. Thanks, Commander.'

The meeting broke up quickly, after Morwell assured the Commander the required money would be with him tomorrow night. He then banged his makeshift gavel once more, signalling the close of business.

As the eleven men left there was no sign of the usual friendly banter and 'goodnight' calls and Judge Morwell did not wheel in the drinks trolley as per normal. The tension of this meeting was almost tangible as each member left, wrestling with his own inner thoughts.

CHAPTER ELEVEN

Mark Stein swallowed the last of his chocolate mousse dessert and pushed the bowl away. He looked across the glass table and noted Jenny had also finished eating, although she had hardly touched her dessert.

'Well, Jen. That's the feed over with. Let's go sit in the lounge and I'll finish the story as I know it. That's if you're ready?'

He managed a weak smile as she stood and re-arranged her stylish blouse.

Using his contacts with the high-class restaurant on the ground floor of his building, Mark had presented Jenny with chef prepared leek soup, followed by sea food platters, French bread and they finished off with the mousse dessert. Along the way they had consumed two bottles of Hunter Valley Hock, and he was feeling light headed.

Jenny had arrived at his apartment a little over two hours ago, dressed in a bright red slack suit, with the silk blouse underneath and red 'wet look' stilettos. The slacks were skin tight around her shapely back side, and she wore no brassier. Mark had had difficulty taking his eyes from her and she teased him further by kissing him on his lips and pushing her breasts into his chest. He had eventually composed himself and stood aside to allow her entry.

Throughout the meal and the light-hearted conversation, Mark had been constantly battling his inner self to focus on the beginnings of a wild story. All the while her sexiness and flirting had combined with his own expectations to form a massive distraction. He had heard several of the office womanisers describing their experiences on a night with 'Sexy Jen', but he was never sure if it was fact or fantasy.

He followed her into the small lounge room, where a stereo was playing several long-play records of soft mood music.

'Drink?' he asked her.

'Sure,' she smiled. 'A Vodka, if you've got it.'

He crossed to his small liquor cabinet and poured two vodkas.

Jenny kicked off her stilettos and sprawled on the sofa. Mark turned off the record player and handed her the drink.

'Before we get up to anything else,' she whispered, 'Sit here beside me and give us this hot story you've got your teeth into.'

He almost stumbled and spilt his drink as he took in her meaning. Mark had had many young women visit his apartment, and usually managed to complete the night with a sex romp. Most of the girls put up the mandatory token resistance, but his charm, good manners and natural good looks always served him, and the women, well.

Jenny was different. Despite her age, her stunning looks and appearance matched or even surpassed any other female company he had enjoyed, and she was making no pretence at wishing to avoid close physical contact with the younger man. In fact, during the meal she had made several references to the subject as if it was a foregone conclusion and a natural part of the evening. He lowered himself onto the sofa beside her and immediately she turned sideways and placed her long, shapely legs across his lap. He gulped a swallow of the vodka and gently began massaging her thigh. She smiled at him and wriggled further into the cushions.

'Ok, Muscles. Tell me about this red hot scoop WE are going to work on.'

'It all started when my little brother enrolled in a S.C.U.B.A. course, up the coast where he lives with Mum and Dad. He's just about finished his apprenticeship as a motor mechanic, and as such is interested in all things mechanical, especially motors. While he was out on this dive boat, he got curious about the engines she was powered by. When the skipper, who is also the Diving Instructor, was underwater, he snuck down to the engine room for a peek. While he was in there, he stumbled on some books and stuff, including a couple of manila folders. One had a short type-written note which said something like 'Termination by the nineteenth of December' or something similar. There was also two colour photos. One was a picture of the late Albert Tuckey, the other was the back end of a Jaguar sports car, which showed the number plate clearly. Well, little brother Dennis had seen Tuckey's ugly mug on television, although he couldn't quite place when and where. He memorised the number plate, returned everything to where he found it, and then when I went home for the weekend, he told me all about it. He was just curious because he'd seen Tuckey's face before, but couldn't place it. When I found out who the Jag was registered to, and told him, I also told him the story of Tuckey's demise. We were both prepared to let it go at that, when it dawned on both of us. What is a dive boat operator doing with pictures of a bloke who was not only a known underworld figure, but had just found himself horribly dead in his big flash car? And, why was there photos of the geezer, and his car in the folder? Then there is the cryptic note, "Terminate by nineteenth of December". It just happened to be the seventeenth when Tuckey and his Jag took on the freight train, and lost.'

Jenny squirmed in her seat and removed her legs from Mark's lap.

'Ok, Sherlock. It's a most intriguing tale, so far. What happened next?' she asked.

'Well, that's when I checked with the news boys, and found out the Coroner's Court had yet to determine cause of death. I knew you had good contacts down there, so that's when I asked you to stick your pretty little nose in for me.'

She flashed him her devastating smile and slowly undid two of her blouse buttons.

'Flattery will get you everywhere, Spunky! Ok, so I found out Tuckey was probing into the mysterious deaths of half a dozen crims. And the strong rumour from around the traps is that the well-known flashy lawyer, Larry Kind, hired him to do it. Why? We don't know, yet. Ok, first up, let's go through the crims Tuckey was so interested in. You write, I'll give you the facts.'

He hurriedly rose and found his large notebook and a pen, then dragged a coffee table over to the sofa and resumed his seat beside her. Jenny snuggled closer and linked her right arm with his left. He leaned over and they kissed deeply for a full minute.

Jenny broke away and said hoarsely, her voice full of tease and promise.

'Ok, more of that later, Hunk! Let's get some facts down before our pants.'

Mark took a steadying drink and prepared to write, his concentration divided between the notebook and the wide opening in Jenny's blouse. She reached into her pocket and took out a small notepad, filled with shorthand writing.

She smiled again, and began to read her notes aloud.

'First there was one Edward James Miller, a known thief and fence. He was over seventy years old, pissed most of the time and was eventually found dead in the sand dunes at Cronulla. He had his attack dog, a huge German Shepherd with him, and the Coroner was unable to determine cause of death. The cops were mystified as to why this great big dog didn't attack who-ever or what-ever bumped old Eddie off. Still no cause known, but sand suffocation ruled out. Next came Thomas Fergus McCleod, better known as Scotch Tommy. He was a dope peddler, and known to indulge in the gear himself. He was arrested for consorting and larceny, got off, spent

heaps of time ridiculing the Newtown Detectives, even going to the trouble of taking out half page ads in the tabloids, proclaiming his innocence and bagging the cops.

Then he is found dead in his truck, parked in Quay Street. Again, dope was suspected, then ruled out. As of two days ago, no cause of death recorded by the Coroner. Two weeks later McCleod's best mate, the notorious Bruce Thompson, better known as Brother Thompson, why I have no idea, was acquitted of serious charges. These included assault, sexual assault, living off immoral earnings and attempting to bribe a couple of Detectives. He gets off, scores an interview with Charles Yetman's current affairs television show, and proceeds to accuse the cops of fitting him up, planting evidence and falsifying his statement. After that he books himself a sleeping berth on the overnight mail train to Dubbo, where his family lives. On arrival at Dubbo, good old Brother is found dead as mutton, still in his pyjamas, with not a mark on him. An autopsy is performed at Dubbo, and no cause of death can be established. His worthless body is brought back to Sydney, to the university, and another, deeper autopsy is done. Still no cause, except the three scientists all agreed his organs simply shut down, for no apparent reason. Still an un-explained death. Now we move to the vicious Errol Mayberry, the best known stand-over man around Redfern. He, of course, was better known as Redfern Errol, surprise, surprise ! Among his other talents, Mayberry was renowned for his fitness and swimming prowess.

He was graded by the South Sydney Rabbitohs in nineteen sixty-nine to play football. He only played half a season before getting lumbered for bashing a couple of queers near Redfern railway station. He got a twelve month stretch for that, so Souths tore up his contract. After his release, he resumed his violent existence around Redfern, stealing, bribing, threatening and running several protection rackets. His favourite leisure activities were swimming hundreds of laps at P.A. public baths, and bashing poofters up at the cross. He loathed the queers and used to go belting them up simply for the pleasure it gave him. Nice type, was old Errol. It was well known he had a girlfriend in Manly, the daughter of a well-to-do real estate agent. The notes say he was on a ferry, on his way to Manly to see his girl, when he slipped overboard and drowned. No-one saw him actually fall, but his body was found by a following ferry about ten minutes after his boat had passed Fort Denison. The Water Police were called, fished his body from the drink, and he was carted off to Glebe. Again, two autopsies, three inquests, and still no cause of death. Drowning was ruled out, and several criminals, coppers, relatives and others all testified to his fitness and swimming ability. His case remains open, although no-one really gives a stuff, especially the local poofs. Next came Billy Greene. A nasty bastard if ever there was one. Lived in a flash pad in North Sydney, was into every type of crooked activities you could name,

including prostitution, drug peddling, bribery and probably murder. He was run over by a Government bus, right outside Wynyard railway station, during the afternoon peak hour. He had two of his thugs with him, but witnesses said he just keeled over, right in front of the moving bus. He, too had just escaped a lengthy jail sentence, spent time bagging the police and proclaiming his innocence then performed his impersonation of a speed hump for the bus. Old Billy joins his rotten mates at the Coroners Court, autopsy and inquest, but no cause of death. His organs also shut down, apparently just before the bus left it's tyre prints all over him. His case is also still unsolved, and an open finding is listed by the court.'

Mark was busy writing the list of facts into long hand and continued for several minutes after Jenny stopped talking.
He finished and studied his handwriting.
'Shit, Jen. This is starting to look like we are onto something big. And you got all that from talking to one bloke at Glebe?'
'No, I talked to two. My contact and the scared and frightened Mister Shortall. You remember, the one Tuckey frightened the crap out of?' she replied.
'Right! Ok, apart from Tuckey himself, are there any others?' he asked without looking up. Her open blouse and provocative gestures were distracting him.
'Yes, there is. A slimy creature from Wollongong called Carter. A real estate agent, entrepreneur, drug dealer and con-man. He was charged with keeping an illegal immigrant, a fourteen-year-old girl, as his private sex slave. He was caught red-handed, or should that be "red-dicked"? He was bonking this poor young girl at a beach car park. She was drugged to the eye-balls, and the cops had him dead to rights. When the case went to court, how-ever, he and his legal team produced film of the girl operating with a Vietnamese drug gang in Melbourne, a doctor's report showing she was at least nineteen and that she had been doing drugs and having sex for at least ten years. It was all bullshit, of course, but the judge had no option but to throw it out. A few weeks later, he was having a morning swim at Scarborough beach when he suffered the same fate as the previously mentioned bunch of low life creeps. After yet another fruitless autopsy, the inquest left his case open, and no definite cause of death is recorded. And to top it all off, they are now saying the same thing about your good friend Mister Albert Tuckey. Despite being smashed into mincemeat by a speeding train, his organs show they were in perfect working order, with no heart attack, kidney or liver failure or any other sign of

ill health. So, another open finding, and no cause of death. That wraps the bundle for us, Marky my man. Where to now?'

Mark finished writing these last details and grinned at her. He dropped his pen and note pad, then unbuttoned his shirt, showing his lean, muscular physique.

'I'd like to suggest the bedroom, Sexy!'

'Suits me. Lead the way, 'Randy Andy'.'

Jenny slipped off her tight-fitting clothes, leaving on only a pair of black panties.

He grasped her wrists and they half ran, half stumbled to his bedroom where she lay on his king size bed, watching him hurriedly disrobe. He stood in front of her, now fully naked, his manhood hard and erect, glowing with colour and excitement.

Jenny rose to her knees, slipped out of her panties and leaned her smiling face towards him, while he panted with anticipation.

The tall, bearded man leaned nonchalantly against the side of a soft drink dispensing machine. He had watched at least ten suburban trains arrive or depart from the three platforms, and each time he felt a degree of sympathy for the well-dressed office workers who piled into each carriage. As one train departed platform two, full of yawning city workers, another would arrive on either platform one or platform three, and from seemingly nowhere hundreds of people swarmed along the length of the train, seeking the perfect seat. When a train departed, the platforms appeared almost empty, with just a few individuals either sitting on the many bench seats provided, or a few couples descending the concrete stairs from the overhead concourse. Campbelltown Rail Station was a hive of activity for three hours every weekday morning, with numerous suburban electric train movements, as well as several long distance and interstate trains adding to the bedlam.

The tall, bearded man was waiting for the arrival of a particular long distance train.

The man pretended to read a morning newspaper which he held up near his face. He took note of his accomplice, a short, Asian woman, seated on one of the long stools adjacent to the stairs. The woman's face was barely visible under her hooded coat and scarf. She also wore supple leather gloves, dark glasses and a long woollen skirt. Her ensemble was completed by knee-length leather boots and matching handbag.

The man shuddered slightly as a gust of icy wind roared along the platform, and he snuggled further into his ex-army greatcoat.

A loud speaker above him had been constantly telling the intending passengers which destinations the next train would convey them to. The voice emanating from the device was irritating, and sometimes almost unintelligible. The tall man smiled to himself as he pictured the voices' owner, probably the resident Station Master. He imagined the man would be short, rotund and balding. He would be nearing retirement age, seen it all, done it all, probably highly qualified in railway skills and knowledge, but found himself still broadcasting train arrivals and departures to the common herd.

His self-amusing thoughts were interrupted by the annoying voice once more.

'Next train on platform two is the Goulburn-Sydney Express. This train does not pick up. Passengers are forbidden from joining this train. Stand clear, platform two.'

He looked up the line and saw a bright headlight approaching from the south.

This was what he and his accomplice were waiting for. He saw her rise, open her handbag and stroll slowly to the foot of the large stairs. These led to the overhead concourse and also gave passengers access to the other platforms.

The platform beneath him vibrated slightly as the big diesel locomotive rumbled past. The train was slowing and the squeal of brake blocks on steel wheels sounded from the bogies. When the train ground to a complete halt, the loud speaker repeated the earlier announcement, reminding passengers not to board the carriages. Despite the warnings, several men opened the doors and stepped inside, scurrying to vacant seats and pretending nonchalance as railway staff on the platform glared at them.

Around two dozen people disembarked the train, and the tall man soon spotted his target. Four men, all wearing silk suits, loud ties and shiny shoes, walked briskly and arrogantly along the platform towards the stairs. The tall man identified his mark easily, noting he was a perfect likeness of the individual depicted in a series of photographs he carried in his shirt pocket. And to make things even easier, Luigi Magetti puffed away on a thick cigar as he swaggered along the platform. Each of the four photos he held showed Magetti with such a cigar either clamped in his teeth or in his hand.

The enormous form of Bruno Allasotti strode ahead of Magetti, and two other swarthy skinned types followed behind. The human shield which the three bodyguards thought they were providing had a couple of major flaws. Head-on attack, and assault from the rear were well covered, but both sides were open. As the quartet passed him and began ascending the stairs, the tall man fell into step beside them. He was only two metres from Magetti as they all climbed the steps, but none of the thugs seemed to realise his proximity. And, unknown to the four Italians, the little Asian woman had positioned herself directly behind them, and had lined the secondary target up nicely.

As the group reached the first landing of the stairs, the tall man took one step to his right, narrowing the distance between himself and Magetti to one metre. He placed a small tube to his lips, aimed at Magetti's thick neck and blew hard. Then he stepped back to his left and continued up the stairs.

Magetti ascended one more step, then uttered a soft groan, before collapsing face first onto the stairs and lay unmoving. The two thugs following tripped on Magetti's feet and both tumbled to the concrete surface, cursing loudly in Italian. Several other people stopped, looking in amazement at the pile of bodies which suddenly materialised before them.

Allasotti whirled around, saw his boss apparently unconscious, and his two colleagues attempting to regain their feet. Two strangers stopped and attempted to assist Magetti to his feet, but he was a dead weight. Allasotti shoved the two men aside and turned his bosses body over onto his back. He knew instantly that Magetti was either dead, or deeply unconscious. He looked around and saw the tall bearded man watching from several metres away. Instinct told him this man was somehow responsible, thinking he had probably tripped his boss with a well-aimed foot.

'Hey, You. Come here, you. Whata happened just then, eh? You see whata happened?' he asked fiercely, taking two giant steps towards the tall man.

He did not see the Asian woman range up alongside him, place a tube in her mouth and aim at his huge bare left hand as she puffed hard. Allasotti felt a slight sting in his hand, and a second later his eyesight failed. He heard a few voices and some confused shouting, then the world went quiet for him as he joined Magetti in the land of the non-living. Two railway porters hurriedly descended the stairs, one asking the crowd of onlookers to stand back. The other felt for a pulse in Allasotti, and, finding none, moved to Magetti, where he obtained the same result.

The tall man and the little Asian woman slowly moved further up the stairs as more people

joined the onlookers and another railway man, dressed in a smart uniform adorned with gold braid, shouldered his way through and stopped at the unmoving bodies of Magetti and Allasotti.

'What happened, Tony?' he demanded of the elder of the two porters.

'I don't know, Sir. We were on the barrier when a bloke told us some-one had collapsed on the stairs. When me and Jimmy got down here, there's two of 'em.'

'Checked their pulses? Are they breathing Ok?' the officer enquired.

'No, they're not, Sir. I think they're both dead. I tried but I couldn't feel no pulse in either of 'em, and they ain't breathing, neither. I dunno what happened but there don't seem to be no marks on either of 'em. Will I call an ambulance?'

The Station Master stooped and felt for Magetti's pulse. He moved to Allsotti but Moscano and Andre restrained him before he could touch the big man's body.

'Yes, call the ambulance, and the police. Call the police first, Tony. Then get the booking clerk to call the Railway Police.'

He shook off the grips of Moscano and Andre, angrily facing the two thugs.

'Let go of me, you two, or I'll see you both arrested. Now, stand back, out of the way. Do either of you know these two?'

He assumed control as the two Italian thugs became less and less sure of themselves.

While this drama was playing out, the tall man with the beard and the little Asian woman walked slowly away, through the vacant ticket barrier and out onto the car park. They entered a light blue Valiant sedan which sported a hire car company logo on the back windscreen. As the Valiant drove slowly from the car park, it was keenly observed by the Commander, seated comfortably in the back seat of his pale green Holden sedan.

He placed his powerful binoculars on the seat and said quietly to the driver,

'All right, Harold. The show is over, or at least the best part. Let's head home.'

Harold started the engine and drove the car out onto the street. He turned left into Queen Street, and followed the signs indicating Cambelltown Road.

The blue Valiant was up ahead as they passed a large sign proclaiming 'Liverpool 28 klm'

CHAPTER TWELVE

∞

Mark Stein awoke slowly and stretched out his arms. He was surprised to feel nothing but the silk sheet covering his mattress. He sat up and saw Jenny's red slacks, white silk blouse and her short coat folded neatly on the dressing table. Her shiny red stilettos were placed on the floor, perfectly aligned as if on display for sale.

He threw back the top sheet and blanket and lay naked for a further two minutes before he became aware of the hissing sound of his coffee machine in the adjacent kitchen. He heard the refrigerator door open and close, then the rattle of crockery. The smell of fresh brewed coffee wafted into the bedroom and he rose to his feet as if the delectable odour was calling him. The wall clock told him it was nearing nine am.

He stood for a few seconds, admiring his naked physique in the full-length mirror attached to the back of the bedroom door and noted with satisfaction his excitement was returning as he thought of the previous night with Jenny. Grinning to himself he walked from the room and into the kitchen. Jenny was pouring coffee into two large mugs, and turned to face him when she heard his feet slapping on the cork tiled floor.

She was wearing only her skimpy black panties and her firm breasts pointed at him, her nipples hard and as erect as he was.

'Well, well, well. Good morning Stud. You sure know how to use that monster, and I see it's ready for further action,' she said, smirking and raising her eyebrows.

They had enjoyed each other's sexuality during the night, starting with twenty minutes of the best foreplay he had ever encountered. Eventually they had both expired around three o'clock in the morning and he had drifted off into a deep sleep.

Now, here she was, daring him, tempting him to have another attempt at satisfying her. He reached for the coffee, unable to take his eyes from her superbly proportioned figure, including her breasts.

'Well, Mate. How about it? Want one last shot at the title?' she said, holding her coffee in her left hand and gently rubbing her flat stomach with her right.

Without a word, he put down his coffee, took hers from her and gently pushed her to the sofa. Giggling, Jenny wriggled out of her panties and within a few short seconds they were thrashing and gyrating together, resuming with the same intensity they had experienced the night before.

When they both had slowly drifted down from the sexual high, Mark rose to his feet, and entered his en-suite bathroom. He expected her to join him but when he left the shower cubicle Jenny was sitting at his dressing table, brushing her hair and applying some make-up. He noted she was fully dressed, right down to her red stilettos.

'Not showering, Love?' he enquired, encircling her neck with his wet arms.

'Already had one, while you were still in the land of nod. Besides, I'm off home to change and I'll have another then. Hurry up and put something on. What will the neighbours think? And it's your turn to make the coffee. Mine went cold.'

He hastily donned shorts and a shirt, before kissing her neck and then heading to the kitchen. He made a fresh pot of coffee and slipped four slices of bread into the toaster.

He was stirring sugar into his drink when Jenny appeared, fully dressed, made up and her hair was perfectly brushed into a neat pony tail. He pointed to the toaster.

'Some nice golden brown toast about to pop, My Love. What would you like on it?'

'None for me, thanks, Mark. I'm in a bit of a hurry, actually. I have an appointment with a contact for a story I'm doing about homeless war veterans. I'll just guzzle the coffee and love you and leave you,' she replied, picking up her coffee mug.

'I thought you were going home?' he asked, slightly perplexed.

'I am. I gotta shower, change, and meet this geezer at eleven o'clock.'

'Well, hang on, Darling. I'll drive you,' he suggested.

'No, thanks. I'll grab a cab. And listen, Mark. Please don't call me "Darling", ok?'

'Ah, sure. At least let me give you the cab fare?' he said. She immediately placed her mug in the sink and glared at him. Her sudden anger shocked him.

'Listen, Mark. I'm not a bloody hooker! You don't have to pay for my company, you know. I do what I do because I enjoy it, that's all. Just like you randy blokes, only it's all right for men to want to screw anything around, but a woman isn't supposed to, right? Well I'm different. I'm not a 'nympho', I just love a good shag, and I try to get as much as I can. If that makes me something you don't like, well tough shit! That's me and to hell with it!'

He was shocked into silence for a short time, then managed a stammered reply.

'Gees, Ah...I'm...I'm sorry if I offended you, Jen. I didn't mean to. I'm really sorry. I thought we had something great going here. What are you all steamed up about?'

She calmed down but still looked angry.

'Ok, Mark, but let's get something straight. We had a great time last night, and I enjoyed myself immensely. But that does not suddenly make me your girl or your darling. I belong to no man, ok? I know you've heard some of the other wankers in the office telling all about the great screw they had with me, and I'll tell you now, some, in fact most, are true. I love sex, but I won't be tied down. We had our fun, we may even have some more in the future, if you can accept that I'm just in it for the screw. As I said, I realise it isn't supposed to be this way, but it is, and that's that.'

He nodded and smiled at her. She relaxed and returned his smile.

He reached out and took her right hand in a normal handshake as he said,

'Well, that has certainly put me in my place. I sure never meant to insult you, Jen. I admit I did think we were getting into something special, but I guess not, now that you have explained it all. Ok, I can accept it, as long as we stay mates. And, can we still work together on the Tuckey and friends matter?'

'Of course, we can. I'm looking forward to getting my teeth into that one. And we're still mates, even though I expect to hear rumours around the office soon about what a wild night you had with 'Randy Jenny' or what-ever it is they call me now,' she said.

'No way!' he said forcefully. 'I would never do that to you. If any bludger says anything along those lines, I will job the bastard, rest assured. Any stories you hear will be made up by the story-teller, and definitely not from me.'

She laughed and stepped forward to hug him.

'Ok, Sir Galahad. But it's a bit late to start defending my honour, especially around our gossipy little workplace.'

She picked up her handbag and they walked to the front door of the apartment. He opened the door and she kissed him lightly on his left cheek. He squeezed her hand and was about to wish her goodbye when she spied his newspaper on the floor of the corridor. She bent down and picked it up, before glancing at the front page.

'Oh, thanks, Jen. It's the late morning edition. I know.......'

He trailed off when he saw her staring at the headline, wide eyed.

'Look at this. "Two mysterious deaths at Railway Station this morning", it says. I wonder if there is any connection with what we were talking about last night?'

He looked over her shoulder and they both read the article. The report told of two well-known underworld figures suddenly dropping dead at the same time on the stairs at Campbelltown Rail Station. The reporter went on to name the two as 'Luigi Magetti', recently released from prison after mysteriously being cleared of a double murder, and his body guard, former professional wrestler Bruno Allasotti.

'This is too much of a co-incidence, Mark. It fit's the same bill as those scumbags we were analysing last night. It's got to be connected,' Jenny said, a little breathlessly.

'Absolutely!' he agreed. 'I'm going to add this to our file. Any chance you can get down to the Coroner's Court and work your magic on your contact down there?'

She finished reading the article and nodded.

'I will, for sure, but after my other meeting I told you about. Look, meet me at the office around one-thirty, and we'll do some digging. Right?'

'You got it. Christ, this is getting interesting, isn't it. Ok, see you at one-thirty,' he answered enthusiastically. She left via the elevator and he returned inside, gathering his notebook and scribbling down details from the newspaper. He had written three pages of notes when he put the pen down and went to the kitchen and made himself a cup of tea. In the sink were the two coffee mugs and the toaster had the four pieces of toast poking out of the top, now stale and cold.

He looked at the lipstick mark on Jenny's mug, and smiled to himself as he thought of the irony of being a healthy young man with a large sex drive, and also being an investigative reporter. It was almost as if last night with Jenny had not happened.

Lindsay Johnson watched the condensation drips slowly making their way down the sides of his glass. He sat on a round stool, leaning against the wooden bar as he waited for Mike Walker to join him. He had consumed two glasses of beer already and had deliberately slowed his drinking of the third. The conversation he intended to have with Mike would require him to have all his wits about him. Depending on the outcome of the talk, he would either consume at least a dozen more glasses before calling it a night, or leave the total at three before making a clandestine telephone call to Sydney. He checked his ornate pocket watch and was returning the timepiece to his shirt pocket when Mike walked in and sat beside him.

'Sorry I'm a bit late, Sarg! Bloody 'phone never stopped ringing and I couldn't get away.

Thankfully the night crew came in, and I handed the lot over to them and pissed off. So, Sarg, what do we need to talk about?'

Johnson signalled to the barman for a beer for Mike, then picked up his own glass.

'Let's go over to the window. We need to keep away from any ears, OK?'

Mike picked up the beer which the barman had placed in front of him and followed the larger man to a table attached to the front wall of the bar. When they were both seated, Johnson stared out of the window for a few seconds, then turned to Mike.

'Mikey, I'm gunna get straight to the point. Please listen, don't interrupt 'til I've had my say, then I'll answer any questions that I'm sure you'll have, if I can. Right, here goes. Mike, it is known in certain other places that you, with the late Chief Inspector Muscatt, were probing away at the deaths of a few Sydney crooks. It is also known that you two stood on some very big toes doing it. If you can figure out whose toes they were, good on ya, but I won't be confirming or denying anything, so don't ask me. It is also known that your previous best friend, that farmer from The Rock, was implicated. Again, don't ask me to comment on that, 'cause I won't. Now it seems you have been sticking your nose into things again. Well, you are living dangerously, my little mate. Very dangerously. So, listen carefully to me. Some very powerful people want you to back off, and drop it. "Butt out", is the current expression, I believe. There are forces at work here that you and I and a thousand other good coppers couldn't hope to topple. I have been asked…..no, that's not right….I've been ordered to give you this final warning. Forget it, Mike. Stick to being the bloody good Detective you are becoming, and keep right out of the other business. Clear, mate?'

Walker sat staring at Johnson, with complete shock registered on his face. The glass of beer in front of him remained untouched as he digested Johnson's words.

Eventually he took a small mouthful of his drink, and asked quietly,

'I don't know quite what to say. Who ordered you to warn me, Sarg? Was it from Sydney, or was it local?'

'Don't matter, Mike. I'm not at liberty to tell ya, even if I wanted to, which I don't. Just trust me, the warning is genuine. If you don't take heed, you'll regret it.'

'Ok, so what do these powerful people intend to do? I mean, I don't like being threatened, and I'm not particularly scared of too much,' Mike replied with genuine offence.

He didn't scare easily and he was not completely convinced Johnson was giving him the full story. The big Sergeant grabbed Mike's sleeve and tugged.

'Listen, Mikey. They are not playing. You may not be scared of them, but they aren't scared of you, either. Mate, these are mighty powerful people. You could find yourself patrolling the streets of Wilcannia, or cleaning shit from the horse stables for the Mounted Police, or worse. You wouldn't be the first honest copper to get fitted up with a few charges and finish up in Long Bay Jail. Or even worse, personal harm could find you. You've got to listen, Mate. Back off, behave yourself, and understand you've come under the eyes of people who could make you, or break you. Please listen, Mike. I like you, and I like workin' with ya, but I'm not gunna jeopardise my own well-being just because you want to be a stubborn bloody mule. Besides, you're too good for that.'

Mike took another sip of beer and looked Johnson in the eyes.

'I take it, then, that you're saying what happened to Allan and Heather Muscatt was organised by these bastards? A bloody good cop, and his totally innocent wife, were bumped off because he dared investigate a few murders? Is that it, Sarg?'

Johnson drained his beer and placed the empty glass on the table as he said, 'I honestly don't know anything about that, more than was stated in the bulletin. But it seems to me it should at least tell you how fair dinkum they are. You can't fight them, Mike. You have no idea how high up the food chain they are. Just tell me, please, Mikey, you'll drop your probing and stick to what we, you and me, do best, eh? Please, Mate, I'm begging you.'

Walker realised he had never heard Johnson say 'please' for anything before. The realisation surprised him. He sat thoughtfully for a few seconds before speaking.

'I would like to know one thing, Lindsay. How has all this come out? Where did I slip up, if I have slipped up? Is there any proof? Did I leave something laying about?'

Johnson sat thinking, drumming his thick fingers on the table. Eventually he nodded to himself and smiled thinly at Mike. Without speaking he reached into his shirt pocket and took out Walker's personal notebook. He threw it on the table in front of the junior Detective and studied him for a re-action.

Mike slowly picked up the little book and flipped to the pages where he had made the

entries concerning Andy and Anita Keyes.

'How the hell did you come by this? Did I drop it during the riot, or leave it openly in the office for any bugger to find? Shit, I must be getting careless. How'd you get it?'

Johnson shook his head.

'Don't worry about how I got it. Just be grateful you've got it back. But rest assured, other people know about it. Look, I'm not gunna tell you anything else, Mike. I just want you to think about what we've talked about and do the right thing by yourself. If you go the other way, there is nothing I can do to help you, Ok? For now, drink up and I'll buy you another. Then we both better 'sorff home. And don't ever call me by my first name again. It tends to breed disrespect. It's 'Sarg' or DS Johnson to you, right?'

Mike declined the second beer, and left the bar as soon as he could. Normally they ended the week with a few drinks and a handshake, but Mike did not feel too friendly towards Johnson this afternoon. He crossed the street to the Police Station yard and went straight to their Police car, then drove home slowly. Johnson's words were ringing in his ears as he considered what to do next, and how much, if anything, to tell his wife, Carmen.

Johnson cursed to himself as he watched Walker leave. He had held high hopes his information would shake his young colleague enough to extract a promise of letting the matter go. He had not received the response he wanted, and now he had to telephone a secret number and report the situation to his superiors.

The big tough Detective Sergeant ordered another beer and considered how he would word his report.

He thought back to over three and half years ago when he had been summoned to Sydney and told to report to the Commissioner's Suite. Johnson and the current Commissioner had joined the Police Force and the same time, and they had remained friends as each rose to their respective ranks. Johnson was satisfied with Detective Sergeant, but was not surprised to see his former classmate continue up the ladder to the very apex of the job.

When he reported to his old friend he was given a secret additional duty to add to his Wagga Wagga investigations. It was the appointment to a special watching brief on a newly arrived farmer in the district. He was told roughly what tasks this farmer, and his Malaysian wife, would be undertaking from their farm out at The Rock, a small town twenty-five kilometres from Wagga Wagga. The farm was called 'Rocky Crop' and on certain given days, Johnson was to discretely drive out to a spot near the farm and observe the couple depart for the local railway station. A day or two later he was to check that they returned safely and didn't keep close company with anybody else.

He was paid several hundred dollars every month for keeping this watching brief and, knowing the tasks which the pair were completing, he felt justified in doing his part and accepting the payments.

It had been a co-incidence of the worst kind when Mike Walker had not only become football and cricket team-mates with the farmer, but the wives had become firm friends as well. He often saw or heard about them socialising or visiting each other.

When the keen young Detective Walker had started noticing things he shouldn't, and asking questions he shouldn't, Johnson had warned him to leave the matters alone.

He had thought his warning had been heeded, but a few late night telephone calls to Johnson at home had confirmed the worst.

Now, he was faced with betraying a likeable, dedicated and honest young colleague or placing himself in the firing line by admitting complete failure.

He left the bar and walked slowly across the street to the Police Station, mulling over his unpalatable choices as he desperately searched for a third alternative. He climbed the outside stairs and entered the office, relieved to find the entire floor empty of other personnel. The cleaner had just finished her jobs and was leaving by the inside door.

Johnson followed her and smiled a greeting as she turned around. The Chinese lady smiled back and began descending the internal stairway, dusting as she went. When she was out of sight, Johnson stepped back inside the office, locked the door and crossed to his desk.

He bypassed the switchboard by dialling 'O' before the Sydney area code, then the secret number. When a gruff voice answered, he gave his verbal report on his conversation with Mike Walker.

'Right, so that's how he wants to play it, eh? Well, let me tell you, Johnno, this boy has just stepped on a land mine with both feet. Ok, now leave it to me.'

Johnson had one last attempt to diffuse the situation.

'Listen, couldn't ya leave it with me? I mean, I know the bloke very well, and I don't reckon there's any real harm in him. What can he do, really? All our tracks are covered, and if he tells anyone about my talk to him this afternoon, I'll simply deny it. I've done that before. Shit, we all have, haven't we?'

'You speak for yourself. No, this young dickhead has had a few warnings, and a few chances to behave. He's run out of rope. But don't you worry, it's my problem now!'

There was a loud click and the telephone went silent.

Johnson replaced the hand piece into it's cradle and sat looking sadly at the instrument for ten minutes. His mind raced as he tried to decide what to do.

Eventually he came to the conclusion there was no more he could now, except warn Mike once again, and tell him to either take some leave, or prepare for a very bumpy ride into the future.

CHAPTER THIRTEEN

∞

Mark Stein steered his Ford Capri GT smoothly through a pair of bends and planted the accelerator as the road rose in front of him. Although ten years old, the powerful vee-six engine was still in perfect order and the sporty coupé gathered speed as it ascended the hill. The car was Mark's first motor vehicle and he was as rapt in it now as when he had collected it from the Ford dealer in nineteen seventy-one. He gained immense pleasure in driving the car, and also found it somewhat of a magnet for girls. The purple metallic paint combined well with the cream, leather interior and the stylish magnesium wheels. He had paid the dealer many extra dollars from his cadet journalist meagre pay packet for these extras when he placed the order the car. People, usually girls, often stopped and looked the machine over. This frequently led to introductions, a swapping of telephone numbers, followed by brief romances in return for a few drives around in the Capri.

Normally he would be completely enthralled in the drive from his city apartment to his parent's house at Toukley, on the central coast of New South Wales. He would be admiring the scenery, enjoying shifting the racy four speed gearbox up and down, and watching for errant wildlife emerging from the scrub beside the Old Pacific Highway.

On this trip how-ever, his mind was occupied with other thoughts. The wild night of unbridled sex with Jenny still played on his mind, but even dominating those thoughts was the story they had worked on together. The sub editor had read their first drafts, made very little alteration suggestions and given the go-ahead for publication of the exposé in Thursday's edition. All three newspaper people knew more research was required to complete the series, and Mark intended to do just that this weekend. The sub editor agreed a four-part series was the best way to present the story. Jenny was also in agreement, and would be the major contributor in part two. Most of her information would come from her contact in the Glebe Coroner's Court. Mark was intent on interviewing his brother's diving instructor about the mysterious photographs and the note regarding the late Mister Albert Tuckey. Dennis had agreed to introduce him to Alex, as soon as he arrived at Toukley for the normal Stein family weekend get together.

Mark had begged Jenny to accompany him for the weekend, but she had declined emphatically, despite his many requests. He had been hoping to not only show her off to his family, but also use her excellent interviewing skills on the diving instructor. Jenny eventually convinced him she had other plans, hinting her weekend was to be taken up in the bedroom of her next lover.

Mark finally got that message and realised his was fighting a hopeless cause, resigning himself to travelling alone.

He was nearing Toukley now, and automatically slowed down to the town speed limit of sixty kilometres per hour. He drove along the main street, watching with pleasure as several young women eyed his car, and him. He reached the Golden Fleece garage where Dennis worked and pulled onto the service driveway. Dennis himself emerged from the workshop, clad in greasy overalls and work boots.

'Good afternoon, Sir. Would you like me to piss in your tank for you, Sir?' he asked with an effected accent and a snappy salute.

'Very funny, Greaseball. How are ya, Mate, all right?' Mark replied as the two shook hands. 'Yeah, fill her up, carefully. One scratch or one drop of spilt petrol and I'll beat you senseless, you young punk.'

'One tank of go-juice, no scratches, spills or bashings. Certainly,' Dennis said as he fitted the petrol pump nozzle into the filler. 'You're a bit early, Brother. I've got at least another hour before I can get away. And that's with two services to do on those two cars on the hoists. I would have been finished by now if some useless pricks didn't keep coming in wanting bloody petrol,' Dennis said teasingly.

'Just fill the limo and stop whining. I'll go for a bit of a stroll and a perv through the shops while you're paddling in your grease,' Mark replied.

When the tank was full Mark parked the Capri beside the workshops and left Dennis to finish his work. He ambled along the footpath, peering disinterestedly in the windows at the displays of merchandise. He came upon the Newsagency, and cast his casual glance along the banner headlines. Nothing he didn't already know about here and then he spied a large notice board attached to the display windows. There were numerous trades and services offered, from baby sitting, lawn mowing and odd jobs, to building works, cars and caravans for sale and many others. In the centre of the board a colourful notice had several cards attached, and he smiled to himself as he read 'Sandy Coast Fishing and Dive. All your fishing, boating and S.C.U.B.A. gear. Diving certificate classes. Expert tuition by Angie & Alex (ex S.A.S).'

The advertisement went on to list a telephone number and a small map telling any takers where to find the shop. Still smiling, Mark took one of the cards and slipped it into his shirt pocket.

When he returned to Dennis' workplace he found his brother showered and changed, waiting for him near the Capri. Mark showed him the card.

'Yep, that's the place. Alex is the big bastard I was telling you about, who runs most of the dive courses. Angie is his missus. A gorgeous little Asian chick. She's a real cracker, especially in a bikini. Absolute stunner, she is,' Dennis told him.

Mark laughed as they both entered the car. He started the engine and as he was driving away from the garage he said to Dennis,

'All right, Casanova. I get the picture. If she's so hot, why don't you make a move?'

'You kidding?' he asked. 'Not only is her hubby, Alex, a big bugger, he's an ex commando from the S.A.S. You know those blokes. Kill a wild steer just by looking at it. And I've heard some blokes say Angie herself is ex commando from China or Malaysia or one of them chink countries. Either way, I'm content to look, but no touch.'

They discussed various women and nationalities as Mark drove. He told Dennis about Jenny and his desire to continue their meetings. He also mentioned she was his partner in the series about the mysterious deaths of the state's biggest criminals.

By the time he had filled in all the details he knew of, they had arrived at the dive shop. Mark parked and locked the car, after gathering his notepad and a pocket sized magnetic tape recorder. They walked to the shop and entered.

Alex was showing a customer a long spear gun and Angie was behind the counter, dealing with an elderly couple who appeared to be interested in fishing rods.

The two brothers looked around for five minutes as other customers came and went.

Eventually the deep voice of Alex sounded behind them.

'G'day, fellas. Can I help you with anything......oh, hello there Dennis. How ya going?'

'G'day, Alex. We..ah, um, we're here because Mark, here, wanted to talk to you. This is Mark, he's from the big smoke. Mark, this is my dive instructor, Alex.'

Both men shook hands and said 'pleased to meet you'.

Alex looked Mark over closely before asking,

'What can I do for you, then Mark? What dya wish to talk about?'

'Well, can we talk somewhere private, Alex? I would like it kept between you and me, if we possibly could.'

Alex took another long look at Mark as he decided whether or not to participate.

'Righto,' he said. 'Come with me, out to the charging room. There's only air cylinders in there, and I don't think they'll say anything. This way.'

Mark indicated for Dennis to stay in the shop. They saw Alex motion to Angie, letting her know where he was going. Once inside the room, Mark looked around. There were several shelves loaded with air cylinders, numerous wetsuits hanging on pegs, and many other items of diving and fishing equipment. One wall was dominated by a stainless-steel tank, which was divided into cylinder sized compartments. Six hoses were protruding through the wall, all attached to cylinders submerged in the tank.

A large gauge was mounted adjacent to each hose. Alex checked each gauge then sat on a steel bench. He indicated Mark to sit in an office chair and looked at him, eyebrows raised in question. Mark withdrew his notepad and pen.

'Well, Alex, it's like this. I am a journalist. An Investigative Journalist, actually. That means I find the trace of a story, dig beneath the surface, and if it's worth writing about, and my bosses approve, I get stuck in and do the full story. Now, sometimes these types of stories are not palatable for some. Sometimes they even hurt people, or worse, get them thrown in jail. It might not sound too great, but that's what I do.'

'Who do you work for?' Alex asked, and Mark noted the suspicion in his tone.

'I write for the 'Sydney Daily News', which I'm sure you've heard of. Although our masthead says Sydney, we are sold and read all over New South Wales.'

Alex grinned at him, despite the tension between the two men.

'Sounds like a radio commercial for your paper. Yeah, I've heard of it. And I read it.'

'Good. Always nice to find a satisfied customer,' Mark returned Alex's grin. 'What I want to talk about is a story that has come my way. It concerns matters going back over three years. About half a dozen of the state's most crooked criminals have all died in mysterious circumstances. And a distinct pattern has emerged. First, these bad eggs get charged with serious offences, ranging from drug dealing, prostitution and theft, right through to assaults and even murder. Then these crims somehow get off, via a dozen different means. Then they go to the media, either the papers or television, and skite about their so-called innocence and usually criticise and poke fun at the cops. Then they die suddenly. Usually it appears as if the death is logical, and easily explained, such as drowning, car crash, train crash or what-ever. But, and here's the twist. The Coroners or Police Surgeons or even Professors at the universities cannot state definite causes of death. Each case says almost word for word the same thing. Something like "all organs and faculties were working normally at the time of death. Therefore, cause of extinguishment of life is unexplained". Now, this has been a recurring pattern for such crooks as Billy Greene, Brother Thompson, Redfern Errol, Scotch Tommy McCleod and a few others. Only this week there were two Italian bastards who suffered the same fate down at Campbelltown Railway Station. Same thing. They appear to have just stopped living. And a few weeks ago, a notorious stand-over man by the name of Albert

Tuckey went west. He apparently drove his nice new Jaguar into a fast moving goods train out near Lithgow. He is rumoured to have been probing into the mysterious deaths of the afore-mentioned bad guys. And, even though he was smashed into little pieces by the train, the coroner will not state a cause of death, because tests have proven his organs had all shut down before the locomotive pulverised the bloke. So, you tell me, how do you drive a big car like a Jag with all your organs shut down? All up, counting the two dagos at Campbelltown, there is at least eight of these unknown or unexplained deaths over the last three years.'

Alex leaned forward and tapped his big fingers on the table beside Mark.

'That is definitely one of the most interesting yarns I have ever heard. But why are you telling it to me? I mean, what possible interest could I have in a bunch of dead crooks? I'm a dive shop operator, not a copper or a private dick. What's it got to do with me?'

Mark stared at the larger man, looking into his clear eyes, trying to gauge his depth of feeling, and searching for signs of discomfort. Years of interviewing guilty criminals and corrupt officials or Police Officers had given him a good insight as to what signs to look for. He was sure he detected the slightest of wavering in Alex's voice and something in those clear eyes told him the big man was rattled.

He spoke slowly, deliberately, while watching Alex closely.

'Well, Alex, it gets back to the tough guy, Albert Tuckey. A few days after his demise, some intriguing articles were found on your boat. Inside an unmarked folder were a couple of photographs and a sheet of paper. The photos showed Tuckey sitting on a park bench seat somewhere, and the other one was his Jag, complete with the number plate clearly showing his rego number. The typed sheet of paper said something along the lines of "complete termination by such and such a date". Now, what do you reckon about that. Why would you, a dive boat operator and not a copper or a private dick, want with pictures like that? And what did the note mean, do you think?'

Alex was clearly uncertain now. Mark noticed his big hands shaking slightly and even with the thick beard he could see the face was slightly paler.

'I would think that folder, if it was found on my boat, would have been dropped by a student. I find all kinds of stuff after some classes. A lot of my pupils are uni students and they are always carrying folders and text books etcetera. If some-one found those photos on board, it probably belonged to a dive pupil. I don't know. That's all I can put it down to. By the way, who found the stuff, and how come you know about it?'

Mark felt he was in familiar territory now, and in complete control of the interview.

'I'm not at liberty to reveal my sources, sorry, Alex. I don't mean any offence here, so please don't take any, but don't you think that's a pretty thin excuse? The folder dropped by a student? Come on. I reckon we both know there's a bit more to it than that. For a start, why would you hang onto it? Why not find the owner and return it?'

Alex took several deep breaths and then stood up. He towered over Mark, even when Mark also stood. Alex leaned down slightly and said, with the slightest trace of threat,

'Listen, Mister. I said before, I am not a cop. Neither are you, so stuff you. You asked me a question, or two, and I gave you honest answers. Now you won't answer my questions, so that's it. Enough chin wagging. Unlike you, I have some fair dinkum work to do. So, I'll ask you in the nicest possible terms, piss off, and scram out of my shop. I don't know what you're probing, and I don't care. Some dimwit left a miserable folder on my boat, and you want to make a federal case out of it. Well, Buster, go make your case elsewhere. Buzz off, and don't waste your breath asking me any more of your silly bloody questions. Goodbye!'

The sudden swing in Alex's mood told Mark he had hit a nerve. Alex's size, obvious muscular physique and threatening mood also told him he would be wise to leave.

He tried one last time.

'Ok, I'm going, Alex. But could you at least hazard a guess who might have dropped the folder on your boat? Anything at all will help.'

'Nope!' came the emphatic reply. 'I've said all I'm going to. Piss off, Newspaper Man. You have outstayed your welcome.'

Mark put his notepad away and nodded. He offered his hand but Alex ignored it and pointed to the door. With a shrug of his shoulders, Mark left and re-entered the shop.

He saw Dennis leaning on the main counter, chatting to a beautiful little Asian woman. He guessed she would be Alex's wife, Angie, who Dennis had told him about. Both looked at Mark, she smiling beautifully and waving.

Mark waved back and signaled to his brother to leave. Dennis said a quick goodbye to Angie and joined Mark at the door.

'How'd it go, mate? You get the answer from Big Alex?' he asked.

'No. I almost got a thick ear from Big Alex, that's what I nearly got. Tell you all about it in the car. Come on, let's get to hell out of here.'

Dennis frowned but followed him to the car. Once they were out of the shop's car park and motoring along the road, Mark told his brother of the conversation.

Dennis was astounded, particularly when Mark mentioned Alex's sudden mood change.

He asked Mark if he had taken any notes. The journalist grinned evilly.

'I haven't done four years at University, a three year cadetship and seven years of snooping and prying in this game to come away empty handed, Brother. I took a few notes, just to make it look good, but here's the real deal.'

He took the tiny tape recorder from his shirt pocket and switched it to "Play".

Dennis listened to the entire conversation, totally spellbound as the voices came in clear and crisp. The change in Alex was patently obvious and he said to Mark,

'Gees, he got off his bike quick, didn't he? And you are right. That's a piss poor explanation about the folder. I tell you, Mate, it was jammed up tight on a book shelf, mounted on the forward bulkhead of the engine room. And I'll tell ya something else for nothing, now I think about it. There was at least two or three identical folders with the one I dropped. Bloody hell! Do you reckon he's hiding something?'

Mark nodded vigorously as he turned into Peel Street.

'Oh, he's hiding something all right. And I'm starting to think I might know what it is. A bit more research by the lovely Jenny and me, and we might blow this wide open. Oh, boy, I can't wait to talk to her and our boss. One thing's for sure, Brother. Your diving instructor, good old Alex, is in something deeper than any ocean he's ever dived in. And I reckon his cute little missus might have something to contribute as well.'

Dennis grinned and laughed with his head tilted back.

'Oh well, good thing I've finished the course. Hey, by the way. You didn't tell him I was the one who found the folder and blabbed to you, did you?'

'No, I didn't. But, I'm thinking, he's a smart cookie. If he gets to thinking about it, and talks it over with his little Asian cutie, it won't take him long to figure it out.'

'Shit!' exclaimed Dennis. 'You're right. I mean, we did think to disguise the fact that we are brothers, at least? But he'll soon connect us together, eh? What a pair of nitwits.'

They had arrived at the family home and Mark turned into the enormous open carport.

'We'll cross that bridge if and when we come to it. I guess he's got your full name and address in his records. Would that be right?'

'Yeah, that's right. Shit, I might start planning a long holiday, to buggery away.'

Mark looked grim as he nodded agreement.

'That might not be a bad scheme. Not a bad idea at all.'

CHAPTER FOURTEEN

Carmen Walker pressed the starter button on her motor scooter and selected first gear. As the scooter began to move she kicked up the stand, folding it away under the slim chassis. She was anxious to get home after a long instructional session with a class of second year university students. Her lessons had been well received but this particular class contained several members who insisted on questioning almost every aspect of the science. Carmen was a patient and thorough lecturer and usually enjoyed the challenge of a class room sniper. This class was well known around the university for having four students with extremely high Intelligence Quotients, and every teacher and lecturer encountering them prepared for additional questions and challenges.

Time had eventually rescued Carmen and she was looking forward to getting to her home, enjoying a shower and a glass of wine. Mike should only be an hour behind her, and they could go for their usual evening walk while they discussed their respective work days. As she turned the scooter out of the University gates she became aware of her helmet chin strap flapping loosely beside her face. She knew she should stop and fasten the strap, but the draining day at her work and the promise of the chance to relax in her home made her continue down the long straight road to the highway.

Nearly four hundred metres from the intersection, a white Toyota Land Cruiser was parked behind a derelict roadside fruit stall. Two men sat in the four-wheel-drive vehicle, both wearing tight fitting surgical gloves and disposable masks. The engine was running and the men watched the road closely. They had parked in this same location, at the same time, for the previous three days to ensure their quarry passed by within a standard time frame. The taller of the two was behind the wheel, while the other man, smaller and older, sat in the left rear seat of the vehicle. This man wore a pale blue safari suit and a white straw hat. His left hand held a typewritten note, folded in half. His companion was dressed in smart, casual clothes. He wore a pair of dark glasses and his head was covered by a faded blue baseball cap.

When Carmen passed by, her red scooter buzzing and emitting a thin trail of blue, two stroke smoke, the Land Cruiser swung out from behind the fruit stall and accelerated after her. In half a minute the four-wheel-drive was easily cruising behind the scooter, with only twenty metres separating the two vehicles.

'Make sure there are no cars about, Harold. We have to time this to perfection,' the rear seat passenger said. 'That spot near the culvert we saw yesterday will be ideal.'

'Gotchya !' the driver acknowledged. 'Coming up to it now. Here goes.'

The driver accelerated slightly, bringing the front bumper bar of the truck to within a metre of the rear of the scooter. As the twin white guide posts marking the concrete culvert drew level, Harold let the front bumper-bar gently nudge the back of Carmen's scooter.

The move was designed to unbalance the scooter, and hopefully tip the rider off, into the grassy water drain beside the road. They had estimated a reasonably fit person, wearing a padded leather coat and a helmet, would only suffer minor bruising and a fright. The old man was clutching the typewritten note which bore the words, "Take this as your 1st and only warning, Mrs Detective.

Loose everything you have on the Malaysian Beetle Venom, and never mention it to anyone, especially Mr Detective. Our next action will not be a warning. Remember the Muscatts".

Their plan was to ensure Carmen was only slightly injured, but sufficiently frightened. They would then deliver the note to her and leave her to her own devices.

The plan went awry immediately the Land Cruiser nudged the scooter.

Being totally unaware of the proximity of the truck, Carmen felt the bump, glanced into her right rear vision mirror and panicked. She stepped hard on the rear wheel brake pedal and pulled the front wheel brake lever full on.

The scooter stopped almost completely, and the Land Cruiser hit hard.

Carmen was thrown high into the air, and her loose helmet left her head, spiralling away to her right. As the four-wheel-drive ran over the scooter, completely wrecking the little machine, the men inside watched in horror as Carmen landed in the culvert, her bare head smashing violently into the earth, and her body rolled rapidly four times before colliding with the concrete pipe.

Harold brought the truck to an emergency stop and ran to where Carmen lay.

He scrambled down to her, and saw blood running from her ears and nose. He gently rolled her onto her side and checked for her pulse. He detected a faint throb and listened to her ragged breathing for a few seconds.

'Is she still alive?' the old man's nervous voice came from up on the road.

Harold looked up, grimacing as he removed his surgical mask.

'Just. She's in a bad way, but there's a faint pulse and she's breathing. What now?'

'Let's get away from here, and call an Ambulance. But, give her the note first.' the old man ordered. Harold checked her other injuries and straightened her bleeding legs. He took one last look at her, shaking his head sadly, before tucking the warning note into her handbag which was somehow still attached by it's strap to her shoulder. Then he hurried back to the truck and they drove quickly from the scene. After reaching an intersection, they turned right and drove towards the big inland city of Wagga Wagga. A roadside café appeared and Harold pulled the vehicle into the small car park.

The old man said excitedly, pointing to the side of the building,

'There's a phone! You go buy something from the shop, I'll call the Ambulance.'

He left the truck and entered the open telephone booth where he quickly dialled three 'O's and, when connected to the Ambulance Control Centre, reported the crash as an accident. The emergency operator asked for his name, he replied 'Tommy Jenkins' as the first name which came to him. He hung up the instrument just as Harold emerged from the shop, carrying two bottles of soft drink.

Without a word both men entered the Toyota and continued towards Wagga Wagga.

Fifteen minutes later, just as they reached the outskirts of the city, a white ambulance came speeding towards them, red lights flashing and siren blaring. It quickly disappeared in the mirrors and Harold slowed down as they entered the streets of Wagga Wagga. He drove directly to the converted service station from where they had hired the vehicle four days earlier, and parked at the kerb. He tossed the keys onto the floor as the old man removed their two suitcases. Without looking back they walked together to the nearby railway station. Harold checked his watch.

'That was good timing. The train should be here in about ten minutes,' he muttered.

'Let's hope the bloody thing is on time. We need to be out of this joint, pronto!'

Harold nodded and muttered, almost to himself,

'Shit! What a stuff up! It all went wrong because the stupid bitch jammed on her brakes. Why don't they teach women to drive properly?'

'Nothing we can do about it, Mate. You're right, it is a stuff up but it's no use crying over spilt milk. I just hope she recovers and takes heed of our message. We've had other stuff-ups before. Gee, I hope this train's on time,' the old man said, donning his white straw hat as they trudged onto Wagga Wagga's railway platform.

Mike Walker picked up a newspaper from the pile on the Police Station's front counter. The civilian clerk typing at a nearby desk looked up and smiled.

'Hello, Mike,' she said. 'I've got a telephone message for you. It just came in, from your good lady wife.'

Mike read the message. It said simply Carmen expected to be home a bit late, but should still beat him home. He smiled and folded the note as he walked up the internal stair case and into the Detectives' office. After stripping off his suit coat, he placed it neatly over the back of his chair. There was no-one else in the office so he crossed to the sink, filled the electric kettle and returned to his desk to wait for it to boil. Turning his attention to the newspaper, Mike sat down to relax, but jerked to attention as he read the large, block lettered headline.

"WHO IS KILLING OUR TOP CROOKS....AND HOW?" the headline read.

The article was by-lined Mark Stein and Jenny Bates. Underneath the by-line were pictures of Albert Tuckey and Billy

Greene. He read the entire article, which took up the whole front page, then turned to page five as instructed. The article continued for most of page five with pictures of Ian Carter, Scotch Tommy McCleod and Redfern Errol. The writers teased him with snippets of information about the mysterious deaths. The reader was told of the complete absence of known causes of death, and how all the scientific minds in the state were engaged in finding out just how all these men died. It explored the possibility of a previously unknown poison being used. It also posed the question, who was killing these criminals and why. The writers pointed out the common theme and a regular pattern consisting of charges, acquittals, press conferences then unexplained deaths. A stoic "No Comment" was recorded from the Chief Coroner and the Minister for Justice. The reporters went on to suggest these killings may be semi-officially sanctioned, or at least a blind eye was being turned. The article ended with the promise of more in tomorrow's edition as well as parts three and four to follow.

Mike's excitement grew as he read the entire article a second time. He was reading it for a third time when he heard the heavy tread of Sergeant Johnson ascending the outside stairs. He quickly folded the newspaper and shoved it into his brief case.

The kettle had boiled and switched itself off while he was reading so he crossed to the sink again and re-activated it. Johnson flung open the door and entered the office.

'Oh, G'day Sarg. Just in time for a cup of mud. Want one?' he called cheerfully.

'Yeah, right-o. I could do with a strong one. I feel a bit buggered. Listen, we have to get more statements from old Louis Daley about the cigarettes Monk and company knocked off. Now that Monk and his mates are disputing the amount of cartons, we have to get Daley's double guarantee the count is right. Soon as we finish this brew, we'll go down to Copland Street and interview old Louis and his head storeman again. And while we're down that way we need to get the rego papers and insurance on that heap of shit Transit truck they also knocked off.'

'Ok, Sarg. I can't wait to get this one back into court. I can't see Monk or his two Sydney mates getting out of this one,' Mike answered.

Johnson grunted in agreement and reached for the mug Mike handed him.

It was nearing four o'clock that afternoon when the two detectives had collected all of the statements and other paperwork. Mike drove back to the Police Station while Johnson sorted the sheets of paper into their correct order. They went straight to the office and Mike was just about to sit at his desk when the uniformed figure of Sergeant Brady burst in.

'Mike!' he said. 'I thought it was you. Listen, Mate. Carmen's been in an accident. It happened about an hour ago, out on the Coolamon Road. She's up at the hospital, Mate. They've only just identified her.'

'Oh, shit!' Mike exclaimed, grabbing his coat. 'Any word on how she is, Lenny?'

'I don't have any details, Mike. Wendy Good is up there with Wayne Burley. They're both waiting for you in Casualty. You got transport?'

'Take our car, Mikey. I'll get a lift home with some other bugger. Go on. Go!'

Johnson told him. 'Hope she's all right, Mate. Give her my best.'

'Yeah, mine too,' Brady called as Mike ran out the doorway and leapt down the stairs three at a time.

Johnson looked at Brady and asked,

'What time did all this come in, Len?'

'The original call was from the 'Ambos' around forty minutes ago. Wendy was on the phone to me when you two drove in, so that's the first I knew that it was Carmen.'

'And, tell me, Mate. Is there any real word on her condition? Do ya know anything else about how bad, or not, she is?' Johnson asked suspiciously.

Brady grimaced and sat down at Mike's desk.

'Wendy put a doctor on the phone when she rang. This quack said it was bad, real bad. It looks like a hit and run. Some low prick knocked her off that silly bloody motor scooter she rides, and left her for dead. This doc reckons she's got massive head and internal injuries. I asked him if they are life threatening and all he said was "we'll do what we can". Wendy said she looked a proper mess when she saw her. Poor bugger was covered in her own blood and both her legs looked broken.'

'Christ!' Johnson exclaimed. 'Poor little bugger. Poor bloody Mike, too. Hey, who's nvestigating the hit 'n' run?'

Brady stood to leave as he answered,

'The boss originally gave it to Highway, and got Tate and Potter to assist. When I just told him it was Mike's missus, he said he's gonna get a couple of blokes from Accident Investigation to do it. Fair enough, too. Too close to home, this one.'

Mike parked the Holden Police car in an ambulance bay and ran in through the wide glass doors marked CASUALTY. He went to a nurse sitting at a desk and said, panting.

'Sorry to interrupt, Nurse. I'm Detective Mike Walker, Wagga Police. You have my wife Carmen in here somewhere. Whereabouts is she, please?'

Before the nurse could answer, Constable Wayne Burley appeared from a side door.

'In here, Mike. She's here. There's a mob of doctors and nurses with her but they said you can go straight in.' Burley pointed to a closed door as he spoke.

Mike pushed the door open and froze. A bloodied, bandaged figure was lying on a hospital bed, with several tubes attached to her arms, an oxygen mask over her nose and mouth and a nurse was operating the demand valve, essentially breathing for Carmen. He knew it was Carmen instantly by the shock of red hair protruding from a head bandage, and the freckled skin on her two long legs sitting in stainless steel cradles. Constable Wendy Good was standing near the door, her eyes red and her uniform blouse damp with tears. Three white coated doctors turned to look at him when he entered. A fourth was shining a tiny but powerful torch into Carmen's eyes, speaking loudly to her as he sought a re-action. Two more nurses were attaching an electronic device to Carmen's finger. Mike addressed the entire group.

'What's the score, Doctors? I'm Mike Walker, her husband.'

The tallest of the white coated figures walked around the bed and came to Mike.

'I am Doctor Willard, Mister Walker. Your wife's had a very severe accident. At this stage we are conducting some tests to tell us the extent of her injuries. She has lost a lot of blood, both her legs are broken, as is her right wrist. She has suffered severe trauma to her head and neck. We'll know more when we complete the tests. Meanwhile, we will keep her in an induced coma to help her avoid some pain. I can't tell you any more than that, Mister Walker. I'm sorry.'

Mike looked at him and saw the saddness in his eyes. He knew instantly that the doctor was keeping something from him.

'How would you describe her condition, then Doc? Severe?' he asked.

'Um, No, Critical would be nearer the mark. But, it's early days yet,' the doctor said.

Wendy came over to him and hugged him, tears falling from her eyes again. Burley joined them and gripped Mike's shoulder.

'How about we go sit down, and let these good people do their best for Carmen, eh Mike?' Burley asked gently.

'That would be best, Mister Walker,' Doctor Willard said. 'We'll keep you informed, I promise. If there is anything you can do, we'll come get you, Ok?'

Mike stared at Carmen for a while before nodding agreement. The three police officers left the room and a nurse showed them to a small kitchenette that was normally reserved for Ambulance staff only. They sat in hard chairs around a square table. Shock had begun to take hold of Mike. He watched as Burley made a pot of tea, and Wendy Good held his hands in hers as she cried.

Despite his shock, Mike soon realised Wendy and Burley knew more than he did.

'Hey, Wen. Settle down, Love. Did those doctors tell you anything more than they told me? Wayne, what about you? You know anything?'

Burley shook his head slowly but Wendy looked up and said,

'We shouldn't say this, Mike, but we heard them talking before you arrived. One of them said he would be surprised if she made it through the night. Another said he thought she would be disabled if she did. I'm so sorry Mike, but I can't lie to you. It looks really serious, Mike.'

CHAPTER FIFTEEN

The Commander waited patiently for his call to be answered. He looked around his well-appointed lounge room, with genuine antiques crowded on every shelf, and original oil and water colours hanging from all walls. An independent valuer had once calculated that he had invested close to a half million dollars in this art and antique collection.

He began a mental re-appraisal but was interrupted by an answer to his telephone call.

'Hello. Judge speaking,' said the gruff voice.

'Hello, Sir. This is the Commander. We have a problem, I'm afraid. Are you free to speak?'

'Yes, Commander, I'm alone. Did the Wagga mission go ahead?' the gruff voice responded.

'Yes, it went ahead, but with a less than desirable outcome, I fear. As I said at our last meeting, the main Operative Team refused to participate, so I was obliged to use my other Operative. I accompanied him on the strike, but, alas, I have to report an unfavourable result. It was agreed only small injuries were to be inflicted, and the stern warning delivered. Well, unfortunately it did not pan out that way...'

He went on, explaining Carmen's unexpected re-action, the subsequent harder than anticipated collision, her helmet flying free and the resultant severe injuries.

When he had finished his report the Commander waited for a response.

'Well, that is most unfortunate, as you say, Commander. Do you think we should call another emergency meeting?' the leader of the Retribution Committee asked.

'I don't see much point. My Operative placed the warning note in her handbag, and I spoke to the local Wagga Wagga commercial radio station just before calling you. Apparently, she is in a critical condition in Intensive Care, and her husband, the curious Detective, is with her. I would dare to suggest we adopt a watching brief for the next week or so, and sort of play it by ear. Do you agree?' the Commander said.

'Yes! Right!' the gruff voice replied. 'That's what we'll do. Failing any dramatic developments, we will leave it at that, but you will need to construct a full written report for the group, to be presented at the next scheduled meeting. That is in over three weeks time. I will contact our friend, the Commissioner and give him the details. That way he will have time to find out more from his staff at Wagga Wagga. It will also give him a chance to calm down. He was dead against this operation, so expect him to vent his spleen on you at the next meeting. I don't see the need for him to know you were on that operation personally, do you?'

The Commander was grateful for this last suggestion.

'No, I don't think he need know that. Thank you, Judge. Is that all?'

'Yes, that's it. Goodnight Commander.'

The telephone went dead and the Commander replaced the hand piece.

He sat in his lounge chair, thinking over the last few days events, and the telephone call to the Judge "I think I've just about had enough of this lark" he thought to himself.

Breaking from his usual temperate existence, he poured himself a triple malt whisky, and slowly sipped his second alcoholic drink of the year.

Mike Walker stared down into the pale face of his wife. She looked peaceful, despite the myriad of apparatus, tubes and wires attached to her body. Her legs were wrapped in thick plaster, and her left arm was similarly bound. Some of the bruising and scratches had disappeared over the last few days, but she still sported a heavy bandage around her head and several lighter bandages covered cuts and abrasions on her right arm, neck and torso. In the four days she had lain in the Intensive Care bed, he had not heard a sound from her. This morning when he entered the tiny IC ward, the on-duty nursing sister told him Carmen had groaned softly when the nurses had repositioned her at around six-thirty that morning.

'It's a good sign, Mister Walker, honestly it is', the sister had said, smiling to him.

'It means she is regaining some feeling, somewhere. Doctor Willard came up straightaway, and was very pleased with the news. You should be too.'

Mike had nodded agreement and thanked the senior nurse.

He then took up his usual position on a high stool next to Carmen and clasped her right hand in his own. He talked quietly to her, reminding her of some nice holidays they had taken, and reassuring her of the plans they had discussed for the future. He told her he was certain now to take her back to her homeland of Ireland, to visit the areas she had known as a small child. He said they would take the trip as soon as she recovered. And she would recover, he told her over and over, just like the doctors had suggested. The Police Chaplain had visited daily, and he, too, assured the unconscious woman she would recover, adding it was God's will, and He will assist her.

Inspector Fisher visited yesterday, accompanied by the Sector Commander, Superintendent Alfred Worthing. Mike was touched by the attention of these high powered visitors, and thanked them warmly. Sergeant Johnson was a daily visitor, and numerous personnel from the Police Station, the Fire Station and some Ambulance Officers all called at the IC front desk, leaving cards, flowers or hand written messages. Most of Mike's football team mates did the same, with some of them leaving a football signed by the rest of the first grade team, and glued to a polished plinth of red gum timber. Mike was touched by all this goodwill and thoughtful wishes, but he was also interested in the investigation by the crash team from Sydney.

The only information they had passed on to him was they were investigating the possible involvement of a four-wheel-drive vehicle, hired from 'Big River Car & Truck Rentals', of Edward Street, Wagga Wagga. Things were becoming difficult, however, as it had now become known the name and address given to the hire car clerk was false, and the fee was paid in cash. The security deposit of one hundred and fifty dollars had not been collected on return of the vehicle. The truck was simply parked out the front of the converted service station which now served as the hire company's premises, with the keys on the floor. Detective George Somersby had swept the entire vehicle for fingerprints, but found none. He opined that the vehicle had been freshly wiped with methylated spirit, a known fingerprint remover.

There was evidence of some flecks of red paint on the bumper bar, mounted on the front of the truck, but not enough to prove useful.

Just after ten o'clock a nurse handed Mike a refreshing cup of tea. As he sipped on his drink he replayed the recent past in his mid. Johnson had visited around nine, left another posy of flowers for Carmen and told Mike a further two weeks compassionate leave had been arranged for him. It was after the big Sergeant had left that the nurse brought him the tea, and he was still sitting beside Carmen's bed. As he thought over the recent past, he recalled the conversation he had had with Johnson in the bar across the road from the Police Station, a little over a week ago. The veiled threats, the information that he and Muscatt had "trodden on some very big toes", and the fact Johnson had been ordered to warn Mike away from the murder cases, all slowly swirled around in his head until a frightening thought formed. He shook his head, trying to force the thought from his mind, but it would not leave. As it became firmer and clearer in his mind, anger also began to rise in him.

"Did these murdering bastards do this to her? Have they somehow found out about her knowledge of the deadly little Malaysian beetles?" he thought to himself.

At first he could not think anyone would deliberately harm Carmen. She had never spoken a harsh word about any other human, as far as he knew. Her wild sense of humour and easy going nature endeared her to anyone who met her. But the thought kept returning, and then he remembered the Crash Investigation Officers who had visited him at home two nights ago. They told him it was evident the crash was a 'Hit and Run' type, and a stranger had telephoned for an ambulance from a public telephone situated at 'Linda's Kitchen', a popular roadhouse located not three kilometres from where Carmen and her smashed scooter were found. The caller had given an unknown name, but the proprietor of the road house recalled a white Toyota Land Cruiser leaving her car park in a hurry at the time of the triple 'O' call was made. They were sure a false licence had been presented to the hire car clerk, as the address recorded turned out to be a vacant block of ground in Sutherland.

Gradually some wild thoughts settled down in Mike's mind. He recalled the newspaper articles about the mysterious deaths which he and Allan Muscatt had been probing. He had read the first article but the remaining three newspapers were laying unread in his lounge room. Checking his watch, Mike decided he had to follow up these disturbing thoughts, and those articles were the first step. He rose and said to the nurse who was sitting at the other side of Carmen's bed,

'Listen, Bronwyn. I'm going home for a spell. You'll call me if she wakes up or does anything, won't you?'

'Of course I will, Mike. You go and try to get some rest. We'll be right on to you if anything occurs, believe me. Off you go, get to bed,' Bronwyn smiled as she spoke.

Mike left IC and took the elevator direct to the ground floor. He hurried to his car and was soon motoring quickly towards his home in the suburb of Glenfield Park.

During the drive he thought of Sergeant Johnson's warnings, both recent and when he first mentioned the patterns of the deaths. He remembered the day he went jogging and was followed by a strange car. This turned out to be an unmarked Police car, operated by the dreaded and loathed Internal Affairs Division. Then there was Allan Muscatt being warned off by his supervisor, and the subsequent suspicious death of Muscatt and his wife, Heather. This was all backed up by his discovery of his best friend Andy Keyes's massive wealth, with large deposits into his account corresponding with the deaths of the criminals. Carmen's discovery of the deadly little Malaysian beetles was significant, especially when it became known the beetles were native to only one tiny area of Malaysia. Keyes' Malaysian wife, Anita, originated from that same tiny area. The final fact was the strange disappearance of the Keyes from their working farm at The Rock, twenty-five kilometres south of Wagga Wagga. After searching the farm and homestead, Mike and Carmen had chanced upon Andy's cricket kit. Among the various sporting paraphernalia was Andy's brand new bat, with a cryptic note to Mike attached. This note had virtually confirmed Mike's suspicions, but also warned him to leave the matter alone, and simply be a good, honest Detective.

He was collating all of these facts when he drove into his driveway and stopped the Falcon in front of the garage roller doors. He was suddenly very keen to read those other articles in the Sydney papers. If he was correct in his assumptions, the reporters who compiled those stories might have information to contribute regarding Carmen's trauma and he was intent on finding out what they knew.

He unlocked his front door and ran to the lounge room. Quickly locating the three papers he was looking for, he sat down and began to read. It soon became apparent that the reporters were following the same path as he and Allan Muscatt had. They had noticed the deaths of some of New South Wales' most notorious criminals, and they also laid out the pattern of events. Criminal is charged with serious offences, Criminal gets off the charges in court, usually under dubious circumstances. Criminal goes to the media, claiming innocence and Police corruption or incompetence. Then the criminal is found dead, and every scientific mind at the disposal of the Coroner is put to work, trying to establish a definite cause of death. And finally, no cause of death is recorded.

The reporters added that Coroner's Court staff confirmed the intense investigations which took place after each death were conducted by Professors from every university around the country, as well as forensic examiners from the Police, and even two scientists from the American F.B.I. had been called in. The result was always the same. Open Finding, as all organs were obvious working pre-mortem.

Mike noted the reporters wisely neglected to name their sources, but suddenly one little paragraph caught his attention. "A small dossier on a recently departed individual was found on a charter fishing boat. This discovery led to the present investigation by this newspaper…..". No details of the mystery boat, it's owner or it's location were given, but it struck Mike as a loose end to be tied up.

Mike re-read each instalment of the story several times, writing down some details in a new notebook. He copied down the names Mark Stein and Jenny Bates, and the business name and address of the editorial offices of the paper.

He was convinced now that Carmen's accident was no co-incidence. Who-ever he was dealing with were ruthless, deadly, and obviously confident they would remain anonymous. The fact that they were prepared to possibly kill to protect themselves was now all too apparent. Then it suddenly dawned on him why Carmen was targeted.

She was the only person, apart from the criminal killers, who knew about the poisonous beetles from Malaysia.

"But", he wondered, "how could they find out Carmen knew about the poison?"

He thought hard, until an awful truth came to him.

"Bloody Internal Affairs ! It had to be".

He remembered the night he thought he had heard the front gate squeak. Then the next morning, Carmen found strange shoe prints in the soft soil in the front garden.

Some spying must have taken place, and he and Carmen were the targets.

Johnson had told him he had been ordered to tell Mike to back off, and no-one gave orders to big Sergeant Lindsay Johnson, unless……unless it was from the Police Hierarchy ! That same hierarchy who controlled Internal Affairs.

So, poor Carmen had to suffer for his obstinance, and reluctance to take a warning.

Thinking of Carmen made him picture her, dressed in hospital robes, swathed in hospital bandages and lying unconscious in a hospital bed.

He looked across the room and saw the pile of her bloodied clothing and belongings he had brought home from the hospital the second night after her smash. He rose and crossed to the lounge chair where the things had landed. Her smart leather coat was torn and covered in her blood. So, too was her tiny skirt and blouse, although her university identification card, complete with portrait photograph, was still clinging to the collar. The helmet was scarred and had mud clinging to it. Her ankle boots were muddy and one had a broken heel. Then he saw her handbag. It was red and white patent leather, one of her favourites. The strap was intact and the zip fastener was still closed. Slowly, sadly Mike unzipped the fastener. Some dried mud fell to the floor and he watched the tiny flakes scatter into the carpet. He reached in and clutched her money purse and withdrew his hand. The purse did not appear to have been opened, so he left it that way. There was some lipsticks, a small make-up compact and a folding knife which he knew she always carried. Then he found a single sheet of paper, pushed into a corner of the handbag. Frowning, he withdrew the sheet and opened it from it's folded position. He gasped as he read the typewritten message:

"Take this as your 1st and only warning, Mrs Detective. Loose everything you have on the Malaysian Beetle Venom, and never mention it to anyone, especially Mr Detective.

Our next action will not be a warning. Remember the Muscatts" Mike's anger rose instantly as he read the threat.

"The rotten bastards!" he thought. "I was right. My poor little darling was targeted just because of what she found out about those stinking beetles. And that proves what happened to Allan and Heather. Christ, what low bastards."

He refolded up the note and kicked out in pure rage. The lounge chair was moved nearly a metre across the floor. Then he picked up the nearest object, a tableside lamp, and smashed it into the wall. The sound of the breaking glass in the lamp brought him to his senses, and his anger was gradually replaced with a cool determination. Still shaking, he walked to the kitchen and grabbed a can of beer from the refrigerator. He swallowed the beer in three gulps and reached for a second. Before he opened the can, he stopped, his mind racing as he thought of how best to topple this self-styled bunch of do-gooders who had hurt his beloved Carmen.

Tossing the unopened can into the sink, he returned to the lounge and retrieved his notebook. He underlined the newspaper office address as a plan formed in his mind.

With a rough plan determined, Mike ran up the stairs and grabbed a suitcase and quickly packed four changes of underwear, four shirts, two pairs of trousers and a pair of casual shoes. He threw in a jumper and a few toiletries before snapping the lid shut.

He decided he needed to refresh himself so he quickly showered and changed into sports trousers and a short-sleeved polo shirt. Before donning a casual jumper, he slipped on his shoulder holster and fitted the Smith and Wesson revolver into it, then clicked on his watch. When he checked his wallet, apart from his Police Badge, Driver's Licence and two credit cards, the wallet contained nearly three hundred dollars.

Satisfied, Mike lifted the suitcase and hurried down the stairs to the lounge room. After collecting the notebook, newspapers and the threatening note to Carmen, he went out through the front door and tossed the case into the boot of his Ford Falcon sedan. Before leaving he checked the back door, all windows on both levels and locked the front main door and fly screen.

He drove to the hospital and parked in the public car park before entering the building.

CHAPTER SIXTEEN

Detective Sergeant Lindsay Johnson parked his unmarked Holden Police car in the section of the Wagga Base Hospital car park which was sign posted :
'Emergency Service Vehicles Only All Other Vehicles Will Be Towed Away'.

A Police cage truck and a large white ambulance occupied two of the other three spaces provided. He grasped a bunch of red and white roses and a large box of chocolates from the front seat and stepped out, remembering to lock the car doors.

He trudged slowly to the double glass doors of the main entrance and took the elevator to the fourth floor. He approached the Nurses' Station at the entrance to IC. Three nurses were completing paper work as they sipped on cups of tea and coffee.

'G'day, you hard working girls. Just here to see Carmen Walker 'n' drop these here flowers orf, Ok? The chokkies are for you girls, though. Here ya are.'

'Oh, Sarg,' the senior nurse replied. They had all got to know Johnson since their star patient had arrived from the Operating Theatre nearly a week ago. He visited daily and always brought flowers for Carmen and chocolates for the nurses.

'I suppose Mike's in there, keepin' up his bedside vigil, as the press call it?'

The senior nurse took the box of chocolates and smiled her thanks. A dark-haired nurse with light brown skin and tired eyes answered him.

'He was here from about seven-thirty this morning. He left about nine, and he called in about an hour ago. He sat with Carmen for only about ten minutes, then he left again. He said he had to take an urgent trip and wouldn't be in for a few days. We all thought it a bit weird, because he's hardly left her bedside since she's been here.'

A strange, almost panic stricken look came over Johnson as he listened to the nurse.

'About an hour ago, you say? Did he happen to say where this trip is to? Did he give a clue, or say what it is about?' he asked, trying to make his voice sound normal.

'No. He just said it was urgent and important, and he would be a few days,' she replied. 'He did say he would telephone every few hours to check on her condition. That's all, Sarg. Sorry.'

Johnson thought for a moment, then, as he realised what his next actions would have to be, he smiled roughly at the three women.

'Ok, thanks, girls. Could ya give these here to Carmen for me? I just remembered I got a job I have to do straight away.' he handed the roses to the senior nurse and waved good bye as he left, walking quickly to the elevators.

Once back in the car, he drove as fast as he dared to the Police Station and bounded up the stairs to the Detectives' Offices. Two other detectives were at their desks, each thumping at typewriters. They greeted Johnson and asked if there was any news on Carmen.

Johnson told them she was still in a coma, but there was no other news. As soon as the two returned to their tasks, Johnson went to a spare desk at the other end of the room, where he was certain the others would not hear him. Fumbling in his coat pocket, he withdrew his official notebook and flipped it to the last page. On the inside cover a Sydney telephone number was printed in erasable pencil. With slightly shaking fingers he dialled the number and waited for it to be answered. After ten rings an unfamiliar voice answered.

'Commissioner's Suite. Acting Inspector Parkinson. Who is this, please?'

The voice sounded full of authority and self-importance. He had not expected anyone but the head man to answer, and Johnson was momentarily stumped.

'Ah, yes. Mister Parkinson. Ah, could I speak to the Commissioner, please. It is rather urgent and important. I am not at liberty to give you my name, sorry.'

There was silence from the other end, then the voice said sternly, 'If you cannot identify yourself, then I cannot help you. Who is it, and what do you want, Sir?'

Johnson became totally frustrated as he pictured some skinny, intelligent officer who had probably never made an arrest or been on patrol. A near useless Brainiac, as the field officers called these computer literate, academic and clever men.

'Look, Mate. I can't tell ya who I am, but the big man knows me. How else would I get this number, eh? Is he around or not?' Johnson grated.

'He is at an important meeting with the Fire Brigades Chief Officer, if you must know. All I can do for you is take a message. Would you like me to do that?'

'No!' Johnson barked, louder than he intended. 'Any idea what time he will be back, then? I will have to call him again.'

'He is due back here for lunch with some retiring senior officers at one o'clock.'

'Right, I'll call back then. Thanks, Champion,' Johnson growled and hung up.

He checked his watch. Nine forty-five. By the time he could speak to the Commissioner Mike would have the best part of four hours start.

Johnson had a good idea where Mike was heading, and he grinned to himself as he thought of the start he had. By the time the search started, which Johnson was certain would be the case, Mike should be almost in Sydney, or no more than an hour and a half from it. He decided he would muddy the waters as much as he could for Mike, without actually jeopardising himself or his own position.

Mike Walker turned off the Hume Highway and stopped in a side street. The throaty growl of the big vee-eight engine dropped to a rumble as he applied the parking brake and selected neutral. He knew he was in the suburb of Liverpool, and there were several different routes into the city of Sydney from here. Mike picked up the street directory from the passenger seat and plotted the simplest and most route for his direct journey.

Selecting the Newbridge and Canterbury Roads route, he memorised the major intersections and landmarks before resuming his journey. The first set of traffic lights he came to were showing red, and he brought the car to a smooth stop well behind the solid white line. As soon as the car stopped moving, a fully marked Highway Patrol Holden Commodore drew to halt beside him. He glanced at the Police car and noted two stern looking individuals looking him and the Falcon over. His car sported wide, chrome plated road wheels, additional driving lights and a black badge which told all and sundry the machine was powered by a huge five point eight litre engine. The four speed gearbox and throaty twin exhausts added to the car's sportyness, but he knew it automatically drew the attention of Traffic Officers.

The Officer in the passenger seat reached out and tapped Mike's window. When Mike looked at him, the Officer indicated he wanted him to pull over once the lights turned green and both cars were clear of the intersection.

"Just what I don't bloody need", he thought grimly. The lights changed and Mike drove through the large intersection and pulled into a short side street. The Police car parked behind him and Mike left his car and walked quickly toward the Holden. He wanted to speak to the two Officers before they radioed in his registration number or any other details. Once that message was logged, his whereabouts could easily be made known. He was hoping to keep a very low profile on this trip, as far as other Police were concerned. He neared the Police car and the passenger quickly stepped out, his right hand resting on his holstered pistol butt.

Mike decided on the friendly approach and smiled as he raised both of his hands.

'Hold on, Mate. Leave it in it's home. I'm in the job.'

As he spoke he reached into his shirt pocket and withdrew his wallet, opening the first flap to reveal his Police Badge.

The driver of the Highway Patrol car alighted and peered at Mike's badge.

'Name and rank, thanks Sir. And what section?' he asked pleasantly.

Mike noted the other Officer had visibly relaxed and now joined his colleague.

'Mike Walker, Detective Senior Constable, Wagga C.I.D. And up until a year ago, of Wagga Highway Patrol, all right?'

'Oh, right. Walker, was it?' the driver asked, smiling at Mike and the second Officer.

'That's right. Mike Walker. You blokes "routine-ing" me?'

The driver looked sheepish as he admitted,

'Well, this beast caught our eyes, actually, Mike. She yours or a company car?'

'No, she's mine. Got it new eighteen months ago. I know she tends to stand out a bit, but I love it. That does not mean I go Hooning in her. Want to see the rego papers?'

Both Highway Officers shook their heads and smiled. They took turns in shaking Mike's hand and apologising for interrupting his trip. He nodded as he said to them,

'That's Ok. I'm just on my way to see my dad. He's a bit crook and I haven't spoken to him for a while. Look, boys, I'd like to continue, if we're finished, Ok?'

The two men both assured him he was free to go, and both wished his father the best.

As he U turned and drove away, Mike thought it ironic he used his father as a reason for being in Sydney. His father had died in Canberra in nineteen sixty-two, and as far as Mike knew, had never set foot in Sydney.

He concentrated on navigating his way through the suburbs of the bustling city until he found the main thoroughfare which would lead him almost to the door of the newspaper offices. He turned off Broadway into Wattle Street, then made a right turn into MacArthur. He saw the large neon sign bearing the name of the newspaper attached high on the front of a six storey office building, and searched for a car parking space. Finding no vacant spaces, Mike drove a complete circuit of the block, arriving back at the newspaper offices in time to see a large van pull in front of him from an open loading dock. Without a second thought, he drove into the dock and parked. The driveway was wide enough for two large trucks, so he stopped the Ford well over to the left, allowing any delivery vehicles sufficient space to back up to the double loading stage. He collected the newspapers, his notebook and the crumpled warning note. After locking the car, he walked briskly around to the front entrance and consulted the directory mounted in the foyer.

As he travelled in the luxurious elevator to the fourth floor, Mike planned his actions.

The doors opened with a loud chime, and he stepped out, taking in the glass walled offices and rooms. To his right a pretty blonde girl of around twenty sat a desk, clicking away on an elaborate electric typewriter. A gold embossed plaque above her head bore the words 'SYDNEY DAILY NEWS' and proudly stated in smaller letters, "Getting to the Truth is What Matters Most".

He walked to her desk and waited until she finished typing and looked enquiringly at him. He gave her his most pleasant smile and said,

'I'm here to see Mark Stein and Jenny Bates, please.'

'And you are?' she smiled at him, but her smile was as fake as her fingernails.

Mike had anticipated this question and had put some thought into his reply.

'I'm a friend of theirs from the Coroner's Court at Glebe. They asked me to bring them some confidential data.'

'Oh, I see.' The girl's attitude immediately improved. 'I don't think Jenny is in, but Mark should be. Please hold on a moment. What was the name, please?'

'Duncan. Duncan Biscuit,' he answered with sarcasm.

His joke was lost on the girl as she dialled an internal number. He heard the call ringing, then a loud click as it was answered.

'Hello, Mark. I have a man called Duncan to see you or Jenny. He says he's from the Coroner's Court and you asked him for some data. Yes? Ok, I'll tell him.'

She hung up her telephone and smiled at Mike again.

'Mark is coming straightaway. Did you say your name is Biscuit?'

'Yeah, that's right. B.I.Z.C.O.T. It's Yugoslavian,' he told her, hiding his smirk.

Then he heard a voice behind him.

'Ah, Duncan, is it? I'm Mark Stein. You told Amanda you had something for Jenny and me?'

Mike turned and saw a young, smartly dressed man, wearing an expensive suit and shoes, hair neatly cut and combed, a pair of sparkling gold pens protruding from his coat pocket and a large gold watch attached to his left wrist.

The two shook hands and Mike steered the younger man away from Amanda's desk.

'Mr Stein, we need to talk. Privately, like. It's in relation to the articles you and your colleague wrote regarding the unexplained deaths of all those crooks.'

Stein looked Mike over, obviously deciding what to do next.

'Just who are you, Mate? Who do you represent? I'd like to know who I'm dealing with before I lock myself up in secret conferences.'

'Look, this is vital. I'll tell you all about myself if you tell me some things I need to know. I am not here to harm you, and I can't do you any nasty stuff even if I wanted to. But we must talk, and it must be completely private. Now, you got somewhere?'

Stein hesitated again, but something about this stranger excited his curiosity.

'Ok, Mister. Follow me. We have a sound proof room where we sometimes talk to informants or witnesses. You want a coffee or something?'

'I could go a cup of tea, if you wouldn't mind. Black with one, if it's ok.'

In five minutes the two men sat opposite each other in a room measuring no more than four by six metres. There were no windows, just a table, three chairs and an empty book shelf. On the table sat a large, twin tape magnetic recorder. Two identical microphones were plugged into the machine, one each facing the two chairs.

Both men held china mugs from which a gentle column of steam rose.

Mike reached across and unplugged both microphones, and checked the power lead to the tape recorder was also unplugged from the wall socket.

'You're a cautious man, Mister....er. Say, what is your name? I thought Amanda said it was Duncan, but I'm betting that was bullshit. Am I right?'

Mike grinned at him and shrugged.

'I told her my name was 'Duncan Biscuit' but spelt B.i.z.c.o.t. We'll get to my real name, maybe later. Right now, let's talk about these deaths. What gave you the first inkling something weird was happening, Mark? I can call you Mark, can't I?'

'Sure, you can call me Mark, but only if you tell me your real name. Just the first name will do for now, Ok?'

'Fair enough. It's Mike. And that's fair dinkum,' Walker informed him.

'Good, good,' Mark said quietly, almost to himself. 'I was also thinking about how you were speaking. You sound like a cop. Are you a cop, Mike?'

Mike stared at the man, trying to decide how far to trust him. Eventually he said,

'Look, it's not about me, just yet. We may be able to help each other, massively. I am looking into a certain matter, a matter which involves severe personal injury to some-one very close to me. I aim to get to the bottom of it, and you could finish up with a cracker of a final episode for your story. Fair enough? You talk to me, and I promise, I'll talk to you. By the way, where's your partner-in-crime, this Jenny Bates?'

The reporter laughed ironically and shook his head. He said with a wide smile,

'Firstly, we have already wrapped up our story. It's finished, published, printed and forgotten about. As we say in this game, today's front page story is tomorrow's fish and chips wrapper. As for Jenny, she's a busy reporter, covering several stories at once. We all do, Mike.'

'Yeah? Well you're wrong about the story. It is far from finished. You two only scratched the surface, and you didn't solve or prove anything. No offence intended, but your articles did nothing more than make a few vague allegations. I might have a hell of a lot more information which will show you how little you actually revealed. But first, I want you to tell me all you know, and how you first sniffed out the few facts you wrote about. What dya say? We dealing?'

Mark was too curious now to let the conversation end.

'All right, Mister Mike-with-no-last-name. Let's see if we can help each other.'

'Great! How about we start with this charter fishing boat where the dossier was found? The dossier was on one of our dear departed friends, I assume?'

'Who said it was a fishing boat, Mike?' Stein asked, testing Mike's information.

'You did. In the third instalment of your story. Want me to show you?' Mike asked.

Stein laughed and shook his head.

'Ok, you win. Right, I'll tell you what I know first, then it's your turn.'

Mark decided to open up completely, but leaving out the details of his brother, Dennis. He told Mike of "a friend" doing a diving course, finding the dossier, and involving Mark. He added the information Jenny had provided, via her contact in the Coroner's Court. They had compiled the list of criminals who had suddenly died, after beating serious charges then ridiculing the Police. Both men agreed the biggest mystery was why Mark and Jenny had not been hauled in by the Police to explain where they obtained their information. Their final article had concluded a vigilante style individual or committee was responsible, and probably had high connections and was protected by a powerful force or forces. They even hinted at Police or political involvement, but had drawn no hostile response from anywhere.

Mike had made a few notes during Mark's revelations, and, following the loose terms of their agreement, handed his notebook to Mark to allow him to proof read it.

The reporter handed back the little notebook, raising no objections.

'Ok, Mike. Your turn. Start with who you really are, and what your interest is. As you said earlier, maybe we can help each other.'

Mike nodded thoughtfully as he slid his notebook into his shirt pocket. He withdrew his wallet and opened it, showing his badge.

'I'm Mike Walker. Detective Mike Walker. I serve in Wagga, and currently I'm on compassionate leave from the job. Why? Because my wife is in Intensive Care at Wagga hospital, after she was knocked off her motor scooter in a gutless hit and run. Some time ago, not long after I left the Highway Patrol and went into plain clothes, I happened to notice this pattern emerging. Exactly like you did. But I was warned off, told to stop sticking my nose into it. By my direct supervisor, no less. My boss is a grizzled old bastard of a Detective Sergeant who has taught me heaps, but is a bit rough and ready. You know, real Old School. Sometimes he would rather give a crook a belt around the ear or a shirt full of broken ribs, than do things by the book. A bit of a worry but a good cop, nevertheless.'

He went on to tell of his contact with Detective Inspector Muscatt, the subsequent mysterious deaths of Muscatt and his wife, and finally his suspicion of his best friends, Andy and Anita Keyes. He described his wife's work and her discovery of the deadly little beetles from Malaysia. The decision to confront the Keyes was explained when Mike told Mark of the huge amounts of money deposited into their bank accounts. Then the totally out of character disappearance of the Keyes from the farm, and the cryptic note left by Andy. He finished with Carmen's crash, and the warning note the perpetrators had obviously stuffed into her handbag as they callously left her badly injured on the side of a lonely country road.

'So, Mike. You think your friend, or ex-friend, as he is now, was not only the hit man, but he might have whacked your good lady wife as well?' Mark asked quietly.

Mike nodded, absently staring at the empty book shelf.

'Yeah, looks like it. All the time they were enjoying our friendship, socialising together, Andy and I playing footy and cricket together, they were probably going around injecting this deadly poison into blokes, killing 'em off. Admittedly, they were probably doing society a big favour, but it's still murder. And they either killed a bloody good, honest copper and his innocent wife, and have all but killed my lovely, innocent missus, or they are closely associated with who-ever did. And I intend to find them, and they will need a bloody good explanation to stop them getting a dose of the same, I guarantee you.'

Mike's last sentence sent a slight shiver down Mark's spine. Something in the look on the Detective's face told Mark he meant every word, and could easily carry it out.

'What does that mean? What would you do if you found them and they were guilty?'

The reply came slowly and was almost a whisper. Mark had to strain to hear it.

'They will get the same as they gave Carmen, Al and Heather Muscatt and the crims.'

Again, the cold shiver went down the reporter's spine, but he felt sympathy for Mike.

Then he had a sudden thought. He snapped his fingers and asked the other man.

'Mike, can you describe this Andy Keyes? And his missus, too, if you can, ok?'

Mike looked at him and knew straightaway the man had additional information.

'Sure. Andy is about six feet four or five. Massive broad shoulders. Built like a tank, but surprisingly fast on his feet. He's got a high forehead, clear blue eyes perfect bloody teeth. Oh, and he's got a Malaysian Special Forces tattoo on his left forearm. It's in the form of a banana leaf with two knives sticking through it. Anita is about five feet tall, a pretty little thing with medium dark skin, wide set brown eyes and her right ankle has a small tattoo of the Australian S.A.S. logo. They once told me they got each other's unit's tat for the fun of it, and to show their so-called love for each other. Why, Mark? Do you know where they are?'

'That's a bloody good, thorough description, Mister. You sure about the details?'

'I'm a bloody Detective, man. We're trained to notice things about people. I repeat, do you know where they are? You had better tell me if you do!' Mike said forcefully.

Despite Mike's obvious superior strength, and his state of mind, Mark held his nerve.

'Look, Mike. I might, and then again, I might not. Please don't waste your time threatening me. Let me sleep on it, and I need to talk to Jenny, and possibly my boss. If you meet me here tomorrow, about eight, I'll tell you what I can. I just want to make sure I'm right. I'd hate to drop some innocent bugger in it, especially into your hands at the moment. Is that fair enough, Mike?'

Walker suddenly rose and grabbed the reporter by his shirt. His raised voice sounded even louder in the sound-proof room.

'Listen, Fancy Pants. My poor innocent wife is laying in a rotten hospital bed, probably dying because of what those filthy scum did to her. I'm going to find the prick, or pricks who did it to her and deal them the same cards. If you know where these mongrels are, you tell me now or I'll......'

'What the friggin' hell is going on here?' a shrill female voice sounded. 'You, tough guy. Let him go or Security will be here. Step away or I'll spray this shit in your eyes.' Both men whirled around to see Jenny Bates in the doorway, aiming a small container of pepper spray at Mike. Her left hand was hovering over a large red button protruding from the wall adjacent to the doorway. The words 'EMERGENCY' was on a small plaque above the button.

Stein shrugged out of Mike's grip and backed away. There was silence in the room for five seconds before Mike dropped his hands and sat down again, his eyes never leaving Jenny. Mark straightened his shirt and spoke to them both.

'It's ok, Jen. I think he's calmed down. Have you calmed down, Mike?'

'Yeah, I'm calm. Sorry, Mark. I shouldn't have lost it like that. It's just the thought of Carmen, you know? It sort of set me off. It won't happen again. Sorry.'

'Who the hell's Carmen? What's happening, Mark?' Jenny asked as she slowly, cautiously entered the room and let the door close behind her.

Mark explained the situation to Jenny, and introduced Mike to her. After shaking her hand, Mike felt obliged to show her his Police Badge.

Jenny placed the spare chair at the table and to two men brought her up to date.

She immediately began scribbling in her note pad, as she absorbed all the details.

'So, you two. What happens next? What's our next move, please?' she asked.

Mark Stein assumed control, feeling more at ease with Jenny in the room.

'Well, I had just suggested to our new friend here that we sleep on it, and if I get his assurance he's not going to head straight out and kill anyone, I might introduce him to a man I know, if you get my drift. And of course, that's if old Boil-Up gives us the go-ahead. Boil-Up is the sub editor, our boss, you see, Mike. He always wants one of us to boil up the kettle, so he can have another coffee. Drinks gallons of the stuff. Ok, we agreed? I'll do what I gotta do, and we'll meet here at eight tomorrow morning. And, Mike, if it goes against your wishes, no more rough stuff, ok?'

Mike smiled and offered his hand to both reporters. They all shook hands and he said,

'Sure, Mark. Again, I'm sorry. Right, I'm getting out of here. Got to find a decent motel. See ya both at eight, tomorrow.'

They left the room and Mike took the elevator to the ground, and headed for his car.

Jenny turned to Mark as they were walking to the sub editor's office,

'You trust him, Marky?'

'I don't know. But I'd hate to cross him. Thanks for the rescue, Jen.'

She grinned at him then knocked loudly on the glass door of the sub editor's office.

CHAPTER SEVENTEEN

∞

Commissioner Roger Simpson listened as Sergeant Johnson finished his story.

'So, Johnno. Where do you think the silly bastard has headed to? I'm assuming you have a pretty good idea what he's up to.'

'Do you really want me to tell you that, Roger?' Johnson asked.

'No, I require you to tell me, Johnno. And that doesn't mean he's in for any sort of punishment. I was dead against this action from the get-go and I reckon, in his place, I would be out to square the ledger, too. I just want to keep an eye on him, that's all.'

Johnson nodded to himself, then breathed a massive sigh.

'All right, Mate. I am fairly sure he's headed for the offices of that bloody newspaper, ah what's it called? The one who published the story about your mob.'

'The Sydney Daily News, you mean?' the Commissioner answered.

'Yeah, that's the one,' Johnson agreed. 'I read the story. It was in three or four parts, and I know Mikey had copies of each paper, 'cause I saw 'em on his desk. I reckon he's put two and two together and he's taken orf to chat to the reporters who wrote it.'

'Yes, that would seem likely. I think the part about the dossier found on the fishing trawler would be the key to young Walker's enquiries. If that's so, then he's in for a surprise. The group's operatives have resettled somewhere on the coast, and they have a boat, but I know for a fact it isn't a trawler. Our Commander is the only one who knows exactly where they are, and what they're doing, so I can't see how a dumb bloody reporter would know their whereabouts.'

Johnson tried one last time to obtain assurances for Mike's welfare.

'Can you promise me, Roger, that Walker won't be harmed, or set up or anything nasty come his way. Despite what we know he did, he's still a bright young Detective with a great future. He'll eventually fall into step, you'll see.'

'I've already told you, Johnno, he's going to be fine, as long as he stays within the law, and Police Regulations. I'll give him this week to empty the bile from his stomach, and return to Wagga. If that happens, I'll schedule an inspection of the Wagga Section, and make sure I have a nice private, cosy chat with him. Meantime, you keep him under your wing when he gets back from his fruitless mission to get revenge, Ok?'

Johnson agreed and they ended the call. He looked over at Mike's desk and muttered,

'I hope to hell I can keep a lid on you, me little mate. I can't fight the world for ya.'

The little old man listened intently as The Judge passed on the latest information.

'Now, Commander, I've just this minute got off the phone from Roger. He's very worried about this young Detective of his from Wagga Wagga. He told me his man in Wagga knows where the young bugger is headed, and why. We assumed that pair of nosy bloody reporters from the NEWS had come up empty handed, but it seems our friend in Wagga Wagga also reads newspapers. He has apparently decided to have a chat with the reporters, and that will spell trouble for us. I think you should hang around near the paper's offices, and keep an eye on things. And if it goes badly, be prepared to take what-ever action is required. Do you fully understand, Commander?'

'Yes, Sir. I understand. I am wondering, though, as I said to you privately last week, if we haven't taken this whole thing as far as we dare? Have you or any of the members given that any thought at all?' the old man answered.

There was a quick intake of breath followed by a loud cough from the other end.

'Well, as a matter of fact I did carry your thoughts to one or two members. They will provide feedback at our next meeting. And don't worry. I didn't say it came from you. Am I correct in thinking the situation concerning the Detective's wife is the catalyst for your reservations about continuing?'

'You are one-hundred per cent correct, Sir. That went horribly wrong, and I still have a nasty taste in my mouth from it. It made me think it is time to draw stumps. After all, we have accomplished a great deal, don't you think, Sir?'

'Yes, I suppose there are positives and negatives. Anyhow, in the meantime, you know what to do. Keep a keen eye on the grieving young Detective, and intervene as you see fit, if necessary. You right with that, Commander?'

'Yes, Sir. Leave it with me,' the old man said resignedly. He hung up from the call and immediately dialled another number. The call was answered instantly.

'Harold, get the car ready, thanks. We need to leave my place very early and drive into the city. From there, who knows, but I rather fancy we may be heading up the coast. See you at four-thirty.'

Mike Walker parked his Falcon in the same loading dock as he had yesterday. Before he could get out of the car, Mark Stein was standing beside him.

'Good morning, Mike. Ready to go?' Stein said pleasantly.

Walker stepped out of the car and showed surprise.

'How you going, Mark? Does that mean you're going to take me to this mystery boat operator? If it does, then, yeah, I'm rearing to go.'

'Right-o, then,' Mark said. 'First, a few rules. Let's call them, agreements. Number one, old Boil-Up said only one of us is to go, so Jenny isn't coming. Second, we go in my car. Leave this thing here. It'll be safe. Besides, if my man is one and the same as your ex-mate, I'm betting he'll recognise your car and we'll lose the element of surprise. Third, I get to take any notes, pictures and tape recordings I want, to help compose my story. And last but by no means least, there must be no violence or any form of law breaking. I know you're a copper, and sometimes cops think they can break the law, but we anticipate the shit hitting the fan when we publish this, so Boil-Up said, and I agree with him, we are going to be squeaky clean. Ok, agreed?'

'No pictures!' Mike said firmly. 'I'll agree to everything else, but no photos. I got my reasons. And as for the law, if any laws get broken, it'll be by me, and possibly the other party. I see no need for you to be in a position where you become an offender.'

Mark nodded and grinned at Mike.

'Ok, fair enough. Let's go. That's my Capri over the road.'

They walked across the street and Mike nodded appreciatively.

'Nice. Very nice. Vee-six GT, eh? We must have a race one day, what d'ya reckon?'

'No thanks. I treasure her too much. Hop in,' Mark replied, unlocking his doors.

The two men entered the coupé and before he started the engine, Stein said,

'Ok, Mike. I have my boss's permission to accompany you on your quest for answers. He wants the whole story, but he stressed that if any serious law breaking takes place, I am to clear out, and leave you behind if necessary. So, I need to know, what if this person I'm about to take you to turns out to be your murdering mate from Wagga Wagga? What if it was him who hurt your wife, and organised that car crash which killed Chief Inspector Allan Muscatt and his wife of twenty-three years, Heather?'

Mike was startled at the level of information the reporter knew.

'Yes, Mike. We have been doing some research overnight. We know all about the car crash, which you reckon was staged. The Police press release said, and I'm paraphrasing here, that Allan Muscatt's body revealed the presence of a high percentage of alcohol in the blood. Same for his wife. Don't you think that might have been the prime cause of the crash?'

Walker stared straight ahead at the line of parked cars. Pedestrians trudged up and down the footpath and courier's vehicles were constantly pulling to a halt opposite, with the drivers rushing into the buildings carrying small parcels and envelopes.

He said nothing for twenty seconds, then he turned to Stein and said grimly,

'You would think it could be the cause, except for one little fact. I had known Al Muscatt for around seven years. Played football with him, worked with him, and recently even visited him at his home. In all that time, I've never known him to touch a drop. He hated grog, and Heather had only the occasional small glass of wine. But Al never drank at all. It was well known around the job. Some idiots even distrusted him, saying something stupid like "never trust a man who doesn't drink". Bloody stupid thing to say. No, Allan and Heather were sacrificed because he had decided to continue to investigate these criminal deaths. I got him started, that's why I feel so guilty about it. And now the mongrels have whacked my lovely wife, too. Well, they're going to pay. We, that is Allan Muscatt and I, were warned off. Someone high up the ladder knew what we were doing, and instead of helping us, or encouraging us, they chose to warn us away. I took the tip, and tried to get Al to do the same. But he is, or was, a brave and stubborn bloke. And an honest copper. I am certain Internal Affairs were used to spy on us both. I even think my phone was tapped and my house bugged. Illegally, I might add. That's the only way the bastards could have known Carmen found the details of the poisonous Malaysian beetles. This hit and run they did on her was probably meant to warn her off, as well. Whether they intended it to go as far as it did, well, I'm yet to find out. But as I have often said, "You hurt me or mine, I hurt you back twice as hard". Now, to answer your original question, about what if this boat man of yours turns out to be Andy Bloody Keyes, well I'll certainly feel like killing him. But I'll hear what he has to say first. I have no desire to finish up a guest of the government for twenty-five years myself, so I might just hold him, until the local police arrive and I tell them my story. It will probably cost me my job, but with the facts revealed by me in court, and you reporting things as they happen, we should put the arseholes out of business, and maybe a few in jail. Or, you and me might finish up going deep sea diving with cement flippers on. If that prospect hasn't scared you out of it, then let's get going, all right?'

Mark started the engine and selected first gear. As he drove away from the kerb, he said quietly to Mike,

'No offence meant, Mike, but do you reckon you could hold him? He's a big unit, and you said he was an S.A.S. Commando. He might take a bit of holding.'

Mike nodded agreement, then slowly opened his jacket, revealing his Smith & Wesson revolver nestling in the shoulder holster.

'This might help hold him,' he said simply.

'Oh, shit! I didn't know you were carrying. Is that wise, Mike? Guns make me nervous at the best of times. Today it seems a bit foolhardy.'

'Just a bit of insurance. Don't fret about it. Like we agreed, if it becomes necessary, you can simply piss off. In fact, I'll insist on it. You need to remember, we're dealing with a pair of mass murderers here. Plus, these former close friends of mine are probably responsible for the severe injuries, and possible murder, of my wife. I'm carrying my weapon merely for insurance, but as I said, if the situation gets out of hand, you piss off out of there. Meantime, just forget about it.'

Mark Stein tried to relax as they drove towards the Sydney Harbour Bridge, but the presence of the gun, even though it was in the hands of a Police Officer, concerned him. He had told the truth when he said he was nervous around firearms. It was the one aspect of city life which bothered him. Every Police Officer and most criminals he had come into contact with seemed to think a gun was part of their natural assets.

They entered the middle lane and Mark accelerated the Capri to eighty kilometres per hour. A large green sign told them they were on the Pacific Highway, headed for the cities of Gosford and Newcastle, and the central coast of New South Wales.

There were only around a dozen other vehicles travelling in the same direction, including a pair of semi-trailers and a bus packed with excited school children.

Most of the traffic was heading in the opposite direction, into the city.

In the next lane to their right, approximately two hundred metres behind them, a pale green Holden sedan kept pace with them. The tall man driving concentrated on keeping the distance between the two cars constant. In the passenger's seat beside him was a little old man wearing a cream safari suit, knee high socks and hiking boots. On the back seat a white straw hat sat beside a set of powerful, military style binoculars and a high-powered radio listening device.

CHAPTER EIGHTEEN

∞

As they entered the dual lane freeway which would take them north, Mike Walker and Mark Stein discussed the known facts surrounding the murders of New South Wales most notorious criminals. They both had a complete list of the names, the dates they were found dead and the locations. Mike referred frequently to his trusted old exercise book in which he had originally entered the details.

They had been travelling along the freeway for twenty minutes when Mike leaned forward and looked in the left outside wing mirror.

He had made a habit of checking every few minutes. This time he frowned, then turned his head to peer out of the rear window.

'What's up?' Mark asked.

'That green Holden in the middle lane,' Mike answered. 'I first saw it just after we crossed the bridge. I noticed it again as we left Hornsby. Now he's just sitting there, keeping the same distance away from us. That's a well-used surveillance technique.'

Mark adjusted the interior mirror and studied the Holden. He returned his eyes to the road ahead before answering.

'I can't see anything special about it. Looks like there's two blokes in it. You sure you're not getting a bit paranoid, Mike?'

Mike continued to watch the other car in the outside mirror.

'I could be, but it is a classic trailing method. I tell you what. Turn off at the next exit and stop just out of sight of the freeway.'

'Right-o. Here's the Berowra turn off. I'll take that. There's a nice little café on the old highway that I usually stop at when I go home. Let's see if our friends follow us.'

Mark changed down to third gear and indicated left. Immediately the Holden indicated left and moved to the kerbside lane.

'Looks like they want to play follow-the-leader,' Mike said.

Mark steered the Capri up the exit ramp, and onto the Old Pacific Highway. A small row of shops appeared ahead and he turned in, parking nose first outside a milk bar.

Both men turned in their seats and their gazes followed the Holden as it cruised past. Mike alighted from the car and watched as the Holden pulled in under the shade of a large tree, around two hundred metres from them.

'Well, that proves it!' he declared. 'Who-ever is in that thing is very interested in us, or at least, where we're going. Come on, Mark. I'll shout you a drink and a snack, then we'll take off again, and see if we can lose them.'

They entered the café and each ordered a sandwich and a milkshake. They sat in one of the Nineteen Fifties style booths attached to the side wall as they ate.

'So, Mike, who do you reckon our friends are? Cops, or what?' Mark asked.

Mike shook his head.

'I got a good look at the geezer in the passenger's seat. He looked like a little old bastard. Too old and too small to be a copper. Could be a Private Dick, though. The Police sometimes use them, believe it or not. But, my instincts are telling me a couple of things. One, they're definitely following us. And two, I don't reckon they're cops or Privates, but I wouldn't mind betting they're something to do with our vigilante mob.'

They finished their meals and walked nonchalantly back to Mark's car. The green Holden was still parked in the same position. Mike noted the entrance leading back to the freeway was almost directly opposite the café.

'Here's what we'll do,' he said. 'Once we get moving again, drive past the bastards as if we haven't seen them. Assuming they pull out and start following us again, slow down until we get to that roundabout you can see in the distance. They should be reasonably close to us by then. Instead of going straight ahead, go right around the roundabout, head back this way and turn back onto the freeway. If they come after us, we'll know for sure they're tailing us. When you go around the roundabout, floor it, will you? Really see what your little rocket can do. Same when we turn onto the entrance ramp. Really gun it. Your Capri should leave their shit box for dead.'

Mark grinned across at him.

'I gunna enjoy this. The only thing that'll stop us is if one of your Highway Patrol mates joins in. What then?'

'We stop,' Mike said firmly. 'One thing we aren't going to get into is a high-speed pursuit. Besides, no matter how good you think this thing is, our Commodores and Falcons are set up to wallop the socks off ordinary cars like this. Ok, let's go.'

Mark reversed the Capri out of the parking space and turned the car north. Both men looked straight ahead as they drove past the Holden, and Mike grunted with satisfaction as he watched the pale green sedan pull out behind them. Mark slowed to twenty kilometres per hour and the Holden driver had to brake suddenly to avoid getting too close. As soon as they entered the roundabout, Mark changed down to second gear and accelerated harshly, turning sharp right as he did. The Capri's rear wheels spun momentarily but soon gained traction. Mark snatched through the gears as the car reached seventy, then eighty kilometres per hour. Watching through the rear window, Mike saw the Holden stop briefly, then also swing a hard right and follow, accelerating in a vain attempt to keep up with the sporty coupé.

'Hold on, left turn coming up,' Mark shouted as they reached the freeway on-ramp.

With considerable skill, he changed down two gears and feathered the throttle, allowing the car to drift left, tyres screeching in protest.

Mike kept watching through the rear window but the Holden did not appear at the top of the ramp. The Capri reached the lanes of the freeway and Mark glanced at his dials.

'Looks like we lost 'em,' Mike muttered. 'Make sure you stick to the speed limit. We don't want any extra attention.'

Mark grinned at him.

'Certainly, Officer. No way you'll catch me hooning around.'

Mike smiled in spite of the seriousness of the situation.

'Nice driving, I must say. You'd almost get a start with the Highway boys.'

Mark laughed and said,

'No thanks. I prefer an honest living.'

In the Holden the two men had watched in shocked surprise when the Capri had abruptly U-turned in the roundabout and sped away. Harold had initially pressed the accelerator pedal to floor, even though he knew his sedan was no match for the coupé.

Then he heard his companion say loudly,

'Forget it, Harold. It seems they've clocked us. And I doubt this car will catch that one. Still, no matter. We know where they're headed to. Just rejoin the freeway and we'll make our way to the dive shop as quickly as we can.'

A large sign informed the two men they were about to enter the City of Wyong.

In reality it was a large suburb of the area known as the central coast of New South Wales. So many of these coastal towns and suburbs had morphed from stand alone localities into one long "city", it was difficult to know one from any other.

They drove through a busy business district, with the main route lined with shops, offices and eateries. Many tanned, healthy young people crowded the footpaths.

Mark turned off the main thoroughfare and stopped the car. Wyong railway station was to their left, and the sea side could be seen to their right.

'Well, Mike. We're nearly there. The dive shop is at the end of that little side street up ahead. Exactly how is this going to be played out?'

Mike looked ahead, noted the street, then turned to look through the rear window.

'No sign of our sneaky pursuers, so that's one thing we can be grateful for. I think the best way is this. I want you to enter the shop, find this tall bloke and confront him. Have your little note book out as if you're doing what you reporters do. I want you to ask him "Are you Andy Keyes, former Captain in the S.A.S., and former farm owner from The Rock?" or something similar. You'll know by the look on his face if you've nailed him or not. Ok?'

'But hang on, Mike. Last time I spoke to him, he got a bit aggressive and I got the distinct impression he would've liked to leave the imprint of his big fist on my face.' Mark Stein was not a coward, or a weak man, but he knew he would be no match for this dive shop operator, whether or not he was the former S.A.S. man.

Mike tried to allay his fear and reassured him,

'Don't worry, Mark. Firstly, I reckon he'll be too shocked to think about belting you. Second, I'll be just out of sight, beside the door. He might be a tough guy, but so am I. Plus, I'm armed, and he knows I'm a cop. You just confront him, and then, depending on his reaction, I'll take over. I'll know if it's him as soon as I hear his voice.'

The newspaper man was still not completely convinced.

'Hey, what about this bloke's missus? You said she's a Commando of some sort. She might get involved and want to get physical. How d'ya feel about jobbing a woman?'

'She'll be as shocked as he will be. I'm counting on the element of surprise, more than anything. If it turns to crap, you keep your eyes on her for me and we'll be right.'

Still not convinced, but eager to gather a massive story, Mark drove out from the kerb and turned into the side street. Immediately ahead, slightly to their right a large, colourful sign announced the presence of the 'Sandy Coast Fishing and Dive'.

The building was of weather-board construction, with a low-pitched roof. The front was almost all glass, and many advertising stickers and posters adorned the large panes. The double doors, also mainly glass, carried simply OPEN signs.

Mark parked to the left of the doors, out of sight of anyone inside the shop.

Walker looked around the small car park noting the only other vehicle was a short wheel-based Land Rover. He felt his entire body shaking as he gazed at the familiar car. Any remaining doubts he harbored were removed when he recognised the vehicle. Mark noticed his reaction.

'What is it, Mike. The Land Rover? You know who owns it, don't you?'

Mike did not answer. He summoned up inner strengths, and eventually was able to suppress his wild anger and emotions. Before stepping from the car, he said quietly,

'Come on. Let's do it. Remember what we discussed. As soon as you ask him, I'll be there. And watch Anita. Just yell if she starts to approach me, Ok?'

Stein also alighted from his car.

'Anita? If you mean his cute little Asian wife, it's Angela, not Anita.'

'Want to bet?' was all Mike said in reply.

He loosened his revolver in it's holster and stood to the left of the doors.

Mark gulped, took out his small notebook and tucked a pencil behind his right ear. He looked in through the glass doors and saw the Asian woman behind the counter at the right side of the shop. As he pushed open the doors, the large figure of "Alex" was a mere two metres away, setting up a display of spear guns and accessories on a slim rack against the left wall. Mark reached into his shirt pocket and switched on his tiny, voice-activated tape recorder. He stepped in and the man turned to face him, a pleasant smile showing through the thick, blonde beard.

'Good morning..........'

The warm greeting trailed off as the bearded man recognised the new arrival.

'What the hell are you doing back here? Didn't I tell you to keep away?'

Mark noted the anger on the big man's face and felt a slight shudder go through him.

'Ah, yeah, you did. Sorry. Ah...look...ah... I just have one more question for you.'

He looked around and noted with relief the woman was busy counting coins into a cash register and did not appear to have noticed him.

'No questions, Newspaper Man. I told you last time, I'm not interested in your bull shit and I won't answer any questions. Also, as I said last time, piss off, Dickhead.'

The big man's insults were just enough to spark some outrage in Mark. He knew it was time to deliver his knock-out blow.

'Well, just tell me this. Are you really Andy Keyes, from The Rock, down near Wagga Wagga? And were you not Captain Keyes, Australian S.A.S. And is that your wife, Anita Keyes, formerly of the Malaysian Special Forces?'

The big man's face went completely pale, and he dropped the three new spear guns he had been holding. His mouth opened, but no sound emitted. His hands began shaking and he leaned back against the wall as he stared at Mark, unable to talk for several seconds. Then he whispered,

'Who are you, Buster? Just who are you and who do you work for? Who's put you up to this?'

The door behind Mark opened and Mike stepped into the shop.

'I did, Andy,' Walker said through gritted teeth. 'Remember me, Good Mate? The bloke married to your latest victim.'

The big man stared open mouthed at Walker, total shock on his face.

After a tense ten seconds, he finally croaked through dry lips,

'Mike! What's going on? What are you doing here?'

Mike closed the door behind him and stood with hands on hips.

'It's settle up time, Killer. Time to pay the piper.'

CHAPTER NINETEEN

∞

As the pale green Holden sedan turned into the small car park, the little old man in the passenger's seat noted the Land Rover and the purple Capri.

'Well, Harold, it looks like all the players are here. This should be most interesting.'

'Yes, I see our lead-footed friends and their hot rod have arrived. And we both know whose 'Rover that is. How are we going to work this, Commander?'

'We play it by ear. But, as I told you last night, this will probably be our final episode. If we can avoid violence, or at least minimise it, I hope to get the chance to talk sense into everyone. The number one aspect, though, is not to let on about you being active. If that blasted Detective wants to kill some-one for what we did to his wife, better it be the other Operatives than you and me. Ok, let's go, and see how the reunion is progressing. Remember, let me go in first, and only come in yourself if it turns to muck.

And hit first, then ask questions later. Both these two are strong, fit, trained fighters. So is Keyes' wife. Your Karate skills should be enough to topple them all, but hopefully we won't need you. Just stay near the door and be alert.'

Harold took up a position identical to where Mike had stood, and the old man quietly entered the shop. He saw Mike standing close to Keyes, and the little Asian woman had joined her husband. Both were facing Mike, and Keyes was saying,

'Honest, Mike. We refused the job, and even told our handler that if it went ahead we would blow the lid on the lot of them. That's the God honest truth........'

He stopped talking when the Commander entered. Not knowing the little old man, he said quickly, 'Sorry, mate. We're temporarily closed. Sorry, could you leave, please? We'll re-open soon.'

'No, sorry. I won't be leaving, Mister Keyes. I think you need me to help convince Detective Walker here of your innocence,' the old man stated.

He immediately had the undivided attention of Mike and both the Keyes. He had not noticed Mark Stein standing just inside the open doorway.

'And who the bloody hell are you?' Mike said forcefully.

The old man stepped further into the shop, but then Andy Keyes spoke.

'I think I know who he is. I recognise the voice. Am I to call you "Commander"?'

Nodding, the old man smiled thinly.

'That is the title by which you would know me, yes. What have you been telling our friend here?' He turned to Mike. 'Just how much do you know, Detective?'

Mike drew his revolver and pointed it at Andy.

'I know this lousy bastard and this little bitch have killed at least half a dozen people. And I know my poor, innocent wife is near death. Now you tell me right now, Baggy-Arse, how do you fit in? Are you the gutless mongrel who organises things for them?'

The old man smiled and shook his head. Mike mistook the gestures for arrogance.

He stepped towards the old man and grabbed him around his throat. With a quick back-handed swipe he raked the barrel of the revolver across the man's forehead.

The old man groaned and dropped to the floor. Immediately the shop door was pushed open and Harold stepped towards Mike, arms raised and formed into a fighting stance.

Before anyone else re-acted, Mark punched with all his power at the newcomer's temple. There was a loud crack, and the man joined the Commander on the floor, completely unconscious. Mike stared at the pair of bodies, then looked at Mark.

'Well done, Mate. Good shot,' he told the reporter.

The Commander groaned and sat up, holding a hand across his bleeding forehead.

'Right! Drop the gun, Mike. And listen to what I tell you,' Andy's voice sounded.

Walker whirled around to see Andy holding a spear gun. It was loaded with a shiny aluminium spear, the deadly point no more than three metres from Mike's chest.

Despite the obvious threat, Mike held his revolver, now pointing at Andy's head.

'Don't be bloody stupid. This is loaded, cocked and ready to blow a hole clean through you. You put that toy down, NOW!'

'Don't kid yourself, Mike. This will take you out before you can squeeze your trigger. But look, I don't want to hurt you. Just put the gun down and then I'll put this down. Please don't make me do what I don't want to, Mike. We can talk, then, and I am certain I can prove to you we did not hurt Carmen. That little creep who you just pole-axed will back me up with the truth.'

Anita spoke for the first time, tears running down her cheeks.

'Please, Mike. Andy, my husband, he tells the truth to you. Honestly, he does. We may be guilty of some of the things you say, but not Carmen. Not dear sweet, precious Carmen. She, like you, is our true friend. We did not do this accident to her, I swear. They asked us to do this but we refused. And Andy did tell this Commander person, if anything should happen to Carmen, or you, we will tell the authorities everything.'

Mike held the gun steady, while Anita spoke, and Andy held his spear gun still pointed at Mike. Mark Stein moved slowly out of the line of fire of both weapons.

Mike glanced at the old man as he slowly, painfully regained his feet and looked at his unconscious accomplice. He shrugged and smiled philosophically.

'What about Allan and Heather Muscatt? What about those two innocent people?'

'Who?' Andy answered. 'Sorry, Mike, but I've never heard of them.'

'Al Muscatt was a friend and colleague. And an honest copper. Heather was his totally innocent wife. Al and I were probing into the mysterious deaths of a few crooks. We were both warned off, by senior police. I decided it wasn't worth it, but Al was made of sterner stuff. So some-one killed them both. That left two young boys as orphans. You saying that wasn't your handiwork?'

'I'm saying we never heard of them. I'm sorry for your loss, Mike, but it wasn't us. What-ever we did, it was only to help rid the world of useless scum. We were given a brief dossier on all of the targets. An honest, serving copper was not on our list. Never was, and never would be. Same with Carmen. Look, Mate, you've got to believe me.'

'All right! Enough banter,' the Commander's voice sounded from behind Mike.

Mike turned and stepped slightly to his right. Mark was already several metres away, and when Mike stepped, Andy and Anita had a clear view of the old man.

He was standing with his back to the door, and he held twin automatic pistols. One was pointed at Mike, the other at Andy.

'Now, both you gentlemen kindly place your weapons on the floor. Do it now, please, and I will fill in a few blanks for you both. Please don't make me use these things, but if I have to, believe me, I will. Drop them, gentlemen. Now!'

Mike looked at the pistols, saw they were both off safety and cocked. Then he looked at Andy. The bearded man nodded to Mike and they lowered their weapons in unison.

Both men squatted and placed them on the floor.

'Good, good. That's better,' the old man said, smiling despite the trickle of blood running down his face. 'Now, Young Man,' he indicated to Mark. 'Would you be kind enough to change the OPEN sign to CLOSED, and lock the doors? Then pull the blinds down so no sticky-beak gets a free show. Next, I would like you to obtain some cold water and see if you can coax Harold back into wakefulness. Ok?'

As Mark went about his tasks, Mike pointed to the prone figure of Harold.

'And just who is your mate, "Harold"?' he asked.

'He is my driver and bodyguard,' the Commander said, not taking his eyes off Mike and Andy.

'Yeah? I hope he drives better than he bodyguards,' Mike said with heavy sarcasm.

'Indeed,' the Commander answered. 'A lucky hit, that's all. Now, you all need to listen to me. I will tell you all I can, or am able to, but there will be some details you will have to live without. Mister Walker, I am the person who set up this operation, recruited this charming couple here, and organised the targets. I did this on behalf of a committee. A very powerful committee. I will not reveal the identities of any members, but you must believe me when I say their power is beyond the reach of any of us here today. Among the other tasks they perform, they also raise a lot of money between them. They pay me, and our operatives most handsomely, but they also see that victims of some of the worst criminals are looked after. The criminals who are targeted are most deserving of their fate, and Mister and Missus Keyes here have done the country a great service, ridding us of these parasites. Again, I stress the power and influence of this committee knows no bounds, so please dismiss any thoughts of reprisals. Do you have any questions so far?'

Mike spoke up straight away.

'Yeah, I got one. Am I to take it you are confirming that these two had nothing to do with what happened to my wife, and the Muscatts?'

'I whole-heartedly guarantee they did not. Nor did I,' the Commander answered.

'Then who did, Mister? That's all I want from you. Give me the bastards who hurt my wife, and you can all go to buggery, as far as I'm concerned,' Mike said angrily.

'I'm afraid I don't know, Mister Walker. I had nothing to do with either operation, and I was not told of the implementation of either. I passed on Mister Keyes' refusal and threat, and the next thing I knew, I was directed to follow you today and intervene if necessary to prevent us all going to prison,' was the confident reply.

'Directed by who? Who is it told you to follow us?' Mike gritted.

'Again, I do not know. I correspond with a voice. I receive my orders, directions and advice from a telephone caller. I then do my research, a feasibility study and finally work out a plan. I send a summarised version to the Keyes via mail, observe the hit if possible, then arrange payment as appropriate. I do not know the names of the committee members, but I do know some of the positions they hold in society. And you can beat me to a pulp, torture me to the depths of beyond, but I will not reveal these positions to anyone. Please accept that. You see, I, too have special skills and training. You would be dead or in prison before that information passed my lips. Can you accept that, Mister Walker?'

Mike stared at the man for some time before his shoulders slumped and he said,

'Ok, I guess. And I believe most of what you say.' he turned to Andy and Anita.

'So, what about your mysterious and sudden departure from Wagga? We went to the farm and everything was gone. The only thing we found was your cricket bag.'

For the first time Andy smiled. He looked at Anita, and she began smiling too.

'Well, that's one thing off my mind, Mate. I take it you got my little note?'

'Yeah, I got it. I didn't like it, but I got it. I thought we were better mates than that.'

The Commander's voice cut through the conversation.

'Right, we seem to making progress. I think we're ready to approach the final scenario.'

Mark re-entered the shop through the kitchen door carrying a jug of water. He poured the entire contents onto Harold's face, and squatted beside the man. patting him gently on the cheek. Slowly Harold's eyes opened and he sat up, groaning and working his jaw open and closed.

'What happened?' he asked, looking from one person to another.

'You tripped,' the Commander lied. 'If you're OK, Harold, go and sit in the car. There is some aspirin or paracetamol in the first aid kit. Wait for me there. I won't be too long. Off you go, Mate.'

They watched as he stood painfully and, with a final glare at Mike, trudged over to the Holden and entered via the driver's door.

'Poor Harold. He's never been bested before. And certainly not by a journalist.'

The Commander seemed amused, but he was the only person chuckling.

'So, Mister. What happens now? I still want to find the gutless prick who hurt my wife. I'm not totally convinced you know nothing about it,' Mike said heatedly.

The Commander lowered his pistols and placed them back in his belt.

'You must believe me, Sir. I know nothing of the matter. You will have to leave it to your own Police colleagues. Now, if you have no more questions, any of you, I propose to scuttle this committee and their operations. When we first commenced, I took on the task based on the firm understanding that when I call "enough", then all matters cease. No replacements, no continuance, and no reprisals. I have mentioned it several times to my contact that I feel the need to retire. Co-incidentally, Mister Keyes has also told me, via telephone, of his wish to halt proceedings. It can be stated here that the Keyes' and I have not met before today, and only spoken on the telephone a handful of times in four years of operations, apart from the large envelopes I send them regarding details of their next mission. Right, back to the present day. At the very beginning I, in conjunction with the head man of the committee, developed a special code for when either of us decide the time has come to cease. I intend to deliver that code, via telephone, right now. I have to repeat the call in a certain time frame to ensure it is authentic, then he will deliver it to the other members. That, people, will be the last act of the committee who happen to refer to themselves as The Retribution Committee.'

'The Retribution Committee?' Mike muttered with disgust. 'A bunch of murdering bloody hypocrites, more like. A mob of cowards who put themselves above the law.'

'Perhaps, Mister Walker, perhaps. But all done with the best of motives,' the Commander replied.

'Yeah? Well tell that to my wife! And Allan Muscatt's two orphaned sons,' Mike said bitterly. 'Why did they have to suffer, if you were only after crooks?'

The Commander shrugged and spread his thin, bony arms wide.

'I wish I could answer you, Mister Walker, but I have already explained that I cannot. I am now about to implement the termination, if everyone is agreed.'

No person replied. Mike simply glared at Andy and Anita, who in turn were watching the Commander. Mark Stein was scribbling furiously in his note pad, flicking his gaze from one player to the next.

Without another word the Commander crossed to the counter and picked up the telephone. They watched as he dialed a Sydney number and waited. They all heard a gruff mumble as the call was answered. Then the Commander spoke into the handset.

'Commander. Finite, Finite, Finite.' He hung up the instrument and turned to face the others and looked at his watch, smiling to the four people watching.

Mike looked at his own watch and noted the time. Still no-one spoke.

After checking his watch again, the Commander picked up the handset again and dialed the same number. Mike checked his watch and saw it was exactly two minutes since the first call. They heard the same gruff answer and the Commander spoke slowly and clearly into the mouthpiece.

'Second and final Finite! Meeting and report at usual place, tomorrow. Goodbye'.

He replaced the telephone in it's former position and turned to face them all.

'That is that, then. By the time I leave here, which will be very soon, The Retribution Committee will no longer exist. Young man, Mister Journalist. I trust you will not mention any real names, or this particular business address when you print your story?'

Mark looked around the shop, and at each person before he answered.

'Agreed. No names, just vague descriptions. But, what about the Police? I mean, when this story hits the news stands, surely the cops will want to investigate it, won't they? Let's face it, it's a ripper

420

of a yarn, and finally explains why the crims got so busy dieing. What am I to tell the coppers when they grill me?'

'You will not be grilled. You won't be questioned and you won't even be contacted. Unless you say something stupid in your writings, Young Man. Then, I'm afraid, no-one will be able to help you. Just do your job as best you can, and you might win a prize for your great journalism. Just be careful, is all I can say. You are safe for now, you have my personal guarantee.'

Mike found it impossible to pass up the opportunity for one last dig.

'Be extra careful, Mark. I got a guarantee just like that once. Me and my wife. And look what happened to her. Come on, let's get out of here.'

He stooped to the floor and picked up his revolver. After securing the weapon in his shoulder holster, he tucked in his shirt, then nudged Mark, indicating for him to move.

Mike and Mark started for the door, but Andy approached, his right hand extended.

'Please, Mike. Let's still be friends. You know now we had nothing to do with Carmen's injuries. And you must believe us, we thought we had prevented it. Please, Mate. We go back too far for it to end like this.'

Mark had already stepped outside the shop and he turned to watch Mike's reaction.

Mike looked at Andy, then at Anita, then the huge hand.

'Get stuffed, you hypocrite. Both of you can go to hell and burn.'

He strode to the Capri and roughly opened the left door.

Mark joined him and started the engine.

'Hurry up, get me to bloody hell away from here. I can't stand the stink.'

Mark drove the car out of the car park and pointed it south, towards Sydney.

CHAPTER TWENTY

∞

Mark skillfully piloted the Capri through the city traffic as they re-entered Sydney. After crossing the Harbour Bridge he turned down numerous side streets, completely confusing his brooding passenger. Suddenly they were drawing to a stop outside the newspaper office. Mark switched off the engine, and turned to Mike, offering his note pad.

'I've written a fair piece on what we both just witnessed. Do you want to read it first, and delete anything you find distasteful or out of order?'

'The whole bloody situation is distasteful, as far as I'm concerned. My wife's still badly injured, I've failed completely in finding out who the gutless arsehole was who hurt her, and I've lost the best friends we ever had into the bargain. And worse, as a serving bloody copper I cannot do anything about half a dozen murders, and the pricks are getting away scot-free. And to even top that shit off, I now know another great mate, Allan Muscatt, and his lovely wife, were sacrificed for bloody nothing. Two innocent people killed, one innocent lady badly hurt, a heap of no-good crims murdered, I pretty much know who is responsible, and I can't do a damn thing about any of it. I tell you, Mark. I'm seriously considering packing it all in.'

Mark was silent for a time, still offering his notebook. Mike looked at it and shook his head.

'No, Mate. You know what to write and what not to. Far be it from me to tell you how to do your job. But remember. No mention of names, particularly mine. I will chase you if that happens.'

'No chance. I owe you too much as it is,' Mark re-assured him. 'So, what now? You heading straight back home to Wagga Wagga?'.

'I'm going back to my motel for a few hours kip, a feed and a shower. But I'll ring the hospital first. I have to know if my darling has shown any improvement.'

'I really hope she's on the mend, Mate. I know you said you feared the worst, and there wasn't much hope, but try thinking positive, Mike. Give her my best, even though I've never met the lady. And, one other thing, Mike. Can we keep in touch, Mate? I've sort of come to like you, and perhaps even admire you, if you know what I mean.'

Mike smiled grimly at him and offered his hand. The two shook hands warmly.

As Mike alighted from the car, he said,

'It's been good to know you, too, Mark. I don't make friends easily, like most cops. And of course, I owe you for clouting that Harold bloke. Probably saved the whole situation from turning to shit.'

'First bloke I've ever belted. One hell of a lucky punch. Take care Mike, and please keep in touch.'

'Yeah, Ok, I will. See ya, Mate,' Mike said as he closed the door and walked to his own car.

Walker fitted his key into the motel room door and pushed it open, then threw his coat onto the double bed. As he slowly undid the buckles on his shoulder holster, he stared into the wall-mounted mirror, noting his blotched skin and tired, red eyes The heavy gun and holster made a dull thud as it landed on the bedside table.

He moved to the main table and picked up the telephone. A bright voice answered.

'Reception. Yes room 231?'

'Yeah, g'day. Could you get me Wagga Wagga Base Hospital, please. I don't have the number on me,' he replied.

'No problem, Sir. I'll get it for you. Will this call be charged to your room, Sir?'

'Yes, yes. I'm checking out early tomorrow and I'll settle up then,' he said abruptly.

He waited while the line clicked and buzzed, then a female voice answered.

'Please put me through to I C, thanks,' he said politely.

After ten seconds a familiar voice said,

'Intensive care, Nurse Whitmore.'

'Hello Sharon. It's Mike Walker. I'm up in Sydney at the moment. How's my girl, Love? Any good news for me?' he asked hopefully.

'Hello Mike. No, sorry. No change. They removed the bandages from her left leg today, because it was only a greenstick fracture. Her right leg is still in plaster, of course. She still can't breathe on her own, and so we've have kept her in a coma. When will you be back in to see her, Mike?'

'Tomorrow. I'm leaving this joint about five, and with luck should be in Wagga around eleven or twelve. No improvement, eh? I was hoping for better news than that. Oh, well, I'll keep my fingers crossed,' he said sadly.

The sympathetic nurse said quietly,

'You know, Mike, Doctor Willard has been keeping a very close eye on Carmen. He said he thinks if you were here, and talked to her, it would help. Yesterday he brought a psychologist and a brain injury specialist with him. They all agreed it would be a big help if you talked to her. You up for that, Mike?'

'Of course!' he snapped back. 'I just had to do this visit to Sydney, you know. I didn't just shoot through for the fun of it.'

'I know, Mike, I know. I wasn't suggesting otherwise. Please don't get angry. We are all doing what we can for Carmen. I just wanted to make sure you knew, that's all.'

He regretted his outburst and apologised. She accepted his apology and wished him a safe trip home. After the call he rang reception again and organised a meal to be sent to his room.

While he was waiting, he stripped off, and gladly entered the shower cubicle. He stayed under the warm water for fifteen minutes, feeling the different parts of his body slowly start to relax. He was dried and getting dressed when a loud knock sounded on the door.

'Coming,' he called. 'Just leave it by the door, and I'll grab it in a minute, thanks.'

There was no answer and he assumed the waiter had heard.

Then the knock sounded again, heavier and longer.

'Just leave it, thanks. I'm getting dressed,' he said, louder this time.

'Can't! Open up, please,' a deep, gruff voice said.

By now Mike had his trousers on, so he opened the door angrily.

'What the f...?' he trailed off as a huge man shoved him back into the room. Another big man followed him in. Both were dressed in suits, and Mike noted bulges under their coats, suggesting shoulder holsters. The men sported "Pork Pie" hats pulled down low over their foreheads.   The first man spoke as the second one tossed a white envelope onto Mike's bed.

'Here, Detective Walker. A love letter for ya. Wait five minutes until we're gone, then open it, read it, understand it, then destroy it. Ok, Pal? See ya later.'

Before Mike could stammer a reply, the men left and closed the door. He heard a car engine start and the sound of tyres crunching on the gravel driveway of the motel.

He pulled the curtain back and looked outside into the semi-darkness.

His instincts told him the two big men were Police Officers. His one glance at the departing car also suggested Police.

And common thugs did not usually use shoulder holsters.

Ignoring the warning to wait five minutes, Mike picked up the envelope and tore it open.

A single sheet of typewritten paper fell out. He carefully unfolded the note and read.

Detective Walker. We are very sorry about the mix-up with your wife. We hope she recovers fully and returns to good health. We will monitor her condition in secret, but you will not know. Please remember everything the Commander told you today. It is so vital to the well-being of quite a few people, including your good self.

Your reporter friend will be left alone, provided he compiles his story as per the agreement. Despite earlier undertakings, you are now completely safe. Just be a good Detective and forget all about 'The Retribution Committee'. We wish you and Carmen all the best, and trust you are more receptive to our goodwill than Mr Muscatt was.'

'Christ! The bastards are still not finished,' Mike angrily said out loud. 'The mongrels are like some three-headed dragon. You cut one head off and it grows another one.'

He read the note again, then slipped it into his old exercise book.

Despite everything that had transpired today, including the two visitors to his motel room, he decided to keep all of his evidence secure.

He realised he was dealing with powerful people, and they could take him down any time. But if they tried, he'd find a way to fight back, at least for a while.

The outskirts of Forest Hill appeared in front of him, and Mike Walker felt an overwhelming sense of homecoming. He had spent a restless night in the motel, with half hourly dozes interrupted by similar periods of wakefulness.

After an early morning shower, he had downed a cold breakfast of cereal and juice, before calling in at the reception and settling his bill.

It was just after six when he had pointed the bonnet of the Ford Falcon west along Parramatta Road, marveling at the amount of city traffic already clogging the east bound lanes. When he had reached the suburb of Ashfield, the Hume Highway had taken him left, heading south through Liverpool and towards his home town and Carmen.

Now, as the big Ford rumbled along the Sturt Highway towards Wagga Wagga, his only thoughts were of Carmen, laying alone in a hospital bed, with numerous machines and devices connected to her fragile body.

He saw the small general store on the highway at Forest Hill, and decided he could use a cold, refreshing drink, although he was anxious to be reunited with Carmen. Stopping the car, he sat for a moment, thinking of what to say to her, what memories to invoke as he whispered their secrets into her ear. The medical staff were certain the sound of his voice would help her, and he recalled hearing of similar occurrences in the past. He was still thinking of the words he would say to her as he entered the old shop, where he ordered a cola soft drink and a small chocolate bar from the young girl behind the counter. He turned to leave and caught sight of an advertising poster for the region's local newspaper, secured in a wire frame attached to the flyscreen door.

'LOCAL DETECTIVE FOUND DEAD' the headline screamed.

Mike stopped and stared at the poster. There were no other details, which was normal. The posters were designed to catch the attention and urge you to buy a copy instantly.

He turned back to the counter and barked at the young girl.

'A copy of the local rag, please love. That poster, that's for today's paper, I take it?'

The girl shrugged and said,

'I think it's for yesterday's, but I'm sorry, we haven't got today's papers yet. We only get a few copies.'

'Well, did they give the name of the Detective? Did it say anything about what happened? Anything at all?' he asked anxiously.

'I haven't a clue, Mister, sorry. I didn't get a chance to read one and they were all gone by the time I started work. You should be able to get a copy in town.'

He was already hurrying for the door as she was speaking.

As soon as the engine started, he drove from the kerb and accelerated the car along the Sturt Highway. For the first time in his life he hoped a Highway Patrol would spot him and pull him over. His inner senses were telling him he was in for some terrible news, and he drove towards the Police Station as fast as he dared.

The Ford turned right into Tarcutta Street, tyres squealing and engine roaring. He did not know why but his instincts were telling him to get the facts as soon as possible, before he did anything else, including visiting Carmen.

He drove into the back carpark of the station and quickly stepped out. Without bothering to lock the car, he ran to the rear doors of the main public area and burst in.

Sergeant Brady and a young Constable who Mike did not know, were standing behind the counter, perusing some papers and forms.

'Mike!' Brady exclaimed. 'Where the bloody hell did you spring from? We've been trying to contact you since yesterday. You all right, Mate?'

Ignoring the Constable who wore a surprised look on his face, Mike said urgently,

'G'day Sarg. I've been for a bit of a drive. I just read the newspaper headlines. What's going on? It said one of our blokes was found dead. Is that right? Who is it?'

'Ah, you better go straight up to Mister Fisher's office, Mikey. He wants to see you as soon as we found you. Go straight up, Mate,' the kindly old Sergeant said.

Mike looked at Brady for a few seconds and his instincts were roaring a warning to him. Without another word, he went to the internal staircase and took the steps three at a time. He arrived, panting slightly at the frosted glass door of Chief Inspector Fisher's office. Straightening his shirt and trousers, Mike knocked firmly on the glass.

'Come!' was the single word answer to his knock.

Mike opened the door and walked into the spacious room. Fisher was seated at his enormous desk, and a uniformed Inspector was sitting in a chair off to the side.

'Hello, Detective Walker. I'm very glad to see you,' Fisher said as he stood up.

The uniformed man remained seated, peering at Mike as he stood to attention in front of Fisher. The Chief Inspector smiled sadly and waved at a spare seat.

'Relax, Mike. Stand easy. Actually, drag up a chair and sit down here. We have to have a chat. This is Inspector Banko. Inspector Banko is from Head Office. First, any news on Missus Walker?'

'Uh, no, Sir. I telephoned last night and there was no change. I was on my way to see her when I saw yesterday's paper. Or, at least, the headline. Who is it, Sir?'

Fisher glanced at Banko, pursing his lips as Mike moved a chair closer and sat down.

'Well, I'm sorry to say, it is Sergeant Johnson. Terrible news. The entire section is in some degree of shock. Terrible, terrible news.'

Mike's shoulders slumped as he absorbed the situation. He bowed his head and his mind swirled with confusion as he tried to reconcile his emotions.

Sergeant Lindsay Johnson had been his partner, mentor, coach and even his friend, although lately Mike had come to think the grizzled old cop had known more about The Retribution Committee, and their operations than he would like anyone to know. He had even contemplated confronting Johnson about Carmen's accident.

All that seemed shallow now. Finally, he looked up, and asked the Chief Inspector,

'What happened, Sir? Has there been any details found? I mean, was it an accident, or a heart attack, or what? Do we know anything, Sir?'

Fisher again looked at Banko first, then thought for a few seconds before answering.

'It appears to be suicide, Mike.'

'Suicide?'

'Yes, suicide. I can give you some facts, if you would like,' Fisher said kindly.

Mike nodded, too emotional to speak.

'Well, here's the preliminary report,' Fisher said as he picked up a sheet of paper and read aloud. 'Sergeant Johnson was rostered to commence duty yesterday at fifteen hundred hours. He was to assist in "Custody" and at the counter. When he hadn't appeared by sixteen thirty, after the station staff had rung his number more than ten times, a car was sent to his residence. Senior Constable Burley and Constable Buchanan attended. The car crew found the Police vehicle in the driveway, locked and secured, but with the Police Radio still switched on. They knocked on all the doors, front, back and side, to no avail. Buchanan is well over six feet six tall and he was able to see in through the high window of the lounge room. He saw Johnson slumped in a lounge chair, unmoving. After trying to break down the side door, they radioed in. We sent the Fire Brigade down there, and they very smartly got the front door open for us. We also had an Ambulance down there by this time. Sergeant Johnson had suffered a bullet wound to his right temple, causing severe trauma to both sides of his head. The Ambulance Officers declared him deceased at that time. Sergeant Johnson's service weapon was found on the floor beside his chair, with one round discharged. An opened bottle of whisky and an empty glass tumbler were on a side table.'

There was silence in the room as the three men all entertained their private thoughts.

Mike was the first to speak.

'Why? Why would he do that?' he asked, almost to himself.

Fisher shrugged and said,

'That's a good question, Mike. I think Inspector Banko might like to talk to you now. We have a recording for you to listen to.'

Mike looked at Banko, who stood up and placed a portable tape recorder on the desk.

'Detective Walker, as you would probably know, most suicides leave a note, either explaining why they took the drastic action, or accusing some-one of forcing them to do themselves in. Well, Sergeant Johnson did not leave a note. He did, however, leave a tape recording. He mentions you a number of times, along with some other things, as well as your wife. We are wondering why this should be so. Any ideas?'

Mike took an instant dislike of the senior officer, but was careful not to display his feelings. Banko had not mentioned

Mike's sorrow and shock, or even Carmen's situation. He seemed intent on settling the suicide case and cared about nothing else.

'I have no idea, Sir,' Mike answered. 'Perhaps if I heard the tape it would help.'

'Precisely why we're here, Detective. Please listen closely, without interruption, and we'll have questions, and hopefully answers, when the tape is finished.'

Mike felt an almost overwhelming desire to smash his fist into Banko's stern face.

The tape machine was switched on and for the first few seconds a faint buzz was heard, then the unmistakable tinkle of glass, and the pouring of liquid. Mike pictured Johnson in his favourite chair, lovingly pouring a good measure of his eighteen-year-old Scotch Whisky into a glass. Johnson's gravelly voice came next.

'Well, I s'pose she's all over now. This 'ere's the last will and all that of Lindsay William Johnson. To any bugger who wants it, they c'n 'ave the bloody lot. Heh, heh. Now, before I leave youse, I gotta say this to young Mikey. Mate, I tried to tell ya, them blokes are bloody powerful, an' there's nuffin you or I could do t' stop 'em, ya know? My job was to watch that farmer bloke, an' t' see he did the right thing. And he did, 'til you an' 'im got to be mates. I tried t' tell ya 'e was no good. At least, 'e was no good t' you, Mike. Now, Mikey, you'r a bloody good, honest Detective, an' one day you should be Commista....Comming.... Commishna, that's it. Heh heh.. Gees, I'm full as a boardin' house dunny. Heh. heh.heh. Now, Mikey, me boy, I just gotta tell ya this. I was ready to go along with the bastards, as long as they left you alone. But then, the pricks did your lovely young wifey a bloody mischief. Poor little Karen, she never hurt no bastard. So, I said to the big man, I said...heh, ya know what I said? I said .. Stuff you, Mate. Ya've gorn too bloody far this time. An' 'e said, he said, Shuddap Johnno, you're drunk. Me? Drunk? No way I said. I'm pissed, that's all, heh heh. Too pissed to be drunk, me. Heh heh heh. So Mikey, that's all I gotta say, and I'm gunna finish this drink, and then go nye nyes..An' if you hear from Barbra, my loving ex bloody wife, tell I spent the Super, and she gets stuff all. You tell 'er that, young Mikey, me best mate. An' I hope I reach them Pearly Gates ten minutes before the Devil knows I'm dead.. Heh, heh. See ya later….'

A clicking sound, followed by a loud report of a gunshot came over the tape.

Banko stopped the tape, rewound it and sat down. He said to Mike,

'Well, Detective. What do you make of that?'

'What am I supposed to make of it, with all respect? Mister Johnson sounded like he was extremely drunk. Other than that, I don't have much of a clue what he's on about. Except, he said Karen, and my wife's name is Carmen. I think he was mixed up about that. The farmer he referred to was a mate of mine. He played football and cricket for my teams, but then he up and disappeared, sold his farm as was gone. How Johnno knew him is beyond me. Neither man ever mentioned the other to me, until that tape we just heard.'

Banko was about to speak, but Fisher cut him off.

'Are you sure there is nothing you can add, Mike? Anything at all?'

Mike ignored Banko and spoke respectfully to Fisher.

'No, Sir. I am as confused as anybody. I don't know why Sergeant Johnson would feel so aggrieved about my wife's accident, and I have no idea who he was referring to when he said "those blokes who done her a mischief " or what-ever it was he said. Right now, all I know is I feel a massive amount of grief. For myself, his other mates, and the Police Force. Because, at the end of the day, we've lost a darn good Police Officer. And I've lost a colleague, mentor and mate. That's on top of my seriously injured wife. So, Sir, if there's nothing further, I would like to go and see her. She is still in Intensive Care. And later, I would like to see who-ever is investigating the hit and run, and hopefully get a progress report. Is that Ok, Sir?'

'Yes, of course. Give her my best, please Mike. And take as much time off as you need. All the best. And I'm truly sorry to be the bearer of the news about Lindsay. I totally agree, he was a good copper, and a fine bloke.'

Mike nodded his thanks, saluted and left, deliberately ignoring Inspector Banko.

He pulled into the hospital car park and checked his watch. Almost two thirty, PM.

After alighting from the car, he checked his reflection in the door mounted mirror.

His reflection looked terrible, with red eyes, blotchy, pale skin and a two-day stubble.

He shrugged and locked the car, after placing his revolver in the boot for extra safe-keeping. Car theft was relatively rare in Wagga Wagga, but you never knew. If a thief stole this Falcon, then he was in for a bonus if he looked in the boot. Such a loss would probably cost Mike his career, but right at this time, he simply did not care.

His wife was far more important, and the news about Johnson was also weighing heavily on his mind. He stopped at the small kiosk and purchased a large bunch of flowers, a box of chocolates and yet another card. After quickly filling in the 'Get Well' card he took the elevator to the fourth floor.

Below, in the almost full hospital car park, a white Holden sedan cruised slowly past Mike's car. It stopped abruptly and a tall, powerfully built man, wearing a grey suit and felt hat, alighted from the passenger's side. He stood fully upright and swung his gaze around the entire carpark. Seeing no-one in close proximity, the man squatted at the rear of Walker's Falcon and reached under the wheel arch. His thick fingers soon located the tracking device, and he pulled hard, breaking the grip of the special putty holding the small metal box in place. Smiling with satisfaction, he strode back to the Holden and opened the left door. Once seated, he flicked a tiny chrome-plated switch on the device and the small red light, which had been blinking rhythmically, was extinguished. He grinned at his colleague and reached for an official occurrence book. As he made several entries, the other man started the engine and drove from the carpark, turned right and pointed the car north, following the highway to Sydney.

'Let's hope that's the end of this shit-fight', the tall man said to the driver.

'Yeah, I hope so, too,' the other man replied. 'I hate this sneaking around in strange places. It'll be good to spend a few nights at home, in my own bed, for a change, as well. Plus, my missus is better looking company than you.'

'Yeah, but don't forget, the Big Man wants a full written report by first thing tomorrow. And, we still have to find that little old bastard with the silly white hat. The Big Fella said he needs to know what happened to him, and this job won't be finished until then. Still, I reckon we'll find him at either his house in Cronulla or at his mates joint where we found their car.'

The driver grinned across at the tall man and said,

'Yep, that's the easy bit. Just follow the pale green Holden and the silly white hat.'

As soon as Walker left the elevator he was spotted by two of the regular nurses.

'Hey, Mike. Come on in, quick. You'll never guess. It's a miracle,' one yelled.

'What is?' he answered. 'What's all the fuss. You lot are supposed to keep things quiet around here,' he returned, walking quickly into the Intensive Care Ward.

'It's Carmen. She's shown some signs. Some incredible signs,' the nurse said, grinning, and taking Mike by the elbow, almost dragging him to Carmen's bed.

Three nurses and two white-coated doctors were crowded around the bed.

He recognised the taller man as Doctor Willard, her original treating doctor from Casualty on the day of the hit and run.

They all turned to face him and he got his first glimpse of Carmen. Despite her two black eyes and swollen lips, he saw a small smile appear on her face. He bent down to kiss her forehead, but she stopped him in his tracks.

'Hello, you rogue. Where've you been, my silly bloody Aussie man?' she said softly.

Despite the presence of the medical staff, Mike kissed her tenderly on her cheek, and allowed his tears to run freely down his unshaven face as he whispered,

'I'm here now and I am never leaving your side again, you mad Irish Beauty.'

Carmen gave a faint smile and whispered through her oxygen supply mask,

'You'd better not. I need you around, you know. I could get hurt, otherwise.'

Walker's muscular shoulders heaved as he sobbed quietly, his whiskered cheek against her forehead. The nurses and both doctors quietly retreated, clear of Carmen's bed, allowing the couple some privacy. Doctor Willard grinned widely at his colleague, his satisfaction and joy clear for all to see.

THE END

ABOUT THE AUTHOR

Terry Richardson grew up in the outback town of Brewarrina, where he enjoyed writing stories and essays. In 1971 he did what so many country boys had done before him and boarded the slow "Mixed" train to Sydney, seeking new adventures. In the big city, he tried various occupations, including training as an auto mechanic, truck driver, a short railway career, and even a two-year stint in Policing as a Constable. In 1982 he joined the then NSW Fire Brigades and served at various suburban and country Fire Stations. In 2005 he was appointed a "Work Place Assessment Officer". This new role required him to visit numerous Fire Stations and conduct the necessary tests and assessments on other Firefighters. He retired from Fire/Rescue NSW in 2011.

Terry and his family are keen fans of the sport of Rugby League, and this game often rates a mention in any Terry Richardson novel. He is a fanatic Cronulla Sharks supporter.

In 1971, aged only 16, he met the love of his life, Linda, aged 14. The two have been together ever since. They were married in 1975 and produced two sons and a daughter. They now reside on the Mid-North Coast of NSW with their two dogs and dote on their eleven grandchildren.

CPSIA information can be obtained
at www.ICGtesting.com
Printed in the USA
BVHW031950190822
645019BV00012B/228